A CARAVAN OF BRIDES

A Novel of Saudi Arabia

Kay Hardy Campbell

 7-12-18

Loon Cove Press
Jefferson, Maine

Quotes from the poem by Muhammad al-Fayiz from "A Sailor's Memoirs (Excerpts from the Twentieth Memoir)" used with permission of Naomi Shihab Nye, co-translator and editor of *This Same Sky: A Collection of Poems from Around the World*, in which it appears.

A CARAVAN OF BRIDES

For information contact:
Loon Cove Press
P.O. Box 413
Jefferson, Maine 04348
looncovepress@gmail.com
www.looncovepress.com

Cover & Map by Louis Roe

FIRST EDITION

ISBN (paperback): 978-0-9990743-0-5
ISBN (e-book): 978-0-9990743-1-2
Library of Congress Control Number: 2017910351

For my parents, Dorothy and Henry Hanson,
who dared me to chase my dreams.

For my husband, Gary,
with all my love and gratitude.

Author Forward

Pronouncing Arabic words can be a challenge for non-Arabic speakers. Arabic vowel sounds can be written several ways in the Latin alphabet, and the language has some consonants that don't occur in English. We have simplified spellings with the reader in mind.

If you would like to imagine a more authentic pronunciation, here are some hints for a few major characters: The protagonist, Fawzia, is pronounced fow-ZEE-ah (rhymes with Maria). Her sister, Ibtisam, is ib-tee-SAAM (rhymes with marzipan). Hisham is hee-SHAAM (last syllable rhymes with rattan, and has a similar emphasis), and Fawzia's brother Tarek is TA-rik (rhymes with market, with emphasis on first syllable).

Fawzia	fow-ZEE-ah	rhymes with Maria
Ibtisam	ib-tee-SAM	rhymes with marzipan
Hisham	hee-SHAM	rhymes with rattan
Tarek	TA-rik	rhymes with market

A more detailed glossary of Arabic terms found in the story, as well as a Book Club Guide and more, can be found on the website: www.kayhardycampbell.com.

Family of Fawzia Bughaidan

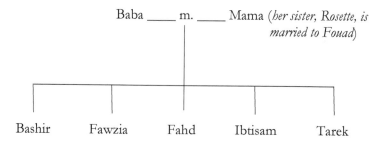

Baba ____ m. ____ Mama (*her sister, Rosette, is married to Fouad*)

Bashir Fawzia Fahd Ibtisam Tarek

Family of Salma al-Shamaali
Tribe of al-Shamaal

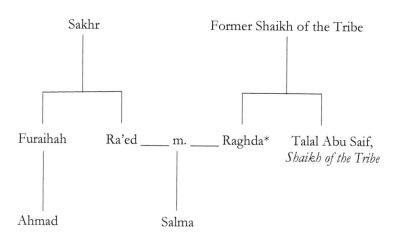

Sakhr   Former Shaikh of the Tribe

Furaihah   Ra'ed ____ m. ____ Raghda*   Talal Abu Saif, *Shaikh of the Tribe*

Ahmad   Salma

* Raghda is the second cousin of Duhaim, Nurah's father (see Nurah's family tree).

Family of Nurah al-Hamdan
of Unaizah

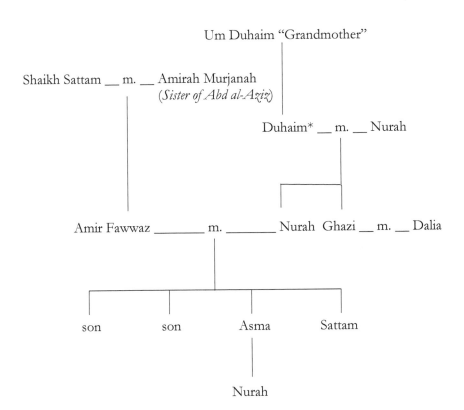

Um Duhaim "Grandmother"

Shaikh Sattam __ m. __ Amirah Murjanah
(Sister of Abd al-Aziz)

Duhaim* __ m. __ Nurah

Amir Fawwaz _____ m. _____ Nurah   Ghazi __ m. __ Dalia

son   son   Asma   Sattam

Nurah

* Duhaim is the second cousin of Raghda, Salma's mother (see Salma's family tree).

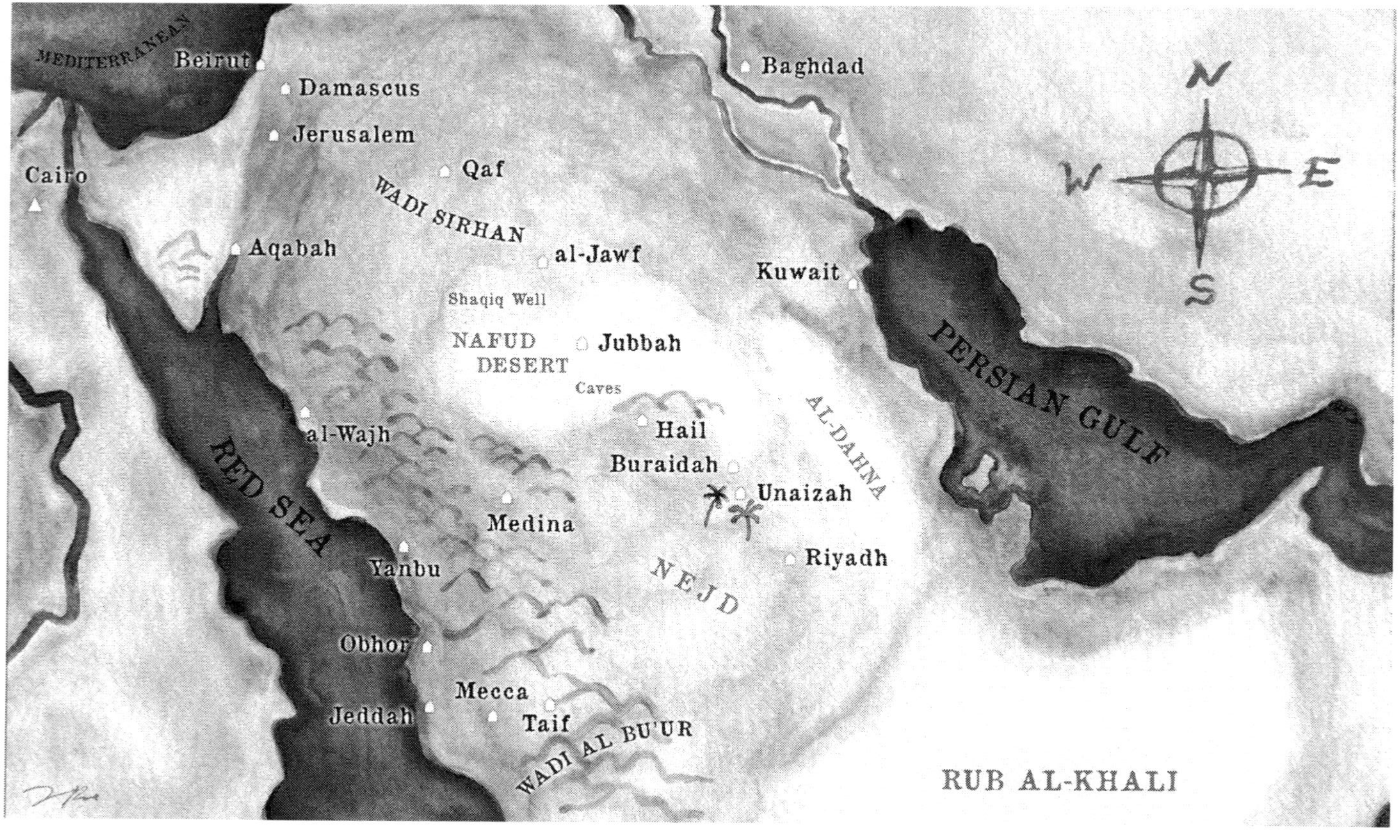
MEDITERRANEAN
Beirut
Damascus
Jerusalem
Cairo
Qaf
WADI SIRHAN
Aqabah
al-Jawf
Baghdad
Kuwait
N
W
E
S
Shaqiq Well
NAFUD
DESERT
Jubbah
Caves
PERSIAN GULF
AL-DAHNA
Hail
Buraidah
Unaizah
al-Wajh
RED SEA
Medina
Yanbu
NEJD
Riyadh
Obhor
Mecca
Jeddah
Taif
WADI AL BU'UR
RUB AL-KHALI

Jeddah
1978

I don't believe in a sun
That illuminates caves
While my home remains steeped
In total darkness.

- A Sailor's Memoirs by Muhammad al-Fayiz

CHAPTER 1

BAREFOOT SAND PRINTS

ONCE THERE was, and oh how much there was, long ago. That's how the old women began their stories. *"Kaan ya maa kaan, fee qadeem iz-zamaan,"* they would say, and, when they did, we sat still and listened. In English, they begin with, "Once upon a time," but I like our way better, don't you? It has this air of mystery, and it rhymes. Sometimes they say only the first part, the rest being implied. *Kaan ya maa kaan.*

Every life has at least one day in which everything changes. The same sun comes up as it does each morning, but on such a day the path of your life shifts, though you might not realize it then. One winter day long ago, I turned onto a new and dangerous road. And it took just an instant. *Kaan ya maa kaan.*

Our laughter filled the marble courtyard as we surged into the cloakroom, then draped our abayas over our shoulders, enveloping our long-sleeved blouses and floor-length skirts in black. We chattered like sparrows, winding dark scarves over our hair and under our chins. As we ran our fingers along the edges of our scarves, searching for stray tresses, our conversations faded to silence.

Wrapped in decorum with our smiles locked away, we hurried through the campus gate into the dusty parking lot, where our brothers, fathers, and drivers, dressed in long white thobes, waited to drive us home. To pass the time, they smoked. A few might get into an argument over rival soccer teams. And there always seemed to be someone leaning on a car, reading the paper.

Dismissal at girls' schools and colleges was a daily ritual, yet it was full of risk. Before long, religious authorities would choreograph the chaotic merging of black with white into an orderly pairing, to prevent what happened to me that day.

Men and women surged past as I walked toward the taxi line. When I reached into my purse for my sunglasses, a man approached. I wasn't expecting to be met, so I avoided his gaze.

"Fawzia," he said, "Let's go, the car's over here."

It was Hisham. He stood before me, the tasseled ends of his red and white ghutra flipped on top of his head. He twirled prayer beads in his right hand and jangled his car keys from his left forefinger. Playing the part of one of my brothers, he frowned, swung his beads one last time, and then winked.

"Come on," he said, marching ahead, expecting me to follow. As I complied, I looked around, relieved none of my students had seen us.

My hands trembled as he opened the car door. He started the engine, straightened his arms against the steering wheel, and leaned back. Closing his eyes, he took a deep breath, then gazed at me. "Finally, Fawzia, finally." His face lit up when he saw my cautious smile.

The car darted out of the parking lot onto Mecca Road. He turned on the cassette player, and the strains of a Lebanese tune filled the air. The accordion and the singer's rich baritone unlocked my memories. I closed my eyes. For a moment, we were with our friends again, our fingers woven and our hands locked tight, dancing a dizzying dabke, snaking in a circle, stomping our feet and laughing.

"Been here the last three days," he said, over the music. "Was about to give up, and I'm back to al-Khobar tomorrow."

Disappointment erased my joy, for his hometown was on the other side of the country, on the shores of the Gulf, hundreds of miles and a plane ride away.

When he reached for my hand, I watched our fingers entwine, still not sure our meeting was real. When the song ended, we tried to converse as we always had in college. But we were far from the American University of Beirut, and the six months since our graduation seemed like years. In Jeddah, we were taking great risks just to have this simple conversation. Riding together in the car like this, we were committing *khalwa*, the crime of an unrelated man and woman being alone together in a private place.

He drove north, leaving the city behind. On our right, the flat Tihama plain stretched toward the dark-cloaked peaks of the Hijaz Mountains. They spun in slow motion as we gained speed. Turning left toward the sea, we passed stretches of whitewashed walls that hid modest cottages and seaside villas.

When we reached the open beach, no one else was in sight. Holding up the hem of my skirt, I tiptoed barefoot in the warm water. Hisham walked beside me on the sand just beyond water's edge, still in his shoes and socks. To the west, the sun dipped into a thickening veil of dust – across the Red Sea to all of Africa. It ripened the sky, the sea, and the sand to apricot.

Waves crashed against the coral reef offshore, and the relentless wind thundered in our ears. How different this was from our strolls on Beirut's Corniche, where music mingled with the laughter of people playing water sports. I let my headscarf fall to my shoulders, setting my long unruly locks free. When a warm gust filled my abaya, I wished the wind would carry it high into the sky.

Though we both had so much to say, Hisham waited for me to speak. Once I began, my words tumbled out. "Sometimes I feel like I can't breathe."

He nodded. "We really *lived* in Beirut. Now it's just going through the motions, counting the days before the next boring weekend, until they marry us off."

I turned toward the sea and watched the waves crash. "At least I'm second in line," I said. "Now my sister's the one in play, poor thing. You?"

"Mother's always mentioning girls, but not seriously, thank God. We're working nonstop at the firm. There's no time to plan a wedding, so at least for now, I'm safe." He fell silent, waiting for a gust of wind to pass. "Besides, there's only one marriage I want."

I turned to gaze into his half-hooded eyes. "You know it was for the best."

"You're wrong." He took my hands in his. "Nothing matters but you and being with you." The wind blew sand around our feet.

Back in the car, he kissed me on the forehead. "I hold you in my eye and my heart. You are my queen, my angel." Then our lips met. "It can never be Beirut again, but let's try. I'll be careful. Please, my sweet." I nodded, smiling. He kissed my teary eyes.

Sitting back, he handed me his business card. "Call me at my office. It's a direct line. No one picks up but me."

It seemed hopeless. All we had was the possibility of an occasional few hours together. Where would it lead?

On our way back, we drove along a nondescript stretch of walled-in beach properties. We came to an old metal gate, painted a faded turquoise. It stood slightly open, and the place seemed deserted, so we stopped the car, got out, and stepped inside. When I was a child, my parents had rented a cottage there. It stood in a cluster with a dozen just like it along a sloping, walled-in beach. On the weekends, we'd socialize there with other families, ignoring the rules about men and women mixing. There were Egyptians, Lebanese, Americans, Europeans, and a few Saudi families. It was a paradise.

As we strolled among the deserted cottages, I remembered the warm seawater streaming through my hair as I spent hours snorkeling, exploring tiny coral reefs. We'd rest during the heat of the day, feasting on freshly caught grouper in our t-shirts and shorts, the sand stuck between our toes, salt caked in our hair. After dark, we'd listen to eight-track tapes from Egypt, Lebanon, and Europe. Later, we'd tune into Radio Monte Carlo to hear the latest hits. Whatever that deejay played, we'd dance to it. Oh how we danced, from toddlers to grandmothers, all of us on our feet, sand flying everywhere. We tied our headscarves around our hips. We'd fling our long hair in arcs like the girls in the desert tribes. We'd dabke, then disco, then switch to Egyptian. All week, I'd practice alone in my room for the next Friday.

We gave up that cottage years ago. My brothers complained it was too hot, and besides, they could swim anywhere they wanted. When we visited the fancy new seaside villas of our family friends, we women had to sit still in our long dresses while the men swam. It wasn't proper for Saudi women to swim in mixed company, unless we wanted to wear our abayas into the water. Would I ever be allowed to swim in my beloved Red Sea again, the warm water caressing my bare arms and legs?

Hisham tried to cheer me up, holding my hand and singing along to the music as we reached the city in the deepening dusk. He dropped me at our neighborhood pharmacy and watched me wave down a taxi. I turned to him as the cab pulled away.

Safe behind my bedroom door, I pulled a cone-shaped shell from my purse. It held the colors of the sunset, the sand, and the sea's relentless wind. I set it on my desk and gazed at it, my heart still pounding. Would anyone notice I'd tracked sand into the house?

CHAPTER 2

Café de la Mer

Jeddah
January 1979

I FOLDED Hisham's business card into a small square and hid it in a corner of my wallet, waiting for the chance to call him. Nearly a week passed before my parents went out visiting friends in the evening. My brothers were out, too, and Ibtisam was immersed in her studies with her door closed. I dialed the number and listened to the phone ring over and over. He wasn't there, and he had no answering machine. In those days, not many people had them. It would be decades before we would have e-mail and mobiles. I redialed, letting the phone ring a long time. I tried again and again, growing more confident with each attempt. Calling a young man was a daring act, and each time I flexed this new muscle, it felt good.

Having no luck at night, I phoned him one morning, and he answered.

"Good morning," I said, just above a whisper.

"Good morning *Fawwaz*! What's new?" He spoke so loudly I had to hold the receiver away from my ear. There must have been someone in the room with him, since he used the male form of my name, which means victorious.

"Nothing much. I've tried calling at night, but you're never there."

"That's right, *mazbu-tation*. You see, unlike you Hijazis who are still living in the nineteenth century, we modern people in the Eastern Province work straight from 9 to 5. We don't take a siesta like you lazy slobs, and we don't work nights unless we're really backed up."

I giggled. This was the way my brothers and their friends teased each other. "I see. Well, any chance you'll be coming to see us lazy Hijazis any time soon?"

"Fawwaz, you're pretty sharp for a guy who takes a nap every day. In fact, I'm due out there next week. Got a job up in Taif. Want to get together? I can meet you at the Sheraton."

"I have classes Tuesday and Wednesday. I'll be leaving school at the usual time."

After I hung up, I snuffed out my grin, remembering I was at home, sneaking a call to my boyfriend.

I picked up a framed photograph from my bedside table. On our last day of classes at AUB, we'd posed for a group shot outside College Hall. We hung off each other's shoulders, our arms entwined. We girls wore embroidered peasant blouses and jeans. We'd pushed our sunglasses up into our layered ebony manes and squinted into the sunshine. Hisham stood smiling behind me in the second row on the end. That was the way he always looked at me. His smile was so big it almost closed his eyes, as if his whole being glowed with happiness. This was the only photo of him I could display safely, since it was part of a big group shot.

I scanned the group, but always returned to Hisham. He stood a little taller than me, about six feet. He stayed on the thin side, since he skipped meals while working on architecture projects. When he wasn't smiling so hard, his dark eyes sat wide apart, rimmed by thick eyelashes.

AUB's campus in the Ras Beirut neighborhood was relatively safe during the Lebanese civil war that tore the country apart in the late 1970s. Of course we had no idea the war would drag on until 1990. The university stayed open during my years there, and the school provided an excellent education even in tough times. Still, it broke our hearts to see the city around us slip into chaos, one bomb at a time, as various political factions fought each other, especially since things were so good back home in Saudi. In the late 1970s, oil wealth was streaming into our country and to our Gulf neighbors. We Saudis were heady with money and optimism, while Beirutis were spiraling into poverty and hopelessness. Young Saudi men with no experience were put in charge of multi-million-dollar projects. Meanwhile, sophisticated Lebanese professionals resorted to selling goods in makeshift, open markets. They spent hours finding enough fresh water so their families could bathe once a week. Others left their families behind and found work in our country.

One night, a Bahraini student invited Hisham to join a group of us dancing dabke in a common room after dinner. Even with the war going on, we still loved to dance. It was cathartic. We took a break to cool off, and I noticed him sitting on a pillow across from me. I admired his straight, chiseled nose.

Someone told a joke, and it felt wonderful to laugh. Hisham put his head back and let out a boisterous *hoo,* as if he hadn't laughed in months, a smile bursting across his face. Then he drew in his breath, groaned in pleasure, and started *hoo hooing* again. I elbowed my friend Samirah sitting next to me, and we started giggling. Soon the room shook with waves of laughter. When we started dancing again, I admired the subtle way Hisham enjoyed every step, stomp and kick. As we danced into ecstatic frenzy, he closed his eyes and that wide grin bloomed on his face.

Hisham began to join us at Café de la Mer near campus. No matter how much they bombed, who was fighting whom in surrounding neighborhoods, this café kept serving coffee day and night.

One afternoon, when I was there alone, someone nudged the back of my chair. It was Hisham, his arms loaded with books. Our coffee turned into a stroll around campus, then a long chat on a bench overlooking the Mediterranean.

That's how it started: by most standards in the world, except those of conservative Arab families, an innocent college romance. Sometimes we walked to Rawshe, twenty minutes south along the beach, and wandered through the shantytown where merchants had set up shop, since their real storefronts were in the battle zone. Then we'd sit by the sea and talk. I'd sketch or set up my easel to paint, and he'd do homework. I had taken an art class as an elective, and was surprised to discover I had some talent, and that I loved drawing and painting.

Hisham let his hair grow just long enough to let him tuck his glistening curls behind his ears. I loved to watch him read a book, his head bent over, his locks falling on his face. Then he'd run his fingers through his hair and push it back behind his ears. I made many drawings of him like this, but I could never quite capture the magic of his curls framing his face.

The back of his neck smelled like the fresh sea air that enveloped us on campus. His voice soothed my soul, but not when he was tired. Then it sounded like pieces of sandpaper rubbing together. If the weather was nice, we'd pretend to study out on the lawn, lying on a big blanket. Before long, he'd be snoring with a book on his face, one hand resting, palm down, on his stomach, his bare feet relaxed and turned out. Most of all, though, I loved it when we danced.

He threw himself into his school projects and drove himself to exhaustion, but he didn't mind the hard work. Nothing was too complicated for him, for he loved challenges. Yet he was sensitive enough to know when I was upset, sometimes even before I did. He'd take the time to listen as I told him my troubles, his arm around me, inviting me to lean into his shoulder. With patience and a few words of encouragement, he'd coax the sadness out of me and make me laugh at my troubles. Just taking a walk with him would clear my head.

An ambitious young architect-to-be from a successful merchant family, Hisham should have been a perfect match for me. But we could never marry. His family was from far outside our social circles, from the Eastern Province. More importantly, his family were Shia Muslims. Like most wealthy families in Jeddah, we are Sunni. While both our families were Muslim, the schism between Sunni and Shia was a sore point in Saudi society. Most Saudis are Sunni, while a small percentage, almost all living in the Eastern Province near the Arabian Gulf, are Shia. Since the death of Prophet Muhammad (peace be upon him), in 632 CE, Muslims have differed over who should govern the community. The official view of Saudi clerics was that the Shia approach is wrong, and some even labeled it heretical. As a result, Saudi Shi`a felt marginalized at best, and some believed they were systematically disadvantaged and oppressed. Very few became successful businessmen in the oil economy. Hisham's family was the exception, but there was no getting around it, they were still Shia.

Though my parents and ancestors were liberal and open-minded about many things, the social differences between our family and his seemed insurmountable, and from the moment he told me his family was Shia, I realized our romance was doomed. Marriages between Sunni and Shi`a Saudis were taboo: very rare and kept quiet. They usually ended in divorce.

Afraid of my family finding out that I was dating anyone at all, and knowing a Shia groom was impossible, I broke off with Hisham just before graduation. I did it one afternoon at the café, with a cold resolve. I hoped we'd get over each other when we returned home. But the sadness in

Hisham's eyes stayed with me for months afterwards. He kept saying, "I love you and you love me. This is the only thing that matters. The rest is nothing." I don't know how I found the willpower to leave him sitting alone in the café. I was certain it could never be, that it was impossible.

Samirah tried to console me on our last night on campus as I hugged a pillow in my dorm room, my tears flowing. I had just thrown out all the drawings and paintings I'd made of him, so no one in my family would find out.

"Even if you never see him again, you're lucky," she said. "Your heart opened like a flower in the sun, and you've felt the touch of a man who loves you. Nothing can take that away. I admire you so much, you followed your heart."

Back home after graduation, my older sister Ibtisam noticed I was changed and asked if anything was wrong. I told her I'd had a secret crush on a boy at school, but that nothing happened between us. She admonished me to forget him.

Even though I'd broken up with him, I fantasized about Hisham all the time. When we waited in an airport departure lounge, or browsed through my favorite perfumery, Gazaaz, I'd look around, hoping his work would bring him to Jeddah and that he'd put himself in my way. And now he had, and we were dancing a new dance together, with danger.

One day after classes, I arranged for our driver Hamdi to take me downtown. I clipped my hair up into a loose bun, threw on my headscarf, and fastened it with a yellow flowered safety pin. As I wrapped my *abaya* over my jeans and t-shirt, I checked myself in the mirror and whispered thanks to my forefathers. My great-grandfather, an educated man who had traveled to Damascus and Jerusalem, had decided the women of our family could appear in public with our faces uncovered. I still think of him with pride. The legend went that he simply stated that nowhere in the Qur'an does it say that women have to cover their faces, so none of us should have to. We've never veiled our faces since.

Hamdi held the car's back door open for me, running the Buick's air-conditioning full blast. He was wiping sweat from his brow as he closed the car door behind me, trying not to slam it. Hamdi, an Egyptian, had been our family driver since we were children. He was like our uncle, and we trusted him with our lives.

He inched the car over the speed bumps on our quiet street. Our neighborhood of small residential blocks had been laid out in the 1960s, and high walls and metal gates shielded luxurious villas with private gardens and swimming pools. Bougainvillea bushes poured over the walls in brilliant pinks and purples. Some trees were tall enough to cast shade on the street, hinting at the beauty and coolness within.

Once we turned onto Medina Road, Hamdi darted in and out of traffic, and we had to slow down to overtake a wooden donkey cart carrying a large chunk of ice. A few decades ago, before anyone had electricity, such carts had carried sweet water and ice to Jeddah's homes. I wondered where they were bringing the ice, which house still didn't have a refrigerator.

Just as we began to speed up, another obstacle loomed ahead. Two late-model Caprices with price stickers still glued to the windows had pulled over at an angle on the left, blocking traffic. Two Saudis in their twenties stood near their cars, shaking hands. Then they hugged and slapped each other on the back, oblivious to the traffic jam they'd caused.

Hamdi rolled down his window and stuck out his arm, "For the love of God, move it!" But they were too far away to hear. With his arm still extended, Hamdi clicked his tongue and shrugged while looking at me in the rear-view mirror. Then he tilted the mirror so he could see himself and smoothed back his full head of salt-and-pepper hair. He'd tried a new kind of hair gel. Was he going for the movie star look?

The air-conditioning was struggling to keep up with the heat as we crept past an old red Datsun covered with tiny dents. It was filled with African office workers smoking cigarettes. I imagined they were talking about sending money back home. Then we passed a Buick with a bald Western businessman in the back seat, reading the English language daily, *Arab News*. Maybe he had plans for a joint venture, or a bid for a multi-million dollar contract in his briefcase. An Indian houseboy riding an old bicycle jumped the curb to our left and rode down the sidewalk, passing us all. He was likely dreaming of his family, far away. A Rolls Royce idled behind us, no doubt carrying someone who had already made his or her millions.

That was Jeddah in the late 1970's. My city had become a magnet for people with dreams of wealth. Money from oil production was funding massive state development and construction projects – roads, airports, bridges, government buildings, banks, and housing. We'd count the construction cranes that loomed over the sprawling city, giving up once we reached 25.

Few Saudi men had the skills needed for all this building, which resulted in a severe labor shortage. Thousands of foreign workers poured into Jeddah, from laborers to executives. Our once sleepy Jeddah had become a boomtown, attracting people from many nations and races. Each was a kind of adventurer, having traveled thousands of miles to take part in the Saudi oil rush. And every time I'd return home from college, the traffic would've grown worse. Stores and restaurants sprouted up everywhere to serve the needs of this new international population.

"Hey, what's your problem! Come on!" a taxi driver yelled. The other drivers started to push down on their horns. Without acknowledging the uproar, the young men kissed each other on the cheeks and drove off, squealing their tires.

As we regained speed, Hamdi pushed an eight-track tape into the stereo – it was a song by Egypt's beloved Abdul Halim Hafez about a fortune-teller who reads a young man's fate in the grounds of a coffee cup. A twangy electric guitar and keyboard jarred against the huge Egyptian orchestra. "O my son," he sang, "Whoever sacrifices himself for love is a martyr. Your life will be filled with love, but you will drown in its sea with no rescue." Abdul Halim had died the year before, and the whole Arab world was still mourning. Hamdi sang along, tapping his finger on the steering wheel. He was still singing as we pulled up outside the Queen's Building. I told him I'd take a taxi home. He nodded, turned up the volume, and drove off.

I've been drawn to the mysteries of Jeddah's dusty alleys since I was a girl. Walking there always did me good, and I needed to clear my head and sort out my thoughts about Hisham. First I strolled through the old gold *souq* behind the Queen's Building, where I loved getting swept up in the crowd. Pakistanis, Indians, and all manner of Asians and Africans, thronged the market. Colorful saris swirled, and towering African head wraps swayed. I followed families, listening to them as they browsed for gold bangles. If they spoke an unfamiliar language, like Urdu or Amharic, I watched their faces and studied how they moved and what they wore.

Pretending to wait for someone, I stood outside the shops, feeling the energy of people surging by. Yemeni boys wove through the crowds carrying boxes of Chinese alarm clocks on their heads. Sudanese office workers strolled hand in hand; discussing which radio they wanted to buy. A group of English ladies, tan from afternoons by the pool, bargained for caftans in simple Arabic and improvised sign language. An old Syrian lady with a cane strolled up the lane, her daughter leading her on her market rounds.

The scent of rosewater mixed with curry, aloeswood, jasmine incense, and ripe mangoes. How far had that mango traveled to be opened up and made into juice? Who woke at dawn to gather the rose petals for this perfume? Why did the dark-skinned lady selling incense on the blanket decide to burn jasmine today?

I made my way up Gabel Street, a shop-lined road where cars were banned. It climbed eastward away from the port, then narrowed as it passed under a new highway. Emerging from the underpass, I reached my goal: the balad, a neighborhood of ancient coral-brick mansions. Built by hand at least a century ago, each old house was held up by palmwood trunks that had been carried on camelback from distant oasis towns. Teak latticework from Asia covered windows even four and five stories up. The latticework caught the breeze and gave women privacy from prying eyes on the streets below. These old houses stood sentinel on Jeddah's only hill of note. All the new office towers, villas, and apartment buildings sprawled to the north and south along the low, flat coastline.

Jeddah is known as the Bride of the Sea, and she stretches out like a woman lying on her side along the Red Sea's eastern shore. Resting on one elbow, she gazes day and night over the water toward Africa, hoping an ocean breeze might waft over her and break the humidity that makes everything, even the dust, stand still.

Once I reached the balad, I liked to sit on a stone wall outside the Nassif House. A century ago, the four-story mansion, with its 106 rooms, was famous for its large library and the fact that the country's first king, Abd al-Aziz, stayed there when he conquered Jeddah in 1925. The Nassif family used to host a kind of salon where dignitaries and diplomats met. Other old houses stood nearby, many in states of disrepair, huddling around the square where I sat, near an enormous neem tree that cast welcome shade.

This was the heart and soul of Jeddah. I always sensed a mysterious wisdom here from the generations who had walked Gabel Street and had lived in those old homes. Sometimes I was sure the city murmured to me, but I couldn't quite hear her. After all, Jeddah means Grandmother. Eve's Tomb, an old walled-up mausoleum where people used to say prayers, stands just down the hill.

Sitting there on the wall, my thoughts soared as free as the flocks of pigeons that circled the sky above the city. I pulled out my little sketchbook and tried to capture the details of what I'd seen that day before I forgot them. I imagined the pilgrims who used to pass this way from Jeddah's old port as they marched east toward Mecca. I listened for the echo of their strange accents and conjured their colorful costumes. In my imagination, tall African tribesmen strode by. Chinese noblewomen rode in red-tasseled litters. Turks on horseback wore tall black hats and long mustaches. Moroccans strode along in pointed shoes and flowing white djellabas.

I looked up at the latticed windows and listened for the voices of ladies who'd gazed down onto the square. Hadn't *they* ever fallen in love? For a moment or two I felt the grandmothers of old were comforting me. I'd been born too late to know my own grandmothers. I never heard their voices, or felt their touch. It was for this that I always returned, relishing it no matter how quickly it passed from my heart. After listening for answers that never came, I walked back down the hill.

CHAPTER 3

SHEPHERDESS

Jeddah
January 1979

AFTER ARRIVING home, I went straight to work in my studio and began sketching what I'd seen in the balad. Maybe, if I brought it to life on canvas, I could discover the key to its mysteries. When my parents learned I'd done well in my painting classes at university, they'd converted a small storeroom near the servants' quarters into an art studio just for me. They thought it would help me adjust to being home after college. Aside from the occasional squawk of wild parakeets in the frangipani tree outside, the studio was filled only with my thoughts and the sound of the brush on canvas or charcoal on paper.

I started painting in the studio at night when I couldn't sleep, thinking about Hisham. Once I stayed up all night, absorbed in painting an old silversmith as he worked in the balad. The dawn call to prayer broke my concentration, so I went outside and stretched. It was quiet, and the marble tile was cool on my bare feet. Everything glowed soft pink. I heard strange, dull "thuds," out in the street, growing louder, and then a woman began to sing.

I ran to the front gate and listened, waiting until she passed by. I inched the gate open and saw the figures of two women walking away, herding goats. One carried a long stick to urge the goats along. She sang a lilting melody over and over. Her black caftan billowed around her, revealing inset panels of brilliant orange, red, and yellow. The other one leaned on a gnarled wooden cane with each step, as she did her best to bring up the back of the little herd.

I started sketching them right away, and, as I drew, I tried to imagine who they might be, these two dressed like tribal women of the desert.

Nomadic tribes had once lived in many parts of Arabia much as they had for centuries, in camel- and goat-hair tents the women wove. Tribal lineage is still desirable in Saudi Arabia, even decades after most desert dwellers settled in the cities, and sent their children to school and university. Even the Saudi royal family has many roots and branches among the various tribes of Arabia.

By the late 1970s, though, it was rare to see women walking in Jeddah dressed like desert nomads, even on a quiet back street like ours. Occasionally we would see heavily veiled women riding in pickup-truck beds with children and sometimes even sheep. They might have been desert dwellers, but Baba told us they were more likely recently settled nomads living in small towns and villages, far from the bustle of Jeddah, or on the outskirts of the city. There they could still keep their herds and pitch tents next to their new concrete block houses.

My curiosity piqued, I waited for them for the next few mornings, with no success. It wasn't until a week later that they returned. I had set up a ladder against the high outside wall so I could see them without being seen.

When I heard the clip clop of hooves coming up the street, I climbed the ladder, and there they were. One sang the same song and wove from side to side, shooing the goats along with her stick. The second woman walked behind, carefully leaning on the walking stick she held in her left hand. She was clearly older. Both of them wore elaborate tribal facemasks of red cloth that extended from their foreheads to below their chins, decorated with embroidery and silver coins.

Still about 30 feet from our gate, the singing woman stopped to retrieve a kid that was hiding under a parked car. "Come here, little one," she said, her voice muffled by the face mask. "What are you doing under there? You want to travel to Riyadh? Come here now." She picked it up and continued on. "I'm sorry there was no water at the house on Medina Road. Somehow, we'll get it for you all. I know you're thirsty."

I pulled the garden hose and set its nozzle under the gate, then turned on the spigot. By the time I estimated that the young shepherdess reached the gate, a puddle of water was spreading at her feet, and I could hear the goats lapping it up.

"Mashallah, it's God's will," the young one said. "Yes, drink, all of you."

I stood there, listening to her desert accent. Then, gripped by a wild impulse, I unlatched the gate and swung it wide open. I pretended to be surprised to see them. "Oh, good morning, peace be upon you."

The woman who'd been doing all the work gasped and backed away, but the older one stood very still.

"And upon you peace," the older one said. She was a little taller, and her shoulders tilted down in surprise. She looked me up and down, taking me in. Then she chuckled, though her facemask muffled the sound. I looked down and realized I was quite a sight in my jeans and painter's smock, splotched with paint. I felt my hair and found a paintbrush resting behind my ear.

I pulled it out and said, "Welcome. Please, Auntie, let your animals drink," trying to make the whole situation seem perfectly normal.

"Thank you, my dear," the older woman replied, laughter still woven in her voice. The younger woman made sure all the goats drank from the puddle that was starting to flow down the street.

"Would you like a drink of water too? Are you thirsty?" Since neither of them answered, I ran to the studio and brought out a bottle of spring water and poured a glass for them, assuming they would share it. I remarked how cool the morning was, and the taller one agreed, still staring at me, her head tilted at an angle.

"Sorry if I surprised you. You're the first tribal women I've ever seen walking on our street," as if that gave me the right to surprise them like I had.

"Auntie, we should be going," the younger woman said. "I don't think we should be talking here."

"No, it's all right. Let them drink a little more."

The older one paused a moment and looked at me, a question seeming to flash in her eyes. She tilted her head back and let out a laugh like a clap of thunder. In that instant, I wondered where she had laughed before, in which tents, in which stretching valleys, under which moons and in whose arms. I was bewitched by the sound of her laughter, like a lazy moth bedazzled by a lantern in the night. I felt dizzy and leaned against the wall for a moment. Regaining my composure, I offered her the glass.

She thanked me and turned to her companion, who shook her head. I waited while she looked up and down the street to see if anyone was watching. Satisfied we were alone, she leaned the cane against her dress, then lifted the bottom edge of her facemask and flipped it back so it rested on top of her head, like a welder setting back his helmet. I could see her face. She took the glass and drank.

Wisps of hennaed hair, gleaming like shiny copper, peeked out from beneath her black headscarf. Lacy and delicate wrinkles covered her skin, more reminiscent of a sedentary life than that of someone from the desert. A faded indigo tattoo of diamond shapes connected her lower lip to the delicate point of her chin. Her dark eyes, rimmed with kohl, sat wide apart and flickered like sparklers. Large silver hoop earrings peeked out below her headscarf.

After a few moments, I regained my composure. I was sure I'd heard traces of something in her voice, then convinced myself I was imagining things, that I was just tired.

"Who are you?" she said. She giggled as she pulled the mask back over her face. "And why are you up so early? You should be in bed, not up listening to street sounds." She certainly didn't sound like a woman of the desert. Her words were those of an educated woman.

"I'm Fawzia. I couldn't sleep, and when I heard you coming, naturally I was curious." I wanted to add that it wasn't every day ladies sing in the street with a herd of goats. "I'm sorry, I hope I didn't disturb you."

"Not at all. But you are an artist, yes? And artists are up at all hours. In any case, I think the world is always best this time of day, don't you? Well then, thank you for the water. And our herd is grateful, too. May God keep you, Fawzia." She turned to her companion. "We must be on our way."

The younger woman gathered the goats into a tight group with her stick and walked on. The older woman fell in behind. They turned up the street toward the older part of our neighborhood, Ruwais.

"In God's protection," I called after them.

Before rounding the corner, the older woman looked back, and I waved. I waited a few seconds after the last of their goats disappeared before I closed the gate and leaned against it, amazed at what had just happened.

My hands raced across my sketchbook. I never imagined such women would talk to me, or that the older one would give me a glimpse of her face. She was at least 70, and she seemed intelligent and educated. And then there was her accent! That was the strangest thing of all. It was an odd blend of our Hijazi style with the central Najd region, but there was something else to it, too, that I couldn't identify. It didn't make sense. Why was an old woman like her out herding goats? And what recently settled nomad would know what an artist looks like, and what kind of hours they keep? I began to doubt she really was from the desert. Yet her face and her jewelry and clothing were exactly right for a shepherdess. I took great care drawing the tattoo on her chin and the sparkle of her eyes. As I sketched, it struck me that she hadn't seemed surprised by our encounter at all. Unlike a woman new to the city, she'd taken my sudden appearance in stride. And I didn't know her name.

CHAPTER 4

FULLY OPEN

Jeddah
January 1979

"MISS FAWZIA?" It was Hamdi, knocking on the studio door. "It's time for lunch." Hours had passed since I'd spoken with the women in our alley. I'd been sketching ever since.

The aroma of stuffed zucchini spiced with cinnamon greeted me as I entered the house. Everyone was waiting for me in the family room. Mama was home from her tennis game. Ibtisam was back from classes. Baba and my brothers were on their mid-day break from the office.

As they all stood up, Baba said, "Well, welcome. I hope you will feel at home here, dear guest." To me, he was as handsome as Omar Sharif, with his dark wavy hair and elegant mustache.

"Sorry, lost track of the time." No one seemed surprised at my answer, for they were accustomed to me disappearing into the studio for hours.

As we made our way to the dining table, my brothers towered over all of us, Baba included. Tarek, the oldest, had Baba's long nose, just like mine. He was an engineer, following in Baba's footsteps. Fahd, the next brother, had graduated from Cairo University in business. The youngest, Bashir, was studying at the London School of Economics. He was fascinated by the latest cars and electronic gadgets.

My sister Ibtisam walked with me, her long navy skirt rustling as she rolled up the sleeves of her white blouse, her long hair swaying. She never wore jewelry or makeup, not even lipstick. But then, it couldn't have improved her God-given glowing skin and perfect smile.

In her mid-forties, Mama wore her hair in a short bob with bangs. I loved pictures of her from her glory days in the late 1960s, when she twisted her long tresses into a towering beehive bun, spit curls on each cheek, framing her button nose and wide-set eyes. I loved her dangling earrings of faceted amethysts shaped like bunches of grapes. They matched a floor-length sleeveless gown of lavender satin. She wore this ensemble to a Cairo concert by Um Kulthum, the night the great artist performed the joyous love song A Thousand and One Nights. It was 1969, and the black-and-white Egyptian television cameras panned the audience and lingered on her and Baba, weaving her youth and her flashing smile into the performance forever.

My parents' schooling in Egypt had instilled in them a cosmopolitan outlook that added spice to their old Arabian heritage. Generations before, their families had moved to Jeddah from Mecca and the Hadramawt on the south coast of Arabia. My father's family, the Bughaidans, always moved with the times. In the 1950s, they'd sold their shops to buy real estate north of the balad, and had started importing machinery.

With his engineering degree in hand, Baba founded a general contracting firm, Bughaidan Ltd. He was the local agent for some Italian air-conditioners and a line of Japanese heavy equipment. He formed joint ventures with friends and bid on government construction jobs. Like most merchants from old Hijazi families, he had more work than he could handle and was awash in cash. He worked non-stop, every day of the week. He had three finance men on the payroll whose only job was to chase down the payments that were owed to him.

"Hmmmmm," sighed Baba, as Halimah brought out lunch. She and our driver, Hamdi, were husband and wife, from the Delta region of Egypt. Although Hamdi was a fine driver, it was Halimah's cooking that got them hired. They'd both been with us since I was a girl.

The boys dined with gusto. Mama just nibbled, since she was always watching her figure. Ibtisam had a bird-like appetite, too. I ate more than those two combined.

We never talked much while we ate, so the phone call didn't interrupt us. Baba was always getting calls at all hours, from all around the world. "Allo? Yes, yes, I'm here… of course… Please, please you are welcome," he said in English, in a full voice. That's how we knew it was an overseas call. He started taking notes on a yellow legal pad and held the phone between his head and shoulder. He rubbed his college ring with his forefinger as he listened.

"Well?" Bashir said, looking around the table.

"I can't tell yet," Tarek answered. It was easy to guess what country was calling because Baba unknowingly imitated the accents of foreigners. He shook his finger at us and shielded his eyes, trying to tune us out and foil our game.

"Of course, of course we will arrange it," he said, scribbling. There was still no hint in his voice. Then, as he said, "Very good, we will see you at the airport, have a safe journey," we all whispered, "Japan!" stifling our laughter.

"Yes, it was Japan." he said as he hung up. "But how could you tell?"

"Baba," Bashir said, "You were *bowing!*" We imitated what he had been doing, bending over his plate of food.

"Well, I finally saw him today," Bashir announced as he sipped his coffee. As was our custom, we had moved to the sitting room where Halimah served us demitasse cups of strong Arabic coffee, spiced with cardamom.

"I saw that crazy motorcyclist. It's true what we've heard—he's some kind of European or American. His blonde curls stick out under his helmet, and he wears his helmet mask down so you can't see his face. He was speeding down Medina Road the wrong way. Only this time, a cop was chasing him, and everyone was pulling onto the curbs. What a mess! And they still didn't catch him. He took off down a side street."

"You'll never guess what I saw today," Tarek said in answer. "Nothing can top this." He relished the silence then said, "A goat wearing a red bra."

After our laughter subsided, Baba said, "You know why they do that? They're trying to wean the kid off its mother's milk, saving it to make yogurt or cheese. It's an old tribal trick."

I told them about the two ladies, and the mystery of the older one.

"She's probably a princess in disguise," Mama said, raising one eyebrow and smiling at me.

"Or a CIA spy in deep cover," Bashir said. "Or no, she's an Iranian spy from SAVAK, sent to scope out the American Embassy on Palestine Road!"

Though it was the most important issue our family faced, we never spoke about Ibtisam getting married when we were all together. The topic was too sensitive.

The problem was that my parents' friends from other elite merchant families like ours thought Ibtisam was too conservative for their sons. They wanted a daughter-in-law who liked to travel to Europe and spoke a handful of languages, yet who would be happy focused on raising the children. Ibtisam was not attracted to the role of a cosmopolitan Hijazi housewife and mother, preferring a more devout life of quiet contemplation, study, and prayer. As a consequence, she did nothing to sell herself as a bride. She told me that God would bring her the proper suitor if and when the time was right.

Many Saudi families still preferred first-cousin marriages, but not ours. Otherwise, I'm sure Ibtisam and I would have married our Aunt Rosette and Uncle Fouad's sons. We'd played together since we were children and remained close. But our families were educated enough to understand the risks of first cousin marriage. Unlike families with famous and high-ranking tribal names who valued their pure family origins, we were of mixed urban merchant lineage and marrying within the family wasn't important.

Even though Ibtisam was modest and naturally beautiful, many religious families wanted a daughter-in-law with pure blood from their own family, or the bloodline of a famous religious scholar, never mind the fact that many of our most revered religious thinkers are of mixed heritage. I suspect that some of these families' reputations would have been tainted if their son had married into a trading family like ours, no matter how distinguished and wealthy we were. Looking back, I wonder if they were intimidated by her obvious, quiet intelligence. No matter, we kept on looking, optimistic that the right young man would come along. Besides, Ibtisam was a natural beauty. That would surely count in her favor.

CHAPTER 5

A MARE THE COLOR OF RIVER STONES

Jeddah
February 1979

AUNT ROSETTE swept into my bedroom and kissed me on both cheeks. "Come, have coffee with your Mama and me, just for a few minutes. Studies can wait!"

Rosette. Just rolling the 'R' at the beginning of her name made me smile. She once took me for a ride in a rented red convertible in the hills above Beirut. Ever the fashion plate, she'd wrapped a crimson chiffon scarf around her short ebony curls, and it matched the car, her lipstick, and her nails. She loved fast cars and fortunately so did my Uncle Fouad, who had plenty of them. He used to take her out driving in the desert and let her take the wheel.

Rosette never held back her startling and infectious laugh. She was always telling jokes, and she loved to dance. When they hosted parties for foreign businessmen and their wives, which they did frequently in those oil-boom days, there was always dancing. She knew all the latest steps and was an expert at Egyptian dance, which she'd learned while in high school in Cairo. She taught me that particular art, insisting it was a social grace that every Arab girl should know.

The three of us sat in the family room. "Any progress with Ibtisam?" Aunt Rosette asked.

"Nothing." Mama sighed. "It's so discouraging."

"We should get her out more, to meet people. In fact, that's why I came today. You and your daughters are invited to a party at Samirah Saleh's house. She's celebrating the engagement of her daughter to the Amir Ahmad bin Majid. There will be people there from entirely new circles. Perhaps it will help expose her a bit more. What do you think?"

As for "entirely new circles," I doubted it. Samirah was a good friend of Aunt Rosette, so there probably wouldn't be conservative ladies who'd find Ibtisam a good choice for their sons. In marrying a prince, Samirah's daughter was moving from her family's comfortable merchant-class status into the Saudi royal family, even though this particular groom wasn't from a very powerful branch.

There are thousands of princes, not to mention princesses, because King Abd al-Aziz, who founded the modern kingdom, married over 100 times, all while maintaining a limit of four wives at a time. Even though there were so many princes, it was still a big step for a girl to marry into any part of the royal family. It wasn't in the cards for us, though. Baba did business with a select group of royals that he trusted, but in general we ran in different circles and steered clear of them unless it was necessary. So the party didn't seem a likely place to find a mother-in-law and a groom for Ibtisam.

And additional exposure for her? My sister always got lost in a crowd, and in these circles it would be worse. She never called attention to herself, never put on makeup. Even at a ladies party, she preferred to blend into the background. In the end, Ibtisam agreed to go, though I'm sure she'd rather have been home reading or researching a paper for school.

This was a formal occasion, so we rustled out of the house in long gowns of taffeta and silk, climbing into Uncle Fouad's new Rolls Royce. Like Baba, Uncle Fouad was a successful businessman, but he and Aunt Rosette tended to be more flamboyant with their wealth.

We turned into the drive-up entrance to the Saleh's sumptuous villa and waited as each car ahead of us deposited ladies at the front door. Once we entered the villa, female servants took our abayas and the hostesses Samirah and her daughter Muna welcomed us.

I'm not a fashion follower myself, but they dazzled us with their glamour in matching caftans of glowing russet silk. Muna was bedecked in a stunning diamond-and-warm-topaz jewelry ensemble, a gift from her fiancé. He had chosen well, as the jewels complimented her gown and set off her gleaming dark red tresses. They ushered us inside to join the throng of women in long gowns and perfect coiffures, enveloped in a cloud of competing expensive perfumes.

The walls of the enormous salon were lined with sofas and cushioned chairs, all upholstered in peach. Matching oriental carpets—there must have been 20 of them—covered the entire floor. It was a group of perhaps a hundred women. A quick scan of the crowd yielded up many familiar faces, and none looked outrageously over-dressed or over-jeweled. I wondered how many royals were there.

We joined some high-school friends and sat together. Ibtisam laughed as she shook hands with two young daughters of an old school chum who had married right after high school.

Women servants carried a charcoal burner filled with hot coals into the room, and set it at one end. Then a dozen women entered, carrying round frame drums in various sizes. They arranged their chairs in a semi-circle and sat down, taking turns tapping the drums over the coals to tighten the drumskins.

"They flew Hind Mubarak in from Riyadh to sing tonight," Aunt Rosette said. "Hers is the top wedding group in Riyadh right now. This is their audition for the wedding party."

The singer entered last, carrying her instrument, the oud. She was a black woman of generous though not unpleasant proportions. Her hair was cut to chin length and swept up to one side, accentuating the roundness of her face. She turned to our hostess Samirah and nodded with a smile, revealing a gold tooth. She sat down in the center chair, flanked by her drummers, and began to tune her instrument.

The drummers pounded the rhythms of old Arabia, and the guests clapped. When Hind began to sing, everyone, from the teenagers to the grandmothers, joined in the old Hijazi love song, "She Waved the Scarf out the Window" about a girl signaling her lover. So many of our song lyrics were about risky love, but who in that room had dared do what I had done? I sang along with gusto, convinced I was the only one who really knew what it was like to have a secret forbidden love. Young women got up and danced in pairs. Some had brought their dancing thobes, and they slipped these colorful loose overdresses on over their gowns. Others lifted the hems of their evening dresses and stepped to and fro. Before long, a dozen girls twirled and danced in thobes of bright green, hot pink, and turquoise, heavy with ornate gold embroidery and sequins.

"Fawzia!" My friend from high school, Badriyyah, rushed up to me, and we hugged. I was so glad to see her, but since it was too loud to talk, we danced together instead. We stepped in circles, past each other, and then mirrored the other's movements. We added little hip slides and tiny shoulder shimmies to make each other laugh. Some girls started to toss their hair from side to side like they do in the desert, and we copied them. Ibtisam sat with her school chum, on the sidelines as usual.

When the band took a break to have tea and re-tighten their drumskins, we slipped outside to get some air, though it was so humid we didn't find much relief. The salon opened onto a private garden of tropical plants and fragrant frangipani trees, crisscrossed with marble walkways lit from below. We claimed a table in a quiet corner. Badriyyah seemed calm, like a horse that had been running free and was content to return its stable.

"What about Hisham?" she asked, looking around to make sure no one was near. She was my only friend in Jeddah who knew about him.

"We broke it off before graduation." Then I leaned over and said, "But he found me the other day and we went to Obhur."

"Allaaah! That's fantastic! Good luck! How are you doing it?"

"We don't have a plan or anything, we've met just once."

She shook her head and smiled, looking down.

"Do you have something you want to tell me?" She turned away, but I grabbed her arm and pulled her back to face me. "I see, there is something. Tell me!"

"I met someone in France, he's from Riyadh. We're trying to make a rendezvous, but so far we're just talking on the phone."

"God help us both."

"Listen," she said, squeezing my hand. "The music's starting again. Let's dance some more!"

We danced for at least another hour. Later, we even got Ibtisam up with her school friend and her friend's daughters. It was after midnight when we were ushered outside to dine at round tables set with elegant crystal, china, and silver. We feasted on roast lamb, chicken, whole sea bass, and all kinds of vegetable dishes and salads.

As was tradition, when the guest of honor—the bride's future mother-in-law—stood up from the table, we rose as well. Servants rinsed our hands in rosewater over gleaming silver bowls and offered us rich perfumes. Opium was the most popular perfume that night, more pungent than usual in the humid stillness. It was a perfect match for the richness of the evening, and for all of Saudi Arabia just then. If we'd had a national scent, like a national anthem, Opium would have been it.

After dinner, we returned to the main salon, savoring the air-conditioning, and took our seats. We had sweets, tea and coffee, and the servants offered European cigarettes from silver trays.

I was just beginning to wonder whether the evening was over when a group of women at the far end of the room stood in a tight circle and began walking among the crowd. In their midst, an elderly woman was being presented to each guest. One by one, they rose to greet her. She kissed some on both cheeks and shook hands with others, always saying a few words. I could only catch glimpses of her, flashes of a vintage thobe of brilliant turquoise silk. Her long silver hair fell in a single braid below her waist. An aged dark-skinned lady by her side sported the old-fashioned costume of Jeddah, namely a tight-fitting yellow coat, a zabun, with a white blouse underneath. Over this she wore a gauze-like coverall in sheer red. Her head was covered in a white scarf. A bejeweled young woman in a Western evening gown of azure blue helped them along, taking their arms to keep them moving through the crowd of well-wishers.

"Do you have any idea who the woman in the blue is?" I asked Badriyyah.

"I heard someone say she's a relative from the groom's family."

"So that would make her some kind of princess," I said.

"I haven't seen her in years," an older guest near us said.

"I didn't know she was still with us," another commented. "God bless her, she must be at least eighty-five."

"Any idea who the younger woman is with her?" I said.

"Amira Nurah," Badriyyah said. "I think she's one of the groom's cousins."

As the group made its way toward us, servants set two comfortable chairs in the center of the room. The older woman's path was slowed when she encountered a lady of her own vintage who couldn't stand. The nearby guests laughed and let out delighted zaghareed in response to something she said.

Finally, the mysterious guest turned in our direction. I was shocked when I recognized the diamond shaped tattoos on her chin. It was the shepherdess, the older one, the one with the walking stick! Instead of the tribal outfit she'd

had when I encountered her in our ally, she wore gold-and-pearl versions of
traditional necklaces I had seen only in silver. Instead of a stick, she leaned
on an elegant polished wooden cane. The coppery henna traces in her hair
framed her chin tattoo and set off those familiar brilliant black eyes. We rose
as she drew near. At last she stood in front of me. Her tribal tattoo danced
on her chin as she spoke to me with that giggle. She recognized me.
"Asalaam-u-alaikum. Peace upon you," she said. "We meet again!"

"Wa alaikum as-salaam. And upon you peace. I am honored."

"Fawzia, is it?"

"Yes, Grandmother." Without thinking, I had used an honorific title for
her.

"I hope this will be an interesting night for you."

"As of this moment, it is."

"God willing, inshallah." She smiled and patted my hand before she
greeted Badriyyah. The older black woman stood behind. No one introduced
her, so I assumed she was a servant.

The young woman with them turned to me. "How do you do, I'm Nurah.
Pleased to meet you. I see you've met Salma before."

"Honored to meet you, Nurah. Yes, I've met her. But she knows nearly
everyone here, doesn't she?"

"Sometimes it seems like she knows every person in the Hijaz," Nurah
said.

"You know her?" Badriyyah asked after they'd passed.

"I met her once." But now I'd learned her name! It was Salma, a classic
and timeless name.

Salma and her companion made their way to the seats of honor in the
middle of the room. Then, one by one, older servants came from the back
rooms and kissed the old lady's hands. With some, she reached out and kissed
their cheeks like an equal. She had kind words for them all. They turned to
her companion and greeted her as well, deferring to her almost as much as
they did to Salma. I was amazed. She was beloved by all, both servants and
guests. She was like a rock star, a real celebrity, accompanied by a princess.
This was the woman who was herding goats down our street? Who was she?

When a servant offered the two ladies cardamom coffee from a modern
version of the traditional dallah coffeepot, Salma reached into a pocket in her
turquoise thobe and pulled out a tiny golden cup, of the old handle-less style,

then drank from it. When she finished, she slipped the cup back into her dress. The facets of her gold jewelry glittered in the light. She was resplendent. All eyes in the room bore down on her, including mine.

A dozen little girls gathered at her feet. "Tell us a story, Auntie!" one of them cried. "Yes, please Auntie, about the girls in the tribes, in the desert!" another echoed. She nodded and put her finger up to her lips for silence, just as the groom's mother walked to the center of the room.

She spoke in a booming voice. "It is a great honor to welcome you all to join us in celebrating the engagement of our Ahmad to the lovely Muna. We look forward to welcoming her into our family. To cap off the evening, we would like to share some heritage with you, stories from the desert told by Jeddah's own storyteller, Salma, who was born in the northern desert." The ladies applauded. Salma smiled and nodded in acknowledgement.

When the crowd grew quiet, one of the young girls called out, "Auntie, tell us about the Great War."

"All right, my dear." Salma smiled, leaning on her cane as she looked down at the little girls before her. "Those were the days when I lived in my mother's tent, among the people of the Bani Shamaal tribe, God have mercy on their souls."

Salma's voice was resonant and full. She sounded like a woman half her age, and her words filled the room. Her voice swept me away to a mysterious place that somehow felt like home.

"It was wonderful to be a young girl in the desert in those days. My hair was so long it reached the ground. It took two servants to comb and braid it each day."

A girl sitting in front stroked her own long hair, as if wondering how long she could grow it.

"It was wartime, and there was danger everywhere. Did you girls know that part of World War I took place right in our own desert, near Jordan? So, when we camped with my father and my uncle Shaikh Talal, may God have mercy on their souls, generals, shaikhs, and princes would visit us. Of course my father and my Uncle Talal were as generous as Hatim of Tayy. They would never turn anyone away hungry, and we organized many feasts."

"Auntie," one of the girls said. "Tell us how you used to ride, how you used to ride al-Sahba." The girls fidgeted with their long party dresses. They crossed and recrossed their ankles, leaned right and left, and briefly rested on their elbows. As Salma continued, their restlessness fell away and they sat still.

Salma held out her cane so the girls could see its handle, an Arabian mare's head carved from bone. "Al-Sahba was the most glorious mare I've ever ridden. She was white, with a mane of pearl and gray, and stockings of gray. They used to call that kind of horse Hajr al-Wadi because she was the color of river stones. My father gave her to me when I was 14, and I used to ride her every day, among the flocks. She was faster than all the others. I used to get her into a run and we would leave the others far behind." With this, Salma had grabbed the girls' attention.

"Those days were full of happiness. Even though the tribes have left their tents for the town, the stories of the desert live on."

"Here is a story from those war days," Salma said. "The great chief of the Ruwala tribe, Nuri al-Sha`alan, came to visit our camp, and he told this tale one moonlit night in spring. Shaikh Nuri had a strong voice so all of us on the women's side of the tent could hear it, too. This is what he said."

"In the name of God, the Merciful, the Compassionate. I heard this story from my grandfather, who heard it from his great uncle Zuwaid ibn Tafas al-Sha`alan.

"Kaan ya maa kaan, there once was, in a time long ago. In those days, the tribes held a market near the northern city of Tayma each spring, when the lambs were young. Every year, the tribes met there to buy, to sell, to recite verses, to dance the dahhah, and to trade news. One year, two tribes went there, one of them big and powerful. Its men were strong, and they had many sons and daughters. They constantly raided the tribes around them, and in this way they amassed great herds of camels and sheep. The powerful tribe had come to market to sell livestock and buy household goods.

"The other tribe was small and poor. They had only 100 sheep, a few camels, and three horses. But God had blessed them in other ways. Their women were famous for the beautiful tent dividers woven from the wool of their sheep and the hair of their camels. The poor tribe came to market to sell the tent dividers so they could buy sheep and provisions for the coming hot summer.

"Five boys from the big tribe sauntered through the market on the last day, when everyone traded in a hurry. They walked by Muqrin, a boy from the smaller tribe. He sat alone on a blanket, selling the last tent divider his sister had woven. She had fallen ill and couldn't sell it herself.

"'Look,' one of the boys said. "This weaving is excellent." Muqrin began to bargain with them, but he kept thinking about how much his tribe needed grain and how his little brother was desperate for a new pair of sandals. He wouldn't lower his price. He urged them to buy from someone else instead, because there were others selling at much lower prices. But none were as beautiful as his sister's weaving.

"The boys began to taunt him. They insulted the size of his family's camp, the manginess of their sheep, and the shabbiness of their camels. How could he be so proud and demand such a price, they asked passersby. A man watched them taunt Muqrin and told them that, earlier, Muqrin had offered the same weavings at a much lower price. This enraged the boys, but Muqrin ignored them and sat cross-legged, looking down. They began to insult the weavings, pointing out imagined faults. Still, Muqrin said nothing.

"Then one of the boys shouted, 'Well what can you expect? Of course it will have faults! Have you seen the cross-eyed one who wove it?'

"That was the limit. They had insulted his sister! Muqrin jumped up to fight, even though he was smaller and weaker. He grabbed his camel stick and tried to chase them away, but they just laughed at him. One of the boys took the stick from his hand. Another grabbed him by his thobe, holding him so another boy could hit him. Just then, Hamid, an older boy from the powerful tribe, happened to walk by. When the bullies saw him, they backed away from Muqrin.

" 'Why are you bothering him?' Hamid asked.

" 'He is nothing but a boy from the weak tribe. He has the nerve to try to sell us this weaving for such-and-such a price, and he won't lower it. He was willing to sell to other buyers at a much lower price this morning!'

" 'Is that true? Did you give us a higher price than you asked this morning?' Hamid asked, standing between Muqrin and the bullies.

" 'Yes, I did, and I'll triple the price now, now that he's insulted my tribe and my family. In fact, I wouldn't sell anything to your stingy people for any amount of money in the Amir's palace.'

"Hamid's eyes grew wide and he stared at Muqrin. Then he turned back to the bullies. 'You have insulted his family and his tribe. To make up for your shameful words, I will pay him the price he demands. How much did you say you wanted?'

"Hamid paid it, gave Muqrin his camel stick, and carried the weaving back to camp. For weeks, the boys were scolded by their elders for forcing Hamid to make the purchase at a high price to uphold their tribe's good name. Whenever those boys saw the divider in Hamid's tent, they remembered their shame."

Laughter broke the storyteller's spell. I looked up and was shocked to find nearly half the guests had left the room, and those who remained were carrying on full-blown conversations. This was not only discourteous to those of us who wanted to hear the story, it was quite rude to show disrespect to an older person, and to the hosts as well.

Salma looked around the room. She had lost control of her audience. She sighed, and the woman beside her reached out and touched her shoulder. Salma cleared her throat and waited, holding her head high but casting her eyes downward. Still, the women took no notice and kept up their conversations, which grew louder since they hadn't realized she had stopped. The little girls, however, who had been paying perfect attention, started looking around at the adults.

Finally, the groom's mother came to Salma's rescue. She stood and clapped her hands once, saying, "Ladies, please. Let us show respect to our elders and to our heritage."

The talking stopped, and the remaining audience refocused its attention on Salma, who nodded at her rescuer before she looked around the room and continued. She never acknowledged their rudeness, but carried on with her story, this time holding their attention.

"The years passed, and fortunes shifted like the winds of a sandstorm. The weak tribe grew strong and rich. God sent rain to their grazing lands, and their flocks increased. Their warriors gained fame for their clever raids. And still, the women in their tribe wove the most colorful tent dividers in the desert. Muqrin grew straight and strong like a palm tree, and he became a courageous warrior.

"One day, Muqrin and his friends went out hunting with his trusted falcon. They caught three rabbits at dusk and decided to camp at a nearby well. When they got there, they found a single tent.

"An old woman came out of the tent and welcomed them. The warriors noticed there was no one at the well but this old woman, a young boy, and a slightly older girl. They were so poor the woman had only a handful of dates to offer her guests. She sent her son to slaughter their only camel. Muqrin grabbed the boy and carried him over his shoulder, kicking and screaming, back to his mother. Muqrin said there was no need to slaughter the camel. Instead, he said, they would share the rabbits.

"After they ate, Muqrin and his men slept next to the fire outside the tent. But robbers attacked in the middle of the night, trying to steal their horses. Now you children know that, in the old days, during a proper raid, women and children were always left alone. But these were common thieves. They ran inside the old woman's tent and started ransacking it.

"Muqrin stormed after them. Once inside, he noticed the same tent divider his sister had made so many years ago. It had been her last weaving, and she had died a few months later. But Muqrin had no time to think about this. He and his men fought off the intruders.

"After chasing the robbers out into the desert, Muqrin asked the old woman about her tribe. She was the last of her once-great people, wiped out by sickness. Her brother, now dead, had left her with his daughter and young son. She was traveling to a town where she had a distant cousin who might help them. 'What was your brother's name?' Muqrin asked.

"'Hamid, God rest his soul,' she said. Muqrin smiled and nodded his head. Some time later, he asked the woman if he could marry her niece. Though puzzled by his proposal, the old woman and her niece agreed.

"At the wedding feast, Muqrin told how he had met his bride's father, Hamid, long ago at the market near Tayma. He wanted to marry the girl because she was a beauty, but also because he wanted to honor Hamid and repay the deed done to him that day. You see, Muqrin used the money he got from the weaving to start his own herds, which became great and prosperous. And so they found their happiness, and may we find ours just the same. And now, my daughters, it is late. You've heard enough of an old woman talk. Go and dream of al-Sahba. Good night, my dears."

As the adults clapped, the mothers of the girls retrieved them. Some fell asleep in their mother's laps as the final round of aloeswood incense was brought into the room, signaling the end of the evening. Badriyyah and I joined the well-wishers around Salma.

"Did you enjoy the story?" Salma asked.

"It was wonderful, truly."

"Please visit sometime. For, after all, as you said the other day, we're neighbors. Nurah can tell you how to find us."

"Then God willing, neighbor, I'll visit soon."

"Do you promise?" she held my hand and squeezed it, looking deep into my eyes. "These things happen for a reason, you know."

I approached Nurah and explained that Salma had invited me to call on her. Nurah seemed very down to earth and approachable in the way she gave me directions. I got up my nerve and said, "Is Salma really from the Bani Shamaal, the niece of the famous chieftain Talal Abu Saif?"

"Yes, she is." Nurah smiled. "In fact, she is our distant relation and has lived with our family for many years now. Salma is like my own grandmother. And if she asked you to visit her, she is serious. She really enjoys visitors, so I hope you will come. It will do her good. I'm afraid these days I'm so busy with my own children, who are still too young to appreciate her."

CHAPTER 6

PALACE IN RUWAIS

Jeddah
February 1979

NOT HAVING a phone number for Nurah's palace, I called on Salma without an appointment and hoped for the best. It was a common way to visit back then, because most people didn't have telephones—the phone company couldn't keep up with the demand for new lines. This was many years before we all got mobiles, much less had the internet.

Nurah's palace was only a ten-minute walk from our house. Standing outside its tall, whitewashed walls, I marveled at the gigantic trees that shaded the whole block. I rang the bell at the front gate and, before long, an elderly man opened it. He wore an old-style wrapped turban, and a cotton cloth wrapped around his waist. His sun-darkened skin contrasted with his white eyebrows and spotless t-shirt. I assumed he was from Yemen or the Hadramawt and had worked many years in the semi-tropical sun.

"Good morning, Uncle," I said, out of respect. "I would like to visit Salma. Is she at home?"

After asking my name, he nodded. "Come in," he said, then beckoned me inside with a small hand gesture. The palace was refreshing in its lack of ostentation. It was more like a large villa than a grand palace. It was a treasure hidden behind high walls, a three-storied stucco structure festooned with balconies and patios. Tropical flowers and vines flourished in the shade of the trees.

The old man led the way, dipping from side to side as he walked, his legs bowed from years of hard work. Instead of bringing me to the main house, he led me to a small building along the outer wall. A miniature villa, it had its own patio shaded by an arbor of brilliant pink bougainvillea. He knocked at its wooden door.

"Yes, I'm coming," a muffled voice answered from inside. The dark woman who had accompanied Salma at the party opened the door.

"Good morning, my name is Fawzia Bughaidan. Is Madame Salma at home?"

"Yes, of course, welcome." She smiled, holding the door and beckoning me inside. I took off my sandals and stepped into a modest kitchen, which led to a small dining area and sitting room. "Please sit down."

Now, you might wonder why she let me inside, just like that. First, that's hospitality. But also, she had sized me up in a moment, and she could tell I was a local woman by my accent and appearance. In Jeddah, unexpected visitors were commonplace, especially among women. She would have no way of knowing my business with Salma, nor would she ask me. That would be impolite.

Salma laughed and clapped her hands when she saw me. "Aha, you did come!" She was wearing a dark purple caftan embroidered with yellow, orange, and red, her hair wrapped in a white kerchief. She shook my hand with gusto and led me to another small sitting room that looked out on a patio shaded by a bougainvillea arbor.

The dark woman brought us mint lemonade.

"Thank you for inviting me to come see you. First, I want to apologize for surprising you that morning when you walked by our house."

"It's all right, my dear. At first I was puzzled about our meeting, although it was hilarious, given your artist's get-up and mine. And then, when I saw you at the Saleh party, I decided we were destined to meet. So I'm delighted you're here."

"But let me explain why I was at our front gate that morning when you passed by."

The serving woman joined us. Most servants would have left the room while their mistress was entertaining, so this surprised me. We still weren't introduced.

"Indeed, sometimes the most interesting things in life are like this, you see, unexpected surprises," Salma said.

When I told them I had intended to paint her and had waited days for her to pass by our house, the ladies began to laugh. As she laughed, Salma bounced in her seat. The other woman leaned to the side and giggled like a much younger person. They set each other off and started up again. Salma stopped for a moment. "Are you sure? Did you really say you're making a painting of me walking in the street dressed like a shepherdess?"

"Yes, exactly."

They started laughing again.

Finally, Salma sighed and took a long drink of lemonade. "I'm sorry. We don't mean to offend you. It's just we never dreamed such a thing would happen. You see, Mabrukah here often comes with me, but on that day, one of the young ladies who lives here accompanied me. I suppose we must have been strange-looking if you felt inspired to paint us."

"No, not strange at all, but perhaps a little out of place in these times. I hope it's all right."

"Yes, yes, perhaps you are right. Our traditional clothing is now exotic even in our own country. Just don't tell anyone it's me that you're painting. Nurah's family would be scandalized if my morning walks were memorialized in a picture!" She was still smiling.

"Of course. I'll keep your secret safe. And by the way, I call the painting, Shepherdess Painting #1."

Salma burst out laughing again. "I am the Number One Shepherdess then?"

"Well, you and your companion are absolutely the Number One Shepherdesses in all of Jeddah."

The ladies dried their eyes and blew their noses. I hadn't laughed like that for such a long time. Not since leaving Beirut.

"I realize I've neglected to introduce you to Mabrukah properly," she said. We shook hands. "Now, tell us about yourself, young lady."

After I told them about my family, Salma nodded. "Ah yes, I remember now. Didn't your family have a fabric store down in the balad years ago?"

"Yes, they did. Did you ever shop there?"

"Oh yes, many times."

"Maybe you knew my grandfather Ahmad."

"Perhaps I did. But I've forgotten so much now. Is he still alive?"

"No, God bless him. None of my grandparents are alive. In fact, I never knew them at all. It's a pity."

"That is a pity. Not to know your own family." Salma's voice trailed off as she looked at her hands folded in her lap. "And now you are back at University?"

"Yes. Studying for my Master's in History and teaching English at King Abd al-Aziz University."

"Bravo. I hope you will be get your PhD one day."

"God willing, God willing."

"But you're not married yet? Engaged?"

"No, not yet. My older sister, Ibtisam, she's to be married first. You see, unlike me, Ibtisam is a very serious student at Umm al-Qura in Mecca, and it's not so easy to find her a groom. Me, I'm different from her a little bit, I'm not so...serious."

There was a little break, so I ventured forth. "So, you enjoy taking early morning walks?"

"Yes, I need the exercise. You see, I was born in the desert, and we always lived in places where I could move, where we could go for a ride or a long walk. You know how difficult that is nowadays, for a woman to stroll in the city. Decades ago, when Mabrukah and I first came to Jeddah, we insisted on keeping goats. In those days, there were no dairies, and we did need the milk, that was true, but mostly we wanted an excuse to go outside."

"From the beginning, we would dress as local tribeswomen, as if we were from a poor family that had recently moved to the city. We'd get our exercise, and the goats would get theirs. So the family always had plenty of goats' milk to drink and to make yoghurt. Now, things are different. There is milk in the market. Lately, I only get out once a week or so, and I've slowed down. Mabrukah walks with me less often now, so my young companion joins me."

She explained that the goats were penned next door, and that the young lady who helped them was from a small village in the north and lived there with Nurah's family. They were all related, part of a large northern tribal family.

"I learned from Amira Nurah that you are the niece of Shaikh Talal. Is that true?"

"Yes, it's true, God rest his soul."

"Did you learn your stories in the desert?"

"Some of them, yes. But I also learned them from other storytellers. Stories used to be a big form of entertainment for everyone among the tribes, and in the towns and cities too. In the old days, I told stories almost every night, to little children, to young brides like you, and to older women. But everything has changed now. The girls still love the old folklore, but they are all in school, learning to read and write, and their minds are going in new directions. Everyone in this country is just too busy with modern life and our oil wealth. Instead of thinking about the old days, they go to the souq in their cars at night. Worst of all, there is that new storyteller in town, the television."

"I'm sorry the women showed you disrespect at the party." This had been bothering me ever since that night. I hadn't intended to bring it up, but the subject had presented itself.

"Thank you my dear, but that was not the first time it's happened. Unfortunately, adults are losing interest in the old ways, the old stories. And who can blame them? Who wants to hear ancient stories from a wrinkled old woman when you read Paris Vogue and fly to London for the weekend?"

"But this is wrong. Your story was marvelous. I loved every word, and how you told it, too."

She didn't respond, even when I took a slow sip of my lemonade, so I changed the subject and asked about her accent, noting she was obviously an educated woman.

"I was born among my tribe, the Banu Shamaal in the northern desert, near what is now Jordan. Along the way, I had the chance to learn to read and write. So when I tell a story, I sometimes play the role of a tribal storyteller, and sometimes a town or city storyteller. I use different accents, depending on the situation and the story itself. I even have costumes for particular occasions. Mabrukah is excellent at making sure my appearance is just right. As for my own speech, well yes, you are correct. Our pasts leave traces in our words, do they not?"

"Has anyone written down, or recorded your stories?"

Salma shook her head.

"Such a shame," I said. "They shouldn't be lost. When you told your story of the two tribes and the weaving, you took us on a journey to our own past. It was unforgettable."

She looked down at her hands again and shook her head. Then she seemed to take deliberate control of herself and sipped her lemonade. She gazed at me as if searching for something in my eyes. "Young lady, they are not my stories. Others told them to me over the years, and I memorized them all. But they were never meant to be mine. When a story is told, it passes to the one who hears it, but only for a while. And unless the story gets retold, it dies. Right now, they are with me, but they are not mine. And there is no one to learn them now. Like our old way of life, like the few old-timers left, these stories are disappearing. My memory for stories used to be like a bank vault. But it is weaker now and I fear they will be lost."

Mabrukah reached out and took her hand in comfort. I objected, saying how impressed I was by her prowess.

"The important thing is, these stories are ours. They belong to us all, and they are part of our history. They make us who we are. Now that you've heard it, that story is yours."

Then she fell silent. I was embarrassed at having brought up such a difficult subject on my first visit. I took my leave shortly after. On my way out, she held my hand and said, "Do visit again, you are always welcome."

CHAPTER 7

Dancing with Danger

Jeddah
April 1979

HISHAM AND I began to meet every time he came to town. He'd pick me up at school, and we would visit Topkapi, a Turkish restaurant that served tea in the afternoon. The waiters always ushered us to a table where potted plants formed a kind of privacy screen. Back home in Turkey, they would no doubt also have needed to be discreet when they met with respectable young ladies. We talked, held hands, and were so reckless that we even tried to sneak kisses.

We craved our hours together, because our love was forbidden and because when we met, we laughed. Despite the risks, just about anything could set us off. Once we were in a café, and Hisham raised his eyebrow so I'd look up. Hanging above us, was a huge pink disco ball covered in mirrors. There were no discos in Saudi Arabia, and just seeing it there got us laughing. But we had to be careful, because Saudi men and women didn't often laugh together in public.

Inevitably, talk turned to whether he could propose marriage with any hope of success. No matter how hard we wished for it, we could foresee only risks. If he asked for me formally, he would have to admit that he knew me at college. This alone could get me in trouble if my parents suspected we had been a couple at school. And then there was the much more significant problem that his family was Shia. A proper courtship seemed hopeless, impossible. So we made the decision to keep seeing each other in secret. We knew we only had limited time together before one of us got engaged to someone else "more appropriate."

Wherever we went, Hisham always had a backup plan, in case we should run into my family. He took care to drive on quiet streets where we were less likely to get mired in one of Jeddah's massive traffic jams. At restaurants, we always sat near a side door, with my back to the entrance. Several times, we had to leave a restaurant when I saw family friends or colleagues from school. I'd signal to Hisham with a slight shake of my head, and he'd whisk me outside to his car, parked so we could make a quick getaway. If this happened in the middle of a dinner, Hisham would leave a wad of bills on the table. The waiters were always discreet and nodded to Hisham when this happened, as if they knew the dangerous game we were playing.

Meanwhile, I often visited Salma after school. Though I was drawn to the world of her stories, she never offered to tell me any more, and we stuck to small talk. I waited for her to bring up the topic, but she never did.

It was during those visits I realized she had an unusual circle of friends. Reem Mutair, one of the country's most prominent poets, was a regular visitor. Sometimes I would stop by and find Salma was out visiting her friends. They were intellectuals, famous authors, musicians, and even royals. At my next visit, she would share their news with me, as if I was part of her circle.

"Are you all right, dear?" Salma asked, during one of my visits. I was watching her mouth move as she spoke, but my thoughts were far away, in Hisham's arms.

During the hot summer months, Salma and Mabrukah went to Taif, and I'd tell Mama I was visiting her each time Hisham and I had a rendezvous. In late summer, Hisham's family firm won a large contract in the Hijaz, so he convinced his father to open an office in Jeddah and to let him run it. I was thrilled we would be living in the same city, yet I knew this would also give us more opportunities to get caught.

He rented an apartment about a mile from our house, north of Palestine Road. Through his business connections, he got a phone line, so I could call him. But he still couldn't call me. I'd pretend to visit my friend Badriyyah in order to see him. Hamdi would drop me off, and I'd go inside her house for a few minutes. Then I'd catch a taxi and meet Hisham at the supermarket, and we'd go from there. Badriyyah wanted to help us any way she could.

Hisham knew every minute of my routine, and, at least once a week, he would drive alongside or ahead of Hamdi on our way to the University. He would let the car drift back next to me and would give me a quick smile and a wink before speeding up and going to his office. Hamdi never noticed the same maroon Impala alongside us on the road. One time, I had a hard time not laughing, since he'd written "I'm dreaming of you" in the dust on the side of his car.

Hisham and I had always argued over Saudi soccer teams. Ever since I was a girl, I'd been a fan of Jeddah's al-Ahli, while he cheered for al-Ittifaq of the Eastern Province. Once, when the clubs had a match in Jeddah, Hisham bought tickets. Women couldn't attend soccer games, so I went disguised as a man. First, I had to change clothes in Hisham's car, which was an adventure in itself. At the stadium, I was nervous at first, but the drama of the match drew me in, and I cheered along with the crowd. No one noticed me. Hisham gloated for weeks about al-Ittifaq's overtime victory, even though I told him that in the Hijaz, hospitality rules, so we let al-Ittifaq win.

As he got to know Jeddah, Hisham became fascinated by the old villas built in the 1950s and 1960s that imitated seaside homes in Miami and Monaco. Most were in disrepair, since posh new residential neighborhoods were being built north of town. These older villas were in quiet neighborhoods, where the trees were lush and tall. He fantasized about buying one to restore and update with modern conveniences. Every time we met, he'd show me his newest discovery.

After a while, we only visited restaurants where we rarely saw anyone we knew. By then, I'd started wearing what we called the burqa back then, a black face veil with openings only for the eyes. I wore it to avoid being recognized when we were in more risky situations, but I hated eating with it on. It was such an inconvenience to have to lift up the veil each time I wanted to take a bite.

We frequented a quiet Chinese restaurant that would seat us in a small booth, far from the eyes of other patrons, where I would sit facing the back and leave my face veil folded up during the meal. As we entered and left the restaurant, I would cover my face with an extra layer of veil, walking out behind Hisham like a modest wife or sister.

One night, as we were leaving, we met a college friend from AUB coming into the restaurant. It was Rashid, a guy who'd worked much harder on his social life than his studies. Hisham had rekindled a friendship with Rashid since moving to Jeddah. Even though I wore the mask over my face, I feared

Rashid would guess it was me. Fortunately, he followed Saudi custom and didn't speak to me at all, and Hisham didn't present me to him, either.

"He guessed it was you under the veil," Hisham said during our next conversation, and I felt my face flush. "Nothing to worry about, though. I never admitted it."

When we met next, Hisham told me he'd gone to a party at Rashid's place. "You wouldn't believe it, you'd think we were back in Lebanon. There were women from Beirut, Egypt, the UK. Stewardesses mostly, and a few nurses. Everybody was dancing, like a real disco. I only stayed until midnight, and I didn't drink because I was afraid of getting stopped on the way home. I've been to a few parties here and there, but this was something else. There were about 50 people, and they were drinking Johnnie Walker and homemade wine. I really felt out of place in my thobe. Nobody else had one on. Rashid told me to wear slacks and a shirt next time."

I was shocked that Hisham had even gone to that party, but tried not to show it. "Does he have a girlfriend?"

"That night he was with a British stewardess."

"He doesn't have a Saudi girlfriend?"

"No, he says it's too dangerous. He asked me about you. I told him we get together to talk, that's all we can do now. He invited us to come over there anytime if we need a place to be alone."

I had been dreaming of the simple pleasure of enjoying Hisham's company completely unveiled, with no one bothering us, just like in Beirut. Hisham kept pushing the idea, promising he'd make sure it was completely safe. Eventually, I gave in. We went to Rashid's flat when he was abroad on business. As usual, I pretended I was visiting Badriyyah. After the driver dropped me off, and we had a cup of tea together, Hisham picked me up.

Though Rashid lived alone, he had a Filipino manservant who also cooked for him. Rashid said we could trust the man, because he thought Saudi social taboos about men and women mixing in public were cruel, and he wanted to help young couples any way he could.

The servant prepared dinner for us, then told us that he'd be in his flat just across the hall if we needed anything. Once we were alone, Hisham turned on a cassette of Fairuz love songs. His eyes smoldered as I uncovered my hair and gazed into his eyes. He took off his headdress, and we could really see each other for the first time in months.

In each other's arms, we recaptured our lost pleasures. I leaned against his chest and listened to his heartbeat. In Lebanon, we always had an easy familiarity, like two close friends. There, you could walk arm in arm. A fellow could even put his arm around a girl and go unnoticed. Not so in our country. As a result, in our desperate situation, even the slightest physical contact was charged with passion.

The evening flew by, and all too soon we were back outside, in the world where we couldn't be married, yet where, in front of strangers, we had to masquerade as a married couple, or as brother and sister. After all, it was a crime for an unmarried couple to be together in a private space like a car. I was grateful for the anonymity my abaya gave us as we drove around Jeddah.

We met at Rashid's apartment several times. Though we could talk and laugh there, I was growing uncomfortable. In some ways, it was safer because it was a private space, and no one could see us together. Yet at the same time, it was far more dangerous because, if I were caught, my punishment would be much more serious. Being alone with a man in an apartment was about the most dangerous taboo I could have breached. Would I, like others caught in that situation, be beaten, forced to drop out of school, or married off immediately? So far, I had kept myself pure – that one limit was absolute – and fortunately Hisham respected it.

CHAPTER 8

DISCOVERED

Jeddah
November 1979

WE WERE in a car accident. We'd just had dinner at the Chinese restaurant and were waiting at a stoplight on Macaroni Road when a taxi rear-ended us. He didn't hit us hard, and we weren't hurt. But Hisham's rear bumper was damaged.

Hisham got out of the car and confronted the pot-bellied cabbie whose car was peppered with dents and scratches. They started arguing. In those days, nobody wanted the police involved in traffic disputes, because many people drove without licenses or had expired visas. Drivers would argue a bit before agreeing on fault and damages. Cash would change hands and they would leave the scene. But that night, the other driver refused to admit fault. Even though the damage to Hisham's car was minimal, he was furious.

Traffic backed up behind us, and a few drivers got out of their cars to watch. There were Saudis, Ethiopians, and a couple of Egyptian laborers wearing long galabeyas. Everyone was siding with Hisham, but the stubborn cab driver wouldn't concede.

"You're wrong," a young Saudi told the cabbie. "If you hit him from behind, and he's standing still at a red light, you're the one at fault!"

"No, no," the cabbie answered. "The rule is, he who gets hit, has to pay." The crowd laughed.

"Well, if that's your logic, then night is bright and day is black," Hisham said, drawing approving laughter from the onlookers.

"Whatever you say about night and day, you obviously don't know your traffic laws," he answered. "And I'm not paying you one halala, that's that." He folded his arms, daring Hisham to do something. "In fact, you owe me 500 riyals."

To my horror, a police car pulled up, lights flashing. I wanted to get out of the car and run away. But that would only call attention to me. It was too late. I was stuck. Worse, on this night, my cover story didn't give me any leeway to be late. So, in a growing panic, I watched them through the cosmetics mirror, my veil pulled over my face so no one could see me. At least no one would bother me, since I was fully covered and was with a Saudi man. They would assume I was Hisham's sister or his wife.

The policeman ordered the cabbie to either pay Hisham 500 riyals for the damage or to get in the car with him and go to the police station. After weighing his options, the taxi driver pulled out a wad of folded money and laid five 100 Riyal notes into Hisham's palm with defiance and pain. Seeing justice had been done, the crowd dispersed. After Hisham got back in the car, the policeman tapped on his window.

"One piece of advice, young man, don't pick a fight with these cabbies if you can help it. Especially since you're not from around here. I can tell from your accent."

"OK, sir. Thanks." And the cop waved us on.

My heart wouldn't stop pounding. "Hisham, I was so scared. Why did you confront the guy? We could have just driven off!" I was furious that he'd taken that risk, that he'd put me in more danger.

"Well, think about it. You're totally veiled. There's no way a traffic cop, or anyone else, is going to question who you are. To the world, you're like my wife when we're out like this, and I'm not going to act guilty about the fact that you're with me. You're off limits to them. Besides, that fellow is crazy, and I wasn't going to be taken advantage of just because he's an idiot."

He was right, but his behavior was still risky. The cop and the men would leave me alone because of Hisham. He was a respectable-looking young Saudi. In those days, no one would question someone like him. So as long as they were focused on him, they didn't care who I was. But if any one of those men had known I was a single young Saudi girl out with my boyfriend, they'd be outraged and, at the very least, they'd be driving me home to my father in an instant. As long as the focus was on him, we were safe. But the fact remained I was still late. And, as it turned out, too late.

Hisham drove me to the women's center where I was supposed to be that evening, selling my artwork at a charity fund-raiser. Earlier, I had dropped off three paintings at the show and asked Badriyyah to sell them for me. As I came in the front gate, I was relieved to find the event was still going full swing. But my relief dissolved into cold fear when I noticed Ibtisam across the room, standing in front of my paintings, talking to Badriyyah. I wove my way through the show and bought a few small items, as if I'd been there for a while and had just walked away from my paintings when she stopped by.

I kept an eye on Ibtisam, who also moved along opposite me, around the perimeter of the tables displaying handcrafts and artwork. It was clearly a successful evening. A talkative crowd of Saudi and foreign women had bought and sold from each other. Laughter wove through the chatter in a dozen languages. As I worked my way toward Badriyyah, I noticed Ibtisam was one of the only women who'd kept her headscarf on. With her glasses on, she seemed about ten years older. How on earth was she ever going to impress a future mother-in-law looking like that?

When she approached me, I smiled. "A great event, isn't it?"

"Yes indeed, a big success. Check with your friend Badriyyah, you'll find that while you were out, you sold all of your paintings. We'll go home together. Hamdi's coming for us in half an hour."

She knew! But I had to pretend nothing was wrong. I was quite an actress that night: friendly, cordial, even charming. My paintings had raised 3,000 riyals for the cause. Yet how hollow that success was compared to the fear growing inside me. I was furious, because if we hadn't gotten into that car accident, I would have made back it in time.

The women who bought my paintings complimented my work. Only Badriyyah and I knew why my paintings had become more alive. They were full of passion for Hisham, my fear of getting caught, and my defiance.

"I'm so sorry," Badriyyah said. "Ibtisam was very direct and asked where you were. I said you were away for a few minutes, and that you were around somewhere, that you'd be back. She seemed to accept that, but she waited for an hour, wandering around the bazaar, occasionally looking over at me. Later, she went to the front desk. I don't know if she asked there whether you'd come or not. But I did see the woman at the desk shake her head, stand up, and look around the room like she was looking for someone. I hope you're okay, and I'm so sorry."

"There's nothing more you could've done. I'll deal with it."

"In God's protection," she said as I walked away.

Ibtisam approached us and said, "Let's go, the car's over here, come on."
She was silent all the way home and slipped into my bedroom behind me.
She shut the door before she spoke. "So, where were you?" She was clenching
her teeth, trying to control her anger. I'd never seen her like this, she was
always so docile and sweet.

"I was having dinner with a friend, a friend from college. We had to meet
at a restaurant, and we had dinner. It's the only way we can talk in person.
It's someone I've known for a long time."

"Is it the same boy you were crazy about in college?"

"His family business has an office in Jeddah now, and he wanted to have
dinner so we could talk."

"So you could talk? Do you know how much trouble you'd be in if you
were caught?

"I know. But it seemed like a simple thing, to meet and have a meal
together, to drink coffee, like my friends and I used to do in Beirut all the
time. There it's normal."

"But you're back home now, and living in your father's house. I don't
believe you did this right in front of everyone!"

I kept quiet, letting her fume.

"I'm so disappointed in your judgment, that you'd risk everything, your
future, our reputation. Baba and Mama give us so much freedom because
they trust us. They think we're good girls, busy with our studies and our work.
They would never suspect you're out with a man! If they found out, what
would they think of you!"

I nodded and covered my face with my hands, imagining the shame and
the punishment they would give me for smearing our family name.

"We'll talk tomorrow. In the meantime, consider what you've done, and
what you've risked."

I lay on my bed for a long time. I was numb with fear, not knowing what
my fate would be if she told my parents. They were liberal compared to most
of my friends' parents. Yet at the same time, they wanted us to marry properly
within society. If word of this got out, I'd have no chance of that. My
reputation would be tainted. I'd be considered a loose woman, and I could
forget any chance of marrying Hisham, or anyone else for that matter.

I knew my brothers had girlfriends abroad, and we all assumed they even
dated foreign women in Jeddah. That was acceptable, because they were men,

and they were meant to be wild until they settled down. But we women were held to a different standard, and the consequences were serious.

For instance, a friend of mine from high school was caught seeing a young man. He was from a decent family and could have married her. They'd met while their families were on vacation in London, and, once back home, they took walks along Jeddah's Corniche together. She was totally veiled of course, so no one could tell who she was. Yet one of her brothers saw them and recognized her from her shoes. He dragged her home, and they made her drop out of high school. Even though the headmistress pleaded with her parents, they wouldn't give in. They kept her in the house until they married her off to an uneducated cousin from Yanbu. She lived in a square, walled-in villa set out in the middle of nowhere. She was the third wife and lived in the same villa as the other two.

Of course, I never forgot the story of the princess who'd tried to run off with her lover by pretending to drown herself at Obhur. She and her man were caught sneaking out of the airport. Despite the King's personal pleas that she be spared, her own family insisted the couple be executed in public to erase the shame.

Still in my clothes, I lay on my bed with the lights out, thinking. Hisham would never know why I'd broken contact. He'd only learn that I married. He'd mourn for a while, before his parents came forward with a perfect match for him with no complications. We would never see each other again. We always knew we couldn't marry, but I'd never expected it to end like this.

"Your sister left for school very early, and she seemed upset," Mama observed the next morning. I drank my tea at the kitchen table, reading the paper. "You didn't sleep well, did you Fawzia? You look tired. What's wrong with you girls?"

"It's just stress over schoolwork. I have a lot of studying, and I'm not keeping up very well."

Since I didn't have classes, I stayed home all day. I tried to study, but I couldn't concentrate. When Ibtisam didn't come home for lunch, I began to worry about her.

Just before sunset, she came into my bedroom and sat on my bed. She spoke in a low voice. "I've been praying and thinking all day. And I'm sorry. This is all my fault." A wave of relief came over me. At that moment, I began to have hope, hope she would keep it a secret. "I shouldn't have been so selfish, and should have just agreed to get married. Then you could become a bride and this risky time would have passed."

I didn't know how to react to this, for I couldn't believe she was taking the blame for something I'd done.

"It's true," she said. "I've been so focused on my studies that I've tried to avoid marriage. I should just face the facts. The only realistic future I have in this world is as a wife and mother. Mama is beside herself with me, begging me to wear makeup when we have visitors, urging me to make more of an effort. But I don't want to be married and have kids. So you see, I too haven't been the best daughter. And I'm not setting a very good example for you, am I?"

I never dreamed that it would be my turn to console her. I put my arm around her and patted her shoulder. "You are a perfect daughter. I don't know why you're taking the blame for something I did. You're innocent, and all you want is to dedicate yourself to studying religion. What could be better than that?"

"I'm like a stranger in my own family," she said. "Even among my friends at school, none are as serious about their studies as I am. I just want to live in the library, pouring over the old legal texts. I want to be a legal scholar, one who knows the sharia and all its nuances. I just want to study and write. I should have lived a thousand years ago. Can you imagine a bigger misfit than me?"

"And I don't blame you for wanting to see your school friends," my sister added. "The way we were raised, all those foreigners at Obhor, our trips abroad. You spent four years of your life outside, how can you be expected to give all that up? In many ways, I'm much worse. I won't ever fit into their world. I can't imagine being married and living a life like that. I'd be so miserable!"

She'd never spoken to me like this before. I kept quiet, stretched out sideways on the bed, toying with the hem of her dress. She was so naïve about life and men that she would never suspect that Hisham and I had been carrying on for months. She would never dream that we'd been alone together in a private apartment. The saddest thing was she was in her late twenties and had never known love.

When she seemed calm, and had had her say, I sat up. "I think you should pursue this dream of becoming a legal scholar. Don't you think Baba would let you? He'll have plenty of grandsons through the boys. And Mama only wants you to be happy."

"Are you joking? I can't imagine their reaction. Mama is already wishing for grandchildren and none of us are even married yet."

"But they've never stopped you from studying, have they?"

"No, you're right. But they see my degree as the end of it. In fact, I think they have a groom in mind."

"Who?" I was surprised I hadn't been informed of this. Then again, I had been so focused on Hisham I hadn't been paying much attention.

"Haven't you noticed they've been talking a lot about the Bahamid family lately? Mama mentions them when we have coffee nearly every day. She tells me they have a young man finishing law school in England, and he's also got an Islamic legal degree. He wants to combine a commercial legal practice with his knowledge of the sharia."

"Come to think of it, you're right, she has been talking about them a lot. But you'd have a lot in common, your love of the prophet's wisdom and the law."

"That's true, but surely he'll want a very traditional wife, so he can pursue his legal practice and studies. He'll just need a maid. I don't think his type would even consider discussing religious law and wisdom with a woman, much less his wife."

"Have you met his sisters?"

"Not yet, but they're coming for a visit soon. I agreed to be the dutiful daughter and serve them tea and sweets. Will you be there to support me?" She seemed terrified of being put on display in front of women she might be obliged to live with for the rest of her life.

"Of course," I said. "Of course."

"Now, we have to make some decisions about you. For my part, I'm willing to move forward and think about marriage. But you have to start behaving better. It's not just damage to our family name. I'm more worried about you and how this could affect your life."

She stood up, clasped her hands behind her back and looked at me with a piercing gaze, as if she were a judge delivering a sentence. "First, you must stop seeing your friend. Concentrate on your studies and your artwork. Your paintings are wonderful, and I think you have a strong talent."

She paused for my reaction. I nodded and she continued.

"I don't want your future to be ruined, so I've decided to tell Baba that they should consider marrying you off before me. I know you want to be married someday. But first, you must promise me you'll stop seeing your friend. Before God. And after this, I'll watch your every move. If I find out you're seeing him again, I'll go straight to Baba, no more chances. You've been taking too many risks."

She grabbed my copy of the Qur'an and set it on my lap. "Your right hand," she said.

I put my right hand on the book and raised my left.

"Bismillah al-Rahman al-Rahim, I promise to never see him again." I resigned myself to the fact that our risk taking had become too much. Perhaps this was for the best. We had crossed a line, and we weren't going in the right direction. We just kept scheming for more dangerous ways to see each other in secret instead of working out a plan to get married. Yet I knew I would never stop loving him.

When Ibtisam hugged me, I said, "Aren't you going to tell Baba?"

"No, no, my dear. It would just do more harm. This will be our secret, and only God can forgive you for what you've done. I advise you to pray for His forgiveness." She patted my shoulder, as I sniffled and shed tears of relief.

"My discretion comes with a price. You must follow our religion more closely. I want you to pray with me here at home every morning and evening. Also, you mustn't go out in the evenings at all unless it's with one of us, or with Hamdi. The temptation is too great for you now. I'll also make sure Hamdi picks you up at school each day. That way, you'll have no chance to go anywhere dangerous. I'll get rides from school with my colleagues."

We prayed together in my bedroom. Though I wasn't very religious in those days, I asked God to help me understand what was happening to me, and asked for the strength to do the correct thing.

I couldn't call Hisham, because he was out of town on business. A week later when I walked out of my classes, looking for Hamdi and the car, Hisham approached me. I shook my head once as I walked by him toward Hamdi, who was re-reading an old copy of an Egyptian newspaper that he'd spread out on the trunk of the car. Hisham watched as we drove off. He knew my school schedule, so the next time I came out of class he did the same thing. He could see Hamdi there, so he stood back like he was waiting for someone else. I glanced at him and then looked down, without even a shake of my head.

When I finally got him on the phone, I just said, "Ibtisam found out."

"Allaaaah. I can't live without you. What am I supposed to do?"

"You're supposed to forget me. Ibtisam's going to ask Baba to marry me off before her."

He said nothing.

"We took too many risks, so it was bound to end like this. I have to go now, someone's coming. I love you, may God protect you." I hung up before he could answer, my heart bursting. Back in my room, I stifled my sobs.

CHAPTER 9

GUNFIRE

Mecca
November 1979

A COUPLE of weeks later, after the annual pilgrimage had finished, Ibtisam proposed the family visit the Grand Mosque in Mecca. We would spend the night in meditation and then pray at dawn on the first day of the month of Muharram, which marked not only a new year on the Islamic calendar, but the beginning of a new century. The year would be 1400. On the western calendar, the day would be November 20, 1979. Traditionally, the Saudi king prayed there at the dawn of each New Year. His royal presence would make our visit more exciting for me, though I'm sure it was irrelevant to Ibtisam. Baba was in London on business, so the rest of us made plans to go without him.

Since we weren't performing a pilgrimage, we didn't don the ihram, the white pilgrim's garment. Instead, we wore our normal abayas over long dresses, and the boys had on their usual thobes.

The mosque was easy to find. Its eight towering minarets shone bright in the night sky, like heavenly beacons. We had all performed our ritual ablutions at home, so we entered the mosque straight away. As we passed through one of its many enormous gates, each of us whispered the traditional prayer, "Lord, open the doors to Your forgiveness."

We found a place to pray in the vast open-air courtyard built around the Kaaba, a large cube of stone wrapped in an embroidered black cloth. Muslims around the world face this very spot when praying. It is the holiest place in Islam.

As we arrived, nothing seemed out of the ordinary, although no visit to the Grand Mosque could be considered routine. Even though thousands of people were there that night, the vast courtyard and the two-storied terraces held us all, and it didn't even feel crowded.

Thousands of families spent the night there. People prayed in long rows. Others curled up and slept on woolen rugs or on mattresses they'd brought with them. The worshippers came from all over: There were Persians, Turks, Pakistanis, Africans, and Asians, as well as Arabs from many lands, all focused on their devotions. Dozens of languages filled the air.

In the center of the courtyard, a steady flow of worshippers performed the tawwaf, the ritual counter-clockwise circling of the Kaaba, in their bare feet, shuffling on the pearl-colored marble worn down from the footfalls of the millions who had come before.

Many Saudi men in the crowd sported long beards and wore thobes that came to just below their knees, with white pants underneath. I thought nothing of it at the time. I dismissed them as tribesmen, villagers from remote parts of the country, or perhaps ultra-devout men, like the religious police. Some men wore black thobes and carried coffins around the Kaaba. This, too, was common – to bring a recently deceased loved one to the Grand Mosque for prayers before burial.

My eyes drifted upward. Despite the lights, I was dazzled by the night's beauty. The crescent moon that marked the New Year hung like a dainty sliver, surrounded by bright planets and stars. God's presence seemed so near.

Mama, Ibtisam, and I sat behind the boys on red carpets and got ready to meditate and pray. Right away, Ibtisam began reading a prayer from an old book she'd stumbled on in the university library. She'd made photocopies of it for all of us. Mama followed Ibtisam's lead and began the ritual prayer. The boys, like me, sat in silence, awed by the atmosphere.

After a while, we moved back to the lower of two arched colonnades that surround the courtyard. There, we had a midnight snack of tea and sweets. We had a perfect view of the entire courtyard and of the Kaaba.

"Ibtisam, this was a wonderful idea," Mama said. "God bless you, my daughter."

Despite the fact that there were thousands of people there, it seemed like we had it all to ourselves. This is the real genius of the mosque's design. It combines enormity with total spiritual intimacy. I felt as if all of us, and at the same time each of us, was alone before God. I will forever cherish those moments of peace.

Later, we returned to the open courtyard and spent the night in prayer and contemplation. I prayed for a solution to my impasse with Hisham. I asked for forgiveness for my sins and thanked God for Ibtisam's wisdom and kindness. I prayed she would find happiness and a true husband who would appreciate her. When I wasn't praying, I let the richness of the night cover me like a blue velvet blanket. As the stars glowed above, the crescent moon slid toward the horizon. Then I read the prayer Ibtisam had given me.

Almighty God, I stand in Your Presence, humbled, alone, beseeching Your forgiveness. I am weak and suffering from the bitter harvest of the sins I have sown. Please forgive me and give me the strength to live in righteousness and wisdom and to choose the path of light. I bear witness that You are the Almighty and All Powerful. Praise be to You, Lord of all the worlds.

I was sure Ibtisam had brought that prayer especially for me. As I finished it, I felt washed of my sins, and had a faint glow of hope for my future. Ibtisam had been watching me, and when I finished praying, she put her arm around me. It was clear she had organized the whole evening for my sake, so I could ask forgiveness in this holy place. She meant for it to be a life-changing night. And it was, but in a way none of us could have imagined.

Later, as Ibtisam and Tarek performed the tawwaf together, I curled up and slept. I felt God had forgiven me and that I was safe there in the community of faith. I was looking forward to the coming day. After the dawn prayer, we would go to a nice hotel for breakfast.

I was in a kind of half-sleep when Ibtisam nudged me. "Fawzia, wake up, dawn prayer will be in a few minutes." She was so energetic, even though I'm sure she hadn't slept that whole night. One by one, she coaxed us awake. We were a herd of sleepy camels, and she was our caravan leader, preparing us for the road.

The loud speakers clicked on, and then the muezzin chanted, "Allaaahu Akbar! Allaaahu Akbar! God is great!" The worshippers organized themselves into prayer lines. "Come to prayer!" the muezzin called. His voice was so gentle and deep, I felt he was calling to me, to our own family, to rise and be grateful to be there, right there at the Kaaba, for dawn prayers on the first day of the new Islamic century. We lined up as before, the women in back, the men in front, and began to follow the ritual prayer led by the mosque's imam. He stood near the Kaaba and spoke into a microphone, ending with the traditional blessings of peace.

That's when gunfire shattered the calm and our world changed forever. Ibtisam and I instinctively grabbed Mama's arms as if she would protect us. Everyone around us stopped moving. We listened.

"What's happening?" an old woman cried out. "My son, what is going on?" No one answered her. We looked to our right and left. Everyone around us was stunned, trying to see, to understand.

"Look, over there, those men have rifles!" someone said, pointing to a group of men who were pulling weapons out of a coffin they had been carrying. They were walking toward the Kaaba.

"Where is the King?" someone said. "Is he here?" I couldn't help but fear it might be an assassination attempt, remembering the horrible day just four years before in 1975, when a young royal had killed our beloved King Faisal.

Panicked words in many languages hummed around us as we tried to listen for anything coming over the loudspeakers. Thousands of the worshippers didn't understand Arabic, and we were all terrified.

"Let's get out of here," my brother Tarek said. "Come on!" We abandoned our belongings and walked toward the nearest exit. Many others did the same, and we swarmed in confusion like a flock of swallows. Someone ahead shouted that the gate was chained shut. Sure enough, three tough-looking armed men in tribal dress were guarding it from the inside.

"Who could they be, Ibtisam?" Mama said as we walked on toward the next gate, trying not to panic.

"God forbid," Ibtisam said, worry written on her face. "I had heard rumors about this pilgrimage, that something was going to happen because of the new Islamic century. But it's an abomination, God strike them down for shooting off weapons in the Grand Mosque." She didn't seem to care that her voice had grown loud.

"God strengthen you," an old man said as we strode past. The next gate was locked, too. We managed to stay together. Other families didn't have such luck. Many elderly and sick struggled to walk, some with canes, calling out for help to the people streaming past. Others remained seated on the ground, sobbing and praying as worshippers flowed around them.

"Please, what is happening?" a man with a group of confused-looking Indonesian pilgrims said to us in English.

"We don't know," Bashir answered. "Just try to get outside."

"But the gates are locked!" he protested. We went to the next gate, only to learn that all 51 gates were locked tight. We were trapped. I could smell fear in the crowd.

Everyone started chanting, Allahu Akbar, Allahu Akbar, the urgent prayer we Muslims recite in dire circumstances. We joined in, and soon everyone in the mosque, thousands of us, chanted together, our pleas rising in a crescendo. Then it faded away. We strained to hear someone speaking over the public-address system from the microphone at the Kaaba.

"What's he saying?" Mama asked. "Can anyone understand him?" It was hard to make out the words, because the man spoke in a strange tribal accent.

Tarek pointed to the arched colonnade, where several men with rifles were forcing worshippers at gunpoint to roll up massive oriental carpets, stacking them against the insides of the gates. Another man got a group of dark-skinned pilgrims, many dressed in their ihrams, to carry heavy boxes.

"Look, gunmen in the minarets!" Tarek said, pointing skyward. Gun barrels poked out of all eight minarets of the mosque. At first, we hoped they were from the Saudi armed forces, but there were no military men in the area.

It was inconceivable that anyone would take over Islam's most peaceful and holy place, filled with ordinary people, the infirm and the elderly! What did they want?

"Do you think they're Shia?" Tarek asked. The Iranian Revolution was in full swing, and some had said the Iranians, who were overwhelmingly Shia and anti-Saudi, would attack the Kingdom during the pilgrimage.

"No, they're definitely Saudis" Ibtisam said. "See how they're dressed, like the old desert fighters of King Abd al-Aziz."

More shots erupted from a roof behind us overlooking the courtyard. A shower of gunfire answered. People screamed. A uniformed guard fell off the balcony above and landed, lifeless, on the courtyard floor. We all screamed and backed away in panic.

"Sit down, sit down and listen!" a voice shouted over the microphone. Foreign worshippers gathered around anyone who could interpret for them, and the throng in the courtyard settled to the ground, at full attention.

"Mecca, Medina, and Jeddah are now in our hands," the man said. There were gasps all around us. In the distance, we made out the form of the man at the microphone, dressed in the short thobe of the ultra-religious, with a long beard.

Another man took the microphone. He spoke in classical Arabic. "In the name of God, the Merciful, the Compassionate," he intoned, before setting off on an hour-long sermon about how this group of Saudi men believed they were going to save the Kingdom from the unholy rule of the Saudi royal family. While we pretended to listen, we watched the crowd around us for any signs of possible escape. I fought back waves of panic, terrified by what might happen next.

The man claimed the long-awaited promised one, the Mahdi, had come, and was in the mosque, fulfilling an ancient prophecy from the prophetic traditions. I was confused by this. Most Sunnis didn't believe in the coming of another messenger after the prophet Muhammad, upon him peace. Who were these men?

Ibtisam grew furious as the speech progressed. "Don't listen to him! He's twisting the prophet's sayings, it's shameful!" She was too loud to be ignored. Heads turned toward us.

Tarek reached out to her. "Ibtisam, please keep quiet. These guys are crazy and there's no telling what they might do!"

But Ibtisam wouldn't be deterred. "These men are sinners. Don't listen to them!" Then she began praying aloud, "God save us from these evil whisperers, protect your people in this holy place."

"Let her, let her," Mama said, when Tarek tried to quiet her.

"Yes, let her speak, the brave woman," a Pakistani woman said in accented Arabic. "We shouldn't listen to them. After all, look what they are doing!"

"Shshsh!" her husband said as he grabbed her arm. "You must keep quiet! These men are insane! Think of the children!" He led his family away from us.

Others standing near us also seemed afraid that Ibtisam might cause a scene, and they distanced themselves.

"Ibtisam, I beg you, keep quiet now," Tarek said, his hand on her arm. "We'll get out of here and then you can talk about them for ten years if you like."

The man at the microphone introduced the supposed Mahdi. His name was Muhammad Abdallah, and he was said to have the sign of the expected one, a red birthmark on his cheek. They led out a young man carrying a submachine gun to stand near the Kaaba. He looked young, barely seventeen or eighteen.

Then the first voice, the one with the strong accent, called out, "In the name of God, the Merciful, the Compassionate, pay allegiance to Muhammad Abdullah al-Quraishi."

"That was the Prophet's name, peace upon him," Ibtisam said. "How dare they? These men have to be stopped! Where are the guards? God protect us, Allahu Akbar, Allahu Akbar." She started again. Others in the crowd were chanting the prayer, too. Unbelievably, others were shouting things like, "Thank God the Mahdi is here!" and "The prophesy has been fulfilled!"

Then some of the armed men stepped forward and kissed the supposed Mahdi's hand, pledging their loyalty. Fearing for their lives, many worshippers did the same. We surrounded Ibtisam and tried to pull her back so we could disappear into anonymity.

I couldn't believe my eyes when they passed out guns and rifles to worshippers who had just sworn allegiance to the Mahdi. The man at the microphone said they expected to be attacked, and they would have to hold off a siege of the mosque from the government forces. Then they handed out brochures in Arabic explaining who they were and what they were trying to do. These pamphlets said they wanted to overturn the Saudi government and return Saudi Arabia to a pure Islamic state.

They started walking through the groups of worshippers, taking identity cards from the Saudis and ripping them up, insulting them, calling the Saudi state illegitimate. At that point, people started ripping up their own identity cards, and soon the mosque floor was covered with pages of passports, cards, and tiny fragments of photographs. Men carrying prayer beads dropped them immediately. The rebels considered them ungodly and were confiscating them.

The sun rose higher in the sky, but that nightmare of a day dragged on. It was still only morning. Since it was late November, it wasn't terribly hot, but the crowd was getting restless. There was no sign of government forces. Didn't they know what was going on in there?

During a long lull, when nothing seemed to be happening, a Saudi man walked by us and said in a low voice, "Come this way, my brothers. Over here, they're letting people out downstairs."

"Are you sure?" Tarek said as we all stood up.

"Yes, as long as we pretend to be in allegiance with them, and to tell the outside world what they want us to say, then we can go."

As soon as we got up, the nearby foreigners followed us. We streamed down a ramp to a lower gallery level of the mosque. Two gunmen stood by, allowing people to climb up onto a raised windowsill about eight feet off above the floor. From there, they could step to the outside. People had to climb on each other's shoulders to get out. It was slow going. One by one, we watched people ahead of us gain their freedom.

As our turn neared, I prayed for our escape. Fahd went first. Then Bashir and Tarek lifted Mama up and pushed her out of the window. She turned to pull up Ibtisam. But as they began to lift her, Ibtisam said to one of the rebels, "You know this is a great sin! God shame you, and curse you and your cohorts for desecrating God's house!"

"Ibtisam, quiet!" Tarek said. They kept lifting her up and tried to push her out, but one of the rebels came running over.

"Can't you keep your woman quiet?" he yelled at Tarek.

Ibtisam jumped back to the ground and said. "I am a Muslim and I cannot stand to see what you are doing to this place, to all these innocent people!"

"He has a gun, Ibtisam!" Tarek said in a desperate hiss, pulling her back toward the window.

"Yes, but I know what's right. They can't do this. It's beyond forbidden!" she said, standing tall, refusing to budge, right in front of the man who had his gun pointed at her. She glared at him in defiance.

"Daughter, please just come out the window. You can't change their minds!" Mama said, beseeching her with her open arms.

"There is no time for this," another rebel said, approaching in a hurry. "Just take her upstairs. If she doesn't want to leave, fine. There will be plenty of work for women to do." The gunman grabbed her arm.

"Noooo!" Tarek said, lunging toward her. But the other man turned and shot him in the shoulder. Worshippers around us screamed as he slumped over in pain. In that same second, the other man yanked Ibtisam away as she shouted, "Why did you shoot him, he did nothing wrong!" As we tried to comfort Tarek, I looked up to see the man leading Ibtisam back up the ramp. She kept scolding him that they were wrong, that they would never succeed. As they passed down the line of worshippers behind us, I could see visible shock on their faces, from Ibtisam's defiant tirade and the swift reaction of the rebels.

"Ibtisam!" I shouted. She looked back once as he pulled her along. She kept arguing with him, and I was sure she had no fear. They went up the ramp and disappeared around a corner.

"If she doesn't come over to our point of view, God will make her a martyr and she will see Paradise soon," one of the rebels said. "Now you filthy cowards, get out of here." He pointed his gun at us. Meanwhile, people streamed around us and crawled out the window in rising hysteria.

We pushed Tarek over the ledge, and he howled when he hit the ground outside. Then Bashir pushed me out to the ground.

"But what about Ibtisam?" Mama cried. "We can't just leave her! Where's Bashir!"

Fahd grabbed Mama's shoulders and looked in her eyes. "We have to get Tarek to the hospital. Bashir went back to find Ibtisam." Tarek was writhing in pain on the ground.

By that time, all social barriers had broken down. All around us, men and women were weeping and crying as they moved away from the mosque to safety. A middle-aged man dressed in the white pilgrim's ihram approached us. "What's wrong?" he said to Mama.

"They shot my son!" she said between heaving sobs. "My daughter is in there, Sir, my dearest oldest daughter. She is a pure Muslim and they've taken her hostage. God protect her and all of the rightly guided Muslims! And they shot my son!"

"I'm a doctor," he said, kneeling down. He reached around Tarek, feeling his back. "The bullet is still in there. We have to get him to the hospital. Where is your car? If you can take us all, then I can help you at the hospital. I'm sure they'll need every doctor's help today."

Fahd and the doctor led Tarek to the car. Mama and I trotted along, both of us crying as we ran. Mama and I sat in front, and Fahd drove like a racecar driver.

"God protect us! Protect my daughter, my Ibtisam!" Mama sobbed as we drove through the empty streets of Mecca. The doctor tried to calm her.

We were the first people from the mosque to reach the hospital. The emergency room staff had heard there had been a disturbance at the mosque, but couldn't believe what we told them. Our rescuer Dr. Farid took charge, as if he was on staff. "Call the director of the hospital, now!" he said to one of the nurses. "You'll need to get all the doctors in here as soon as you can."

Dr. Farid wheeled Tarek right into surgery. He and the only emergency room doctor on duty managed to extract the bullet from his shoulder. Tarek had one broken bone, but nothing had shattered. He was lucky.

Dr. Farid stayed on at the emergency room, which was filling up at an alarming rate with the injured. They came by car and taxi, wearing vacant stares of disbelief at what they had witnessed.

While Tarek was in surgery, Fahd called Uncle Fouad, who in turn woke up Baba in his London hotel. He would take the next plane home. Baba somehow got through on the phone to Mama at the hospital. She got so hysterical while talking to him, and trying to explain what was happening, that I had to take the phone from her. "Go home as soon as you can," he said, "And don't leave her side until I get back."

CHAPTER 10

VEIL OF EVIL

"IBTISAM, my daughter, my daughter!" Mama wailed as the car sped home. I held her, wishing I could stay with my brothers in Mecca, to do something, anything, to get Ibtisam out of that mosque.

We all believed the crazy people in the mosque were no match for the Saudi armed forces, and that it would all be over in a few hours. I prayed over and over for God to protect Ibtisam. I knew she would resist. She was so versed in the prophet's sayings and in the law. She knew right from wrong, and would not be swayed to join them. But the dangers she faced now were much greater than faulty doctrine.

Mama calmed down by the time we got home, but she became hysterical again while standing in the doorway of Ibtisam's bedroom. "Animals they are, how could they do this to her? God protect her!"

Aunt Rosette spent the night, and I don't know how I'd have managed without her. First, we had to get Mama to change into her nightclothes, and then to bed. We sat with her and read from the Qur'an together. We prayed before we shut off the lights and talked in low voices until Mama slept. We curled up alongside her in the king-sized bed. It was good to lay my head on my father's pillow, which smelled of him and his cologne. It was my only comfort that night as I lay there listening for Mama's and Aunt Rosette's breathing to become rhythmic at last. Only then did I dare to let my thoughts free. I relived the day over and over, remembering my last glimpse of Ibtisam being led away. I couldn't imagine what she was experiencing. I kept hoping she had managed to slip out with the rest of the worshippers, that she'd find Bashir and Fahd, that they'd come home any minute. Then I imagined her a hostage. Could she sleep? Did they even have food there?

The next morning, we were shocked to hear nothing on Saudi radio or TV about the siege. Someone from the office came by to say that all the international phone lines had been cut. We were in some kind of news blackout. Even the mid-morning BBC broadcast had only sketchy information.

By noon, the phone started ringing. At first we ran for it, hoping for good news. But the calls were from friends, trying to confirm whether what they'd heard about Ibtisam was true.

When Fahd and Bashir walked in the door at noon, Bashir shook his head, took Mama's hands, and sat her down. "I looked everywhere for her. They've taken the women hostages somewhere hidden. People kept climbing out of the windows like we did until about midnight. I waited until the last moment, then I had to come out. I'm sorry, Mama."

Baba made it home just before dinner. He'd flown to Amman and rented a car, driving for many hours to reach Jeddah. He held Mama, then led her to the bedroom and shut the door. I could hear her crying as he tried to console her.

The next day, our friends began to visit, bringing rumors about what was happening. While it is taboo to talk politics in public, in private it's almost a national sport. In our protected salons, drinking coffee and tea, the network of women seemed to know more than the men who spent their days in a Mecca hotel that had become the government staging area. Some insisted the rebels were Shia, but we didn't believe that, because we had seen them wearing the typical costume of the Ikhwan, who were opposed to the Shia. We were right. The rebels and their so-called Mahdi were from the Bani Utaiba, one of Saudi Arabia's largest tribes. They came from a village called Sajir, once an Ikhwan settlement. So their grandfathers were probably some of the original Ikhwan fighters who King Abd al-Aziz, Saudi Arabia's first ruler, subjugated back in 1929. Maybe they were taking revenge for their defeat fifty years earlier.

Rumors spread around the world, as it was shocking to Muslims everywhere that the Islam's holy site was under siege. Iran's Ayatollah Khomeini blamed the incident on America, causing a violent demonstration at the American embassy in Pakistan, in which a US marine was killed.

After a few days Baba brought news that troops were gathering outside the mosque itself. This was important, because no one was supposed to fight inside the holy places. So the government asked senior clerics for a fatwa, a religious ruling that would permit them to retake the mosque by force. Once they'd issued the fatwa, we were sure it would be just a short time before rebels would be captured and the hostages freed.

At first, we were mystified about why the incident dragged on, but as the days passed we learned the rebels had made plans long in advance to take advantage of the mosque's complex layout. Underneath the mosque lies the Cellar, a warren of underground rooms, halls, and tunnels, where a religious school operated. Most of the hostages were taken down to the lower levels. The rebels had stored supplies there, anticipating a long resistance. We also heard they were using water from the mosque's famous Zamzam well.

A veil of evil fell on the place. We heard that, when a rebel was killed, their women and even their children would shoot off the face of the dead man, so he would be unrecognizable to the authorities. And when the rebels killed a Saudi soldier, their women would mutilate that man's body, too. It was horrific and shameful for such things to be happening in Islam's holiest place.

Tarek came home from the hospital a few days into the siege. Though he was still weak and couldn't leave the house, he was on the phone with his contacts, who passed on rumors and information. He and I would play backgammon late into the night, tuning into the BBC on our shortwave for the news. Saudi TV and radio kept reporting that the mosque was back in government control.

For most Jeddans, life continued as normal. Businesses and schools were open. People shopped in the markets. But at our house, normal life was suspended. We were on vigil, waiting for Ibtisam.

Either Baba or my brothers waited at the hotel in Mecca 24 hours a day. They planned to be there when the authorities defeated the rebels and rescued the hostages. The atmosphere was tense. People came and went at all hours of the day and night, but no journalists were allowed. Baba often insisted on staying in Mecca all night by himself, returning exhausted and disheveled, still convinced that Ibtisam would be out any day.

Finally, the government regained control of the ground level, so the Kaaba and the mosque courtyard were cleared of rebels. Now the rebels just moved below ground, and the government tried all means to root them out. They shot tear gas down into the Cellar. They lit tires on fire and threw them in, hoping to smoke the rebels out. They even flooded it with water and put in live electrical cables. Nothing worked. We heard rumors that a company of French Commandos was in the country, poised to finish the job if asked. Though we were glad to hear of these efforts to get the rebels, we knew the hostages were probably in greater danger each day. Who could survive all the tear gas, flooding, and electrocution? And yet they fought on, giving us hope that Ibtisam, too, might still be alive.

As the days passed, we reassured each other that they'd get Ibtisam out safely. Yet I think we each had our doubts. The fighting was getting worse, and the rebels resisted. No one knew how long they would hold out and what they would do to the hostages. They must have known their cause was lost. Why didn't they just give up?

Despite my misgivings, on those long nights of waiting, I clung to hope that Ibtisam would come home safely. I kept back my tears to bolster my courage and dreamed of welcoming her home. I would bring her coffee every morning for a year. I would buy fresh flowers for her room each week. I began saying my daily prayers in her bedroom to feel closer to her. Mama sat in her room every day, praying and crying. One morning, I watched through the doorway as she held pages of Ibtisam's hand-written notes between her palms. Though we kept hoping, our hearts ached.

Two weeks from the morning of the takeover, government forces captured the last of the rebels and their leader, Juhaiman. The television broadcast showed the authorities leading him out of the mosque. With his long disheveled hair and scraggly beard, he looked like a wild animal. His bony face had been blackened by the tire smoke that had filled the tunnels of the Cellar.

"Praise God!" Mama said. Then, echoing our thoughts, she began to wail, "What about the hostages? What about the hostages! My daughter, where are you?"

When an hour passed and no one called, our elation dissolved. After two hours, we grew silent and sullen. Mama retired to her bedroom and closed the door. Aunt Rosette, Tarek, and I waited in the sitting room, barely talking.

Baba, Uncle Fouad, Fahd, and Bashir got home at nightfall. Their faces said everything. Baba held out his arms to Mama and shook his head, then pulled her to his chest. She was by then so drained of tears that she was silent.

Uncle Fouad took Aunt Rosette in his arms. Then we circled around Mama, hugging each other, our arms interlocking. We stood there for a long time, saying nothing, crying in silence, trying to get comfort from each other's touch.

"May God have mercy on her soul, our purest rose," Mama said. My father drew her away to the bedroom. While trying to be strong, we all broke down as our hopes dissolved and our hearts broke. How could God let this happen?

"She survived until the last day," Fouad said after a while. "She was caught in the crossfire as the government took control of the Cellar. She was trying to protect two small girls, children of the rebels. She threw herself on them to keep them from getting hit. She succeeded, but gave her life for them."

"How did you hear this?" Tarek said.

"A young man, another hostage, a Meccan named Marwan al-Batarji. He sought out your father to tell him. He said she was brave the entire time. She argued with the rebels at first, when they tried to convince her of their ideas. But she refused, and told them they were violating the holy site, that they were committing great sins. As more of the fighters were killed, she began to concern herself with helping the innocent children of the rebels. She was hit by stray bullets in one of the final battles. Marwan said she was the strongest of all the hostages, that she was an inspiration and an example to them all."

The doorbell rang. The news had spread fast. It was the imam of our local mosque, paying his condolences, so the men left to sit with him. He would lead a prayer session for Ibtisam the next morning.

"Auntie, she was so much better than me," I said to Rosette as we sat in the family room together in shock. "How could God let this happen to her? She was so good, so perfect."

Aunt Rosette wasn't very religious most of the time, so it shocked me when she said, "May God be praised for creating this brave and pure Ibtisam who gave her life for two innocent girls. What bravery and sacrifice, up to the very end. She is a true Muslim. Please God, prepare a great welcome for her in Paradise."

"God." I prayed aloud with her. "Please tell Ibtisam that I love her, that I will do my best to follow her example. Please tell her not to worry, we'll take good care of Mama. But I will miss her. God give me strength to bear this sorrow, to help Mama bear it."

Then we both prayed in silence. I called out to Ibtisam in my mind, tears streaming down my face, telling her that she was the best sister one could ever have.

An ambulance brought Ibtisam home that evening. My brothers carried her on a stretcher into our washing room, where they had laid out thick boards to make a wide table. A woman named Shafiqah came from the hospital to help Mama with the ritual washing. She was from an old Medinan family that had plied this somber trade for generations.

At first I couldn't bear to join them, or even smell the aloeswood incense they were burning as it wafted into the sitting room where we waited. Later, I asked if Mama and Shafiqah would like some tea. Only then was I strong enough to enter and to look at my sister's body. Shafiqah was winding a white cotton shroud around her. They'd already bathed her and brushed her hair.

"She is almost ready," Mama said. She was much calmer, having spent those hours with Ibtisam. Shafiqah's presence seemed to have helped, too. "Come, Fawzia, see how beautiful she is."

Mama was right. Even in death, Ibtisam was a beauty. Her long eyelashes were still as thick as ever, her eyebrows arched perfectly. Her lips were full, as if any moment she would take a deep breath and sit up. They'd folded her hands across her chest. Mama placed her hands on Ibtisam's hands, and I put my hands on Mama's. Then I felt Ibtisam's cold cheeks. Mama cut a long lock of Ibtisam's hair, wrapped it around her fingers, and slid it into her pocket.

Shafiqa turned her onto her side to wash her upper arm, and some of the shroud fell away. We could see the four bullet wounds across her back, just below her shoulders. The doctor had said that each bullet had hit a vital organ. She'd had little chance of surviving, even if doctors had been close by.

Aunt Rosette and an old friend of Mama's joined us after a while. We read from the Qur'an over Ibtisam while Shafiqah finished with the winding sheet. When she was finished, we thanked her and gave her a handsome tip, then Hamdi drove her home.

The men came in and paid their respects, then moved Ibtisam to the women's majlis. She was still on the boards, shrouded except for her face. We kept vigil until the dawn prayer, when we prayed together with her body laid out sideways in front of us, between us and Mecca. It was the last time we were all together in this world.

Mama lingered alone with Ibtisam that morning. This would be the last time she could touch her, because after the prayer service, Ibtisam would be buried right away. We dressed in traditional mourning colors. Mama wore black, and Aunt Rosette dressed in beige and gray. I wore navy.

As we left for the mosque, Mama spoke. "We must be strong, this is God's will, and He is comforting her now. We all come from God and unto Him do we return."

A discreet white station-wagon ambulance drove Ibtisam, and the rest of us followed. At the mosque, we women prayed in the women's balcony above the main prayer hall. Mama was very strong that day. She didn't cry once.

The men buried Ibtisam in an old graveyard in Ruwais, a couple of blocks from Salma's house. My grandmothers are there too. In keeping with our local custom, we women didn't go to the cemetery. Bashir and Fahd lowered her into a grave and marked it with a nondescript stone.

Later, we received our female friends and relatives in the order dictated by tradition: first Mama, then me, then Aunt Rosette. The first visitors brought more mourning clothes as gifts for us to wear for the next four months. They were caftans and headscarves in dark blue, brown, and grey. Even now, I avoid these colors, for they still bring back memories of those very painful days.

We hosted many condolence mornings at home, and the stifling scent of fresh flowers filled the house. Though nothing was written in the newspaper about Ibtisam's death or about the fate of any of the hostages, word of my sister's courage spread through the University and across the city. Ibtisam's student friends visited, and it was through them that we began to appreciate who Ibtisam was, and who she might have become had she lived. To me, she had seemed extreme in her approach to living as a good Muslim woman. But I was proud of the way they spoke about her. They said she was the best student in her class.

One day, two of her professors called on us. Ibtisam's professor of jurisprudence assured Mama that Ibtisam was gifted, both in the sharpness of her memory and in her wisdom in interpreting how the law's logic might apply to modern problems. The other, a professor of history, likened Ibtisam to A'ishah, the prophet's wise third wife, because of her ability to reason and to convince others through logic.

Was Mama comforted knowing this? I can only imagine what was in her deepest heart. Sometimes, she would sigh. "What a rare and beautiful girl she was, I am so proud of her. But why was she taken so young?"

We were honored when women of the royal family visited, including the Amir's wife. These were women of the family of the king and former king who lived in Jeddah, and they were especially kind to Mama. One of the older ladies, well acquainted with personal loss, told Mama that, in time, God would relieve some of her pain. "But," she said, "The loss of a child always leaves deep scars on a parent's heart. You can only stop it from bleeding. The scar will always remain. May God give you strength."

When Salma, Mabrukah, and Nurah visited us, the sun shone in my heart. Salma hugged me and I imagined my grandmothers might have held me like that. "When you are ready, come for a visit," Salma said. "I miss you, my dear."

How did Mama cope? She tried to be strong, to set an example to my brothers and me. She kept up the regular family routine. The condolence calls helped, because she had to be up and dressed, no matter how she felt. The countless good wishes and kindnesses of the women seemed to hold her together. But she was still so weak. Each day, she would visit Ibtisam's room, read her Qur'an and weep.

Baba's wound was just as deep, but he was used to dealing with death. Years ago, he had lost an older brother, my uncle Muhsin, in a car crash. He seemed stronger than Mama and worked hard to get the household back on a normal routine. Meanwhile, the family businesses were booming, and my brothers were soon involved in new projects at work. Even Tarek went back to the office full-time.

As for me, I didn't recover so well. I didn't go back to school that spring, and I even avoided Salma. I couldn't concentrate on anything, and memories of that morning in the mosque replayed in my mind day and night.

Should I, or any of us, have run after Ibtisam when they led her away? Were we cowards for not doing it? And why hadn't any of the other people stood up for her?

Since that day in Mecca, I hadn't set foot in my studio, and I'd locked it so no one else could get in, either. The world was gray and brown, like our mourning clothes. The concrete of the city reminded me of the simple stone that marked Ibtisam's grave.

Guilt over my sister's death overwhelmed me, but I couldn't talk about it with anyone. She would never have proposed that midnight prayer vigil if it weren't for my indiscretions with Hisham. Most nights, I couldn't sleep. I just tossed and turned, wavering between sleep and wakefulness, as if I'd had a cup of coffee just before shutting off my light. I didn't want to recover from my loss. It didn't seem right. Ibtisam had lost her future because of me, while I still had a future that I didn't deserve.

My mind was numb, and I lived in my bedroom in a gauzy cocoon of mourning. The sheer curtains and the hum of the air-conditioning filtered out the colors and sounds of the world. Even the city herself seemed to mourn with me. The dust and haze in the air were her veil and mourning clothes. She and I both hid our faces from the sun and the sea, preferring to stay silent and hidden.

It was almost noon when Halimah knocked on my door one day. I was still in bed. "Miss Fawzia, Mabrukah is here with a message from Salma."

I threw on a caftan and washed my face. I'm sure Mabrukah could tell I'd just woken up. "We've been worried about you. You haven't visited us for so long, and we miss you. Can you come for lunch tomorrow?"

I started to yawn and stretch my arms over my head. But since this would make it obvious I had just woken up, I pulled my arms back down and folded them. But I couldn't stifle the yawn. "Yes, of course I'd love to come."

After she left, I showered and got dressed. It was time for lunch, but I wasn't hungry. As I pulled on my jeans, I realized I'd lost a lot of weight. The pants were at least a size too big. I looked in the mirror and noticed dark circles under my eyes. My face had a pasty yellow hue.

I sat at the table to have lunch with the others for the first time in months, and forced down a few bites.

"Good girl, you're eating. Have some more," Halimah said. The boys were silent, concentrating on their food. Baba was rushed. He took two calls at the table.

As usual, we all settled into the family room for a round of coffee. The boys lit cigarettes, and everyone perused the papers. But in the months since Ibtisam's death, I hadn't read a newspaper, and I didn't play backgammon anymore. I had a cup of coffee, but my thoughts always returned to Ibtisam.

Later that afternoon, the color of the sky drew me to the dining-room window. The sun was trying hard to shine through, but yellow dust-laden clouds insisted on blocking its rays. Something was brewing, maybe a storm from the north. Could it be rain? This was the time of year when storms blew in from Egypt and Jordan. But then again, it could stay like this for days, churning up nothing but dust and sand.

I walked around the swimming pool barefoot. The water reflected the strange yellow tint of the clouds. A fine layer of dust had settled on the glass patio table. I sat down, wishing I'd brought my sunglasses, because the glare was giving me the beginnings of a headache.

The swirling clouds stirred up the dull grey haze in my mind. Everyone else in the family seemed to be doing better. Not me, though, because that morning at the mosque was always with me. No one was pushing me, either. They were leaving me alone to heal. Maybe that was the problem. Yet, in a way, I didn't want to be pushed.

After a while, I went back to my room and tried to write some of my feelings in a journal, but it did nothing to dull the ache in my heart. Without thinking, I pushed the play button on my cassette recorder and listened to music for the first time since Ibtisam's death.

Fairuz's velvety voice sang "O Jerusalem, O flower of cities," about her yearning to wander in that city's ancient streets. The music flowed through me and unleashed my tears. I rolled over and hid my face in the pillow to try to stop them, but the tears still came.

In the silence after the song ended, something began tapping at the window. Raindrops. I dismissed them at first, since many dust storms throw down a few drops here and there, nothing more. Then it began to pour. I slid open the door to my balcony to smell the freshness of the rain. I stuck my hand out and felt the water, the temperature of my tears. The wind whipped the palm branches, and torrents of rain ran along the marble patio below. I went downstairs and walked out into the rain, feeling its full force on my face.

The wind swirled my hair around my head like a writhing wet turban. I held out my arms and let the warm rain soak through my clothes, into my skin. Puddles formed at my feet. I held out locks of my hair, letting the rain wash it. I opened my mouth and drank the sky's tears. Something started stinging my arms and face. It was hailing! I jumped out of the rain to stand in the doorway, and I listened as tiny ice pearls pounded on the marble. I scooped up a handful. They were pure white and rounded, like a child's teeth. A huge sheet of water poured down, and a torrent raced toward the main gate, out onto the street.

"Fawzia, you're soaking wet!" Tarek had joined me at the threshold.

When a loud thunderclap shook the sky, we screamed and ducked inside, our fear turning to laughter. In that instant, my heart jolted back to life. How long had it been since I'd laughed? Upstairs, we found Baba, Mama, Fahd, and Bashir looking outside. I put the hailstones in a tiny bowl in the freezer. Then I wrapped myself in a big white towel and joined the family at the window. We watched Halimah and Hamdi looking out of their ground-level apartment, keeping a worried eye on the rushing water.

A full force rainstorm like this happened once or twice a year, and in some years, it didn't rain at all. Such rainstorms soaked the plants and trees, which survived only by the careful hand-watering of gardeners, or from managing to eke out moisture from the humid sea air. Now, there would be big puddles everywhere, and some minor flooding. While our marble patio glistened with the warm rain, I knew that high up in the balad, the walkways would be very muddy, except where ancient marble bricks and stones poked through to the open sky. I wondered how many roofs on the old houses leaked.

As the rain stopped, low churning clouds hung overhead, dark with the promise of another downpour. When rain like this came to Jeddah, it often continued for days. I breathed the sweet moist air, and felt a refreshing calm overtake me.

CHAPTER 11

CONFESSIONS

Jeddah
April 1980

I TOOK the hailstones with me to Salma's the next morning. It was slow going, since Hamdi was trying to avoid the puddles. Boys threw rocks into the water, laughing as they got splashed. Men emerged from the bakery with their arms full of loaves, their thobes hiked up, hems held between their teeth to avoid getting wet. Scrawny kittens perched on walls and curbs, meowing.

Salma took my arm as she led me inside. "In the desert, we believe hail is good luck. When I was a girl, we would eat it like candy, like this. Here, try some."

Salma, Mabrukah, and I sat for a few minutes in the salon, crunching the hailstones in our mouths. Then Salma nodded to Mabrukah, and she left the room. Salma reached for my hand. How could her wrinkled hands emit such warmth and tenderness? Her touch comforted me, but at the same time, my deepest pain began welling up like a rising river in a flood.

"How is your family now, my dear?"

"Mama is still weak, and she still cries a lot. But she works hard to keep the family going. She's trying to be brave for our sake. Baba and the boys mourn in their own way, keeping busy with work. Ibtisam's room is just as she left it. No one has washed her sheets, or moved her books and notebooks. Sometimes I find Mama sitting on Ibtisam's bed, crying. Then, after a few minutes, she gathers her strength and goes on. And I, too, go into her room when no one is home."

"We have missed you so much," Salma said. "In your mourning, we have worried that you have not been well."

"She was so perfect, and I am so bad compared to her."

"But you're a good girl," Salma said. "God created each of us to be unique, just as He creates each day different from the one before. Some days are quiet and calm. Others are blessed with riotous rain and thunder. So it is with people."

"There's more to me than you think. I haven't been a good daughter or sister."

She was silent for a long time, as if she was debating what to say next. Though I was looking down, I felt her intense gaze, and my cheeks burned.

"Is it something to do with love?" she asked.

How could she know? I bowed my head and shook it to say "no," trying to deny it, but my hand tensed up in hers, and I couldn't hide my strong reaction to her accurate guess. Sobs built up inside my chest. I tried to pull my hand away, but she held on tight.

"It's all right. You can tell me. You are not the first girl to fall in love, or to have your heart shattered by loss."

She reached her other arm around me and held my head to her shoulder, patting me as the sobs came out in waves that shook my whole body.

"Have patience with yourself. Remember, God created love too. It is not an evil thing, but it can be dangerous sometimes. Believe me, I know this from my own experience. Love sings in all our lives at some point. Its melodies, its poems, and its ways are mysterious and, yes, they can be deadly. Tell me, tell me everything. I think it might help you. You can trust me to keep your secrets."

"I've walked so close to danger, and, worst of all, Ibtisam found out before she died. I betrayed her trust, and I think I caused her death. I'm the one who should have been taken. She was blameless, I'm the one who has sinned."

"How have you sinned, my dear? Remember, none of us is without blame, without secrets."

So I told her everything. Salma was silent through it all, nodding her head, and smiling when I explained my feelings for Hisham.

When I finished, she spoke. "Yes, she gave her life, in God's holy place, for the life of children. This is a great sacrifice. She was a wise and strong woman, especially for one so young. But you are not an evil or bad girl. You fell in love, and love is never easy. And besides, you've a sensitive and loving heart. God created you this way, and He also made you strong enough to endure it. You must have faith that, with time and wisdom, He will heal you."

She was quiet for a few moments. "Each year, the rains are our signal that spring has returned to the mountains near Taif. Soon, we will go to my house there, and God willing we will stay for the summer. When you're ready, why don't you come visit us? I think it will do you good."

"Would you tell me more of your stories, and let me record them?"

Salma smiled and paused for a moment. "Yes, to both questions. It will be my pleasure."

When I asked Baba's permission to visit Salma, he approved with one condition. Tarek would drive me up to Taif, and he would decide whether it would be appropriate for me to stay. As for me, I kept wondering: What could Salma know of love?

Wadi al-Bu'ur
1980

Peace to the brazier in winter
Around which are spun the evening tales.

- A Sailor's Memoirs by Muhammad al-Fayiz

CHAPTER 12

SHE OF THE PICKUP TRUCK

Jeddah and Wadi al-Bu'ur
May 1980

THE SEA withheld her breezes the morning we left, and, as the heat rose, humidity wrapped around us like a heavy woolen cloak. We drove downtown to catch Mecca Road, passing through the Yemeni spice market. We idled at a stoplight, as East African women strolled by in long flowing dresses of bright yellow and orange. Tarek boosted the volume on the latest love song by Abadi al-Jawhar, who was singing with a full-sized orchestra. I turned the air-conditioning to high and closed my eyes.

Once past the outskirts of town, road signs marked the shrinking distance to Mecca. Neither of us had been there since Ibtisam died. I was relieved when Tarek announced that he would be driving the long way – taking the bypass road around Mecca – so he could enjoy the powerful engine of his brand-new Range Rover. I realized I hadn't left Jeddah since the night at the Grand Mosque. It had been nearly six months.

Neither of us felt like talking, so we filled the morning with speed and music. We flew through the brown sandy plain dotted with forlorn concrete block houses built right next to the road. Water mirages shimmered all around. I aimed the air conditioning vents directly at my face.

Salma's home lay beyond the ridge of the Sarawat mountains that stood before us in haze. We wound our way up the escarpment road along hairpin turns, joining a fleet of painted pickups and full-sized trucks.

I rolled down my window. The humidity was gone, and the air was noticeably cooler. We pulled off at a turnout and leaned over the wall to bathe in the cool breeze. Three big birds rode the thermals. Baboons stared at us from nearby rocks, waiting to see if we would offer them food. As we continued up the road, I wanted to roll up the sleeve of my abaya and stick out my bare arm. How delicious it would feel! Instead, I leaned my face out the window and held the edges of my headscarf open to catch the wind.

At the top of the cliff, we entered a world of rocky hills dotted with bushes and palms. The sun shone bright, yet the air was cool and dry. After Jeddah's humidity, this was pure delight, a very different world indeed.

"OK, so where's the turnoff?" Tarek asked.

"We take the Abha road south. Then we're supposed to turn right onto a dirt road after we pass a gas station and a small store. It should be about 20 kilometers to the gas station. There'll be a rock painted orange to mark the turn-off."

Music still blaring, we sped south along the Abha road. We passed stone houses two and three stories tall that were huddled in tree groves or tucked up in the rocks. At each bend in the road, I willed the gas station to appear. My worry grew each time we came around a turn or over a hilltop and it wasn't there.

"So tell me," Tarek said, popping out an eight-track tape. "How can an old lady like Salma live up here all by herself? Doesn't her family care for her?"

"Well, she's always with Mabrukah. She doesn't have kids, and I don't think she's married. You can ask her yourself when we get there." I didn't know that much about her myself, and I kept thinking about what she'd said to me about love. Honestly, I couldn't believe my big brother was about to sit down and talk to Salma. Fortunately, due to her advanced age, this meeting would be acceptable to most Saudis, though I'm sure some would still say it was improper for Salma and Mabrukah to meet my brother at all, since they weren't related.

At last, we found the orange rock and turned onto a well-worn dirt track full of ruts and boulders. We inched forward, bumping up and down.

"Heeee! My tires, my suspension." Tarek moaned. We passed in and out of the deep shade of acacia trees. Prickly pear flourished among the rocks. A dove flew overhead, casting a shadow on the hood of the car. The road grew even rockier as it turned down a slope and then right, hugging a hillside.

"What's next? Do we have to cross a river?"

I was starting to feel sick from all the bouncing, my head bumping against the car's ceiling. We came to a full stop in front of a large boulder blocking the road.

"Now what do we do?"

"Allah," I said with a sigh, for I had no idea. "The directions say to park when we come to the big tree next to a large white rock."

"OK but does it say how long before you get there?"

"No."

Tarek backed up and inched around the boulder. The car bucked and bounced so much it hurt. After 10 more minutes of crawling and rocking along while I gripped the door handle, Tarek muttered, "If we don't find that tree soon, we're out of here and I don't care what you or your friend Salma says. You're ruining my car."

He slammed on the brakes inches from the edge of a ten-foot-wide crater. He turned off the car. "That's it. We're going back. This is unbelievable."

Before I could respond, we heard the sound of a motor up ahead. A pickup was careening straight toward us. Tarek got out and waved his arms. The pickup stopped in a cloud of dust, and a woman emerged from the driver's side and dusted herself off. A woman at the wheel! She sported the fitted embroidered caftan of the region and had wrapped a long brown headscarf around her hair, but her face was bare. I'd heard that rural women drove, but until then, I'd never seen proof.

"Yes, my brother. Are you lost?" She approached us with one hand shading her eyes. When she saw me, she turned to me instead. I got out of the car grinning, delighted to be asking directions from a woman driver in my own country.

"We're looking for the house of an old woman from Jeddah. She lives near here."

"Ahh, you mean Salma!" She smiled, her gold-capped front tooth gleaming in the sun. Her voice was loud, but its pitch was warm and low. "I've known Salma for many years, she's like my own grandmother. Tell her you met Farhah on the road and greet her for me, eh? As for her house, you're almost there. First, you have to get around this crater. I'll show you how. Keep going just a little way, then leave your car next to the white rock.

You have to walk from there. Just follow the path, and you'll come to her house."

"Thank you, but how can we…"

"Get around this crater? Come, I'll show you." She pointed out a track that ran a wide course around the crater. "I'll go first, then you can do the same." She paused and looked us over. "You're from the city, I see. Welcome to the mountains, and have a nice visit."

After passing by the crater, she waved and drove off, singing at full volume, the dust cloud billowing behind. Neither of us said a word about the fact that a grown Saudi woman drove up to us, perfect strangers, chatted with us, and gave us directions. We drove around the crater and soon found the rock and parked the car. We got out and stretched.

Tarek swore when he saw the rocky path we'd be taking. "But my shoes." He had on Italian loafers with tassels. At least I'd had the sense to wear running shoes.

"Unbelievable." Before I could call him an idiot, I stopped. "Wait, didn't you go to the beach last weekend?"

"Yeah, why," he said, realigning his ghutra and agal. He stretched out his arms, then twisted his torso first right, then left.

"Well, are your sandals still in the car?"

"Sister, you are a genius!" He opened the back and slipped on his well-worn camel-skin sandals. Even though we were cosmopolitan city kids, we all had pairs of these comfortable hand-made leather sandals in our closets. Even us girls.

The path meandered over small hills and gullies peppered with rocks and trees. We leaned against a boulder in the shade and shared some bottled water. When a bee buzzed by my head, I noticed the deep silence around us. When was the last time we'd experienced this utter quiet, away from air conditioners and car horns? My ears delighted at the cooing of doves and the chatter of sparrows. I took deep breaths of pine-scented air.

"Let's go," Tarek said, standing up and checking his watch. "It's nearly 2 o'clock. We'll never make it back by midnight if we sit around all day." He was assuming I'd be going back with him that day; I was praying I could stay the week.

We came upon a small stone hut. A red and white ghutra was draped over the corner of its half-open door. A walking stick leaned against the wall.

We looked inside. No one was there. It was just a one-room shack furnished with a simple mattress, which also served as a couch, and a tiny kitchen. It was much too small for both Salma and Mabrukah, so we kept walking.

The path brought us alongside a vegetable garden bordered with stones and weathered boards. A breeze carried the scent of a cinnamon-spiced stew cooking somewhere nearby. Could that be coming from Salma's home? Was it Salma's lunch? Our lunch?

The smell of that stew pulled us along the path, until we came to a more substantial stone house built into the hillside, surrounded by acacias and junipers. Embroidered blue caftans swayed on the clothesline as the breeze rose and fell. I hoped this was her house so we could taste whatever was cooking inside.

"I'm so hungry." Tarek leaned back against the wall and turned his face to the sun. "All this way, and she's not even…"

"Yes, just a moment, I'm coming!" It was Salma, striding up the path. She was pushing her pace, defying her slight limp and reliance on the walking stick. "Ah! You made it!" She stretched out her arms to welcome me with a hug.

She squinted up at Tarek, the sunshine revealing every wrinkle on her face and each blue-black diamond of her chin tattoo. "Welcome, Tarek. Please come in. And Fawzia, you can take off your abaya here. There's no one around." She waited as I removed my cloak. Then, with a shake of her hand, she signaled to me to take off the headscarf covering my hair too. I let it fall to my shoulders. "We're out here in God's own sunshine and fresh air, and you should enjoy it."

Cool air greeted us as we stepped inside. Bright weavings covered the cushions lining the walls of the main room, and the whitewashed walls were painted with black geometric patterns filled in with yellow, blue, and red. An equally bright woven carpet covered the stone floor. I peeked into the kitchen, where an old gas stove kept the delicious-smelling concoction simmering in a pot. Tarek rubbed his stomach, then caught himself and smiled. Like me, he seemed delighted we would be tasting that stew after all.

Salma beckoned us back outside to the patio. We sat in the shade of a grape arbor on a wide wooden bench with rush seats. She served us tall glasses of water from an old-fashioned red metal tray festooned with painted flowers.

Below us, the wadi widened to the south. Everything was green and lush. Rocks jutted up here and there. Farms with terraced garden plots hugged the hillsides. Salma pointed out that every farm had at least one beehive and several rosebushes, reminding us that the roses of Taif were famous for attar, a perfume made from their petals. A dozen goats stood on one farmhouse roof, eating the leaves off nearby trees. We laughed as the farmer's wife shooed them away with a broom. Tarek took off his ghutra and agal. I rolled up the sleeves of my caftan and let the cool air caress my bare arms.

Salma joined us on the bench, leaning back and carefully folding her legs underneath her. "We make that drive once in spring and once in fall. It's always an ordeal." As if reading my mind as to whom she meant by we, she added, "Oh yes, Mabrukah is here, she'll be along any minute. We've been visiting the neighbors."

When Mabrukah appeared, she made no attempt to cover her hair in front of Tarek and joined us on the terrace.

"Do you both really spend your summers here?" I asked, hoping it was true.

"Why yes, from the first to the last hot days in Jeddah, we're here."

"But you're not alone, are you?" Tarek said, no doubt assessing my safety if I were to stay. "We saw the hut down the path."

"Ah, that's Salim's place. He helps us when we need him. There are many families here, who are now our dear friends, so we are far from alone."

"What tribe lives in the area?" Tarek asked.

"Bani Thaqeef, mostly. Some Qahtanis, too."

"And you have permission to use this land and build on it, if you don't mind my asking?" Tarek was obviously surprised, as I was, to find women living out in the countryside like that, independently. Where were their male guardians? Saudi women didn't just live alone, they were part of a family group, and these two really seemed to be on their own.

"You can ask me anything. Yes, the land belongs to me. It was given to me many years ago by the wife of one of their shaikhs. I helped her recover from an illness. It was God's will, of course, but she rewarded me just the same. She was pregnant at the time with the Shaikh's only son."

"How do you get water here?" Tarek asked. "Do you have it trucked in? I don't see a water tank."

"Come, I'll show you." She led us around the house and opened a door to a cellar built into the hillside. We stepped into a small, cool room, lit by a single window. A stream was flowing right underneath their house.

"See that? It's a spring. The mountain provides several springs like this in the wadi, and that's how it gets its name, Wadi al-Bu'ur, Valley of the Springs. We don't only use it for drinking water. It can also keep our food cold for a long time. See?" She pointed to a shallow pool in the middle of which sat a metal trunk. "We keep all our meat and yoghurt in there. Here, try some water, it's delicious."

We each scooped a handful. It was cold and refreshing. Back in Jeddah, water was a complicated issue. We drank only bottled water. For cooking, we used sweet water that Hamdi bought in five-gallon jugs. We even had to buy all our washing water for the house by the truckload. Here, Salma and Mabrukah had pure water day and night. It was the ultimate Arabian treasure.

"Where does the water go from here?" Tarek asked.

Salma led us outside, then down a path. There, the stream was about a yard wide and several inches deep. The water rushed over small boulders and stones.

"This is a kind of paradise you have here," Tarek said, sighing. I grinned and turned away. It wasn't often he admitted to being impressed by something.

"Indeed, we thank God to be here, each day, in good health. From here, the stream goes down the hill a little way, then disappears into the mountain again. Now, I think it's time for lunch."

Mabrukah served the stew on a bed of rice. Rounds of flat bread were stacked beside it. We said "bismallah," and all of us ate together on the patio, scooping the stew and rice with pieces of bread. Mabrukah also brought out a bowl of fresh olives and a salad of tomatoes, cucumbers, and green peppers.

"May your table always be this bountiful," Tarek said. After we sat back, sated, Mabrukah and Salma started to clear. I rose to help them.

"Nonsense, young lady," Salma said. "You're our guest."

"What kind of dish is that?" I asked. "I'm intoxicated by the spices."

"I got the recipe from an old friend. I'll tell you about her sometime."

They took the food away, leaving us alone for a few moments. "This cool air is really something," Tarek said. "Wouldn't it be great to build a villa up here?"

More than Tarek could ever understand, I was giddy from the freedom of sitting outside unveiled to the sky. I savored the spice in the air that seemed as ancient as the landscape around us. For the first time since I was a girl at the beach, my face and hair were bare to my own country's breezes, open to its sounds, its smells and its sunshine. I could feel my spirit coming to life again, like a desert flower that can only bloom after spring rain.

Yet this feeling was bittersweet, because enjoying this happiness for longer than an afternoon depended on a man's permission. This time, it was my own brother—speed-loving, Italian-shoed Tarek—who would make my choice for me as to whether I had to go or could stay the week. That's the way it was. Men made our decisions for us. They were in charge.

Mabrukah led us around the side of the house to wash. She opened a spigot of cold spring water and we washed our hands, then dried them with a sun warmed towel.

When we returned to sit, Salma offered us orange sections. "From one of the villages to the south," she said, pouring tea.

A gruff man's voice called out. "Salma! Mabrukah!"

"We're outside!" Salma said.

A man came around the corner like a water truck barreling down a mountain road.

"Aha! Hello! I saw the car and wondered if you had guests. Welcome, welcome," he said, pumping Tarek's hand with a grin as he was introduced. This was Salim. Then he turned to me, still shaking Tarek's hand, and greeted me with a nod. I had been so relaxed that I had forgotten to cover my hair, and wound my headscarf over my head to cover.

When Salim released Tarek's hand, a set of red amber prayer beads slipped down his sun-browned arm, and he caught them just in time. He joined us, sitting next to Tarek. Once his customary four sugar cubes had dissolved, he slurped his tea and said, "It was quite a day in town today, but they still don't have those dates you asked for, Salma. Inshallah, tomorrow."

"No matter, I can be patient, for they are worth the wait," Salma said.

When he finished his tea, Salim turned to Tarek and said, "Come, let me show you around the hills. You should stretch your legs after all that time in the car." They were gone in a moment, and Salim's sudden disappearance left a great silence.

"Well, my dear, what do you think of our mountain chalet?" Salma said.

"It's so quiet and peaceful, like heaven really."

"I'm glad you like it. We always find peace in these hills among our friends. So my dear, can you stay for a few days? We have plenty of room for you. It would be our pleasure."

"Baba said it's up to Tarek. Truly I would love to, but it's his decision."

"My dear," Salma said, patting my hand with a bit of admonition. "Sometimes, even though you think you have to ask permission, you don't really have to. Try this. Tell him you'd like to stay, and ask him to inform your parents of your decision. Believe me, men grow tired of having to make our decisions for us. I think they really want us to tell them our preferences."

"I'd like to stay the week," I announced when the men returned. "Can you tell Mama and Baba everything is fine up here and that I'll be safe?"

"Sure, no problem," he said, smiling. "Wish I could stay, too. This is fantastic, it's the Arabian Alps." Salma winked at me.

"When you return," Salma said to Tarek, "come a day or two early and spend the night here. You can stay in Salim's hut, and he'll show you around the area some more."

As we kissed goodbye on both cheeks, Tarek said, "Don't worry, Mama and Baba will be fine about this, I'll explain everything. Have a good time." His voice had a tenderness I'd never noticed before.

CHAPTER 13

Country Girl

Wadi al-Bu'ur
May 1980

"LET'S GO for a walk," Salma said, shortly after Tarek left. "Or are you too tired?" I stood up smiling, ready to go. Salma looked at my shoes and nodded before she sat down and tied on a pair of running shoes over a pair of white anklets. Grabbing her walking stick, she led me toward a meandering path behind the house that went up the hill.

I wondered how she would manage, with her limp. So long as she was in front she would set the pace. Within a couple of minutes, I was out of breath. Salma was the one with the limp and walking stick, but she still had more stamina than me. She noticed and beckoned me off the trail. "Come, let me show you something." How could an old woman like her be so energetic?

She led me to an opening in the bushes that looked over the valley. "Our property extends there, to the top of this hill then down about half a mile. It isn't suited to farming. But as you can see, those farms do well. Their soil is excellent and we get good rains."

Salma sat down and leaned back against a boulder, closing her eyes and enjoying the sunshine. I sat down near her and looked down into the wadi. I felt so small there, hidden among the bushes, the white clouds billowing high above.

I shut my eyes and listened to a bird twittering nearby and the breeze caressing the small pines. I don't know how much time passed before Salma nudged me. She pointed down to a large brown rabbit crouching on the path. We didn't move until it hopped away into the bushes. Before that day, I had never sat still and listened to the natural sounds of my country.

Like most Saudi women, I'd had very few chances to be out in the open air, experiencing nature. City girls could visit a park or at the beach with their families. If they were lucky, they might go on a picnic at night in the city when the weather cooled. But to be on a trail in these green hills, away from the eyes of gossips and strangers, was a rare thing, and it was something I had missed since my childhood, and my college days in Lebanon.

At the top of the trail, Salma stopped. "From here, you can see the top of the wadi. Just beyond it, the hills roll up to Taif. And to the south, this wadi goes all the way to the Asir." She started poking around in the bushes with her stick. "Fawzia, come see this."

She pointed to a small patch of deep purple flowers with four delicate petals like miniature hibiscus blossoms. Each had bright white pistils jutting out of their black centers.

"These are rijlat al-gharab," she said, picking a stem with two blooms. She tucked it behind my ear. "Now you're a real country girl."

Circling the north side of the hill, we joined the trail Tarek and I had walked to get to the house. Salma pointed her walking stick toward the nearest farm below. "Those are our neighbors, Um Saleh and her husband Samir." The large whitewashed house had several added wings. A swath of pastel colored girls' dresses hung on a clothesline on the roof, undulating in the breeze. "They have five children: two boys and three girls. They visit almost every day."

As we walked back down the hill toward the house, she slowed and picked her way carefully among the rocks. I saw her wince.

"Are you all right? Do you want to rest?"

"Let's stop a moment. My hip, it's been bothering me for the last year. It used to come and go, this pain, but now it seems to want to stay. But the doctor told me to keep walking, so I do as she says. Actually, being more active up here in the wadi helps more than anything. Thank God for this place."

When we got back, I admired my flower in the tiny mirror that hung on the outhouse door. "Hah – indeed, a country girl," I murmured, imagining what it would be like to grow up there.

As I walked back to the house, I heard young girls' voices. "But Auntie Salma, you said you'd tell us a story today! We've been waiting all week! Please?"

"As I said, girls, we have a special visitor. In fact, here she is, you can meet her. This is Miss Fawzia, who is visiting all the way from Jeddah. Please, girls, introduce yourselves."

The three daughters of Um Saleh were blessed with long wavy black hair, and bangs curled across their foreheads. They had small button noses, set between deep brown eyes. In their bright cotton dresses of yellow, orange, and red, they looked like a set of Russian nesting dolls.

The oldest girl stepped forward and extended her hand. "It's an honor to meet you." She had a lady-like grip.

The next one shook my hand with a little more strength, unafraid of a lady from the city.

Last but not least, the littlest one stepped forward. Her handshake was almost electric, like she was a lively little beetle about to fly off as soon as our hands separated.

"Now girls, Fawzia would like to take some tea. We need to rest."

"What about the story?" the youngest said. "You promised!"

"I know I did," Salma said, "And I intend to follow through. But you see our visitor is tired now and it's almost time for the sunset prayers. Why don't you ask your mother if you can come after the last prayer tonight? Then, inshallah, I will tell you a story."

The girls looked at each other, and the oldest said, "All right, we'll ask her. If we don't come tonight, we'll come back tomorrow and then you can tell us. But we will try for tonight, then."

"Inshallah," Salma said, smiling widely at their obvious enthusiasm for her stories, a perfect contrast to the party in Jeddah. We waved goodbye as they skipped down the trail.

"Where do they go to school?" I was wondering what it would be like to live in such a rural place.

"Their father takes them to the village school each morning and one of the neighbors brings them back."

"And their brothers?"

"They are good boys, and they work just as hard as the girls, like most boys on the farms up here."

We drank our second cup of tea, and I noticed the shadows from the hills were scaling the side of the wadi. After a few minutes of quiet contentment, Mabrukah said, "Let's get you settled so you can unpack your things."

Mabrukah led me to the bedroom. "Please, you will use this bed." She pointed to one of two single beds, dressed in colorful woolen blankets and comforters. I could see a mattress rolled up in the corner.

"I'm happy to sleep on the mattress," I said.

"No, no no. That's for me. You're a guest."

"But I'm a young person, and this is nothing to me. I would be so much happier if you slept on your own bed. I'll be fine."

"On your first visit, we want you to be comfortable. After all, you are far from your family and your home." As she smiled, the sunset cast a tangerine glow on her dark skin.

On the contrary, dear Mabrukah, I thought. I think I have only now reached home.

We prayed together at dusk on the patio, our prayer shawls wrapped around us. We faced northwest toward Mecca, with our backs to the wadi. Not since the night in the Grand Mosque had I prayed out in the open air, and I felt so much closer to God. As we finished, a star came out. Then the moon rose over the ridge to the east.

I stayed out on the patio awhile, relishing the changing sky. Inside, Mabrukah lit an oil lamp and set it on a low round brass table in the main room. After we dined on stew left from lunch, Salma lit a fire in the stone fireplace, and the flames set the room aglow.

"Do you feel safe up here all alone like this?" I asked, transfixed by the flames.

"Yes, absolutely," Salma said. "But we really aren't alone. There's Salim, Um Saleh and her family, and all our friends here. In many ways, I feel safer up here, with hardly anyone around, than I do in the big palace in Jeddah."

"Hello, Auntie Salma, Auntie Mabrukah!" The children stood outside in a tight group, and one of them knocked on the half-open door of the hut. We stood to greet them. The boys shook hands as formally as their sisters, under the watchful eye of Um Saleh, a housewife with the same button nose as her children, and a proud, wide smile. Her voice was warm and friendly,

"Welcome to the wadi, Fawzia. Inshallah you will have a nice visit." They presented Danish butter cookies in a big round tin of midnight blue.

The girls helped serve tea and cookies, and, before long, we grew quiet, waiting for Salma to start. I loved watching them, but then my heart broke when I remembered Ibtisam and I would never sit together in someone's salon. We would never be together again. I wiped my tears before anyone could see them and pushed the button on my tape recorder. Salma stared into the fire, gathering her thoughts. This time, her audience was transfixed, and we didn't move until she had finished.

"Kaan ya maa kaan fee qadeem iz-zamaan. Long ago, there once was a little girl named Samirah who lived in an oasis. Her mother and father were farmers, and all year long the family was working and working, because there were no schools then. Her brothers helped her father harvest the dates, and they planted wheat and alfalfa. Samirah helped her mother at the sawani, which is an old system where camels were used to bring water up from a well to irrigate the crops. Samirah brought alfalfa to the camel as it walked back and forth at the well, bringing up water that flowed into the irrigation system. All day Samirah did this, carrying alfalfa, listening to the creeeaaaking sound of the sawani, all morning, all afternoon, until her mother said it was time to go home.

"Samirah worked so hard that she had no time to play, but she was happy and sang songs with her mother. When her mother's friends came by, she listened to their talk, but always kept her eye on the camels and the sawani. If they brought their daughters, she could sometimes sit and talk to them. But she always thought about her work – the sawani, the water, and the alfalfa.

"One day, a group of travelers appeared at the farm. They were from Morocco, far to the west. Do you know about Morocco, children? Of course you do, you've seen it on a map in school.

"These travelers spoke Arabic, but they left off so many vowels that it sounded like their tongues were always turning somersaults. They rode on camels with purple and red saddles. The women wore dresses made of sewn-together ribbons.

"They'd been attacked by robbers, who didn't find their money but tore up one of their tents. So they asked permission to camp nearby for a few days while they made repairs. Samirah's father welcomed them, and they set up their camp near the sawani. Their tents were green, like the alfalfa Samirah carried all day. And wouldn't you know, they had a daughter the same age as Samirah named Amel.

"Amel watched Samirah working, and, without words, Amel began to help her. The girls worked together all day long. They got the job done faster, and, for the first time in her life, Samirah had time to play. Amel taught her how to hop like girls do in Morocco. Like this. Stand up, my dears, and I'll show you how.

"Excellent! Well done. Samirah took her new friend to the streams and secret pools deep in the oasis. When they lay down in the grass and looked up at the palm branches silhouetted against the blue sky, Amel told Samirah about the grand bazaars of Cairo and the boats that sailed on the Nile. Samirah sighed, wishing she could be released from her life of work, wishing she could venture beyond her small oasis world.

"The strangers finished their tent repairs and prepared to leave, for they were traveling on to Baghdad. On their last night in the oasis, they hosted Samirah and her family at their tents. After supper, the women shared stories, knowing they would be told again in new places and times.

"Amel gave Samirah a small silver bracelet. 'This is from Cairo,' she said. 'Remember me when you lie under the palm trees, when you long for adventures.' Samirah gave Amel a little woven bag she had made on her practice loom. 'Use this bag to hide your jewels from thieves on the road. It will protect your most precious things. When you hide them, think of me, and the safety of the oasis.'

"The next day, the travelers took their leave. The girls hugged each other and Samirah ran down the road behind them until her father called her back. She waved as hard as she could until the caravan turned out of sight, and then she felt the silver bracelet on her arm. Riding behind her mother on the camel, Amel waved back at Samirah until they were out of sight. She reached inside her pocket and felt the little woven bag that kept her most precious things safe.

"Samirah stayed in the oasis all her life. She never traveled to Cairo or Baghdad or Istanbul, but her heart flew above the palms whenever she brought out her bracelet. She imagined her friend, all grown up and married, living in a grand city house, listening to the sound of the muezzin, washing her hair in rose water. Amel never returned to the oasis, and she did live in a grand city palace. Yet Amel always kept her most precious jewels in the finely woven bag, remembering the kindness of the little girl and her family, and the safety of their oasis. May we, like them, find friends wherever we go, and may we always cherish them."

As Salma finished the tale, I felt as if I were waking from a trance. The youngest was curled up on her older sister's lap, asleep. The firelight painted her eyelids vermillion gold.

"Thank you, Salma," Um Saleh whispered. She lifted the youngest over her shoulder. The oldest girl held up an oil lamp and led the way down the path.

Later that night, the crickets woke me, chanting, "Come listen! Come listen!" I wrapped myself in a blanket and tiptoed onto the terrace. The rocky cliffs guarding the valley glowed silver in the half moon's light. I crept up the steps to the flat rooftop and sat on its low wall, just above the grape arbor, my hair flowing free. My heart took up the rhythm of the crickets' call, and I breathed the valley's fragrant scent.

Then a vision of Ibtisam praying in the Grand Mosque came to me, and my eyes filled with tears. How she would have loved this place and its kind people. A dove landed on the edge of the roof's wall. Together, we witnessed the passing of the night. At times, I closed my eyes and rocked back and forth, listening to the crickets, letting my tears flow on and on.

Someone touched my arm. Salma was sitting beside me, her eyes glistening. She took my hand. "Many nights, I have sat here myself just like this. What a gift this place is. This is why we come back year after year. Just let your tears go, my love. Don't hold back."

She stroked my hair. "Only time will heal the loss of your sister. There will be many nights like this, but your heart will grow strong again. God will see to it, you must trust Him."

Salma stayed by my side for a while, taking in the night's quiet grandeur. Gradually a thin band of white spread across the eastern horizon as the moon dipped westward. Salma pointed to the eastern sky. "There is the planet Venus, rising before the sun. Remember her in the dark of night. Often she brings the promise of sunrise long before we can see it."

As the stripe of light widened and turned peach, then orange, the dove began its morning song, coo-oo coo coo, coo-oo coo coo coo. It had stayed with me through the night.

In those quiet hours, I recalled the risks I took with Hisham, and the horror of Ibtisam's death. My decisions had been foolish and selfish, and because of them Ibtisam was gone. What had I been thinking, sneaking around, making bad decisions, lying to my parents and leading Hisham on when I knew we couldn't be together?

When the rooster began to crow, when daylight touched each bush and rock, revealing the color of the valley, I turned toward Mecca and prayed for forgiveness. In answer, the birds sang all around me, the sun rose higher, and the breezes caressed my teary face. The wadi stilled my sadness. Then I crept back to bed and slept.

The smell of cardamom-spiced coffee woke me later that morning. I felt refreshed, as if I'd slept the whole night. My hostesses were already up and dressed. As we savored sliced cucumbers and bread with yoghurt and raw honey, Salma said, "Today, we'll work a little in the garden. Then we'll go to the village market."

I knelt on the earth with them and pulled weeds from around tender zucchini and eggplant vines, my hair uncovered in the sunshine. This might not seem like much, but I had never worked in a garden before. At home, we always had gardeners.

"Have you learned to drive yet?" Salma asked as we walked to the truck later that morning.

"Aunt Rosette let me take the wheel in Lebanon once, but I never got an international license."

"Well, if you stay here long enough, Salim could teach you."

"Do you drive?"

"I used to, so did Mabrukah. But we're too old now, especially with all those speed-crazy young men on the road."

I remembered to mention that we had met Farhah. "Yes, many ladies of the wadi drive," Salma said. "They've been doing it for years. But now they try to stay away from the big highways."

"The police don't bother them?"

"No, they don't seem to care. Out in the desert, anywhere in Najd, north or south, you'll find women driving pickups, trucks, everything."

"Well, I hope I can drive someday."

"Oh, you will my dear, you will."

"That's what my Aunt Rosette keeps saying." The possibility that the authorities would ever permit us to drive seemed so remote. They kept saying our society wasn't ready for it. If you ask me, it's the men who aren't ready for it.

Salma sat with Salim in front, so Mabrukah and I climbed into the open truck bed. Mabrukah nodded. "So now you'll ride to the souq like a real desert girl!"

Foam cushions helped us endure the bumpy ride on the dirt road. My abaya served as combination sunhat and sunglasses, while protecting me from the dust that billowed up around us. Once we reached the smooth blacktop, it felt like we were flying.

We stopped at an outdoor market where farmers and their wives sold vegetables from pickups.

"Here, come see the weavers," Salma said. At the market's edge, three women sat on woven palm mats selling fist-sized skeins of black and white wool. One stood nearby, twisting and winding brown woolen threads around a long wooden spindle. Mabrukah sat on the ground talking to others who were selling finished weavings.

"Excellent work, Um Sawsan," Mabrukah said as she examined a woven panel, striped in red, black, and white. The weavers, she explained, were from the Ghamidi tribe near Taif. Most of them lived in villages, but they still kept flocks.

"See these designs?" she said, pointing out geometric figures and patterns woven into the panels. "Each is a wasm, a tribal marking. Sometimes they weave a tribe's camel brands, like those, the ones with the circle and jagged lines. Others come from the weaver's imagination. Look, there's an incense burner. And on this other weaving, here's the symbol for our wadi, two arcs for the hills and the zigzagging line for the streams. It's not a wasm, really. The weavers in the valley use it as a mark of pride, for our wadi has some of the finest weavers in the Hijaz."

With our purchases piled in the truck, we stopped at a butcher in the village for a leg of lamb. The hamlet was quiet except for a few people visiting the butcher shop and the little store next door.

As we waited for Salim, I asked Mabrukah how he had become their caretaker.

"He was on the crew that built our house. But, from the first, he treated us like we were his own aunts. His wife died a long time ago, and his children are grown and married. We are his second family in a way. Make no mistake, he gets paid for his work. It's a good arrangement."

We passed the small village mosque on our way out of town. I realized that, in the wadi, there was no mosque within hearing distance, so there was no call to prayer. There were very few places in Saudi Arabia where you couldn't hear it. It was a comforting sound, marking the passing of the days and nights, and I had missed it already. Just as we drove past the mosque, the muezzin tapped the microphone on the loud speaker and began his call, Alaaah-u-Akbar.

Out on the highway, Mabrukah touched my shoulder and pointed up. Two shepherd girls were prodding a flock of sheep along the side of a rocky hill. Their bright pink dresses caught the breeze, and they were easy to spot among the rocks.

Back in the wadi, I savored the coolness of the sliced cucumbers as I tossed them into a bowl with lettuce, lemon, garlic, and olive oil. The smell of onions lingered on my fingers, and the juice of ripe tomatoes stuck to my hands. We ate our salad and fresh bread from the village bakery out on the patio. Um Saleh was working in her garden. She stood up and waved to us, and we waved back. Then she let out a big, cheerful zaghrutah that echoed down the wadi. We answered, and our laughter bounced off the hills.

I asked why they didn't have electricity, since utility wires linked the other houses in the wadi.

"We lived most of our lives without it," Mabrukah said. "To us, it is a new convenience and is certainly wonderful in the city. Here, we prefer the buzzing of bees to the radio, and the glow of the stars to the glare of the television screen." How could I have argued with that decision, enjoying the peace of the valley, far from the troubles of the world?

That afternoon, in the shade of the grape arbor, I sketched things I'd seen. The two ladies would pause from their work to look over my shoulder, taking care not to disturb me. And for the first time since Ibtisam's death, I mixed my watercolors and began to paint.

The aroma of lamb cooking on a spit broke my concentration. After we dined on the patio with Salim, the neighbors joined us once more. It was a warm evening, so we stayed outside and sat around the fire.

CHAPTER 14

SHAIKHAH'S DAUGHTER

Wadi al-Bu'ur
May 1980

SALMA SAT still, as if listening across the decades, then said, "Owing to our special visitor, I am going to tell you a very special tale, one that I have never told anyone before, so you will have to bear with me.

"Normally when I begin, I say, 'Kaan ya maa kaan fee qadeem iz-zamaan,' but this time I will not say it, for this is our own story, the story of how Mabrukah and I came to be here with you on this night. Instead, I'll begin by saying, "In the name of God, the Merciful, the Compassionate."

I was riveted in that moment. She was not going to tell a folktale. Not having known my grandmothers and never having heard such stories from them, my heart opened up in an instant as I realized the gift Salma was about to give us all. It was so rare for a woman to share her true story, for details of her life could be used by gossips and troublemakers. Exposing our personal lives to strangers was dangerous, as it might reflect badly on the whole family. As a consequence, we women were cautious about telling of our own lives. We boiled things down to minimal acceptable facts, but in the process, we omitted nearly everything. Salma was about to tell us her life's journey in total confidence. Given what I knew of her so far, I was certain she had quite a story, and I was sure we were the perfect audience.

"I was born in the winter of 1901 in the northern desert that is now part of Jordan. In those days, long before oil was discovered in Arabia, there was no Saudi Arabia. The Ottoman Empire ruled most of the Middle East, and the Banu Hashim family ruled the Hijaz. This was before the European countries divided up Syria, Lebanon, Palestine, and Jordan in 1919 into the countries we know today. It was a very different time."

Salma paused and wrinkled her brow. "When I'm telling one of the old stories, I know exactly where to start. But this is different."

"Perhaps it will help if I ask a question or two," I said. "Tell us about your family."

"God rest their souls. My father was Ra'ed bin Sakhar. My mother Raghda was the favorite sister of my uncle Talal, shaikh of the Bani Shamaal. They were so close that people used to call him "Akhu Raghda," the brother of Raghda. Among the tribes, a man might be known as the father of so-and-so and also as the brother of so-and-so, if his sister was a great personality."

This amazed me. In my time, most Saudi men never even acknowledged their sisters' existence in public. Yet a hundred years ago, tough tribal warriors might have been called by their sisters' names.

"And you, Mabrukah?" I asked. She and Salma seemed as close as sisters, more than mistress and servant.

"They say my parents were from the Sudan, and that I lived with them in Medina. I don't remember them, because they died when I was a baby. After that, an old couple cared for me until I could walk and speak. I wasn't alone; many children like me lived with them. The old people seemed kind, but when we were old enough to understand, they told us we were servants and that God had ordained we would always serve others.

"Later, someone from the Bani Shamaal came to Medina looking for servants, and before long I was riding on a camel, wrapped in sheepskin against the cold winter of the northern desert."

Salma took up the story. "My father and mother said they had a great surprise for me, and they called me into the tent of my aunt, the Shaikh's wife. Mabrukah stood there like a frightened lamb, all wrapped in sheepskin. Her curly hair fascinated me. My mother said, 'This is Mabrukah. She will be your helper. You must be kind to her, for she will be with you for many years.'"

"From that day on," Salma said, "she has been at my side, like my own sister. In those days, it was customary for a high-born girl like me to have a personal attendant. I was the youngest daughter, you see, with no sisters or girl-cousins close in age. They were all married and living elsewhere by the time I could speak. Mabrukah kept me company, and we grew up together. My father had raised many sons and daughters, but I was the last child of his third wife. His first wife died, and he was divorced from the second before he married my mother. He taught me how to ride and shoot, because my mother wanted me to learn these things, just as she had. By the time I was eight, I rode my own horse, and so did Mabrukah."

"So your family lived the nomadic life?"

"Yes. We raised camels, sheep, and horses, too. We visited the grazing lands in the northern deserts. Our tribe, the Banu Shamaal, was great, even famous then. We numbered in the thousands and spread all across what is now Jordan, Saudi Arabia, Kuwait, and Syria, and sometimes ventured to what today you call Iraq."

"And your mother, what was she like? If your Uncle Talal was known as her brother, she must have really been something special."

"Oh yes. She was a striking figure. She was tall for her day, and, like her brother, she stood very straight, like a spear. She had wide-set eyes and never needed any kohl at all. She wore her hair like me, in long braids. She would talk politics with uncle Talal as if she were a shaikh herself. In fact, she was so wise that people used to call her shaikhah.

"She taught me to think for myself; I learned the value of my independence from her. She used to say that was the most important thing for girls. And she was right, because in those days you couldn't rely on your husband. The men went off raiding and hunting, and many people died young. We had no doctors, so sickness could wipe out a whole family. If she was clever, a widowed or divorced woman could find another husband and have more children."

Salma rose and stood at the edge of the terrace, staring into the night. "But that was not to be my fate." We waited for her to go on, the crackling of the fire filling the silence. She remained there a while, then returned to her seat.

"What is your earliest memory?" I was eager to hear more about those early days.

"There was a great wedding. One of my cousins was to marry a man from the Bani Harb. The tribes gathered to celebrate, and the nighttime campfires sparkled all the way to the horizon, mirroring the stars above. Days it took to prepare the bride. My mother let me watch them henna her hands and feet and the young women danced. The older ladies contorted their faces and called out zaghareed. One stuck out her tongue and wagged it from side to side, like this, loolooloolooo. Another smiled, raised her bony hand above her mouth and yodeled out a high-pitched yeeyeeyeeyee. And a third shouted leeleeleeleelee. I practiced on my own in a dark corner. Then, satisfied with my own leeleeleeleeleee, I raised my voice among them.

"In those days, there was an honor code among the tribes. Men respected women, and boys behaved toward girls. The tribes have a word for this, hilm, self-control. It's a pity young men today seem to have lost it.

"Then there were the raids. Warriors raided other tribes to steal camels and horses. Raids were men's business—women and children were usually left alone in their tents. Most injuries were minor, fatalities were rare. It was like a game for them. Those who had been raided would plot revenge, and the game continued.

"Life wasn't all weddings and raids. Daily living was hard work, even for the leading households. The boys and girls had flocks of sheep to take care of. In winter, Mabrukah and I went out alone with the flocks for days at a time. It was dangerous, but not because of other people. Each night, we had to set up camp and light a fire to keep the wolves away. Once I woke to find a wolf crouched not twenty feet away, watching me, its yellow eyes glowing. I pulled a burning stick from the fire and chased it away. Mabrukah offered to take the night watch, but I couldn't sleep, so we both stayed up until sunrise.

"My father used to say we were lucky not to have faced lions. At one time, they killed men in Arabia, you see. Fortunately, by the time I was ten years old, they had all been hunted. My grandfather kept the pelt of one he had killed. When he laid it out in the guest tent, I remember staring in horror at the gleaming pointed teeth in its gaping mouth.

"The women taught us young ones how to weave, cook, and sew. You see, the women wove the tents we lived in from goat and camel hair, one panel of cloth at a time. We sewed and embroidered our dresses by hand, and made our own camel-riding canopies. Each one was unique. We'd decorate them with ostrich feathers, beads, wool tassels, and leather braids.

"Those years had a natural rhythm, as old and as natural as the seasons themselves. In winter, we grazed our flocks, and the Solubba lived among us, trading their work for food. Do you know the Solubba? I didn't think so. Like the Arab tribes, they were an ancient people, but they weren't of our bloodlines. Some had light hair and were very handsome, others were considered ugly. Legend says they descended from Crusaders captured by

Saladin himself, but who knows? When I was young, they wandered the northern deserts, riding white donkeys known for endurance.

"They traveled among the tribes, working at trades we Arabs didn't, like tinkering and blacksmithing. They played music and were also excellent trackers and hunters. In summer, they went off and hunted gazelle and ostrich in remote places, surviving on water from secret wells only they knew.

"Some people said the Solubba could see the future, that they could influence things through magic. Because of this, many tribesmen feared them, and it was taboo to marry one of them.

"In the heat of summer, raiding was forbidden, and the Banu Shamaal camped together. Old friends and cousins renewed ties. We bought and sold livestock, replenished our supplies, repaired tents, and worked on our weavings. The nights were filled with singing and storytelling. Poets recited verses about battles and love. Love affairs began and ended. People got married. When the Pleiades reappeared in the sky, signaling the end of summer, the tribes would scatter and return to their grazing grounds.

"Our tribe, in fact all the great Arab tribes, lived this way for generations. Until 1914, when World War I split our lives in two. That war changed everything in Arabia. The Turkish Sultans had ruled many parts of the Arab lands, including this very territory, the Hijaz, for centuries. But by the time I was a teenager, the Ottoman Empire was weakening, and they became embroiled in World War I. Remember this was many years before oil was discovered in Arabia. This was a poor country, from north to south and east to west.

"In the Hijaz, a man named Hussein, the Sharif of Mecca from the Bani Hashim family, declared himself ruler of the Arabs and even Caliph, the leader of Islam, and took up arms against the Turkish Sultan. The Turks tried to conscript our men to fight with them, but we Arabs of the northern desert sided with Sharif Hussein. Like him, we aligned ourselves with the English army against the Turks.

"My father and uncle were both leaders in the Arab Army. They fought alongside "Al Auruns," an English army officer who spoke Arabic. I remember those days well, for I was 14 or 15 years old when the Arabs started to fight the Turks."

"So, how did the World War I split your life in two?" I asked.

"I lost everything because of it. I lost my father, my mother, my brothers, and my sisters."

"Were they all killed?"

"No. I was killed."

A breeze blew up, igniting flames in the embers. It was getting late, and a chill had come into the air. I wanted Salma to continue, so I added more wood to the fire. The flames leapt into the night, and the firewood crackled as we waited for her to go on.

CHAPTER 15

WHEN SUNSET PAINTS THE HILLS

Wadi Sirhan
April 1917

YOU ARE all so young. Just a few years from now, something may blossom inside your heart. It is powerful, and it is dangerous, but it is also wonderful. It is love, and it lives like a tiny seed in your heart. Of course, you love your mama and baba, your sisters and brothers. But I'm talking about grown-up love. In every person's life, love can bloom as suddenly as the desert flowers after a rainstorm. Girls, your mother and father, even your teachers tell you to stay away from boys, to keep yourselves hidden, as if doing that will protect you from your own heart. But nothing can save you, for love can bloom anywhere, anytime. You have to watch out, and protect yourself, for love can be dangerous, even deadly.

Even I, an old wrinkled lady, once fell in love, and this love broke my life into pieces. Yet because of this love I am here with you today. Listen to my story and learn. Maybe my tale will save you from my mistakes, and God willing your way will be easier.

Fly with me now on the wings of the night, over the hilltops to the north, high above the glowing lights of Mecca and Medina, over the dark Hijaz Mountains and the lonely campfires of the tribes, and farther still to the northern deserts. Fly with me now to the days long ago when Mabrukah and I were a pair of young gazelles, one brown and one black.

It was the spring of 1917, and World War I, the "Great War," enveloped all the nations of the earth. Our men fought in it, too. We Arabs were fighting against the Turks, alongside the English soldiers. As I said before, Al Auruns was on our side, and he even visited our camps. I saw him with my very own eyes.

But that spring, our family was camped, for safety, in a hidden canyon north of al-Jawf, in a place called Wadi Sirhan that is now part of Jordan. It was a horrible place, so cramped that we lashed our tents together in a tangle of ropes. Before we'd set up there, the only beings living there were green snakes and poisonous asps. Each night, they crept into our camp and tried to reclaim it by nosing their way inside our tents. We slept with sticks by our sides, and each morning we had to probe the ground around us. The rains were relentless and soaked everything.

We were the guests of our cousins, the Ruwala tribe. They were our secret allies in the war. Their shaikh, the famous Nuri al-Shaalan, was double-crossing the Turks. While pretending to be their ally, he fed them false information to give our army cover.

When the rainstorms finally ended, the leaders of the Arab army came to our camp to meet with Nuri. Gossip filled the tents, for Al Auruns had hired bodyguards for himself, made of Ageyli townsmen. They were known to be fierce and brave, but we looked down on them because they were only hired men with no tribal ties. Everyone said they'd do anything for money.

One night, the shaikhs gathered outside my uncle's tent. We women listened from inside and took turns peering out through a seam in the tent wall. My father, Talal, Nuri, and Al Auruns sat together before the fire, leaning on camel saddles.

A crowd of fighters joined them, everyone straining to see the great men. After conferring for a time, they raised their voices so everyone could hear. Talal and Nuri kept addressing Al Auruns as they teased an Ageyli named Abdallah. Nuri said, "Auruns, did you not wonder at how miraculous it was that Abdallah managed to return from Ma'an so fast? He must have traded his camel for one of your English armored cars. Ha! And Auruns, how else could he bring these green almonds all the way from Damascus?" Al Auruns said only, "Yes Nuri," or "You're right, Talal."

The coffee circle rang with laughter, as this Abdallah became the brunt of outrageous jokes about what he'd done on his mission. At first, Abdallah tried to defend himself, but Talal interrupted, making up more stories. "You must admit it, Abdallah," he said. "It was the wife of the Turkish officer who gave you that swift steed."

Talal thrust his muscular arm through the opening in the tent, holding a handful of fuzzy green almonds. "Raghda, taste the fruits of Damascus!"

Mama cut them with her knife and we shared them, our lips puckering at their tartness.

Mabrukah and I decided to go back to our own tent before the coffee circle broke up. To avoid the eyes of the crowd, we walked a discreet path among the tents, staying in the shadows of the firelight and stomping our feet to scare the snakes. Coming around a corner, I bumped into someone.

"Aieee!" I cried. Laughter from the fire circle drowned out my voice.

"Allah, I'm sorry, shaikhah," the man said. I'm sure he called me that because I was coming out of Talal's tent. I was embarrassed, for I hadn't covered my hair, and as I stood in a shaft of firelight, he could see my face and my famous floor-length braids.

Now, in those days, you didn't just hurry away when something like that happened. These chance meetings were the stuff of destiny and poetry. So it was for us, and we stood still.

"Forgive me, my lady," he said. "I am tired from my long journey from Ma'an." It was Abdallah the Ageyli! He turned to Mabrukah and nodded. She smiled and stepped back into the shadows.

"Such an astute scout who brings almonds from afar," I said. "But your reputation is certainly overblown if you can't back out of the coffee circle."

"Ah, but I knew you would be coming, so I planned it." He smiled and bowed his head. "And," he added, as he looked me over, "I see that it is true, there is a bright moon shining over Talal's tents."

"Well, you should not eat so many almonds because your footsteps have grown clumsy." I grabbed Mabrukah's hand and we walked into the dark, giggling as we continued on, stomping our feet.

Then he called out to me: "May my clumsy footsteps always lead me tripping into you." For some reason, I turned back to him. In the dim firelight, I saw he was gazing at me, arms at his sides, the breeze rippling the hem of his thobe.

Mabrukah and I lay in bed together and whispered details of his physique as if to double-check what we'd seen. He wasn't thin like many of the tribesmen, he was muscular, and he stood straight as a rod. His skin was darkened from working in the sun, and his shoulder-length hair fell in glistening ebony curls and waves. He smiled with a wild grin, showing perfect white teeth. His voice was deep and sonorous; every word sang a merry melody. I couldn't sleep that night, for his face swam before me, and his laughter rang in my ears and mixed with the howling of the jackals.

On the rare days when the weather was fine in that wretched place, I would take my mare al-Sahba out for a ride in late afternoon. Have I told you about al-Sahba before? Yes, I thought so. What a beautiful horse she was. My father had given her to me the year before, and she needed the exercise. Like her, I needed to get out and breathe. Mabrukah usually came with me, but that day she was helping someone with a weaving, so I went alone.

I stopped at my favorite lookout and dismounted, letting the horse graze. After checking for snakes, I leaned back against a big boulder and watched the clouds glow in the slanting rays of sun. I closed my eyes for a few minutes and rested. I listened to al-Sahba chew on the greenery and swish her tail. A bulbul twittered nearby.

Sensing something, I opened my eyes. Abdallah stood in front of me, holding the reins of his horse. I stood up in surprise. He had crept up on us, and my horse had been silent. I've always wondered why she didn't whinny to warn me. Could it be she knew?

"Don't you know how to approach someone?" I asked. "I won't speak with you further unless you greet me properly."

"I hear and obey," he said with a smile. He bowed his head and rode out of sight. After a few minutes, I began to wonder if I'd offended him, but to save face and self-respect, I leaned back against the rock and acted indifferent, toying with my braids. I waited for what seemed like hours.

Al-Sahba looked up, pointed her ears toward camp and blew air from her nostrils. I followed her gaze. Abdallah was returning. He stopped his horse a few feet away and jumped down with ease — he was carrying something tied up in his headdress. Even though he'd dropped the reins, his horse followed him, then approached al-Sahba and grazed by her side.

"Peace be upon you, Miss Salma, Daughter of Ra'ed bin Sakhr," he said as he bowed to me. "I bring you a token of my esteem for you and your good name."

"And peace upon you, Abdallah of the Almond." A sweet honey flowed through me from my ears to my toes, and as he drew closer it got sweeter and warmer.

"For you, a rare present I have carried a great distance." He untied the headdress. In it sat a big fat gray lizard with a spiny tail, a dhubb! Back then, they were harmless and plentiful in the desert. Mabrukah and I used to play with them when we were little. They were also a desert delicacy when roasted.

"Never has anyone brought me such a gift. I shall treasure it always. A thousand thanks, generous one." I picked it up and held it. It didn't move, for dhubbs are slow and sleepy creatures. "And it's obvious this isn't just any dhubb. Why it's the shaikh of the dhubbs. See how it looks at you with superior disdain? And how thick and muscular his little legs are? He is the great Shaikh Dhubb bin Dhubb bin Dhubb al-Dhabbi." I petted it and set it down on a rock, where it rested a while before crawling away.

I admired Abdallah's mare. Her coat was a warm brown that hinted of red. Her tail danced high, and he'd braided her mane in several places. I added another braid and tied it off with a tiny strip of bright yellow cotton I ripped from the end of my sash.

I lost track of the time in my confusion and pleasure, until the deepening dusk brought me to my senses. I clicked my tongue three times. Al-Sahba nodded her head and stood next to me, waiting for me to mount her.

He laughed. "Meet me like this each day, until Al Auruns takes me away."

I mounted al-Sahba, turned in a complete circle, and pulled up next to his mare. I ran my fingers over the braid I'd made and patted his horse's neck. "Until sunset paints the hills," I said, and galloped back to camp. No one was the wiser.

Abdallah was 20 years old. Like most Ageylis, he was a townsman. He came from Unaizah, an oasis town far to the south, in a part of Najd known as al-Qasim. He'd been trading horses between Baghdad and Cairo when he heard that Al Auruns was recruiting men and that he paid well, so he signed on.

We met for ten days. Even though I was an elite member of our tribe, until then my whole world was our tribe and the desert. And though we traveled hundreds of miles each year, and though the great and powerful came to meet with my father and uncle, Abdallah spun tales of the world beyond. He had climbed the pyramids, explored the back streets of Jerusalem, swum in the Euphrates, and slept beneath the great cedar trees that clung to the mountains in Lebanon.

"In all my travels," he said, "I have never met a gazelle fawn like you. The roses of Isfahan hold nothing to your soft cheek." He took my hands in his. How warm and strong his hands were, like the paws of a great lion. He pulled me to him, and I rested my cheek on his chest. He put his arm around my shoulders and held me there. Though his heart pounded, he took long slow breaths, as if trying not to frighten me.

Perhaps I fell in love with him and the wider world at the same time. Of course my young heart was confused about what I loved. But Abdallah embodied everything new and exciting. And how handsome he was! At night I would dream of him speaking to me, and in the daytime I would relive our conversations. I would conjure up the feeling of his hands and the open-air smell of him that I breathed when I nuzzled his chest. Certain things repeated in my mind, and I couldn't concentrate. Each day it seemed the sun took longer to reach the western cliff in late afternoon, when I could see him again.

How impossible it was that I had fallen in love with an Ageyli! I knew it was hopeless, and that my parents would never agree to us being together. In those days, my mother had been talking about my cousin Ahmad, to whom I was promised, and all the other suitors who would be honored to have me as their bride after the war. Perhaps, she said, I'd be a real shaikhah like her one day, the most important woman in her tribe. I explained all this to Abdallah. Yet he persisted, and we kept meeting.

One day, he caressed the back of my hand with his thumb as we savored the afternoon sun. "This might be our last meeting for a long time," he said. "There is talk of us leaving tomorrow. While it's God's will whether we'll be together, I have a plan. After the War, I will ask for your hand, but only once I have enough money to make me a suitable groom in your father's eyes. For unless I am rich, he will never let you marry an Ageyli."

Even though my head knew this plan was nonsense, my heart answered. "I will grow old waiting for you." He reached around and held me close, resting his chin on top of my head. Then I looked up, and we kissed. The wind blew his curly hair onto my cheeks. I opened my eyes and looked at him, and he at me.

"My soul is blazing. When I look at you, I feel connected to the flow of time, to the past and the future. Your laugh makes me want to clap with joy. This is my oath. By God in the heavens I will come for you."

The stars were still out when the men rode off the next morning. We women gathered at the openings to our tents and shouted zaghareed in waves to wish them success in battle. Mabrukah stood by me, her arm tight around my waist. My father rode by and nodded as he passed among the Ageylis, who followed Al Auruns. Abdallah glanced at me and nodded, then ran his hand over the braid I'd tied on his horse's mane. Holding his gaze, I touched my right hand to my heart, my lips, and my forehead, all in half a moment. We kept up our zaghareed until they disappeared from view. Mabrukah hugged me as I wept.

It was only after he was gone that the full effects of my love craze bloomed. His words echoed in my ears all day, and when I tried to sleep at night, I saw his face. I was in agony at being apart from him. Even though ours was such a brief affair, I felt the full fiery love of the great poems and songs.

In July, we learned that the Arab army had captured the port town of Akaba from the Turks. But we didn't celebrate the victory in our tents, because Uncle Talal lost his only son, my cousin Saif, in the battle. Then the army went south along the Red Sea and began attacking the Turkish railroad – the Hijaz Railway that ran between Ma`an and Medina. It seemed the war would never end, and our men would never return home.

Later that summer, we moved our camp to another hidden canyon. This one was much better, with room to spread out our tents, and high cliffs that gave us cool shade. It had a well, and, best of all, it was free of snakes. We young people took turns standing guard over the camp from atop the cliff, and the women in camp rotated cooking duties. In many ways, life was easy. Except for me. I was in pain, still haunted by the young Ageyli, Abdallah.

One afternoon in hottest summer, my father rode into camp. Mabrukah and I jumped up from our weaving in excitement. He leapt off his camel and walked straight toward me. "Salma!" he said, his words sizzling. "Inside, now!" I shuddered, for upon my life he had never spoken to me in such anger. Mabrukah disappeared before he could see the fear on her face. He stood before me as my mother lowered the tent walls.

That was the day when I would taste the first consequences of love, and it would also be my wedding day. May God protect you from such a day, and from such a wedding.

CHAPTER 16

SHAIKHAH'S TEARS

Wadi Sirhan
July 1917

BABA STILL held his rifle, as if he was about to start a battle right there in our tent. "We're settling a matter of family honor, and it has to do with you. There is talk among the fighters. They say you sullied our family honor. That last spring, you were alone with Abdallah the Ageyli. Is this true?"

My mother stood behind him, and their four eyes pierced through me. Someone had betrayed us. My heart pounded and my cheeks burned in fury, but I kept quiet, trying to decide how much to reveal.

"Are you still a girl?" Mother asked. "Has he taken your virginity?" She was known for her directness.

Before I could answer, my father said, "Speak, daughter. The truth!"

Though their words were harsh, they spoke quietly, for there were ears all around.

"I met him when Al Auruns came to consult with Nuri. Nothing happened. I swear that I am still a girl. Before God I swear it's true."

Father stepped forward and grabbed my wrist. His grip was hard, and I could feel him trembling. His eyes were flaming red from riding in the harsh sun.

"Yet you admit it, you were alone with him. And not just once?" I refused to lie, and remained defiant, for on one level I believed I'd done nothing wrong. Yet I also knew that falling in love with this outsider was forbidden. I nodded.

My mother stared at me in silence, as if trying to see into my mind. My father took off his headdress and unwound the agal he wore on his head. He grabbed my arm and jerked me sideways, then he whipped me. Hard. Only after he'd hit me several times did I bend in pain.

He kept on, until my mother stopped him. "Enough. It is enough."

"You must never see him again," he said. "Ahmad, your first intended, has returned with me to marry you. God willing, your purity will be confirmed and the rumors will be silenced. Though you are dearer to me than my own heart, if you've been deflowered by that Ageyli, I will not spare either of you one minute of life." He stepped back. "May God save you from any evil fate," he said, and walked out.

I struggled to control my fear at the maelstrom of my father's anger. Mother turned her tear-filled eyes to me, betrayal and doubt written on her face. I'm sure she was imagining my fate if they found I was no longer a virgin.

Before we could speak, Father returned with Ahmad and his mother, my Aunt Furaihah, her eyebrows arched with surprise and shock. When I'd last seen him, years ago, Ahmad was an awkward boy. Now he was a handsome young man, yet anger blazed in his eyes. My mother stood close to me, and held her hand on my back where I'd been beaten, as if to take the pain away.

Ahmad glared at me. "I ask for Salma's hand, exercising my right as her first intended."

"Since you claim you are a virgin," my father said, "you have the right to refuse."

My mother held my hand as I met my father's gaze. I had to agree, because only the man who deflowered me could confirm I was a virgin. Marrying Ahmad was the only way to survive and redeem myself. If I refused, I'd be punished further. I might have even been killed right then, since my refusal would prove I had indeed dishonored the family name.

"I agree and have no objection," I said.

"Today," Father said. "You'll marry this day." Then he marched out of the tent and rode off alone.

Ahmad smiled at me for a moment, then frowned and left with his mother. He had not said a word directly to me.

I refused to yield to my mother's ardent hugs. "I know you're pure, even if he doubts you," she whispered. "Be strong, Salma. Do not show your fear." Then, for the first time in my memory, she began to cry. She wrapped her arms around me, but I stood like a stone statue.

Remember, my dears, romance was everywhere in the desert. Men and women mixed together much more than they do today. Think of all the great poems and stories that celebrate love among the tribes! Majnun and Laila, Abla and Antara. We all grew up hearing their stories. If the families approved, young couples were allowed to spend time alone together. Even when secret love affairs were discovered, relatives might help them marry, because every generation had its legendary romances.

Unfortunately, our affair came to light in gossip among outsiders – lowly non-tribesmen far away at war, and, worse yet, within my father's hearing. An Ageyli like Abdallah was off-limits to me. Being brought up the way I was, I could understand my father's anger, and I knew he had to discipline me. He had to make an example of me, and I would have to steel myself and face my fate. We Banu Shamaal are not cowards.

With mother, my tongue loosened at last. "I will prove your trust in me. Don't worry, I'm still a girl." Only then did I begin to cry.

"I know, I know you are," Mother said. "I'm sorry for your heart. If you do love this Abdallah, may Ahmad be the knight who drives him away. Love is never easy." My mother cupped her hands against my cheeks and wiped away my tears.

"When your purity is clear, your father's anger will subside," she said. "And Ahmad will be a good husband." Then she took a deep breath and pulled up the tent walls, one by one. She stood just outside and announced: "We have a bride and groom! Salma and Ahmad will be wed tonight!" Zaghareed echoed up the canyon walls.

I mustered enough self-control to curtail my fury and my shame. Within minutes, everyone in camp knew the story. It was helpful, given my situation, that we desert brides weren't supposed to act joyful at our own weddings. Instead, we were to be quiet and passive. For most of us, it wasn't an act, as many feared being bedded for the first time and moving away from home. In some tribes, the bride was even expected to fight her groom off, to protect her honor by not giving in right away to his hugs and kisses. Fortunately, I was simple-hearted enough to believe my innocence would be proven, and my name would be cleared.

The men slaughtered a camel for a feast, and the women erected a festive tent for our wedding night. Small and round, decorated with colorful weavings and pillows, it was just big enough for two.

My mother led me to the women's bathing area, where they took care of the welts on my back, which weren't too bad since I had been wearing two layers of cotton. The whipping hadn't broken my skin. They bathed me and rubbed my skin with fragrant dried rosemary. Mabrukah washed my hair. A distant aunt used honey to remove all my body hair. Ouch! It hurt as she ripped it off my skin over and over.

As it happened, earlier that day a group of Solubba had ridden into camp on their white donkeys. Once they learned there was to be a wedding, some of their women came to our tent and serenaded us. They sang love songs and played drums as we got ready. One of them dipped my fingertips in henna and painted simple designs on my hands. The little girls knelt in a circle, watching in awe.

Later, while Mabrukah and I waited for the henna to dry, an old Solubba woman approached our tent. "Bride," she said, "I am Zurfah. May I sing a song of blessing for you? I can also read your fortune." I nodded for her to enter, glad for the distraction.

"Ah, yes," she said, looking me over. "You are a lovely bride, daughter of the shaikhah. Yet there is this question of honor." I didn't respond, too overwhelmed by the day's events to speak with a stranger. The old woman sat down, crossed her legs, and rubbed the surface of her frame drum. She set her drum aside, then drew a small leather bag from her belt.

"First, I shall tell your fortune." She shook the bag and turned it upside down, scattering shells, date stones, and pieces of old pottery on the tent floor. She studied the objects for several minutes. What did she see? Why was she silent? As you know, palm readers chatter like sparrows, drawing a finger on the lifeline, telling how many boys or girls a woman will have. But Zurfah was silent as she moved her hands back and forth, palms down, a few inches above the objects. Then she closed her eyes and sighed.

"First of all, there is no question—you are a virgin. Yet I'm puzzled. You have three lives. Yes, that is what it says. And how can that be? It is as if each one is broken from the next. I see one marriage." When I returned her gaze, I was surprised to notice her left eye was clouded like an eggshell. Interesting that one who could see the future had only one good eye.

"And children?" I asked, words finally returning to me.

She thought a moment before answering. "My eyes have grown weak. I can't tell for certain about children." She added a few more details like, "You will live a very long life," and "You are highly intelligent."

Then she cast Mabrukah's fortune. Hers must have been an easier read, for Zurfah began talking right away. She saw a marriage, then two marriages and three children.

Perhaps to distract me from wondering about my fortune, she picked up her drum and began to sing. Her henna-stained thumb and fingertips danced across the drum skin. With her eyes half-closed, her raspy voice sang the same melody again and again.

We loved, we loved a forbidden love.
I've locked your heart away with two locks,
To keep it safe from the Evil Eye.

It was as if she knew what was in my heart. The tune had several verses, so Mabrukah and I joined her on the chorus. She drummed on and said, "Dance a little, my dears. This is your wedding, after all. Even rushed weddings must have a little merriment."

We danced, stepping toward each other, then backing up and turning around in place. At first it felt strange to be dancing after taking a beating, while my life was at stake and my honor in question. Yet the tune lifted my spirits, and the dance quieted my fears. We turned and spun and laughed as Zurfah played faster and faster. When she stopped, we collapsed in laughter.

"Thank you," I said. "This is a difficult day. You have helped us face our future." At my nod, Mabrukah dropped a coin into her hand.

Others stopped by to congratulate me, despite the rumors that had rippled through the camp. Another distant aunt who had been married for many years placed a tiny sprig of sweet basil in my hair. She put her hands on my shoulders. "Your kisses will make your husband happy. After the first night, don't withhold them. Be sure to speak to him with sweetness, because even the roaring lion loves honey."

My mother opened the woven bag in which she kept her most precious belongings and unfolded a dress of purple silk, with matching pantaloons.

"Here, bride, wear this tonight." Once I'd tried it on, she draped me with silver necklaces and bracelets. She slipped a ring on each of my fingers. Then she wrapped a red silk scarf around my head like a turban and draped it with a headdress of silver coins. "There. You are beautiful, a true shaikhah's daughter." Then she kissed my cheeks and my forehead. "God go with you tonight."

Our two families prayed together at sunset. Out in the desert without any imams, the tribes married in simple fashion. Beside the bridal tent, my father declared us a married couple. Then they left us alone. My father avoided my gaze, because he might have to return with a knife.

We stepped inside and Ahmad spoke. "You will live or die tonight, bride. Either way, I will enjoy you at least once. Never did I imagine we would wed like this." Then he took me with a coldness equal to his words.

We were like animals I'd seen coupling in the desert. Only when he was reaching his climax did he moan, and afterward he lay down beside me for only a few moments. Then he knelt next to me in the darkness and pulled out the sheepskin on which we'd been lying. There, in a dark round stain was visible even inside the tent: the blood that proved my innocence.

"So you will live." He took the sheepskin and left. I laid back and gazed at the night sky through an opening in the tent. Was what just happened worth all the heartache? It seemed a lot of bother for something that took so little time.

Ahmad returned with my mother, who smiled through her tears. She hugged me and whispered, "Thank God, thank God. Go to your groom, beautiful bride." My honor was confirmed, so the singing began, and we joined the wedding feast. I sat next to Ahmad, who was quiet and reserved. I followed his lead.

Later, after the revelers had gone to bed, Ahmad bade me to follow him. The Solubba were already up, preparing to move on at first light. The moon was waxing to full. It lit our way and painted the desert silver.

We climbed to the watchman's post on the cliff, far from the ears of the tribe. Ahmad sat down and nodded for me to join him at his side. Just as I was wondering why he had not brought up Abdallah, he did. "So tell me what happened with you and the Ageyli."

"Husband," I said. "You are my light and my eye. How can I speak to you of this on our wedding night? How can I even think of another man now?"

He grabbed my arm and held it tight. He went on through clenched teeth. "I command you to tell me everything."

"We met by accident when Father and Uncle Talal came to camp with Al Auruns to meet Nuri. No one was dishonored. As you know, the women of our family are not afraid to talk to strangers. My father brought me up to fight, to defend my honor, and to have my wits about me. Nothing happened. We talked, that is all. Why, what did you hear?"

"One of the fighters from the Bani Salim sang a poem about you just as your father walked by. I don't remember all of it, though it was obviously about you. He asked the tribesman who the poet was, and he told him it was Abdallah the Ageyli. Here are a couple of lines, to give you an idea."

She stood by al-Sahba, who hid us from gossips.
    Her form straight and slender, braids dancing 'round her.
Proud, like a falcon, flying free in the desert.
    Whose wings dip and flash in the glow of the sunset.

I was furious. How could Abdallah have composed this poem, using my horse's name, and recited it in the fighters' camp, knowing my own father was there?

"Since Abdallah was one of Al Auruns' men, your father couldn't punish him," Ahmad said. "Talal complained to Al Auruns, who fired Abdallah on the spot. They sent him off with just enough food to get to the nearest town. That was a week ago. I doubt he will get far on his own."

Though I was reeling at the news, I had to keep quiet, pretending it meant nothing to me. Ahmad was silent, perhaps watching for my reaction. He must have known the news would torture me.

After a minute of silence that seemed endless, Ahmad's mood seemed to lighten and he began to give me his views of the war. He told me his own detailed account of the taking of Akaba, and their attacks on the Hijaz railway.

While he talked, my thoughts raced a thousand miles a second as I recalled the brief romance I'd had with Abdallah. Ahmad's voice became a faint buzzing sound, and I couldn't concentrate. Only when he stopped speaking did I return to the moment and regain my composure.

We stayed up all night, talking. I let my guard down a little, yet I couldn't forget how he had gripped my arm to get me to tell him about Abdallah.

As dawn lightened the sky, Ahmad brought me a heavy bundle wrapped in a soft camel hair blanket and placed it in my lap. It was my trousseau. First, in a small pouch of yellow silk, I found seven gold bangles. Two of them jingled with tiny gold coins. In another bundle like it, I found a pair of gold earrings from Damascus that dangled to my shoulders in a cascade of delicate crescents. Underneath, I unwrapped a crimson velvet caftan with gold embroidery. He had also bought this in Damascus, his mother told me later. He had gathered these things over the years for his bride. Had he really intended them for me – or did he have his eyes on someone else?

When I thanked him, he said, "There is a she-camel in the herd, it is yours. The russet-colored one, the one with the diamond patterned wasm on the inside of its rear left ankle."

As camp stirred, he took me again. At the end, I relaxed and shut my eyes. But it was a mistake, for just as he finished he sat up, turned me over onto my stomach, and held me down. This time, the whipping was to my bare back, and I bled immediately. But I kept quiet, biting the woolen blanket next to my face. I only moaned when he stopped.

He stood. "That will ensure your good behavior. If I ever hear of you straying, get one whiff of trouble from you that would sully our name, that will be your end. This is your warning, wife." He left, and I wept in silence and shame.

I soaked up the blood as best I could, dressed, and walked back to my parents' tent. I refused to weep. Instead, I watched my father pack his belongings. I wanted him to acknowledge my virtue. He hadn't trusted me, and our bond, once so close, was forever changed.

Just as he was leaving, my father spoke. "Daughter, your virginity was proven. But our name has been tarnished. I warn you, you are a married woman now, and this kind of rumor and gossip must stop. I'll cut out the tongue of anyone who speaks of you. Meanwhile, wipe that Ageyli scum from your heart." He kissed my forehead before turning to leave.

He paused and glanced at my mother, who reached out to touch his arm. "May God keep you and your sons," she said as he left.

I stood next to Ahmad on his horse, the sun in my eyes. "God keep you until our next meeting, in health and safety. Peace be upon you."

With no emotion, he said, "In God's care."

As they rode up the canyon, my mother stood on my right, and Ahmad's mother, my Aunt Furaihah, on my left. Mabrukah stood close behind. How different this parting was from the morning Abdallah rode away, months before. I felt older, mourning my romance with Abdallah, afraid of my new husband's temper and jealousy. How close I had come to death. Now, in this life, I was separated from Abdallah. Our brief days together had become a dangerous dream that I had to lock deep in my heart.

CHAPTER 17

ZURFAH'S WARNING

Wadi Sirhan
September 1917

SO THERE we were, Mabrukah and me, brand new bride and faithful servant and companion, starting a new stage of life. Unlike most brides, not much changed for me, nor did much change for Mabrukah. We only moved a few tents away, to live with Ahmad's mother, Aunt Furaihah. We were spared the usual hard work of setting up and breaking camp, and each night a different family hosted supper. Even though a war raged nearby, our small world seemed calm and safe. We couldn't know it then, but with the war's end, the old rhythms of life that had ruled our tribe for centuries would vanish forever.

To pass the time, we wove tent panels for our future life with Ahmad. We set up our looms outdoors and worked side by side, hurrying to finish before Ahmad returned. Even then, Mabrukah's hands were far more skilled than mine. With each lift of the warp threads, I tried to pull out my heartache and calm my fear of Ahmad's temper. With each whack of the sword beater against the newly laid weft, I willed my heart to obey, and like it, to be woven tight into the fabric of my new family.

We imagined a happy future as we wove it, thread by thread, hour by hour. Our shuttles flew back and forth, and the panels sprouted like grape vines. We wove black and white triangles and stripes against an indigo background, the color of the night sky. We wove ourselves, Ahmad, and the animals, in stick figure designs, into the panels. And I prayed he would be kind, somehow, after the war was done.

While I tried to focus on the future, my mind kept circling back to Abdallah. One day while we were at our looms, my thoughts billowed up like a thunderstorm and burst out of my mouth. "I still think of him every day,"

I said. I had stopped working, my hands holding a tangle of warp threads. There was no need to tell Mabrukah I was referring to Abdallah.

Mabrukah had been working at twice my speed. "I know you do," she said, taking a rare pause. "But you walked so near to death. Forget him; it's over and he's gone."

"But he still haunts my dreams. Sometimes, during the day when I'm alone, I even hear his voice."

Mabrukah shook her head, then she began to sing, imitating the raspy voices of the old desert bards, each line to the same tune.

In the dawn he departs;
   silently slipping from my side;
After tasting the honey of his lips
   And the protection of his arms.
How silently he comes and goes,
   Like a bright star, he appears, then dips below the hills.
He returns to his people, breathless,
   A rabbit slung over his shoulder.

I sighed and said, "Why are there so many songs and poems about forbidden and secret love?"

That night, Mabrukah and I lagged behind Mother and Aunt Furaihah as we walked hand in hand to the tent where supper was being served. An apricot full moon burst over the edge of the canyon.

Later, as was our custom, we gathered around the fire for coffee. Mabrukah and I settled in for what had become our favorite part of the camp routine. One of the old women began to sing, improvising on a phrase.

"Ya wail ya wail ya wail ya yummah ya yummah."

There was a lifetime of heartache in her voice, yet each note was clear and strong. "Oh woe is me, O Mother O Mother," she sang. Each time she finished the line with a flourish, we answered with a rousing, "Ya wail," to spur her on. Then she started singing a song we all knew, and we joined in, clapping.

Come, bring the moon with you and sing tonight;
        In the coffee circle as the fire burns bright.
My love, your eyes shimmer liquid gold,
        Sending fire-tipped lances to my heart and soul.

Between the verses we clapped loudly, like galloping horses, like this. Come on, try it, children! Yes, yes, it sounded just like that! We made such a noise with our clapping that it echoed up the canyon walls. Then someone let out a zaghrutah. I imagined our song carrying across the desert, so that any passersby would pause at such sounds in the night, wondering if we were djinn of the desert.

After that, the women sang love songs from their youth while we danced back and forth, making circles and figure eights with our long tresses. We danced on until the singers tired and the clappers' hands ached. Only when the last singer begged to sleep did we walk home arm in arm. It was almost dawn.

By summer's end, we'd grown tired of the routine. We longed for the end of the war and the men's return. I was anxious to start my new life with Ahmad. And yes, by then Abdallah was fading from my heart. Most of the other young husbands had slipped into camp to visit their wives, but not Ahmad. I assumed it was because he wanted to be in the thick of battle, for he was known for his courage.

As the days grew shorter and the nights grew cooler, we heard the Arab army had grown to a throng of thousands as it marched north to Jerusalem to liberate it from the Turks. Mabrukah and I hurried to complete the tent. We had nearly enough panels to construct it.

Hoping for our fighters' return, we all looked up when the salukis started barking one afternoon. I'm sure everyone was as disappointed as me when a group of Solubba came down the canyon trail, riding their white donkeys, Zurfah the fortune teller among them. As usual, they set up their tents beyond ours, then made the rounds asking what was needed, whether any animals required tending.

It wasn't long before Zurfah appeared at our tent saying, "O lady of the house, do your pots need mending?"

"No, sister, everything is in good order," Furaihah said.

"But your young bride, what about her?"

"She's weaving out behind that tent there, though I doubt she needs anything either."

We heard all this and stood as Zurfah approached. She wore a patchwork dress of gazelle skin, a brown woolen mantle draped over her head and shoulders.

"Salma the bride, and your dear Mabrukah. I see your honeymoon hasn't had much honey in it due to this war."

"Yes, God willing we will begin our honeymoon soon enough," I said, inviting her to sit with us. We went back to work.

"Pretend we are discussing the repair of your loom. I have news for you."

I stared at her. Although I heard her words, I tried to ignore the seriousness in her whispered voice. "Really, the loom is fine," I said.

"No look, that wooden piece is broken, and you've just tied it up with twine. I can repair that. And you have struck your sword beater so hard it is splintering." Then she whispered, "Salma, I must speak to you in private. You are in serious danger."

"Furaihah's coming," I said. "We'll talk tonight at the fire after supper."

"We've no work for you now," Furaihah said, striding toward us. "Our pots and pans are in flawless condition, and we have more than we can use in five seasons. So thank you, sister. Go in peace."

"All right, but keep me in mind when the time comes," the old woman muttered. As she walked away, her limp tipped her tiny frame from side to side like a howdah swaying high atop a camel.

"These Solubba, by God I have never seen them pester the women so much. They're taking advantage of the men being away." Furaihah stayed with us until dinner, so Mabrukah and I couldn't talk.

After supper, our hostesses announced that the Solubba women were going to sing for us. A dozen of them entered the fire circle in a single line, carrying frame drums tattooed with handprints and crescents in indigo and henna.

Zurfah knelt at the end of the line as the drummers settled into their places on the sand. She was the oldest by far, and the firelight accentuated the way her angular nose and cheekbones jutted from her face. The singer in the center might have been a young bride like me. Her startling eyes matched an emerald green scarf tied around her hair.

The women lifted their drums, and when the girl in the center nodded, they hit their drums all at once, like a clap of thunder, and burst into a pulsating rhythm. She sang first, and the others answered. Their arms and hands moved together in waves, pounding and pounding. Some drums made high tones, others low. When one of them lifted her drum high in the air and played in between the beats, we were swept into a frenzy. Everyone clapped and swayed, and the girls danced as if possessed by djinn. Normally I'd be with them, but I couldn't move, I couldn't even think. The pounding drums flowed through me. The campfire danced, too. Its leaping flames sent sparks flying onto the cool sand.

Then, just as they'd started, the drummers stopped all at once and the dancers collapsed into laughter, waking me from my trance. Zurfah approached me. "Move to the back of the crowd. I'll meet you there when they start up again."

When the musicians gathered again in their line, Mabrukah and I slipped into the dark. The singer crooned a line of love poetry, and the women were transfixed.

"This way, girls. I'm here, behind the bushes. Follow me." Zurfah led us behind some rocks. We sat with her in the dark, watching the long shadows of the women reach to the far cliffs.

"We don't have much time, so I must be blunt. Salma, your life is in danger. You must run away, as far as you can go."

"Why? I have a new husband and a kind mother-in-law. What could possibly make me run away? Can't you see I'm happy?"

"Yes, I see you're happy now. And, God willing, these days of happiness will always live in your memory. But they are about to end. Another poem is circulating, written by the young Ageyli Abdallah. It is so wondrous that it's crossing the desert as if carried by the wind itself. All the coffee hearths are ringing with his verses about you. I'm afraid your family honor has been stained. Your husband plans to take revenge on you for unfaithfulness, to cleanse the family name once and for all. I'm sure you've discovered by now that he backs up his hot temper with action."

I blushed at the way the gossips must have feasted on this rumor, but still I could not believe it.

"Unfaithfulness? How can that be? I've been here with my mother and my mother-in-law since my wedding, at which time it was proven I was a virgin. Every woman in this camp can attest to my honor."

"Well, listen to the poem first. Then decide what filled your husband's heart when he heard these verses." She sat back, smoothing her leather dress, then began to recite in a hoarse whisper. Though she raced to recite it just that once, she branded it into my memory.

> On the rim of the canyon, I stand all alone,
> Silent, watching their camp as the nighttime descends.
> The aroma of cooking wafts up the cliffside,
> Though my hunger is great, my loneliness greater.
>
> There she is, with her servant, strolling hand in hand,
> Like two arrows set in a royal archer's quiver,
> Her face like the full moon, the other her shadow.
> Round one tent they gather, and in silence they dine.
>
> Then the drumbeat begins, and the moonlight glimmers
> On the face of the cliffs that hide them in secret.
> They loosen their locks and their arrows fly freely,
> And dance on for hours in late night merriment,
>
> In silence I wait till they return to their tent.
> Will I sneak down to wake her, to fight her once more?
> Or leave her alone, to her husband unblemished?
> I leave her in peace, she sleeps on in the canyon.
> For a pure maiden's soul she possesses it's clear.
> Like the deepest well in a secret oasis.
>
> With a sigh, I step back and leave them in slumber.
> Mount my horse and pull back from the lip of the canyon,
> My mare whinnies softly, eager to move on,
> From the quiet cliffs and the coals of her campfire.
>
> The night soon surrounds us and the stars glow above.
> We ride on through the night, till the full moon descends.
> Goodbye my fair warrior, go in God's care,
> May my wounds heal in peace, as your joy increases.

The distant drumming echoed around us after she finished. I was stunned at first, as my heart absorbed the beauty and sadness of his verses. Then my tears flowed, and I began to sob. Mabrukah held me as I rocked back and forth. Abdallah had fulfilled his promise and came for me. He still loved me, and the poem was his farewell.

"But how can this poem ruin Salma's honor?" Mabrukah said. "It says she's a virtuous bride, and that he left her alone. What is the dishonor in that?"

Zurfah looked up at the stars and shook her head. "Before God, I swear that in three different camps, we have heard both Ahmad and your father are furious over this poem. In their eyes, it defames you and the whole tribe. They believe you did meet again, and that this poem covers it up in a lie. Especially when he says he left you in peace with your family. They think the opposite happened. Ahmad plans to make an example of you to the other women. I advise you to leave as soon as possible. Do you know anyone who can protect you, far away from here – farther than anyone can find you? I fear this is your only hope. I wouldn't have warned you, it's really not my business. Yet when I heard the poem, I had to tell you."

"But where can we go? I can't imagine living anywhere but here with my family."

"Perhaps you have some distant relatives who can take you in. You're not the first bride to seek a refuge from a harsh husband. You have at least a week before the men return. In that time, plan your escape. I promise I will keep your secret. I see your mare and camel are in good health; you will need all their strength. May God protect you."

I couldn't sleep that night, my tears flowing, my anger welling up like a coffee pot boiling on the fire. But I had to keep quiet or Furaihah would notice something was wrong. Mabrukah held me, whispering what comfort she could. It did little good. I couldn't think straight, as I searched for a solution. Even if we did run away, where would we go? My life was with my family and my tribe.

The next day, Mother sat with Mabrukah and me as we worked on our weaving. I was exhausted, but she didn't seem to notice it, as she was drawn to Mabrukah's excellent skills. After a while, she brought up Nurah, a distant cousin we hadn't seen in years. She was exactly my age, and we'd become great friends when our families met during a gathering. We had laughed and played like sisters. My mother recalled how we tried to teach Nurah to weave, but later had to re-work everything she'd done.

Nurah's family lived in the oasis town of Unaizah, Abdallah's hometown, far to the south, beyond the great Nafud desert. Nurah's father Duhaim was my father's cousin. He had defied tradition and married into one of the town's merchant families. Nurah's mother had died in childbirth, but Duhaim never remarried. I'd always remembered Nurah's description of Unaizah: a beautiful city cloaked in a palm forest, fed by fresh springs.

Could that be our answer? Could Mabrukah and I get there without being caught? And would my cousin and uncle take us in? At first, it seemed totally impossible. And yet with every passing hour, my mind turned it over and over. Because it was so far and unlikely, it just might work. No one would follow us that far.

Now children, despite the harsh law of the desert about a girl's honor, we all revered love. All forms of love, especially the impossible kinds, the forbidden ones. How they fill our poetry and songs, even today!

We were always hearing about lovers among the tribes running away together. How could it be otherwise, when we celebrated the power of attraction in all its forms? Yet running away meant taking great risks, for if you were caught, you might die at the hand of your father or your brother. However, if you did get away, far away, it's possible no one would follow. You might never return to your family, but at least you could make a new life.

In those days among the Arab tribes, a wife who was mistreated by her husband could run away to her family and take refuge. Often the family would help patch things up between husband and wife. My situation was different. I was with my family, so I was actually running away from them, and for fear of being killed by my husband, all over a couple of poems. Ours was a very peculiar situation.

Still, every generation has its runaways, its family problems, and its lovers of legends, of poems and of song. For no one can control the heart. It gives us life, but it can also take it away.

My decision wasn't easy. Could I trust Zurfah's word? She was a stranger, yet I had experienced Ahmad's anger, and I could almost feel it reaching out to burn me. The poem was about my innocence. Why couldn't he see that?

Mabrukah and I talked about it for days as we worked at the looms. We concluded that, even though the poem itself attested to my purity, the mere fact that he'd written about me again, and that my story and our love affair was being recited and discussed at every campfire in the northern deserts, defamed me. That was my crime. With his poem attesting to my innocence, he was tainting my good name and shaming Ahmad. My husband would not stand for it, and I would have to pay for it with my life. And what about my father's anger? Would he stand up for me if Ahmad attacked me?

I had to choose whether to risk dying at my husband's hand or to run away and never return. And if we ran away, I might never see my family again. Perhaps you can imagine how hard this was for me, since I had never lived away from them.

What about Abdallah? Everyone would assume I was going to meet him. Yet how could I still love a man who would do this to me, whose words were tearing me away from my family? It was months since he'd seen us that night in the canyon. He'd gone far away, and I had put him out of my mind. Our brief romance had become a nightmare.

Mabrukah and I talked it through, over and over, circling the issue for days. Together we decided we had to leave to survive, despite the risks we would take. First, we would travel south to the bottom of Wadi Sirhan, to the city of al-Jawf. From there, we would cross the forbidding Nafud desert that stretches across Arabia's belly. Beyond that, we would have to traverse the mountains known as Shammar. Only then could we approach the oasis city of Unaizah.

In addition to the physical hardships, along the way we would risk being robbed. If we were discovered, we might be brought home to face certain death. And in the end, even if we made it to Unaizah, we would have to beg my relatives to give us refuge, and they might turn us away. We decided to put our trust in the custom of giving refuge to family members and, more importantly, we would put our trust in my uncle Duhaim's kind character. He was, I remembered, a man with a noble heart.

After making that hard decision, it was strangely simple to leave. Since we were always organizing things for our new home, Furaihah paid no attention when we packed a few belongings and provisions in some camel bags.

We waited until we had night watch duty. In the quietest hour, we walked up the canyon trail, al-Sahba and the camel in tow. Our only witnesses were the sheep and goats huddled on the ground. They twitched their ears and shook their heads as we passed. The salukis knew us and were silent.

At the top of the canyon where we should have stayed at our watch, we looked down at the sleeping camp one last time in the half moon's light. Someone was walking around, so we backed away from the edge.

"Bismillah, In the Name of God," I said. "Keep us safe from robbers. Heal my mother's wounded heart. Guide us and protect us from evil." With those words, on that morning in the autumn of 1917, we began our journey.

CHAPTER 18

SETTING OUT

Wadi Sirhan
September 1917

AT FIRST, my mare al-Sahba seemed eager for the road, and the camel followed along. As for me, with every passing hour, doubt rose in my heart about our decision to run away. I thought of my dear mother who would soon wake and spend the day in tears. Our actions would wound her, and her heartache might never heal. Yet if we didn't go, I would surely be killed. I never imagined that I would have to make such a choice.

Mabrukah was sniffling, and tears wet her cheeks. Soon we were both crying as we rode on. Al-Sahba pressed her ears back, listening to us. She slowed down, then turned back toward camp. I steered her back, but she turned again. We battled this way for a while until she stopped in her tracks and snorted.

I urged her on, but she wouldn't budge. When I loosened her reins, she turned again and started walking back toward camp, the camel following behind. Then they both broke into a trot, and we couldn't stop them, no matter how hard we pulled on their leads.

I jumped off and jerked on the reins, and she reared up. I stood my ground, turned her back toward the south, and walked on foot for a mile or so pulling her along, fighting her resistance with every step. I cried as I walked, mourning what we were leaving behind, fearing what lay ahead.

The mare forced me to gather my wits. I had to get control of myself. When we reached the edge of a wide canyon that opened to the south, al-Sahba reared up again and whinnied. Her eyes were wide with fear, and foam dripped from her mouth.

I spoke gentle words to her. She stood still, panting, and let me stroke her face as I leaned into her neck. "She can sense my fear, Mabrukah. I'm sure of it. Let's wait here a while, let them calm down." But it was we who needed calming.

After tethering the animals, we sat together and leaned against a rock. We folded our arms over our knees and unleashed our sobs.

"We can still turn back," I said after a while. "We can say that some sheep got lost and we went looking for them. No one would suspect anything."

"No," Mabrukah said. "We must leave, it's the right decision. Ahmad's temper has no bounds." I was grateful for her certainty.

We lit a small fire and talked, deciding once and for all that we had to keep going. Ahmad's temper and the fame of the poem had created an impossible situation. If I wanted to live, we had to run. Once that decision was made, we slept until the warm sun woke us.

Our courage restored, we transformed ourselves into my cousin Badr and his servant Muhsin. We stripped off our gowns and bound our chests with flannel. Then we donned the men's clothes we'd found in my mother's tent and pulled on wool vests to disguise our figures. Mind you, we were young and very thin. There wasn't much to hide!

We stoked up the fire and held up our dresses that we'd sewn and embroidered by hand.

We said, "Go in peace, Salma. Go in peace, Mabrukah," and tossed them into the flames. As they burned, Mabrukah cut my braids with her dagger and threw them into the fire, too. Tears flowed down my cheeks again as I watched my hair crackle and curl. Then it was her turn and soon she too was shorn like a young man. The smell of burning hair lingered on our clothing for days. Dressed in men's garb with short hair, Mabrukah looked like a male desert traveler, and she assured me I did too. But we had no facial hair.

"We'll just have to let the dust and dirt of the road settle on our face," I said.

"And when we're in town, we can cover our mouths with our headdresses, like men do when they're sick," Mabrukah said.

Al-Sahba sensed our new resolve, for she obeyed me after that. Yet I watched her ears as we rode. When they shifted back, I turned to see if anyone was following us. We hadn't covered our tracks, and we knew that if fighters had returned to our family camp, they might be pursuing us on swift mounts and would surely overtake us.

CHAPTER 19

Dipped in Crimson Henna

Shaqiq Well
October 1917

WE RODE south for several days, encountering no other travelers. The war, it seemed, had disrupted everyone's lives. Despite this, we kept up our guard. Each night, we camped among hillocks away from the road. After making a small fire, we would snuff it out and sleep wrapped in our sheepskins.

No one in the busy market town of al-Jawf took any notice of us in our disguises; we were two young Shamaalis riding in from the north. We didn't speak much as we sold my gold bangles and bought provisions. Our purchases complete, we rested in a palm grove on the outskirts of town for a while, then departed at dusk, riding along the rim of the canyon above the town. Cooking fires flickered in the darkening valley below.

We turned from the canyon's edge onto the track to Shaqiq, the last well before the Nafud. Al-Sahba turned her head from side to side as she walked, eyeing the rocks and bushes silvered in the moonlight. The camel's footfalls marked a slow hypnotic rhythm that serenaded us all night. Sometimes, the camel let out a burst of air, or a quiet harrumph. As the sun rose, our gigantic shadows rode alongside. Later that morning, light breezes warmed us.

I was just beginning to relax a little for the first time since we'd left home when a single gunshot rang out. It was muffled, yet nearby. We stopped to listen, but when silence returned, we rode on. A few minutes later, the trail led us around a corner into an open basin surrounded by hills. This was indeed Shaqiq; but we were not alone. Dozens of camels milled about, roaring and complaining, but these were not ordinary camels. They were dark, almost black, and they were gigantic. Their legs were so long we could have stood underneath them and our heads would not even reach their stomachs.

A group of even taller cameleers were trying to corral them. Adding to the confusion, shepherd girls, a full foot shorter than us, were trying to herd some long-haired white sheep that were weaving among the camels' legs. Black and white ostrich feathers decorated their headdresses. The girls darted among the camel legs like quails.

Bang! Another shot. The animals grew quiet. A man shouted. "Get the sheep over there and the camels over there. Now, before we start losing them."

"Well," said one of the shepherd girls, "I think your camels should step back. You're giving us no room at all, Sir."

"You lasses can't even control your sheep! Just do what I say, and we'll sort out the watering later."

The chaos subsided and the herds were separated, which gave us time to study our fellow travelers. The cameleers were not only tall men; they were browned from the desert sun and very thin, like praying mantises, their arms and legs like long sticks. They were so tall they could lean over and rest their elbows on top of their camels.

The man with the rifle approached us and reached a bony hand down to shake mine in welcome, "Peace upon you, sons of Shamaal." His voice sounded like sticks rubbing together on a wood gatherer's back.

"And upon you peace," I replied. "Have you come from the south, cross the Nafud?"

"Yes, my son. And to answer what you are thinking, the road is clear, and the rains have left ample pasturage. We didn't see anyone at all in fact. Perhaps even the robbers are off fighting the Turks. Fahd! Get that young camel over there. It's running off."

"Sir," one of the shepherdesses called out to the cameleer. She strode up to us, hands on hips. She leaned back and looked up to his face. "It's only fair that since we came to the well first, our animals should drink first."

He agreed with a chuckle, and let the sheep drink first. The ostrich girls lowered their leather buckets, let them fill with water, pulled them up, and emptied them into the stone troughs where the sheep jostled to drink. When it was the men's turn, the camels roared as they rushed forward.

After a while, the head cameleer called us over to the well. I looked down, and my heart sank as deep as the well, for I couldn't see the surface of the water. I dropped my bucket, let the rope run through my fingers, then heard it splash and felt it fill. While we both strained to lift it hand over hand, the men beside us had no trouble pulling up bucket after bucket with their skinny arms. Was it obvious we were having trouble? Were we giving ourselves away?

The head man paid no attention. Instead he circled al-Sahba and reached down to run his hand along her face and under her mane.

After we'd retrieved enough water and our animals were drinking, he asked about our journey. I explained that we were bringing the mare as a gift, beyond the Nafud.

"I warn you," he said, "this horse is splendid. You must disguise her, for if word should get out about her along the way, you will be vulnerable to thieves and tribal raiders who might decide you are fair game, since you've no guide. We didn't hire one either, but we never do. Besides, we are many, and you are only two." Then he said, "Why don't you rest with us a while. We're staying until evening."

"Thank you, but we can't. We've got to get to the red dunes before sunset."

"No, I insist," he said, bending down to study my face. Did he suspect we were in disguise? I coughed, so I could look away.

"Not only for reasons of hospitality," he said. "I think I can help you disguise your mare. My method always works. Stay with us a few hours. We can do the job and you can be on your way."

A disguise was a good idea, not only to fool would-be robbers, but to distract anyone who might be looking for two runaways with a splendid mare. But what if he was a robber himself?

Before I could answer, our would-be host, whose name was Nassah, invited the ostrich girls to join them, too. I knew then he was no robber. As we all sat round the fire, I noticed his men were so thin and brown that any one of them could have broken off an arm and tossed it right into the fire, had they needed more wood.

You know children, in the old days it was a pleasure to watch men make coffee for guests. Even the poorest tribesman would do his best to show hospitality this way.

Nassah folded his long legs under his body and ground some cardamom seeds with the coffee beans in his outsized mortar and pestle. A huge brass coffeepot sat on the coals. From a blue velvet cloth, he pulled out a dozen cups, twice the usual size, and stacked them up by his side. When the water boiled, he tossed the ground beans and cardamom into the pot, and returned it to the fire for a few minutes. Then he served us, bending down from his great height to fill our cups.

Though we'd sat at our family hearth a thousand times and watched my father and brothers do the same, I was transfixed by the ritual that day: to smell the aroma of freshly roasted beans, and, for the first time in our lives, to be served by a man.

He asked about our background, but we told him very little. From our clothing, he'd already guessed we were Shamaali.

I asked where they called home.

"Oh, here and there, there and here, wherever the camels take us." And the camels, I asked, what kind were they? "Giant Yemeni mountain camels, of course," he said. I wanted to point out that there was no such thing, but I kept quiet, for, as you know, it is impolite to argue with one's host.

"That mare would fetch a fortune at auction," one of the young men said. "She looks like she was stolen from an Amir's stable."

"Tell me, how did your father come across her?" Nassah asked.

"In battle with the Turks. She is gift of thanks for a great favor of many years ago."

"She is beautiful," he said, staring at al-Sahba as she swished her tail. "The challenge of disguising a mare like this is that we must distract the onlooker from the very features that make her stand out; her mane, the way she holds her tail, her coloring, and her beautiful face."

"What do you propose?" I asked, beginning to worry that he wanted to hurt her.

"First, if I were you, I'd trim her mane and tail, so she'll look mangy."

"That is easily done."

"Then, you should dye her coat with henna."

"Henna, so she'd be red? Like the designs on a bride's hands and feet?"

"Well, I was thinking more like a village donkey. I have some henna with me; I use it on my beard." He stroked his apricot-hued goatee with pride.

Before we knew it, everyone was swearing they wanted to take part.

"It's a henna party! God bless the bride, long live the groom!" one of the ostrich girls shouted. They started to sing and clap, the feathers on their headdresses curling and bobbing. Their voices were so high, they sounded like birds.

> The dove will rest with me tonight
> I'll watch her kohl-rimmed eyes.
> I'll hold her fingers, soft and small,
> Dipped in crimson henna.

With the ease of one who'd been tinting his beard for decades, Nassah poured water into a large wooden bowl and mixed in henna powder with a stick. He beckoned us toward al-Sahba. "First cut her tail, then her mane."

I drew my dagger and grabbed the tail. I hated to cut the mare's long tresses, which flew straight behind when she ran with her tail held high. Two young men joined in, cutting a few strands at a time because her hair was so thick. Al-Sahba looked back and whinnied. She nodded her head and pawed the ground. Mabrukah stroked her snout to distract her while they finished. Afterward, one of them handed me a lock of hair as a memento.

My tears welled up when I saw the horse's tail sheared to a short fringe just beyond the end of her tail flesh, but I couldn't cry, for no young man would never flinch at such a trivial thing. Al-Sahba tried to swish her tail, and then looked back and whinnied. That was the greatest blow to her vanity. Her tail had been her great glory, like a bride's long tresses. And we'd also done her another disservice. We'd taken her God-given fly swatter.

"Now the mane," Nassah directed.

I leaned against the horse's neck and whispered, "Be patient now, we're going to cut some more." I ran my hands through her pearly mane one last time. Then the boys with the knives joined me and, within a few minutes, we'd slashed it down to a mangy stubble.

"Excellent," Nassah said. Then he bent over and poured a blob of henna paste onto her flank and began to smear it over her chest and rump.

"Come, all of you, and help me rub the henna in, like this." Ten pairs of hands massaged the green paste into her midsection. Al-Sahba endured with patience.

"Good." Nassah said, standing back. Then he kneeled down and painted thick rings around her lower legs with his stick. Using their fingers and hands, the rest of them put stripes round her neck and painted delicate lines across her face.

As they put finishing touches on their designs, the ostrich girls stood in a line and began to sing and clap again, leaning back and forth in time to the rhythm. Then one of them leaped out in front and tore off her headdress. She hopped around and swung her long hair in circles. She flapped her arms like wings, flashing her newly hennaed palms. The young men joined in the song.

> O beauty in our midst
> O soft and mild gazelle,
> Don't fear this night of nights
> Your groom will treat you well.

After the last line, we all broke into laughter.

"And now a special treat for the bride," one of the young men said, offering al-Sahba a big bowl of fresh camel's milk. She gulped it down, and with that we bought the mare's forgiveness.

It was only then I realized we couldn't leave for several more hours, for just like at any henna party, we had to wait for the henna paste to dry. I never would have agreed to this scheme if I'd thought things through.

"True," Nassah said, when I explained my concern. "But if you didn't disguise this mare you wouldn't get very far on your own. Don't worry, it will be dry by dark, and you can leave in the morning."

The men mounted their giant camels and rode away. The girls and their sheep followed, waving and calling one last bridal zaghrutah for the mare, their feathers bouncing as they passed out of sight.

Covered in green paste as if she had an exotic mange, the horse grazed until nightfall. And though we were once more alone, we felt safe there. The overwhelming silence of the place surrounded us and lulled us to sleep.

Mabrukah's giggles woke me in the morning. Al-Sahba stood nearby, staring back, shaking her head, shifting the weight between her hind feet, like a woman unaccustomed to new shoes. The henna was drying and flaking off. Mabrukah patted her with reassurance and we rubbed off the rest of the dried paste. Nassah was right. We had to make her look like she wasn't worth anything. So we all had to disguise ourselves, except for the camel. And why is that? You are right, my dears. There is just no way to disguise a camel.

As we filled our water skins, I noticed ours were the only tracks at the well. Just two sets of footprints and two sets of animal prints, one camel and one horse. Where the herds had teemed, the campfire had roared, and the girls had danced, there were now only ripples in the sand. We looked at each other, then down at our henna-stained hands. Whispering prayers for protection, we jumped on our mounts and rode off as quick as we could.

I tell you, my dears, you will encounter strange things on every great journey you make. And don't think such things are not part of our modern world, for they are. God has created many beings and people of all kinds. When you get older and travel, you too will see mysterious things and meet strange people in this world that will astonish you. Just remember we are all His creatures, may He be praised.

CHAPTER 20

THE NAFUD

Nafud Desert
October 1917

IMAGINE YOU are with us on the day we started our crossing. At the edge of the desert, we looked up. A mountain of sand rose before us, glowing carnelian against a sky of Persian turquoise. The Nafud is no ordinary desert, my dears. It's an ocean of crescent-shaped sand waves blown ever westward, grain by grain. Its tallest peaks guard its northern and southern edges. We would have to scale them as we entered it, and again as we left it behind.

Having listened to many tales of Nafud crossings, I knew the trail to follow. If the Almighty favored us, it would take us two weeks to cross. First, we had to reach the halfway point, a town called al-Jubbah, before we ran out of water. Until then, we would have to survive on the water we carried in our waterskins.

Struggling with each step in the soft sand, we led the animals up that first dune and paused on its crest. To the south, a mountain range of dunes stretched before us as far as we could see.

"In the name of God, the Merciful, the Compassionate," I said, but the sand muffled my small voice. A breeze reminded us we had to keep moving. With more than a little fear, we walked down the side of that first dune, leading our mounts on foot. The camel protested, for the steep inclines were difficult for her. Al-Sahba stepped down sideways, enduring with a noble and stoic silence. She didn't know how ridiculous she looked.

Now, don't get the idea that the Nafud was barren of life. Larks called from ghada bushes that clung to the sides of the dunes. Desert rains provided a few patches of pasture for our mounts. Hawks, rabbits, and gazelles made their homes there. Piles of stones and brushwood on the dune ridges marked the trail. And we were not the only travelers who had crossed, for the path was well worn. Yet the silence was unnerving, for no matter how loud we shouted, how high a birdcall or angry a camel's roar might be, there were no echoes. The great sands absorbed all sounds.

Each day the sun warmed us. The evenings were cool, sometimes cold, but we always found fuel for a small fire and slept long before the embers died. As the days passed, the dunes grew smaller and we spied the peaks, A'alam al-Sa'ad. A welcome landmark to all Nafud-crossers, they were the first real proof that we were making progress toward al-Jubbah. The tallest one, Shaikh of the Nafud, was a dark rock mountain, and the smaller hills to its northeast were His Harem. Once we saw them, we knew we had three more days to town. We rationed our water, mixing a full share into al-Sahba's dried milk each morning. The camel went without.

Even though we were young and fit, the journey took its toll. We suffered from the steep riding and walking, and from saddle sores. As the days passed, our exhaustion mounted and our minds turned inward. We spoke less and less and felt utterly alone.

Since the well at Shaqiq, we'd seen only two groups of travelers in the distance, on roads that crossed our track. Each time, we'd hidden until they were long past. Normally, the tribes would be grazing their animals in the desert that time of year, but the war had disrupted even this.

We were making good time until a scorpion bit Mabrukah on her ankle. It wasn't a poisonous bite, but it swelled up, and we had to wait two days for the infection to heal. She drank a lot of water, and we both knew how dangerous it was if we ran out before we got to al-Jubbah. When a sandstorm's wall of towering red clouds raced toward us, we tied the animals down-wind and laid in our tent to wait. It blew the tent down over us and raged into the night. I was sure we would run out of water. But the next morning, we awoke to find that the Almighty had saved us. A swarm of locusts had ridden the back of the storm. They covered the ground in a green carpet, dormant in the cool morning. I jumped up in glee and gathered them by the handful.

Never did locusts taste so glorious as they did when roasted over our little fire. They revived Mabrukah, and al-Sahba, too, ate her fill of them. As the sun warmed the sand, all at once the swarm took flight to the east in a big cloud. Mabrukah's ankle was still swollen, but she was strong enough to ride.

We reached the tall rocks at the outskirts of al-Jubbah at dusk. Set among small red dunes, it was a miniature of al-Jawf, really just a cluster small houses. Despite my fear of being discovered, I was glad to be among people again.

We set up our tent near other travelers, and, in the dark, no one paid us much attention. We kept to ourselves, having bought a small meal of dates and bread. By then our faces were filthy with dust and dirt, and we pulled our headdresses tight around our faces in the cold, just like all the other travelers.

We retired to sleep in our tent and listened to a small gathering at a nearby fire. We learned that our next goal would be the village of Qina on the southern end of the desert, and from there it was one day's walk to the oasis city of Hail in the region known as Jabal Shammar.

The travelers swapped tales of the Ikhwan, zealous fighters who were being conscripted from the tribes to fight against unbelievers. The great tribal leader Amir Abd al-Aziz, from the region of Najd south of the desert, created this army, and they fought for him. He convinced thousands of Arab tribesmen and their families to live in desert settlements. There, they learned to worship according to the teachings of a preacher who had lived nearly two centuries earlier. Today, we in Saudi Arabia follow a more moderate version of his ideas. Those Ikhwan became like a swarm of locusts, wreaking havoc wherever they went.

The other travelers explained how they avoided them, and covered their tracks when they camped. I could only imagine what the Ikhwan would do if they discovered a runaway wife, dressed as a man.

We set out the next morning before dawn and returned to the rhythm of the march. The animals' rhythmic footfalls filled my exhausted mind. Sometimes, even today, I hear its cadence, echoing like a drumbeat deep in my heart. As the days passed, each sand peak loomed higher and each ascent grew more grueling. Meanwhile, the moon waxed to full.

On our fourth day from al-Jubbah, Mabrukah spotted what looked like a hundred men on camels in the distance, coming up behind us at a fast pace. We jumped below the lip of the dune to watch them. They wore thick white cloths wrapped around their heads, and their thobes were cut short – the uniform of Ikhwan fighters. We couldn't outrun them, so we had to hide.

We rode down to the hard desert floor, then turned off the path, staying between the tall dunes. Mabrukah and the animals climbed over some small dunes off to the side, and I followed behind, dragging a blanket to cover our tracks. We hid the animals, and I crawled to the crest and crouched behind a bush. From there, I would be able to see the men ride by without being seen. A long time passed, then the wind died.

When they first appeared at the top of the dune above us, they dismounted from their camels and paused to look around. Had they seen us? They must have had sharp-eyed guides with them, as every army does. We had to stay still. I held my breath. Fear throbbed in my arms and legs.

Their camels roared and complained, as if begging for a break. Then they sat down and rested. We couldn't move. I waved to Mabrukah to keep the animals still. How long could we keep quiet? The men did their ablutions in the sand and prayed.

It seemed like many hours before they walked down the dune, their camels in tow. When they reached the floor of the desert, they got back on their mounts. Then our camel let out a roar, and one of the men stopped to listen. Had he heard us?

My heart pounded as he stood still, listening through the din of the men riding off. He stayed behind them for a long time. I sighed with relief when he rode off to join the others. We waited until the moon rose, giving them plenty of time to advance ahead of us. We rode on for several more hours and saw no more sign of them. Even now, I shudder when I think of how close we came to being caught by those men.

Ahead of us, a cliff glowed in the moonlight, beckoning us to approach. There, we had no trouble finding an inviting cave with remnants of a recent campfire. In fact, there were several caves in a row, each with perfectly round openings big enough for both of us and our mounts. As soon as we'd laid down and covered ourselves with our sheepskins, we fell asleep. I don't know how much time passed before al-Sahba woke me with a low, nervous whinny.

CHAPTER 21

RUNAWAYS

Nafud Desert
October 1917

I HEARD muffled conversation. It was strange talk, and I couldn't make out the words. I nudged Mabrukah awake. She rolled onto her back.

There it was again, two girls talking. Maybe they were cave-dwelling djinn. I drew my dagger, crawled to the cave entrance, and felt my way along the wall toward the voices. I held my breath and listened.

One of them must have sensed me, for she said words that probably meant, "Who's there?" or "Listen."

I didn't move. Then in Arabic she asked, "Who's there?"

"Are you djinn or men?" I said, trying to sound gruff, remembering the strange people we had met at the Shaqiq well.

My answer was a scream, then another, then the caves filled with a hundred ear-splitting wails. Al-Sahba whinnied at full voice and the camel roared.

"Quiet!" I shouted, silencing them all. "We are just travelers, trying to sleep. Who are you?"

"Travelers from far away."

"What's your tribe?"

"Armani. We are Armenians. Who are you? You could be robbers and thieves."

"And you could be djinn, God preserve us from evil. No, we are Arabs from the Banu Shamaal tribe, and we won't harm you." They murmured in their language, then fell silent.

We lit a fire inside our cave, for if they were djinn, they would flee into the darkness. When the first flames cast their light, a young woman appeared. She was wrapped in a tattered woolen blanket, and she shivered as she grimaced and squinted at us. She seemed to relax once she saw we were only two, and I suppose we didn't look all that threatening. We beckoned her to sit. She kept her eyes on us as she approached and sat down, then warmed her hands near the fire.

Her small nose curved like the beak of a hawk. Her cheekbones and chin jutted out like rocks. Her eyes had sunk into her skull, and there was something about her—as if she'd seen death's own shadow. Her clothes were smudged with dirt and dust. Two long matted braids reached her waist.

"Water?" she said, pointing to her mouth. "Very thirsty." Only her voice told me she was about our age. She lifted the water skin to her mouth, her hands shaking.

"Take it easy," Mabrukah said. "Just a little or you'll get sick."

"Thank you." She pointed toward the other cave. "Do you have more? We are ten." She held up both hands. "Ten."

We had plenty of water for two, but for ten? No matter, even though we were runaways in disguise, we were bound by the desert code to aid those in need.

She spoke again in her language, and, one by one, nine more girls joined us around the fire. They were wrapped in torn blankets, their faces dirty, and their hair matted and dusty. Some shivered and coughed. Each took a single gulp from the water skin as we made coffee.

"How long since you ate?" I asked.

"Two days," said the first girl. She was the oldest.

"Here, take two dates each. Eat them slowly, only one at a time." They sucked on the first date and stared into the fire, savoring the powerful nourishment that has saved many lives in the desert.

"Thank you," she said.

"There is no thanks for this. It is our duty,"

"Not all Arabs are good like you," she said.

"Well, then. They are not true Arabs, are they," Mabrukah said, smiling at the littlest girl, who held a small bundle in her arms and stared back at Mabrukah with big dark eyes.

"Don't eat the second one until you've had some coffee. This is how we break our fast at Ramadan."

We only had a few tiny cups, so each girl sipped a cupful and passed it back to be refilled for her neighbor.

"Now, eat the second date." Their hands rose to their mouths as one.

It was cold and several hours to daybreak, so I put more wood on the fire. The flames leapt high, warming the cave. The girls settled in, wrapping themselves tight in their meager blankets, laying their heads on their bags and each other. One girl pulled out a silver cross on a chain. She kissed it and said a quiet prayer as the others listened, echoing her amen at the end. They slept with their faces toward the fire to capture its warmth.

The oldest one stayed up to talk, so I made more coffee. Questions boiled in me like the water in the pot, but she spoke first.

"We come from villages near Marash, a city in Turkey. One day, the government said we had to go, all of us with our families, to Aleppo. When we got there, they put us on trains to other places, very bad places, places like hell. Meskeneh and Deir al-Zor. Then Turkish soldiers made us walk all day, back and forth, for many days. We walked and walked. No food, no water. Many old people died. Younger ones got sick. Then the Turkish soldiers started shooting people, boom." She covered her ears as if to block out the memory. "We were lucky. We ran away, and some tribesmen saved us, God bless them. But they were very poor and had little food. They took us to Damascus and sold us as slaves. Other Arabs bought us. They said they would take us to the Amir of Hail. These were bad men. They hit us and even made the little girls walk when we crossed the Nafud. We ran away during a sandstorm. I don't know how we found these caves. Thanks to God. Running and running, that's all we do now. Please, don't return us to those bad men. I think you are not like them. God willing, you are good men."

"You are safe with us," I said. How pitiful that they would fear us, desperate runaways ourselves!

"Are you from the same family?" Mabrukah asked.

"Yes, some, that is my cousin." She pointed to a girl in the middle with a white scarf. "My sister," she said, pointing to the littlest girl holding the bundle as she slept.

"Is that her doll?" I asked, making a cradling motion with my arms.

"Yes, she has had it since we left the village."

Our own story tried to burst out of my mouth, but I held it back. It was too risky.

"What is your name?" I asked her.

"I am Suresh." We nodded and smiled back. She asked us how far it was to Hail, and explained they would like to stay there, that is if the Amir would take them in, and of course if there were no Turks there. Then she asked us about us about our journey.

I introduced us, but did not share our story. We asked her what happened to her family. She stared at the flames, then shook her head. "Mother, father, two brothers, all died there in Deir al-Zor, killed by Turks. Third brother, I don't know. He is lost." Tears welled up in her eyes and wet her cheeks, but she wiped them away. "I can't cry. I must be strong, for them. But I'm very sad." Just like us, they had lost everything except each other.

These girls were some of the lucky few who managed to escape the Armenian genocide. We learned later that, during the war, the Turks rounded up thousands of Armenian Christians in western Turkey and sent them by the trainload to desolate places in what is now Syria, just like Suresh said. Thousands of children managed to escape and were saved by kindhearted souls, and to this day many descendants of those children live in Lebanon. The evils of that terrible war reached even to the heart of Saudi Arabia.

At dawn, long fingers of powerful sunlight reached into the cave and woke us. Mabrukah cooked patties of flour and dates, the girls helping her as best they could. Suresh introduced them as we ate.

"This is Siran, which means pretty." At the mention of her name, a tall, thin girl nodded. Her long patrician nose gave her a regal presence. Anush and Siranush, young teenagers, were sisters. Suresh's cousin Arpineh was plumper than the rest, despite their desert ordeal. Vartanush was a true beauty. Her name meant rose, and she had woven her long reddish hair into many braids and tied them behind her head with coarse rope. A beauty mark perched on her ivory cheek like an amber jewel. Nazeh jumped up when Suresh said her name. Her short braids flew about as she smiled and bowed with a flourish.

Sarineh was a little younger than Nazeh. As she stood, she looked down at her feet. One was bigger than the other, and she walked with a slight limp. Markar, whose name meant gem, was about the same age. She was sturdy and proud, like a young camel that started walking soon after being born. Last of all, we met little Makrouhi, four years old. She had the same hawk nose as her sister, only in miniature. She held her doll close to her chest, wrapped in a tattered red shawl.

"And is that your little sister?" Mabrukah said, pointing at the doll.

Makrouhi unfolded her arm and revealed the face of her "sister," a doll of faded indigo-dyed cotton with a painted wooden face, and black braids of human hair. Colorful embroidery and buttons decorated its dress.

"Does she have a name?" I asked.

"Maryem," Makrouhi said. While we muffled our smiles, she handed Mabrukah the doll for a moment, then took her back and hugged her.

I beckoned them outside to introduce them to the camel and al-Sahba. Laughter echoed in the caves.

Every step was a battle on those last mountainous dunes. Yet the journey had been transformed, and the desert didn't seem so vast anymore. Perhaps it was the happy singing, or the way the girls pampered al-Sahba and tied colorful scraps of clothing on her lead. Maybe it was their green, red, and blue skirts that appeared when their blankets came off in the warming day. Or it might have been the sight of the littlest girls sitting two and three deep atop the camel and al-Sahba. It was so good not to be alone anymore. We were among kindred souls, and though we kept up our assumed male identities, it was a relief to be among women.

"The Shammar Mountains!" Mabrukah shouted and laughed from the peak of a dune we were all struggling to climb. In a mad burst of speed, she and Nazeh had raced ahead. Once we reached the top, we saw the distant Shammar Mountains glowing like amethysts and emeralds behind the ruby sand peaks we still had to conquer before sundown. Later, we descended into the shadow of the last dune and stepped out of the great ocean of sand, marveling at the flat ground before us.

We reached the village of Qina as dusk faded. The smallest girls took over the tent; the rest of us slept outside. Setting out the next morning, the hills ahead jutted skyward like giant tents. As the road turned a corner, we paused in silence to look back at the towering red sands one last time. Sometimes the end of a great struggle is like this. There is no celebration. You just take a deep breath, smile, and give silent thanks.

CHAPTER 22

ZAID AND HIS MEN

Hail and Shammar Mountains
November 1917

WHEN I look back on our journey, there are some days that remain so vivid in my memory that I recall every minute and detail. Our arrival in Hail is one of those days. Perhaps it was coming out of the Nafud, after having been away from people. Who can say really, why I remember. Perhaps it was the danger, riding into town in broad daylight, exposing ourselves to scrutiny. We were no longer hidden by dusk or night. We could be seen. And we were quite a sight. My strangely decorated horse was odd enough, but the girls were even more unusual. They didn't wear traditional dress, but rather had only colorful tattered frocks. Their hair was matted, and their entire forms were dusty. Even though we could have abandoned them there, and let them walk into town, I felt duty-bound to get them to their stated destination.

Right away, villagers joined us as we rode toward town. Some rode donkeys decorated with henna, though none could compare to the spectacle of al-Sahba. At first, we greeted them, only to receive no response. They must have been suspicious of us — the hennaed horse and the strange girls in the middle of Arabia. The girls stared straight ahead and held their heads high.

A dozen cameleers came up behind us at a fast pace. They slowed down as they passed us on both sides. The young riders laughed when they came alongside al-Sahba.

"Good morning, O moon," one said, smiling at Sarineh. She looked away.

"Sweet jasmine," said another to Vartanush. They broke into song, leaned off their camels, and ogled the girls.

"Move along," I said. "Mind your own business!" The rest of them rode by, smiling and nodding at the dusty beauties.

The last rider pulled up next to me and reined in his camel to match my pace. His white beard jutted to a point beneath craggy cheeks.

"Young man, you have to forgive the lads, for your group's quite a sight. I don't know what is more spectacular; a mare hennaed like a donkey, or all these girls in their bright colors, as bedraggled as they are."

I smiled and nodded. "It's been a long journey."

"For us as well, we've come from Baghdad. Tell me, these are Armenians?"

"Yes, we found them in some caves, one day beyond Qina. We're taking them to Hail to the Amir, where they were supposed to be sold."

"I see. And you? Where are you headed?"

"Unaizah."

He gave me a penetrating gaze that lasted just a moment. Riding at my side in silence for a while, he said, "Go in God's care." Then he pushed ahead and caught up with the rest of his group just as they disappeared around the bend.

The parade of villagers going to market kept growing. Some carried baskets of tomatoes and cucumbers. Others balanced stacks of animal skins or weavings on their heads, or pulled donkeys laden with their goods. Everyone laughed and pointed at al-Sahba, but kept their distance from us.

We bought a watermelon from a little boy and ate it while resting at a turn in the road that looked down on the city. Hail was built around the Amir's palace. We decided to ride straight into town, bringing the girls directly to the palace. I feared for them, for once inside, they might never step outside that place again. But they had little choice, and Mabrukah and I had to get back on the road before someone looked at us too closely.

The girls walked in a tight group, but they couldn't hide from the stares and whispers of the townspeople. Children played in the narrow streets. Chickens and roosters darted this way and that. Some little boys started chanting, "Girls! Girls!" Faces appeared at windows, and women stood at thresholds to see what was going on. The boys pestered us like flies, and a pack of mangy street dogs trotted behind.

"Go on, leave them alone! Get away!" I said. "These are for the Amir! Stand back!" They ignored me and skipped alongside as we walked faster.

"Suresh, we have to hurry," I said. Suresh shouted something to the girls, and they began to run. The little girls held tight as the animals broke into a trot. When the boys started throwing rocks, the girls ran faster.

Once we reached the market square, the boys disappeared. It was chaotic: noisy with buying and selling, braying and bleating. Across the square stood the great wooden gates of the Amir's palace. One door was open just wide enough for a single person to enter. A lone guard sat next to it, asleep despite the din. The girls got themselves ready to walk to their destiny through those doors. They tried to wipe the dust from their faces and clothes, and attempted in vain to make their hair presentable.

Suresh clasped my hands. "Thank you. You are good men. We will never forget you." Her eyes teared up.

Just as she began to lead the girls away, one of the boys who had been chasing us shouted: "Here they are, over here!" He was pointing toward us, leading two men on horseback. The girls huddled behind Mabrukah and me as a crowd formed.

I stepped forward. "These girls are the property of the Amir. We are delivering them to him."

"The Amir? Hah!" one of the men said. He was missing several teeth and scrutinized us with his one good eye.

The other jumped off his horse and approached to get a closer look. "What are these, Armenians?"

"Yes, and they are property of the Amir," I said.

"By God, that one I would like for my wife," the toothless one said, pointing to Vartanush, and they both laughed.

"We'll bring them to him," the second one said. "We're the Amir's men."

"No, they will enter the front door of the palace on their own. Come on," I said, signaling to the girls to back away.

"And who exactly do you think you are?" The one-eyed man scowled and pulled his horse closer. He slipped the rifle from his shoulder into his right hand and rested it on his thigh, pointing the barrel upward. He motioned to his companion, who walked around us and blocked our way to the palace door. By this time a small crowd had gathered to watch.

"I'm Badr bin Mu'tizz ash-Shamaali, delivering the Amir's property to him."

"Very good and well done, lad. We'll take them to him. You have done your duty. Now, on your way."

His friend jumped off his horse and grabbed Suresh's arm. "This one's the oldest, they'll follow her." The one-eyed man raised his rifle and aimed at the girls, and the crowd backed away.

"Wait!" The cameleers we'd met earlier rode up. The white-bearded man jumped off his camel and strode up to the ruffian holding Suresh's arm. He put his hand on the man's shoulder and pulled Suresh away. "Thank you, good man, I owe you a debt! You'll have a fine reward for returning these girls to me."

"But they said they were the Amir's property."

"Yes, well they would say that, wouldn't they? Anything to escape the bonds of servitude into which they were sold in Damascus where I acquired them. I've spent my profits on them. Of course, I will be happy to show my appreciation once you surrender them." The horseman lowered his rifle.

"And you, young men," he said to Mabrukah and me. "We owe you as well, for bringing them out of the desert to safety." He looked at me with the same penetrating gaze he'd given me before, only this time he lingered longer and opened his eyes wide for a moment, willing me to play along.

"No thanks are needed for doing one's duty," I said.

"God will recompense you accordingly," he said, then turned to the horsemen. "May I have a word with you both?" As he talked to them, his young men dismounted and surrounded us. Suresh sent me a questioning glance.

One of the young cameleers grabbed my arm. "Just play along and follow us out of town. We'll be provisioning here, leaving this afternoon. We're also going to Unaizah." Unaizah? I nodded to Suresh and Mabrukah.

The crowd dispersed as quickly as it had formed and the little boys vanished. The older cameleer shook the horsemen's hands and slapped their shoulders. They rode away, fondling shiny silver coins. The Amir's guard slept through it all.

"We leave in one hour," the old man announced. "Hamad, take the girls over there to the other end of the square. Buy them some food and let them drink. I'm going for more provisions." Again he looked at me and nodded.

After watering the animals, Mabrukah and I sold more bangles and bought enough coffee, dates, and wheat to get us another five days on the road. We would go with the group, at least until we left town. We pulled our animals next to the cameleers and sat down, but they didn't notice us. They were watching the girls eat.

"Smell this perfume, it's rose from Jerusalem," one of the young men said, holding a tiny glass bottle for his friend to sniff. "Perhaps the beauty there with the red hair, she might like it." He pointed to Vartanush, who had finished eating and was rebraiding her hair.

"What should we do?" Suresh asked. "Who are these men?"

"Shshsh," one of the cameleers answered. "Where we go is better, better than Amir's palace. Wait and see." Then he turned to us. "And you, keep quiet. We'll talk later."

"Do as they say," I said, trying to instill my voice with confidence.

"That one, she's so lively, like a gazelle," another young man said, pointing to Nazeh. "That's the kind of bride I want someday." She stuck her tongue out at him and he laughed. "She has to grow up first, though!"

The old man returned, his camel loaded with provisions. "Let's go. Fellows, surround the girls and walk on foot with them. Don't let anyone near them. You two," he said to us, "Ride with me in front. No questions. Just hurry."

We headed into the hills, and only after we'd left the last village behind did we stop to rest in a grove of trees.

"Join us," the older man said to Mabrukah and me. The girls sat by themselves, talking in their own language. Once we were comfortable, he spoke. "What are your good names?"

"I'm Badr ibn Mu'tizz ash-Shamaali, and this is my servant Muhsin. We're from the north, on our way to Unaizah. We are going to see my uncle, Duhaim al-Hamdan. This mare, disguised as she is, is a gift for him from my father."

"Duhaim is your uncle?" I nodded. "We have known each other for decades. A good family, the Hamdans."

"And you sir, may we know your good name?"

"My name is Zaid, and this is Hamad, my oldest son." Hamad was a taller version of his father. He shared his father's dark sparkling eyes and his curly hair, cut short. Zaid introduced the rest of them. There were twin brothers returning from their first trip to Baghdad. Fifteen years old at most, they were a matched pair, with identical shoulder-length braids. The others were older and had traveled widely. I don't remember all their names anymore, except for Karim, because he wore glasses, which was unusual then. He had been working in Bombay and Isfahan before meeting up with Zaid to return home.

Like Abdallah, they were all Ageylis, long-distance traders. I wondered if they knew him. Maybe some were even his relatives. Then I wondered if they'd heard the poems, or if they'd heard of two runaway girls from the Bani Shamaal.

After a short rest, we got ready to move on. Zaid insisted that we ride up front with him. Mabrukah and I took two of the smallest girls onto our mounts, and Zaid matched the other girls with the young men, two riders per camel.

That night, I asked Zaid why he'd intervened, given that the Armenians were promised to the Amir. "In a way," I said, "you stole them right out from under him."

Zaid chuckled. "You are right, of course. However, we'd seen the Armenians and their former 'owners' as they were leaving al-Jawf, and I doubt they had any arrangement with the Amir. They beat the girls, even the youngest one, and they used whips. Sons of dogs, they were. As you know, God looks with favor on those who free slaves."

"You don't want them for yourself?"

"No, never. How can such a thing be permitted in God's sight? Besides, if they were my daughters, I'd want them in Unaizah. Believe me, it will be better for them, for we have a serious shortage of brides there. You'll see, they will be well received once we get them to your Uncle's house."

"Uncle Duhaim? Why involve him in this?"

"Well, you saved them from the Nafud, so you are responsible for them. Leaving them at the Amir's palace in Hail would have meant enslavement. This way, you can fulfill your obligation to help them. And we will do our part to get you all there." While I was grateful to travel with Zaid and his men, I feared what my Uncle Duhaim would say when a dozen runaways, not just two, appeared on his doorstep seeking refuge.

CHAPTER 23

O SMALL GAZELLE

Al-Qasim
November 1917

AFTER THE struggle to cross the Nafud on our own, this part of the journey seemed easy. We had no safety worries, and our companions knew the way. We encountered a few other parties, but Zaid and his men protected the girls from scrutiny. Each day, the girls rode with the same boys. Makrouhi saddled up with Mabrukah or me, and tied her doll into a shoulder sling and sang lullabies.

But we couldn't totally relax. Mabrukah and I could have given ourselves away with a girlish movement, a weak handshake, or by using feminine instead of masculine forms of address for each other. But it soon became clear the young men were so fascinated by the Armenian girls that they barely noticed us. Suresh had to bridge conversations in Arabic and Turkish and laughter peppered the hours.

On our last night, Zaid said, "We have shared the road. There is no reason we shouldn't share the bounty of food that God has given us, so let us all eat together." Until that night, the girls had always eaten apart.

The girls sat on one side of the circle and the men on the other, everyone leaning into the food platters to scoop up the rabbit and rice with their hands. After dinner, a silence fell over us as we sat before the crackling fire. I admired the sun-browned faces of my fellow travelers, from Zaid to little Makrouhi.

The girls talked to each other in Turkish, their giggles rippling down the line. "What is so funny?" I asked Suresh. "What are they saying?"

"We will dance for you," Suresh said as she stood up, and the others joined her. They stood shoulder to shoulder, their arms linked, forming a tight chain. Nazeh sang a melody, high and clear, while they dipped their shoulders to accent the beat. Then they repeated her melody in a chorus, leaning back and forth in place, their arms still locked together. The firelight glinted in their eyes, and their smiles flashed. Then the line began to move around us. They turned their heads to the right, then the left, then straight ahead, all moving as one.

We began to clap, and the girls' smiles widened. They danced faster, circling the fire again and again. Then they stood in place, stepping forward and back as the singer repeated the chorus, and we all clapped along until they ended it with a final stomp. Mabrukah let out a girlish zaghrutah, and I elbowed her. The men's cheering drowned it out, and no one noticed.

As if in answer, the twin Ageylis started singing, and we echoed the chorus as they added verse upon verse on a simple tune.

> O small gazelle, o small gazelle,
> Come sing with me tonight.
> The moon's half full, the moon's half full,
> We'll fill it with delight.

Next, they turned to Mabrukah and me. It was our turn to perform something. What would we sing? Mabrukah elbowed me. "Don't worry, you've heard this one before."

She chanted in the nasal voice of a desert poet, in the lowest notes she could manage. The crowd was transfixed by her clear voice as it rose in the night, full of confidence and pride, mixed with true longing.

> In the dawn I depart;
>   slipping from her side;
> After tasting the honey of her lips
>   And the warmth of her arms.
> Her heart sleeps and she dreams of me.
>   I ride away before
> The eyes and ears of her camp
>   Awake to discover us.
> How often I come and go,
>   Like a bright star,
> I appear at night, then dip below the hills
>   I return to my people,
> A rabbit slung over my shoulder.

At the last line, the men smiled and nodded. I turned to Suresh. "It was a love poem."

"I know, I know!" she said. "And very beautiful."

The poem quieted the crowd a little, and another round of coffee was set up. I thought about the coming day, and how I'd have to face Uncle Duhaim. After staring at the fire for a while, I looked up and caught glances flying around like sparks. While I'd been contemplating our future in the embers, the others were moon-eyeing each other. Love was blooming. To see them like this, enjoying each other's company in the open air, broke my heart with both joy and sorrow. How much I would have loved to spend even a few days like this with Abdallah!

That night, I lay in my bedding and watched the half moon, lulled to sleep by the quiet conversation all around. When I woke briefly a few hours later, the moon had set, but the desert sky glowed with starlight. The young people were still up, talking around the fire and in small groups apart from the rest. How many times I have relived that night. In those hours, everything seemed possible, and even though we still faced danger, we were safe, and a group of strangers had become friends. A journey that had begun in fear was ending with more than a little magic.

CHAPTER 24

A Caravan of Brides

I WOKE to the sound of Zaid pounding coffee in the mortar and pestle. Admiring the starlit sky and the horizon's orange glow, I joined Zaid and Nazeh by the fire. Everyone else still slept. We could see our breath.

By then, Nazeh had learned a few words of Arabic, but with Zaid, she didn't need them. They worked well together, as if she were his granddaughter. He signaled when he needed something, and she obliged.

"Most of these young people didn't get much sleep last night," Zaid said, smiling. "I wonder, how many broken hearts will we have to repair after this trip?"

As we sipped our coffee, I tried to burnish that morning in my memory: the crackling of the campfire, the kind face of Zaid, Nazeh kneeling next to me, and all the young people asleep. I knew we would never be together like this again, and I wanted time to stop.

Nazeh went off in search of more wood for the fire, leaving us alone.

Zaid spoke in a low whisper. "I don't know what your story is, Badr, if that is even your real name. Whatever your business is, I leave it to your Uncle. It's obviously a family matter. Believe me, in my years of travel I have met many who are not what they claim to be."

"Have you known all along?"

"No, not at first, but you two have kept apart from the lads, and neither of you seemed drawn to the girls, so I began to wonder. And then there is your mare," he said, looking at me with a smile and a lifted eyebrow.

"We owe you our lives for your discretion."

"You owe me nothing. Some time, tell me the truth."

Nazeh returned just then, and we spoke no more.

At the sun's first rays, Zaid walked among the clumps of sleepers. "Time to get up. Dawn is here. Unaizah today!"

That afternoon, we rounded a small dune and paused to take in the view. Some miles ahead, a green palm forest spread across the horizon, filling a vast shallow valley. The young men called out: "Mother of al-Qasim, Unaizah!"

Zaid addressed us all. "We must avoid making a spectacle today. When we reach the edge of town, all but the youngest girls will walk. I'll ride in front, and you boys surround them. Badr and Muhsin, you bring up the rear. We ride straight to Duhaim's. Come on, let's go. Bismillah, in the name of God."

As we began our final march, a few townspeople joined us on the road. But here I sensed we were welcome, unlike our previous arrival at Hail. A skinny boy rode past us on a donkey laden with firewood. He eyed us without saying a word, but when he got out in front, he turned and shouted at the top of his lungs, "It's a caravan of brides! Lulululululu!" We laughed as he worked his donkey into a trot and rode toward town ahead of us, shouting, "A caravan of brides! A caravan of brides! Lulululululu!"

At the edge of town, we rode along thick stands of palms and tamarisk trees. The squeaking of the sawanis filled the air. Families worked in the alfalfa fields in the shade of the palms.

Mabrukah pulled up next to me and tugged at my sleeve. "Well, we did it. Welcome to Unaizah!" I nodded with tears in my eyes. Her smile helped me regain my composure. We only had to keep our charade up a little while longer.

My dears, Unaizah was no town, it was a real oasis city. It was much larger than I had imagined. Once we entered its gates, the roads grew narrow and the adobe houses towered three stories high, and, in some places, arches reached over the streets. Swirling, spiral-shaped minarets adorned the mosques.

Zaid kept the group together as the roads grew crowded. A man called from the stoop of a store, "Welcome back Zaid! What have you got this time?"

"Brides, we're a caravan of brides."

"Did you say a caravan of brides?"

"Indeed, I did."

Pedestrians passed in a hurry, paying us no mind. Camels, donkeys and mules plied the streets, loaded with wood, sacks of grain, and bolts of fabric. We halted in delays and traffic jams. In the metal workers' street, men hammered on large copper cooking pots and trays, while others worked at forges, making hooks and tools of iron. I had to block my ears from the din. We rode through a market where they hammered camel saddle frames and wooden doors. We passed tailors' shops and tinkers, then a market where women sold spices and homemade cakes.

At last, we entered a maze of narrow streets lined with large houses. We turned into a small alley and halted next to a gate in a high wall. Zaid waved Mabrukah and me forward. As we rode toward the front of the line, passing each rider and camel, I realized our caravan was a living thing. We were the dust we kicked up in the road. We were the noisy jostling of the animals. We were our hunger, our sleeplessness, our longing, and our songs. We were our beating hearts, and our friendships.

"This is your uncle's home," Zaid said, pointing up to a large house that rose above the high wall. "The main entrance is out front. We'll wait, but you must hurry. The men are anxious to be home."

The front door stood partly open, and it led to the men's majlis, a large room with high ceilings. Bright woven cushions lined the walls. This was where the men of the family entertained their visitors. We stepped out of our sandals and entered, surprised that the floor was covered in a thick layer of soft red sand, just like the Nafud.

"Uncle Duhaim!" I said. "Visitors from Wadi Sirhan, your nephews, bring greetings from your cousin!" A sparrow chirped from an upper window in answer.

"Hello!" I called again. Silence. I crossed the room to an interior door that opened further inside. I inched it open. "Is anyone home?"

A woman's voice answered. "The men are not at home."

"When will my Uncle Duhaim return? I'm his nephew, coming from Wadi Sirhan."

The inside door opened a little more. "He will return in an hour. You are welcome to wait, of course."

Once I was sure there were no men around, I changed my tone. "Is Nurah bint Duhaim here? It's her cousin Salma, and Mabrukah."

The door flew open, and Nurah stood before us, her hands covering her mouth in surprise. "But you're dressed like..." I took off my headdress. "Salma! I don't believe it!" She hugged me. "Allahh! Welcome!" Then she stood back, "Yes, you do smell like you've just crossed the desert!"

"We ran away from cousin Ahmad. He's my husband now, and well it's a long story. We crossed the Nafud, the two of us, on my horse and my brides-wealth she-camel."

"The two of you crossed the Nafud alone and you're married?" she said, circling, appraising us. She had blossomed into a classic Arabian beauty – quick, wide-set black eyes, a willowy figure, white teeth, and a perfectly chiseled nose, like a Roman statue. She wore a thobe of dark green wool edged in bright yellow and red embroidery. Her long hair hung free. With each step, her silver ankle bracelet jingled.

"I'm afraid it's not that simple," I said. "We're not alone. We brought ten Armenian girls, too."

"Where are they?" she asked, after I explained.

"In the alley behind the house, with all the Ageylis."

"The whole group? Behind our house?"

I nodded.

"Show me." She led us into the family quarters.

"And another thing," I said. "Even the Armenians think we're men. I'm Badr, and she's Muhsin." Nurah stopped and looked at me. "Please, Nurah, will you help us? I'll explain it all later. But believe me, we're in real trouble, though we've done nothing wrong."

She let out a puff of air and nodded. Without another word, she walked on, more purpose to her step. It was then I was sure she had become the lady of the house. And she was to become a great lady, but I'll tell you about that later.

Peering through a hole in the door, we saw the feet of one of the boys, a camel's belly, and a brightly colored patch of skirt. Nurah shook her head. "Unbelievable."

"Badr? Is everything all right?" Zaid called from the majlis.

"Go back and tell him father isn't home," Nurah said, "and that we'll take the girls inside back here."

I ran back to the salon and readjusted my headdress. Zaid was waiting inside the majlis. "Yes Sir, everything is fine. Uncle Duhaim is at market.

We've been talking to the lady of the house. The girls can enter through the side gate. I'll meet you back there now."

"In the name of God," I whispered as I opened the alley door. "Suresh, all of you, come with me inside." The boys handed them their bundles. The girls nodded goodbye to their new friends, then, one by one, they walked through the doorway and into their new lives.

I stood before the Ageylis for the last time as a man. "Thank you for your generosity and kindness to these strangers on the road. May you receive your just reward, and may God preserve you from your enemies."

I shook Zaid's hand, then we touched our hands to our hearts. "In God's care," we said to each other. The group echoed the blessing. He handed me the reins of al-Sahba and the camel.

Mabrukah and I watched the men ride up the alley and turn onto the main street. And so the caravan disbanded. Though it never formed again, in my heart I always remained a part of it, and it a part of me, and we are always together in my memories.

CHAPTER 25

THE WAY OF LOVE AND YOUTH

AFTER THE gate closed, the arms of the big house wrapped around us. We had been out in the open for so long that, at first, being behind four walls was very strange. Makrouhi's mouth turned down, and her eyes widened. Suresh knelt and took her hand, but she started to cry. Only when Suresh picked her up did she stop.

Nurah stood next to me and looked them over. "How did they ever survive? They are so thin, they're starving."

"Suresh here is the oldest," I said. "She speaks some Arabic. Suresh, this is Nurah, my cousin." They nodded at each other and Nurah said, "Welcome."

Suresh seemed guarded, which was understandable, since so many strangers had betrayed them.

"We'll need to find you some clean clothes. You can bathe later. But first, you must be hungry."

Nurah turned to Mabrukah and me. "The servants are out, but they'll be back soon, so go back to the majlis and wait there. Girls, bring your things over here." She beckoned them to rest in the shade. "Now, off with you two. The girls will be fine with me."

As we walked across the open courtyard at the center of the house, I took in our surroundings. Nurah's home was a grand Arabian mansion. The three-story structure of adobe surrounded the courtyard on all but one side, the side with the gate through which we had entered from the alley. In the courtyard, two stately palm trees reached heavenward. Bougainvillea vines climbed along an arched colonnade. There were fruit trees, vegetables and bright-colored blooms filled garden plots, and a small raised pool marked the courtyard's center. No, I decided. This was no prison at all.

"I think I'm dreaming now," Mabrukah said. "I think we're still out on the Nafud, thirsty and alone, and I'm about to wake up. Is this really happening? Are we here, safe in Unaizah?"

"Yes, I hope we are safe. It will be strange, you know, after all the lies I've told, to speak the truth at last."

Waiting in the majlis, the minutes turned to hours, and we were lulled to sleep by the chirping of the sparrows and an occasional rooster's crow. I woke to the sounds of a crackling fire. An old man was tending the hearth, and from his dark skin, flowing white robe, and turban, I knew he was Sudanese.

"Welcome, Badr and Muhsin," he said, bowing his head. "My name is Umar. Master Duhaim will be along soon. So you've had quite a journey."

A few moments later, Nurah called from upstairs, "Father is coming down the street. He has people with him."

"God help and protect us," I murmured. We would have to carry on our charade one last time, until his guests departed.

Seconds later, shadows crossed the threshold, and we stood to greet our host. Uncle Duhaim had to bend over to step inside. He laughed when he saw us. "It is true! I heard rumors in the market that you were here, young nephew from the north." He shook my hand with a hearty grip.

"Uncle, Sir, perhaps you don't remember me, Badr bin Mu`tizz, and this is Muhsin."

"Welcome, welcome," he said, still shaking my hand. "Well, I haven't seen you since you were about five years old. You are a handsome youth, yes, very handsome, and how is your father?"

"Well, thank God. He is helping Talal defeat the Turks. We brought you a mare as a gift from him. She is tethered in the courtyard."

"Ah! Well, thank you Badr. And meet my dear friends Zahid and Abd al-Rahman." Duhaim motioned for us to sit, then he joined Umar at the hearth to prepare the coffee. In Unaizah as in the desert, a good host honored his guests by making the coffee himself.

"We have heard a strange rumor," he said, "that ten Armenian brides arrived with Zaid Abu Hamad's caravan from the north. It's the talk of the market today."

Umar smiled at me, then looked down. Before I could explain, he whispered in Uncle Duhaim's ear.

"My God, they're here?" Uncle Duhaim nearly dropped his precious bag of coffee beans. The Sudanese nodded. "And you brought them?"

Telling them about the Armenians was easier than I thought it would be. They asked for every detail. I explained that it was Zaid who decided Uncle Duhaim would have to take them in, since we'd rescued them.

"Yes, yes, he's right of course," Duhaim mused, stroking his short black beard.

When the men left, we took Uncle Duhaim to the courtyard where al-Sahba stood, with one hind leg bent, her hoof pointing to the ground. Umar's son Yahya fed her hay, trying not to laugh out loud as we approached. Duhaim chuckled at her disguise as he stroked her forehead and nose. She pricked her ears forward. Yahya whispered as he petted her neck. "Yes, we'll take care of you, gorgeous bride. You are welcome in our house." She nodded her head in answer.

"Ten girls, appearing out of nowhere," Duhaim said to Nurah, who had joined us. "And Armenians at that; unmarried Christian women. We will have to consult the judge and the Amir, certainly. But for now, we must keep them here. Where else can they go? Nurah, do you have enough time to take care of these guests?"

"They don't ask for much, father. Only safety, protection and some simple human kindness. They have seen so much cruelty. Come, you should meet them."

Uncle Duhaim gathered his cloak in his arms and swept up the stairs. Scrambling to keep up, we followed him into a room much like the majlis downstairs, only it was carpeted with bright weavings. The girls stood smiling, lined up in order of size, but Suresh held Makrouhi, who looked terrified.

"They are orphans," I said. "Their parents were killed or taken away by the Turks."

Uncle Duhaim nodded. "You are welcome here, and you are safe. I must discuss your situation with the town leaders. But for now, this is your home."

Suresh stepped forward. "Thank you for your kindness. We will help – work – we can cook and sew." She introduced them one by one, then she said something to all the girls, and they began to repeat, "Shukran shukran," over and over. Uncle Duhaim nodded and backed out of the room as they followed him to the door, still saying, "Thank you, thank you."

As we stood in the hallway, I heard a voice from upstairs. I pulled on Nurah's sleeve. "What's that?" She stepped back to listen.

"Nurah? What's all that commotion?"

"Oh my, how could I forget? Come with me." Uncle Duhaim said, signaling us all to follow.

We stepped into a room where an old woman sat on a raised bed. Even as she lay back against colorful bolsters, she was tall and imposing like Uncle Duhaim. She wore her hair in a single white braid over one shoulder.

"My son," she said in a booming voice. "What strange dreams I've had today. People laughing, shouting, speaking in Turkish! God protect us from evil." Then her eyes fell on me. "Tell me, who is our visitor? A young Shamaali?" She looked me over then smiled. "Are you my great-grandson Badr? I have never seen you, but you look just like your father."

"Excellent guessing, Grandmother," I said as I kissed her hand.

"No, Grandmother, you were not dreaming," Nurah said. "You did hear all those things. You are in for a surprise—well, many surprises."

Suresh entered the room first and introduced the others. Each girl kissed the old woman's hand, then stood back in line.

"They're so thin, God preserve them!" the old woman said. "They look like they're starving." Then she spoke a few words in Turkish. The girls gasped in surprise, and Suresh answered her. She motioned for Suresh to sit beside her.

"I didn't know you spoke Turkish, Grandmother," Nurah said. "How did you learn?"

"Until 1906, there were Turkish soldiers stationed here in Unaizah. You were just a little girl, so I'm sure you don't remember. Even this town was part of the Ottoman Empire, though really just a small outpost. I learned to speak it from a Turkish friend who married into the Zalman family."

Suresh began to tell her story, Turkish words tumbling out of her like a rushing torrent. Grandmother's face folded in horror as she listened.

That night Mabrukah and I retired to sleep in the majlis, still keeping up our masquerade. Uncle Duhaim instructed us to go to the public baths first thing in the morning with Yahya. Then we were to call on him at his office in town before returning home for lunch. In the afternoon, we would take al-Sahba and the camel to the family farm on the outskirts of town.

We had no intention of following this plan. Instead, just before dawn, Nurah nudged us awake and led us to the courtyard bathhouse where a fire was already blazing. Umar's wife Salwa, a servant to Nurah and her grandmother, was waiting for us, smiling. I cried in pleasure as she poured hot soapy water over my bare skin.

We had already bathed and dressed in Nurah's caftans by the time Yahya went to wake Badr and Muhsin. He found only our folded bedding and came looking for us in the courtyard.

"No, you can't go out there," Salwa warned him, as he looked around. "The Armenian girls are bathing now."

"Badr and Muhsin aren't in the men's salon, they're gone!"

"I'll say they're gone," Salwa said with a smile. "Gone forever."

"They left? Well, I better tell Duhaim then."

"No no, that won't be necessary. They will explain it to him themselves."

"But you said they were gone? How can they explain it to him?"

"You'll see."

Later that morning, Duhaim returned from the market, wondering where his young guests were. "Here, they're in here." Nurah said, leading him to us. When I shook his hand, he didn't recognize me, and in that moment I knew our disguises had been a total success.

"Uncle, I am Salma, your niece, and this is Mabrukah. We had to cross the Nafud disguised as my cousin Badr and his servant Muhsin. I apologize for our deception, but we had to do it. Uncle, we seek refuge in a matter of honor. My husband, my first cousin Ahmad, threatened to kill me for adultery. But the accusation is untrue. We had to run away or risk certain death."

He jerked his head as if to take in my words, but said nothing as he studied us. He gazed at me, and his eyes narrowed. "And why does he suspect you?"

"Because of poems that circulated among the warriors, by an Ageyli youth I knew before I was married. While the second poem speaks to my virtue, no one believes it. They believe it masks sin."

"And for this you were to be killed?"

"Well, yes, we were warned to flee or risk death. And now, we seek refuge and protection."

"Recite the poems," he said.

I recited them.

"And who is this Ageyli?"

"Abdallah al-Fusaihi of Unaizah."

"It can't be. I have known his good family for years. I can't believe he would recite such verses in public and let them circulate. And if Ahmad's temper is anything like that of your father and uncle, those verses would have stirred up their wrath into a raging fire. However, would he have killed you over this? And is there another side to the story I wonder?" He turned to me and looked deep into my eyes.

"No Sir, this is the truth. Perhaps you are right, he might not have killed me." Then I explained how he'd beaten and threatened me on our wedding night, and how we made our choice to leave.

Duhaim was silent for a minute or two, and I wondered if we were about to be thrown out, but then he spoke again. "So you disguised yourselves as your own cousin and crossed the Nafud, two girls alone?"

"Yes, Uncle."

"And you found these Armenian girls and saved them, meeting up with the Ageyli Zaid Abu Hamad?"

"Yes, Uncle."

"And Zaid did not sense your deception?"

"In truth, he did suspect we were not who we said we were. Assuming it was a family matter, he kept quiet, though he made me promise I would tell him the truth one day."

He smiled. "Well, indeed I would have been surprised if he hadn't seen through your disguises, as convincing as they were. Does anyone else know of your deception?"

"No, Uncle, no one outside this household."

"And you expect me to take you in, along with all of them?"

"We rely on your generosity, Uncle."

"You've put us in quite a position, bringing us not only ten strangers in need but your troubles as well."

"We know it is a great burden on you, Uncle."

After a while, he sighed and his face softened. "And to think I woke just yesterday morning, grateful for the calmness of the house. God knew better. Yes, my niece, we will give you refuge."

I knelt before him, grasped his hands, and kissed them as a servant would. "Uncle, may God bless you and grant you good health and long life. We will try to be worthy of your protection."

He patted me on the head. "Enough. You're not the first runaway bride to appear at her family's threshold. This town and the deserts all around are full of love and honor intrigues. I must admit, though, those poems are spectacular. I can see how they'd cause a husband's wrath. And a wife's escape!"

"Such is the way of love and youth," Grandmother said when I finished reciting the second poem for her. "Love cannot be tamed and can be more dangerous than the snake's bite. Thank God you reached us. Here, show me your palm."

"Yes, Ma'am," I said.

Her delicate hands were cold, but they warmed as she explored my palms with her ancient fingers. Her white eyebrows jutted out from her proud forehead. Tiny wrinkles circled her mouth and lined her cheeks.

As she examined my hands, I noticed a bookcase filled with leather-bound volumes. Out her window, the tops of two palm trees rustled in the wind. A brown desert dove flew by, in the beating rhythm of flight I knew by heart, reminding me of the great distance we had crossed. She opened up my fingers and gazed at my right hand. With no further comment, she curled up my hands again, squeezed them both, and set them back in my lap. After my experience with Zurfah, I had no interest in learning what Grandmother saw in my palm.

Mabrukah and I went with Nurah to the women's salon. "May we enter?" Nurah asked. She opened the door, and we found the girls busy mending their clothes and trying on hand-me-downs from the neighbors. As we stepped in, all motion and conversation stopped.

"Badr?" Suresh said. "Is that you? And Muhsin?"

I kissed her on both cheeks. "My name is Salma, and this is Mabrukah."

The girls put down their work and stared. Then they all started to laugh and shout in Turkish. As they encircled us, touching our hair, our clothes, and holding our hands, Suresh spoke first. "But why? Why did you wear men's clothes?"

"My husband is very bad," I said. "He wanted to kill me." We hugged each other and didn't let go for a long time.

CHAPTER 26

CUT FROM FINE CLOTH

Unaizah
December 1917

YOU WOULD think that living in town would seem boring after growing up outdoors in the desert and crossing the Nafud as we did. To the contrary, it was a new world for us, full of new adventures and challenges.

"Don't worry, they can't see us," Nurah whispered as we peered down on the majlis. "Many houses in Unaizah have these secret windows, so a hostess knows when her guests need something. See the old fellow with the cane? He's the chief judge. The one with the dark beard, he's the imam of the main mosque. The other fellow, that's the Amir's deputy. Those two are your Ageylis, yes?" I nodded. Zaid and Hamad each sat with one knee up.

Uncle Duhaim knelt at the hearth, preparing coffee with Umar's help. Smoke from the open fire billowed to the upper reaches of the majlis, blocking our view for a moment and adding soot to the already blackened ceiling, the sign of a generous host.

When Uncle Duhaim joined his guests, the conversation began in earnest. We couldn't hear them speak, but we followed their pantomime. At first, Zaid did most of the talking. Uncle Duhaim gestured upstairs, moving his hand from low to high. The officials asked questions, mostly of Zaid. After he answered, they sat back and stroked their beards. The judge shook his head and gazed at the wall. They questioned Uncle Duhaim next, then the imam spoke for a time, and everyone nodded. Smiles and subdued laughter followed. As they left, Uncle Duhaim shook each man's hand. It was over in less than an hour.

After they left, Uncle Duhaim sat alone, staring into the fire. Several sparks popped from the flames and landed at his feet, then went out. He flicked them back and told Yahya to assemble us in the majlis.

"The girls present an unusual problem," he said. "It's not that they are Christian and Armenian. It is that that they have no family, no one to keep them safe here, or anywhere else in Arabia. The judge, who has several daughters himself, proposes requiring the older girls to get married as soon as possible, stipulating that they cannot be divorced and left without support. The younger ones must stay in a reputable home until they are 14 and can marry. The imam's wife has offered to teach them to read the Qur'an. If the Amir approves of us as their guardians, we'll hold classes here."

Just as Zaid had promised, the men of Unaizah were cut from fine cloth indeed. Once the Amir approved the plan, the ladies of the neighborhood welcomed us. Mothers, daughters, grandmothers, and aunts came on foot, on donkeys, or via the second-story walkways that linked the house to the rest of the neighborhood. They loved hearing the saga of how we came to Unaizah and wove us into the fabric of the town as neatly as the Armenian girls could mend a torn blouse.

Uncle Duhaim was aware I had vowed to tell Zaid the full truth of our journey. Yet this would certainly raise a scandal in town, because Abdallah's family lived there, too. We had to minimize the gossip, so when the time came, I recited the poems but disguised Abdallah's identity and said that he was an Ageyli from al-Jawf. Naming him would have disgraced his family and caused Uncle Duhaim's family anguish, too. So the poet's identity stayed a secret, known only to Uncle Duhaim, Grandmother, and Nurah.

After I met with Zaid and told him the tale of our journey, the womenfolk of our caravan mates paid us visits, since by then we'd become town legends. More importantly, they visited to inspect potential brides. Zaid had been right, there was a bride shortage, and proposals soon followed. Studious Karim asked for Suresh. The twins asked for the hands of the sisters Anush and Siranush. Several more matches were agreed to, leaving the youngest five with us: Vartanush, who was just 13, Nazeh, Sarineh, Markar, and Makrouhi.

When the Amir's wife and her mother-in-law paid a visit, we assumed it was a simple social call, for the Duhaims were from the first rank of Unaizah families. They asked about the weddings, and Grandmother explained we wanted to marry the brides off in one night.

"We would like to offer the palace and town guesthouse for the celebration," the Amira said. "Isn't it wonderful how all the brides know the grooms? How often do brides just appear out of the Nafud? Mashallah, it's quite something. Well, Um Duhaim, what do you think?"

The Amir and his family lived at their own home, not in the palace itself, which had plenty of unused bedrooms and large halls for gatherings. It would be a perfect arrangement, and Grandmother agreed. Then the Amira approached all the grooms' mothers, for in Saudi families, the groom pays for the festivities.

The grooms called on Uncle Duhaim one by one, bringing gifts for their brides, so the coffee hearth burned bright each night. Yahya and Umar carried the gifts upstairs, and the young men would pretend to be calm as they sat in the salon, waiting to hear the zaghareed upstairs that signaled their gifts had been received. Elegant silver necklaces, earrings, and bracelets began appearing on the brides-to-be. Colorful new frocks replaced hand-me-downs.

The older Armenian girls knew how to use the treadle sewing machine Grandmother had bought Nurah. They fashioned their own trousseaux: simple cotton shifts of dark green, blue, and black. They also made skirts and jackets in the Armenian style. While they sewed, they chatted and sang. Grandmother often sat with them, joining in the laughter and practicing her Turkish.

The girls kept busy with needlework. They even knew how to make lace handkerchiefs. One day, I was sitting with them as they sewed, and I picked up Makrouhi's doll. The girls often took it in hand and looked at it.

"Why do you all look at Maryem so much?" I asked.

"See the embroidery on her apron? These are special stitches. They are from our home, from Marash. This stitch," Suresh said, pointing out a complicated design that looked like a thick square "t." "This is the Marash stitch. The others come from our villages and our families." She lifted the doll's apron and pointed to more stitches underneath, sewn on the doll's skirt. "And these are the gaght nakar, the secret stitches." She paused for a moment. "When we were coming from Marash on the train, my grandmother Maryem was with us. She brought her needle and thread and sewed all these stitches on the doll. At night, she taught Makrouhi and me how to sew them. You could say Maryem helps us remember."

I turned the doll over and marveled at her human hair braids, decorated with tiny fake coins. Every detail of her costume was hand sewn, down to her red-and-white flowered pantaloons.

Since I was a married woman and Mabrukah was a servant, town custom permitted us to appear in public, so nearly every day we went out on wedding errands. Uncle Duhaim was very generous when it came to the wedding expenses, so, carrying a little purse full of coins, we bargained with merchants for buttons and thread. We hired a woman to paint henna on the brides and found musicians for the party. We bought incense and perfumes, tea and spices.

Our errands gave us an excuse to explore Unaizah's famous markets. We were so lucky that Uncle Duhaim and Nurah lived in this particular oasis city. Even all those decades ago, you could find English clocks, gold earrings, and Indian silk, all within walking distance. Local craftsmen made fine woolen cloaks, swords, and bowls. Even Jeddah and Riyadh of today can't rival the wonderful markets of Unaizah. They used to call it the Paris of Najd, you know.

A few nights before the wedding party, the women from the Ageyli caravaneers' families came for a henna party. The brides sat while henna designs were painted on their hands and feet. Then they had to wait while it dried, just as I had waited, alone with Mabrukah, months ago in the desert. To entertain them, the younger Armenian girls sang wedding songs. Vartanoush and Nazeh danced, twirling their wrists and turning in circles.

The brides and grooms signed the marriage contracts at their respective homes with the judge and imam in attendance. But, just like today, they didn't come together as couples until the night of the zaffaf. That night, we made a procession to the Amir's palace. Yahya walked in front, carrying a pink bougainvillea branch that represented an Armenian Wedding Tree. The brides rode behind on white donkeys, and the rest of us followed on foot. Townspeople stood in the doorways and windows, calling out with zaghareed as we passed.

The windows of the palace glowed with lamplight, and the hearths crackled with fires. The men gathered in the main majlis on the ground level, and we went upstairs to another large salon.

Even in those days, the women's wedding parties were more joyous than the men's gatherings. We wore our best dresses and our finest jewelry. Women singers and drummers performed the Samiri. They knelt in two lines facing each other and danced while kneeling. How I would love to see the Samiri again! Always on their knees, they leaned side-to-side, raising and lowering their instruments as one, as they played and sang. Some girls danced in pairs in the space between the drummers. Later, the grooms and their brides entered the room, surrounded by unmarried girls holding tall candles and singing blessings.

Once the couples were seated before us, we sang and danced for them some more. The grooms shouted to each other over the pounding drums. The ladies roared with laughter when the twins, Hadi and Amr, tried to change seats with each other and their brides held onto their thobes to prevent them from moving.

Just as our eyes got used to the sight of them all together on their wedding night, the golden moment ended, though it lived on in so many memories. They rose and went off to spend their first night of marriage, while the singers serenaded them.

That night, I lay in bed, wondering how Suresh was faring, wishing for her and the other brides a world of happiness I could never have. I did not envy them, for they had seen so much hardship. They deserved their joy. And I was content, for we had all found safety at last.

CHAPTER 27

SHAME'S SHADOW

Unaizah
February 1918

WHEN THE neighbors heard we were teaching the girls at home, they sent their daughters, too. Mabrukah and I also joined the class, and that is how we learned to read and write. It was rare in those days, you know, for girls to have such knowledge. Literacy is a great gift for anyone, and it is a gift we have been thankful for ever since. Most days our voices filled the house as we chanted the alphabet and repeated simple words and verses from the Qur'an.

Our Arabic teacher was the imam's young wife, Amina. She came from an educated Meccan family, and her pronunciation and grammar were as perfect as the imam's, whom we'd heard preach in the main mosque. We wondered whether they spoke to each other at home in the classical Arabic of their lectures and classes.

"Since you came to us," Grandmother said one night, "With your Armenian girls and your desert adventures, I have become young again. Youthful memories fill my dreams."

She began to retell long-forgotten stories, tales that she'd kept to herself for years. Some were ancient, others seemed as fresh as last night's dreams. When she told stories, she would wear a bright dress, or drape a saffron shawl about her neck and shoulders. Her rose perfume filled the room, and her eyes danced with excitement. She sat up straight, and her voice deepened. A lamp glowed inside of her, turning her cheeks and lips to rose. Her wrinkles disappeared with the bloom of each smile.

Her stories helped us pass that first winter. Violent storms blew in from the north. The skies crashed and boomed as if fighting their own Great War.

One night, as we huddled near the hearth with Grandmother, wrapped in shawls against the chill, Salwa burst in. "Miss Nurah, someone is asking for your father. A traveler from the north, a Shamaali, Ahmad bin Fursan. He says you would know him."

I locked eyes first with Mabrukah, then Nurah, then Grandmother. Ahmad had found us.

"Tell him Father will return soon from the market," Nurah said. "He is welcome. And of course, they can stay the night in the majlis."

"No, I will receive him myself," Grandmother said, rising and reaching for her cane. "Girls, go as we planned, right away. I will keep him here, but you must hurry." We peered through the secret window into the majlis. It was indeed Ahmad, and with him, a Solubba tracker. We watched Grandmother enter the room with a majestic air. The men greeted her with deference, and a sickening wave of panic filled my chest. We had to get away.

Yahya led Mabrukah and me through back streets, riding donkeys fully veiled and wrapped in heavy cloaks, as if we were going on a social visit. Even though we had made plans for Ahmad's appearance in Unaizah, I was still in shock that he had found us. None of us doubted his bad intentions.

There was no moon, and low clouds raced above. Yahya lit a lamp at the edge of town and led us deep into the palm forest, to Uncle Duhaim's farm, where al-Sahba and the camel were stabled. The wind rattled through the palm branches, hurrying us along. We came to a simple adobe house, where the farmer Zaki and his wife Zainab welcomed us inside. We hardly slept that night, wondering how he'd found us.

Two days later, Grandmother rode out to visit us. "God knows how strange the world of men is," she said. "The first night was fairly cordial. When Duhaim came home, he met Ahmad and the other one, a Solubba tracker named Thulaij. They talked into the night, discussing the war."

At first, Ahmad said he didn't know why we'd run away, that he and I had had a misunderstanding. When he asked if we were in the house, in perfect truth, Duhaim said we were not, adding that we were under his protection. Ahmad didn't ask to take me back. We decided he was waiting to discover more about the situation before stating his case.

The next morning, the two of them called at the Amir's majlis and explained they were visiting to reconcile me with Ahmad. The Amir gave no indication of surprise, but he repeated that I was under Duhaim's protection.

Grandmother continued. "Last night, they visited again. Duhaim said he knew about the poems, and, for the first time, Ahmad got angry, asking if you'd told him about them, or did he hear them in the bazaar, or from traders coming off the Nafud? Duhaim said you'd recited the poems, that he believed you were innocent. Ahmad insisted you had ruined his family name. He demanded to see you, but Duhaim refused again."

"After that, they moved to the travelers' inn on the town square. God knows what they'll do next." Then she sighed. "I'm afraid I'm not up to making many more rides out here."

The next morning, Zaki and his son left the house to repair a breach in an irrigation ditch. We women gathered in the kitchen. Zainab and Mabrukah cooked, while I told a story to their two daughters.

When a shadow crossed the threshold, I looked up, and the cold metal of fear flowed down my arms and legs. Ahmad stood there, rifle in hand, the tracker at his side. He smiled.

Zainab ran outside with the girls.

"As-salamu alaikum, wife." Ahmad's voice was sweet, his anger well-disguised.

"Wa alaikum as-salaam," I answered. The flash of his black eyes disarmed me for a moment, and made me question everything. Had I misjudged him? Had the Solubba woman been wrong? Did he still love me?

When Mabrukah tried to back out of the room, Thulaij grabbed her.

"And Mabrukah is with you too? Well, well, well. You crossed the Nafud, two women alone. Impressive. And you even brought al-Sahba with you. She looks to be in fine shape." She whinnied just outside; they were stealing her.

"I see you fear me, wife. There is no need for fear. How often I've thought of our only night together as husband and wife." I backed away as he approached, but he kept coming.

"Let me go!" Mabrukah cried, struggling in Thulaij's grip.

"The Sudanese has a lot of spirit."

"Take her outside and tie her up. You can have her later. Now, I want to be alone with my wife." His voice dripped with venom.

He set his gun down and backed me into a corner, grabbed my arms and twisted me around. Then he held me from behind and pushed me into the bedroom. He threw me down on the cushions and tried to claim me as his wife for the second time in our marriage. The more I fought him, the more he laughed. His eyes danced and sweat glistened at his temples.

"Thulaij, get in here!" he shouted. He sat on my legs and Thulaij held my arms above my head. Then Ahmad ripped open my caftan from the top. "See the body of my bride. How beautiful she is." He fondled me and, as I squirmed, he folded back the opening in my caftan. "See her glowing skin." Then he ripped even lower, revealing everything. "Now, look away, while a man takes his wife." He forced himself in me, then pulled away and stood up.

"She is full of lust, just like every other woman."

Thulaij looked down at me and smiled, taking in my naked form. "But she is beautiful."

"A beauty that too many eyes have seen, of whom too many ears have heard. Now she is common, like a watermelon. Everyone knows all about her sweetness." Ahmad drew a dagger from his boot. "Now that I'm finished with you, I'll make sure no other man can ever see you, hear you, or have you." He spread my thighs apart with his boots, even though I tried to squirm away. He crouched down over me and looked over my body. He was deciding where to cut me first.

My heart beat faster, but I pretended to be stiff with fear, like a rabbit waiting to see what terror a predator would inflict. I was planning for the right moment to pull Thulaij down on top of me, but I couldn't let on that I was about to act. Ahmad rolled the dagger in his right hand.

"Nooooo!" Zaki and his son shouted, rushing into the room. I slipped free and rolled over, covering myself. Zaki aimed a rifle at Ahmad, and his son aimed one at Thulaij. "Drop the knife," Zaki said. "Salma is under Duhaim's protection, and this is his property. You have no right to attack her here."

"She's my wife—I have the right to be with her anywhere on this earth. Besides, who is this little soldier with you? He's as tender as many young Turks I killed with my bare hands. You are no match for us, you'll see."

"Not on my property," Uncle Duhaim said in his most booming voice. He stepped into the room behind Zaki, with three of the Amir's men, rifles raised. "Take them to the jail," he said. The Amir's men grabbed them.

"But what is the charge? That I was with my wife?"

"That you trespassed, stole my mare, and were about to commit assault and perhaps murder. You are in a town. This is not the desert."

We owed our rescue to both Zainab and Duhaim. When they attacked, Zainab ran to get Zaki. An hour earlier, the innkeeper's son had told Duhaim that Ahmad and Thulaij left, provisioned for a long journey. Duhaim followed them, having a hunch that Ahmad had found out about the farm.

We were summoned to appear at the Amir's palace the next day after sunset prayers. Uncle Duhaim escorted me into the presence of the judge and the Amir. Then Ahmad and Thulaij were brought in.

The Amir spoke first. "I had hoped that your family could settle this dispute in private. However, since the Shamaali has tried to commit violence to a woman under the protection of a townsman, I had to get involved." He nodded to Uncle Duhaim to speak.

"Last week, Ahmad bin Fursan and the tracker Thulaij came to Unaizah to try to bring Salma back home. She does not want to go with them, because she believes Ahmad will kill her out of suspicion, baseless as it is, of adultery."

The judge turned to me. "Is it true? Do you wish to remain here?"

"Yes I do," I said.

He nodded. "You may leave." Mabrukah was waiting for me outside, and she escorted me to a room upstairs with a secret window so I could listen to the rest of the meeting. We looked through it as Ahmad stated his case. While he did not recite the poems, he said, "I wonder if you know that the poet of these vile verses is from your city. Abdallah al-Fusaihi. Lucky for him, he is not in the city now, or he would have paid for defaming us."

The town leaders looked at each other, no doubt in shock that a man of Unaizah was involved in this scandal. Uncle Duhaim held his head high throughout. As for me, I shut my eyes and covered my face in shame.

"After these poems started circulating, my entire family was disgraced, and they agree with me. She's an adulteress, and her running away proves it. But I forgive her, so I have come to take her home."

This was the first time Ahmad had spoken of forgiveness. But I didn't believe it, having watched him twirl a dagger blade inches from my bare skin.

"I see," said the judge. "And why were you at Duhaim's property in the oasis? Why did you steal the mare, and why were you attempting to harm your wife?"

"We were returning to the desert when I learned that Salma was staying at the farm. As you know, it is my right to take my wife home. Of course, she should ride her own mount."

"Why were you threatening her with a knife, and why was Thulaij holding her arms so she couldn't move?"

"She was resisting, you see. We were going to tie her up so we could get her on the horse. We were going to untie her once we got out of town."

"And why were her clothes ripped?"

"She fought us off as we were trying to get her ready to travel."

"So you say you had no intent to cut or harm your wife?"

"We only wanted to take her back home, for her own safety."

The judge leaned over and conferred with the Amir for a few moments. "In the strictest sense of the law, Ahmad, you can claim your wife and take her home," the judge said. "However, you have violated an important principle of society that extends from town to desert, and that is as ancient as both our people. Duhaim has given Salma his personal protection as long as she is on his property. In addition, three witnesses testified that you spoke of your intent to kill your wife. Furthermore, you were stealing property, since you took al-Sahba without the owner's permission. The mare is Duhaim's now; you had no right to take her. Therefore, you must leave this town tonight and never return. We advise you to divorce Salma, since she does not wish to go with you."

I think it took Ahmad a moment to realize I was about to win, to be out of his reach forever, no matter how much the poems had charred his ego. When he spoke next, his voice boiled. "She is my wife, as you say, and if you want me to leave this town and never return I will comply. I shall never return to this city, and I shall never look at her again, on two conditions. First, Salma must never return to our tribe. After all, she deserted the women and children during war. Second, I will not divorce her. No, she will instead live her life as an abandoned wife, since that's what she wanted in the first place. She'll have no husband, no children, no grandchildren, and no tribe. She will be dead to us. She chose to leave us behind, so she shall have her wish."

"But young man," the judge said. "Wouldn't a divorce sever your ties to her? Why would you want to remain married to her?"

"As long as those poems circulate in the desert and the town, my honor and my family are tied to her. So why shouldn't she be tied to me? No, let her live out what she started. And you, Duhaim, now you and your family can also share in the scandal."

Ignoring the issue of the poems, Duhaim said, "If you do not grant her a divorce, there is no guarantee she will not contact her family and return to them. Even if you divorce her, she still has the right to visit them."

"In any case, I won't divorce her. That is my final word."

"I see there is nothing further to discuss," the judge said. "She remains under Duhaim's protection."

Ahmad must have known I was listening, for as they stood to leave, he spoke. "O woman, you are cursed. You will never have children, you will never return to your family. That poet's words have burned your fate forever. If you should try to return, I will see that desert justice prevails and you will breathe your last."

We slept in the safety of the town guesthouse that night. The next morning, the Amir's men tracked the two men far out into the desert.

After Ahmad left, I entered a season of profound sadness as black as the storms that rained upon us. The fears and sorrows of the last year rose in me. I cried myself to sleep each night as the wind howled. Circles as dark as deep desert wells grew under my eyes. Grandmother and Nurah let me stay away from lessons, but that only worsened my state of mind, for I had nothing to distract me from my sorrow.

Unless Ahmad died and left me a widow, I could never marry. I would never know the joy of suckling a baby, or of teaching a daughter to weave and to ride. I would be dependent on others, and, when I grew old, no one would sit by my bed and watch over me. And how would I learn if Ahmad died? Only Ahmad and Thulaij knew where I was, and I was certain they would tell my family I was dead, or that they'd never found me. And now the poems had pulled Duhaim, Grandmother, and Nurah into my shame.

When I managed to fall asleep, I dreamed Ahmad came for me again. I would scream myself awake, to find Grandmother sitting next to me, her hands on my shoulders, or Amina reading prayers and Qur'an verses over me. In lucid moments, I prayed for strength and guidance, but I heard no answers. There was only blackness and hopelessness.

CHAPTER 28

THE TENT OF MEMORY

FOR DAYS, I locked myself in our room and kept my windows shuttered. When the girls read from the Qur'an each morning, I covered my head to block the sound. I hated for anyone, even Grandmother, to touch me. Mabrukah told the girls I was sick, and needed to rest. Makrouhi even sent her doll Maryem to my bed to cheer me up.

Then one night I dreamed my mother was sitting next to me, her face lit by the glow of a crackling campfire. "Don't be afraid," she said. "I will always love you. Have courage. You will find your way." She reached out and cupped my cheeks with her hands, then she was gone. I sat up in bed. There was no one there. Yet the dream had calmed me, and for the first time in many weeks, the searing in my heart stopped. I opened the bedroom shutters to find the half moon standing guard overhead, and I sat on the windowsill until a bright star rose above the horizon at dawn.

Though I still had no answers about my future, those few loving words in my dream brought me back from despair. Nurah, Grandmother, and Uncle Duhaim knew how bleak my future would be, that a normal life of wife and mother was cut off from me, maybe forever. They didn't question why I was feeling better; they just accepted it.

I was once more in Grandmother's debt, for, while I hid myself away, she and Nurah called on Abdallah's family and told them everything. They had heard of the poems, but had no idea who inspired or who had written them. They were horrified that Abdallah's verses had caused so much trouble to one of the town's leading families. That meeting among the women of the two households was enough to quell the gossips, even though the poems became legendary and were woven into folksongs you can still hear in Unaizah to this day.

One afternoon, I found Grandmother reading from a great volume in her room, a red Kashmiri shawl drawn about her shoulders. She removed her precious reading glasses and folded them in her lap. She closed the book and laid it aside, then beckoned me to sit and asked how I was.

"Aside from helping with the girls, I have nothing to offer the household in return for everything you have done for me," I said. "I can ride, track, and shoot a gun. I can guard a herd for hours, and gather stray lambs with ease. But of what use are such skills in this town? The Armenian brides can sew and cook. They improve their homes every day. I have nothing to contribute."

"Ah," Grandmother said, smiling. "I see you're getting back to your normal self. Your mind is working like a sawani, always going back and forth." Then she paused. "Did you know that Mabrukah has set up a loom? Yes, while you were ill, she started. I'm not implying that you should become a weaver, for that is more suitable for her. She can make a little income and gain some independence."

"But I need that, too," I said. "My parents didn't raise me to live like this. I have to do something."

"I have an idea," she said. "You can't sell it at market, and it isn't something you do with your hands. It's done with your mind, and it will call on all your skills. I want you to learn how to tell stories."

"Tell stories?" My heart sank. Would this be my destiny? I could only envision the old women back home telling tales to the children. Was I to become a hag with missing teeth and cackling voice, waving my bent fingers like a spider spinning webs? When I was a little girl, the storytellers scared me. They told terrible tales of death and revenge, of misguided and bewitched lovers, and of magical creatures that spoke. They warned us of the dangerous world outside our father's tents, so we wouldn't stray far, so that we wouldn't make bad decisions that would lead us into danger.

"I see this proposal doesn't sing in your heart." Grandmother said, giving me a penetrating gaze. Then, she put her glasses on and opened her book. "I wouldn't want to teach you this art if it doesn't interest you."

"I'm sorry, it's just I'm so confused now."

"I see. Well, perhaps I am mistaken about you in any case."

Just then, Makrouhi came to the door. She'd scraped her knee playing outside, and I rose to help her.

We were drinking tea that evening when our neighbor Sherifah called on us. She was hosting relatives from the nearby city of Buraidah for a wedding. She asked Grandmother to tell stories at a ladies' party. Grandmother agreed, adding that I would accompany her.

On the appointed night, we set out on foot, wrapped in heavy woolen cloaks. I carried a lantern and held Grandmother's hand. We walked above the everyday world across the network of rooftop walkways and peered into the courtyards of our neighbors' homes. Most windows were shuttered from the cold, but lamplight shone here and there. Cats crouched on the rooftops. The stars lit the heavens.

When we arrived at the neighbor's house, a servant led us to the salon where a roomful of women, all talking at once, sat on the floor, knee to knee, two or three rows deep. The visiting ladies wore austere dresses of plain dark wool. We Unaizahns were exotic birds in comparison. Our dresses of rich green and dark blue were edged in colorful embroidery. We wore our hair loose, or wove it in braids, our tresses glistening with hennaed auburn tones, our eyes traced in kohl. Shiny silver earrings danced from our ears. Hardly a neck wasn't adorned with a jingling necklace. Few arms were without a row of clinking bangles. All this silver shone bright in the hearth light.

Grandmother was seated in the place of honor, next to the oldest lady visiting from Buraida. It was so crowded that even though I sat far from Grandmother and near the door, I was touching the arms and legs of four different ladies around me. The women grew quiet; Grandmother was about to start.

"In the name of God, the Merciful, the Compassionate," she said. "It is an honor to be here this evening, at the invitation of your kind hostess, one of the most distinguished women of our town. It is also a pleasure to meet visitors from our sister city Buraidah, may it always prosper." Her voice was powerful, as if it were that of a much younger woman.

The visitors nodded at these pleasantries, and, from their smiles, it was obvious that Grandmother had charmed them. When she paused, they shifted around and the sea of women's faces turned to her like a skyful of golden moons.

"I understand that, for many of you, this is your first visit to Unaizah. I bid you a heartfelt welcome. In honor of your visit, I will share a tale or two about our two towns, from generations ago. This first one is older than my great grandmother's mother. She heard this story from her grandmother; may God have mercy on their souls, and the souls of all our mothers and grandmothers.

"Yes indeed," the women murmured. It seemed as if she was calling up their memory, and that their faces hovered above us in the firelight, watching and listening from the hereafter.

"This is a true story. If you doubt its veracity, Amina, the wife of our imam, is here, and she can confirm its truth."

When they turned to her, she tilted her head. "I take refuge in God!"

Everyone laughed, then Grandmother continued. "Yes, it is a true story my dears. Perhaps some of you older ladies have heard this one. It is about the fish and the falcon."

The matron next to Grandmother said in a soft girlish voice, "I haven't heard this story in years. In fact, I can't remember much of it anymore."

Grandmother patted her knee. "Don't worry, my dear. I'll bring it back to you once again. So, if you are all comfortable now, and you are ready, we shall begin."

That night, she told three tales from the intertwined lore of Unaizah and Buraidah. The young were captivated to hear them, many for the first time, and the older people delighted to hear them again. When she finished her third story, the servants brought more tea and pastries. We stood up to leave and made the rounds saying goodbye, kissing cheeks of Buraidahns and Unaizahns alike, all of them smiling and thanking Grandmother over and over. Sharifah walked us to the door and slipped some coins into Grandmother's hand. I was proud to be there with her, to see the magic she wove with her words.

"Remember, stories are not just children's fairy tales," Grandmother said as we crossed the rooftops toward home. "We also tell legends and true stories from history. Stories don't exist on their own. Like the poems the reciters spread through the desert, stories are alive. But they only have a life, and can only exist, if there is someone to tell them. Stories connect us from age to age. We need storytellers in each generation who can remember and retell the stories of those who have come before, so the chain of our stories can live on."

She waited for me to respond. "But how could I do all that?" I asked. "And how do you keep it all straight in your head?"

"I know how your mind works," Grandmother said. "Nothing escapes you. You notice what people say, how they say it, and the way they move and look while they speak. People speak these three languages at once, but only the true listener notices them."

She was right. I did watch and listen when someone spoke. It was something my mother had taught me.

"And you have a good memory. You recounted the names of all the women who were camped with you in Wadi Sirhan, and the lineage of your mother and mother-in-law. And when you recited Abdallah's poems, you imitated the nuances of a desert poet that only a true listener would notice."

"I'll teach you where stories hide, who has them, and how to get people to tell them to you. Then I'll show you how to keep them safe in the tent of your memory. You'll have other teachers, too. Already in Unaizah, one has agreed to instruct you. But we must start right away. Only God knows how long I have left on this earth."

I was silent, overcome by doubt. She took my hand. "For years, I have prayed for someone to take this knowledge, and then you appeared from the desert. Despite your troubles, and the road you are forced to travel, you have the freedom and independence to learn. I have been looking for someone to help me, and here you are. It is God's will."

I began to learn the art of storytelling when I was 17, in the early spring of 1918. Setting off on this new journey renewed my spirit, even though I didn't know where it would take me.

"Let's start with the beginnings of stories," Grandmother said. "Here in al-Qasim, we always say, 'There was one, and God is One, all praise be His.' In other places, the Arabs say, 'Kaan ya maa kaan.' You can choose how to start your stories. So, let's start. Tell me the stories you heard the other night."

I recited the stories, unaware how remarkable it was that I had memorized them after just one hearing. I imitated Grandmother's mannerisms, mimicking her as best I could.

"Very nice," she said, folding her hands. I soon learned that was a sign she was preparing to correct me. "Now, tell me just one of them, and don't imitate me anymore. Say it your own way, but don't leave anything out."

I retold the first story. "Much better," she said with a smile. She taught me new stories every day, and my mind was soon filled with tales of talking animals and all manner of mysterious and magical occurrences. Grandmother also took the time to teach me the history of al-Qasim and legends from the old Arabian cities. Many of these stories had poems or famous sayings in them, perhaps only a line or two, but I had to remember them because they were crucial to the story.

She tested me, asking me to recite a line of poetry from a story, or to tell an entire story on the spot. She'd do this in the evening, or while visiting us in class, if there was something that illustrated a point we were learning. The girls loved it. Soon, they asked me to tell them stories each night.

Grandmother wanted me to learn poetry, too. Poets spun verses so important tribal events would be remembered, for, in those days, nothing was considered real history until it was memorialized in a poem. Poetry reciters roamed the desert, spreading verses among the tribes and towns. When you recite a poem, you must remember its exact words, so events mentioned in them are better preserved. While great poems are difficult to compose, they remain for generations.

My poetry teacher was an old man named Samir who lived out in the palm forest near Uncle Duhaim's farm. He was born in the desert among the tribes, but ran off and signed up with an Ageyli crew going to India, where he stayed for many years. When he returned, he married a girl from town, and they lived on a date farm. He was in great demand at the Amir's majlis, for he was the best poetry reciter in town.

Learning poetry was much more difficult than learning stories, but owing to his patience, I learned. Mabrukah and I would ride our donkeys to their farm after classes. He liked to sit on a stone wall near a small waterfall. His wife would bring us tea, and she would join us. In bad weather, we met in their tiny majlis, the floor of which, like Uncle Duhaim's, was covered with sand from the Nafud. My mind would be bursting full after an hour or two. Then he'd nod his head. "Enough, my dear."

From him I also learned the history of Unaizah. It is an ancient town, always ruled by an Amir from among the townspeople, just as when we lived there. For hundreds of years, its citizens traded and traveled long distances, cultivated their lush gardens, and welcomed pilgrims on their way to the holy cities of Medina and Mecca. In 1818, the Egyptian General Ibrahim Pasha invaded Arabia on behalf of the Ottoman Turks, breaking down the first Saudi state that had expanded into al-Qasim from the southern part of Najd. For nearly 100 years, the Turks kept a small garrison at Unaizah. In 1904, the town swore allegiance to the Saudi leader from Najd, Amir Abd al-Aziz, aligning themselves with his rising star. Abd al-Aziz tolerated the Turkish presence until they left for good in 1906, never to return.

Many days, Samir led us on walks through the palm forest. Even though he was well into his seventh decade, he was still a dashing figure, swinging his walking stick in time with his stroll. He'd lead us along the streamside paths that wound through orchards in the palm groves. He'd pause at the sound of a birdcall, smiling, saying nothing. Later, we would emerge from the palms' shade to feel the full strength of the sun beating down. We'd walk among small sand hills, then we'd climb with him to the top of a dune and look back at the oasis.

You know, my dears, it was from Samir that Mabrukah and I learned the secret to happiness: walking outside in the fresh air, as often as possible, to a pleasant place where you can clear your mind.

CHAPTER 29

The Year of Mercy

Unaizah
June 1918

WE EXPERIENCED more heat in the summer of 1918 than Mabrukah and I had ever known in the desert. That year, the month-long fast in Ramadan occurred in hottest summer, yet the heat couldn't dampen the festive atmosphere. Uncle Duhaim hosted guests at his coffee hearth each night, for, in Unaizah, heat was no excuse for a host to shirk his duty. Grandmother was called to many late-night gatherings to tell stories, and she often took all of us with her. She would have me tell one story, to give me practice.

Summer's end brought two events of great excitement. First, Vartanush married into the highly regarded Ghassan family. Then the Amir of Najd, Abd al-Aziz himself, visited the town. He loved Unaizah for its shady gardens and legendary hospitality. He had visited many times and on one trip, he had married an Unaizahn beauty from the Dhukair family. An acquaintance of Nurah's, his bride still lived at home. She'd borne him a daughter and named her al-Jawhara, after her husband's favorite, most senior wife.

The Najdi Amir had an entourage of a hundred men, most of them soldiers. He also brought Shaikh Falaby, an Englishman who spoke Arabic. While Unaizah was always hospitable to foreign travelers, Englishmen were our most exotic visitors, and they were considered mysterious, legendary characters. Years before, another Englishman, Captain Shakespeare, had visited with Abd al-Aziz. Decades before him, a mysterious man calling himself Khalil wandered into town on his own. Grandmother claimed to have seen Khalil herself, walking in the marketplace. She said he dressed like a poor man, even though he could read and knew medicine.

Abd al-Aziz and his men brought news of the Great War. The mighty Ottoman Empire was about to fall apart. The Armenian girls were giddy with delight, anxious to learn the fate of their families and villages, wondering whether they would ever return.

Meanwhile, Abd al-Aziz continued building his army with fearsome Ikhwan fighters. Trained by strict preachers to carry out jihad against the Amir's enemies, they began attacking everyone, even people from their own tribes, for being less-than-perfect Muslims.

The wise leaders of Unaizah had made an agreement with Abd al-Aziz that the Ikhwan were to camp outside the city. When they entered to buy goods, they were not to disturb the residents. You see, the locals feared the Ikhwan would try to take over the city. You could hardly imagine otherwise, the way they glared at the townspeople.

The campaign of Abd al-Aziz to capture Hail from his rivals, the Ibn Rashid family, began to affect us. Trade between al-Qasim and the Shammar Mountains was blocked to squeeze the Ibn Rashid into submission. Smugglers were everywhere, and auction prices fluctuated wildly, driven by fear of shortages.

Then came the sickness. It blew into our lives in the winter of 1918, with harsh winter winds and driving rains.

It started when several men at the Amir's guesthouse fell ill with fever. One of them had left Riyadh feeling fine, but, by the time he reached Unaizah, he was coughing and turning blue. The next day, five more men in the guesthouse got sick.

At the start, we didn't pay much attention, for people were always getting sick in winter. By the next night, however, we knew this was different. Half the sick men died, and several more travelers staying in the guesthouse fell ill.

At first, no one told us that the victims suffered terrible pain. They bled from their mouths, noses, and eyes, just one or two days after getting sick. Strangest of all, this scourge sought out healthy young adults. Within a week, a hundred people had caught the illness. Some were sick for several days, complaining only of cough, fever, and chills. Most of these got better. But others fell ill and died within hours. Two men at the public auction, bidding on a shipment of wheat, fell over dead like trees cut with a farmer's axe. Soon, five or six people were dying every day. Amina led us in prayers for the sick and dying.

In those days, no one knew how diseases passed from person to person. As the plague spread, the traditional healers would sit beside the sick with their ears and nose stopped with cotton fabric, reading Qur'an verses. Many healers got sick and died, too.

One day, the Sudanese servant Yahya started coughing and writhing in pain. He began to bleed from his mouth and nose. He turned blue, just like the others, and shook from chills, then plunged into a fever. He grew delirious and spoke as if his mother was with him, slipping into his native language. God called him, and he was dead by morning, as if he'd been burned from the inside out.

Coughing punctuated prayers at the mosque, where each morning they read off the names of those who had died. Entire families were wiped out in the course of two weeks. It was as if a swarm of djinn flew through the city, hunting for healthy young people.

We stayed home and burned incense in every room to cleanse the air. Uncle Duhaim closed his business and his coffee hearth. The city auction was cut back to once a week. The few people who ventured outside covered their nostrils and mouths, and plugged their ears.

Each morning, we heard the neighbors wailing over those who had died in the night. The families brought their dead out to the street. Sometimes the corpses were wrapped in just a blanket or cloak, since there was no time to wash and prepare them. The Amir's men piled the corpses onto donkeys and camels and took them to the cemetery. All day, people mourned and coughed, the sounds muffled by the walls and shuttered windows.

No one mourned in public. This was in part because of our stoic faith, but, after a while, it felt like Death itself had moved to town. The souls of those who had gone to paradise seemed close at hand, lingering, as if in shock at the swiftness of their fate.

A little boy from Suresh and Karim's home came looking for me one morning. Suresh had fallen ill and was asking to see me. The boy led me through a maze of alleys into the gardens that divided our neighborhoods. As we walked, I thought of Suresh's new-found happiness. She'd escaped the war, walked a thousand miles to safety, married a kind young man, and was pregnant. And now this.

I found her lying on a cushion beneath a window. Her eyes were closed, and her breath rattled. Her chest heaved and she moaned, talking to herself in Turkish. Blood trickled from the corner of her mouth.

I bit my hand and turned away. Seeing her like this broke my heart. Gathering my courage, I said, "It's me, Salma." I wiped her mouth with a cloth.

She opened her eyes. "Thank God you came. It's horrible, this sickness." Then she started to cough.

"The strangest thing is, when I'm asleep, my mother is with me. I'm back home, and my family is all around me. They are smiling and waving to me, telling me to come closer. Salma, I think I'm dying."

"You must fight, you can pull through this." I dabbed the sweat from her forehead. "I'll bring the girls to see you tomorrow. Get some rest now."

The next morning, after the dead had been taken away, I set out with the girls to visit Suresh. When we reached the gardens, they skipped and sang, enjoying the warm sunshine, defying the fear that had settled over the city.

Karim met me at the door, looking worried. "She is worse. She didn't sleep last night, and now the blisters have come out on her skin. She speaks only Turkish."

"Has she stopped bleeding?"

"At least that is good news."

When I entered the room, Suresh nodded, then looked ahead with a blank stare. I poured her a cup of tea. She sat up and drank it, smiling through her obvious pain.

The girls stood just outside the window and looked in, speaking to her in Turkish. Suresh responded, but at first spoke as if she was dreaming. The girls laughed at something she said, and she leaned forward and looked out the window, as if seeing them for the first time. Nazeh held Makrouhi up to the window so she could see her sister.

"Thank you for this. God bless you," Suresh said, then switched back to Turkish, addressing the girls with a strong voice, girding all her powers of concentration. The girls started to cry. Then she turned to me. "Please, promise me if something happens, take care of Makrouhi."

"Of course," I answered. "She is safe with us."

"Now, if you don't mind, I'm a bit tired." She started coughing again. I couldn't help but notice the blisters on her forearms where her sleeves were pushed back.

The next morning, sharp pains woke me, as if someone was stabbing my arms and legs with a knife. I coughed and strained to breathe. It was my turn to face the plague. Though I'd seen others with the blue lips and the bleeding mouth, my fevered mind didn't recognize what was happening.

Characters from the stories I was learning flew in the window and talked to me. Between hallucinations, the daylight hours passed as if each minute was a day in itself. The Armenian girls prayed over me in Turkish, and incense filled the room. When someone took my hand, or grasped my shoulder, I would emerge from my fever for a moment before spinning back into my dreams. Grandmother had to feed me, holding up the tea glass or the bowl of buttermilk, because my arms were numb and I couldn't move. Each morning, I listened for the wailing, then men's voices on the street below. I would fall back to sleep, relieved that no one seemed to be crying inside our house.

The bleeding stopped, and I gained strength, but when I tried to stand, my legs wobbled and I was unsteady on my feet. When Grandmother brought me food, it was all I could do to smile. I wondered whether the disease had left me mad.

One day, I managed to say, "Grandmother, I'm seeing things."

"Ahh, you can speak! God willing, you'll be fine. Just have patience. He has tested you, and your will has triumphed. Be glad, Salma, you are fortunate."

"Who else…?"

She sighed. "Well, right now Mabrukah is fighting, too. Nurah is sick, but not as bad as you."

"God keep them safe. Uncle Duhaim?"

"He is coughing and very tired, but he has a mild case. May God protect him."

"You?"

"I am fine."

"Suresh?"

Grandmother shut her eyes and shook her head. "I'm sorry, God called her two nights ago. God rest her soul." Grandmother held me close as I cried, my shoulders shaking.

Once my lucidity returned, I spent my afternoons with Makrouhi. She seemed lost without Suresh, her last living relative. She was truly alone in the world. We tried as best we could to surround her with love.

In Riyadh, Mecca, and Medina, the sickness was just as harsh. No family was untouched. Amir Abd al-Aziz lost his first-born son, Turki, as well as two other sons and his favorite wife al-Jawhara.

Desert travelers came upon encampments whose inhabitants had died, their camels and sheep still tethered nearby. Riderless horses and camels wandered into town. Flocks of sheep and goats ran wild in the Nafud. I wondered how my family had fared. Who lived and who had died? Were my parents still living? My brothers, sisters? And Ahmad? Was I a widow, free to marry again?

We learned that the plague had ravaged Europe and India, even America. People speculated that we were being chastised for the Great War, that God had sent this disease to punish Europe for its arrogance. Yet not one country on earth escaped the terror. They say that one in four adults in Unaizah had died.

It took months for the plague to subside, but at last one day it was gone. In the wake of the sickness, the good people of Unaizah opened their hearts to the orphans.

By the time it had passed, World War I was over and the whole world had been chastened. Millions had died from fighting, and then this terrible sickness. We believed that this plague was God's will, and those who died were reunited with their loved ones in Paradise. I'm sure you've heard old-timers refer to it as the Year of Mercy, when God called so many to His side.

CHAPTER 30

NURAH'S CHOICE

Unaizah
March 1919

AFTER THE sickness passed, Duhaim turned his attention to finding Nurah a husband. At twenty years old, she should have at least been engaged, but whenever we suggested a groom, she always had excuses.

"I can't leave Baba and Grandmother alone," she would say. "And now with you two and the girls living here, my place is here, at home with all of you."

Her first cousin, to whom she had long been promised, had been in Bombay for years, and had not written to claim her. So Nurah remained unmarried, even as her married friends had their second and third children.

Little did we know that her life was about to change faster than anyone could imagine. In the course of one week, she was engaged and married. All because of something the Amir's wife said. Just one sentence. Never doubt, my dears, that words can change everything.

The Amir Abd al-Aziz had returned to town to visit his young Unaizahn wife. Memories of the plague were weighing on his heart, and he needed a change of scenery. He brought along his sister, Princess Murjanah and her entourage, and it was quite exciting for such a distinguished lady to visit the town. In her honor, the wife of Unaizah's Amir hosted a ladies' party at their oasis gardens. Grandmother, Nurah, and I were invited.

The party took place on a raised platform covered with fine carpets, set among palms so thick it was like a forest. The hostess and guest of honor sat in French-style gilded chairs, the rest of us on bright-colored woven cushions. The women from the Ghassan family arrived just as we did. Vartanush was with them, resplendent in a green silk caftan that set off her copper-hued tresses. The princess wore a silk tulle gown of deep purple, embroidered in gold. We kissed her hand and greeted her with the special things you say to princesses, like Hayaak Allah, ta'aal amrik, May God give you long life. My dears, can you all try this? Yes, yes very good. Indeed, you are all as elegant as princesses.

It was very rare to be so dressed up outside, sitting on pillows in a palm-forest garden, our faces unveiled, our best jewelry glinting in the filtered sunlight. A bulbul warbled, and water gurgled over a small waterfall in a nearby stream, fitting accompaniment to the ladies' quiet conversation.

Murjanah was married to an Amir from the Ruwala tribe, Shaikh Sattam al-Nawwaf. We learned she was looking for a bride for her son. The young man was a distant relative of ours, since the Banu Shamaal often intermarried with the Ruwala.

Princess Murjanah asked the Amir's wife about each of us. When she reached Vartanush, the Amir's wife explained how the Armenian girls were rescued by two brave Shamaali lads. Noticing that this had captivated the royal guest, the Amir's wife added, "In fact, one of those Shamaali boys is sitting with us this very moment."

"God forbid!" Murjanah said. "What do you mean? Are we not all female here, before God? I see no men!"

"That young lady over there," she said, pointing at me. "She ran away across the Nafud disguised as her male cousin. It was she and her servant who rescued the Armenian girls and brought them here."

"Hah!" the princess said, laughing. "Truly, we have heard many tales about Armenians coming to Najd. So, my dear," she said to me. "And you found refuge here?"

Grandmother nodded to me, so I said, "Yes, may God give you long life. My cousin's family took me in, and Uncle Duhaim gave me his personal protection against my husband, who tried to take me back to the desert to kill me."

"And your husband, did he divorce you?"

"No," the Amir's wife said. "He refuses. He does not want her to remarry, or to have children."

"God protect you. And you, Nurah, you've a kind heart, to give refuge to your cousin."

"She also took in the Armenian girls, all ten of them," the Amir's wife added. "Now she has the four youngest in her home. The imam's wife is teaching them to read and write."

"May God give you strength," the princess said to Nurah.

"Thank you, your highness," she answered. "It is my grandmother's heart that is the biggest."

"Truly," the princess said, smiling at Grandmother. "I can see you have had a lot of tumult in your house. May God strengthen you!"

After that, there was a long silence, and we heard only the sound of the waterfall. No one moved. A breeze caressed our faces. We drank tea, and ate some sweets and fruit, while the older women made small talk. When the princess stood to take her leave, we lined up to bid her farewell.

Murjanah shook hands with Grandmother. "You have a lovely girl here, and her character is written on her face as plain as sunshine. Please come to us this evening, and have supper with us. And bring your granddaughter and the young Shamaaliyyah and her companion along, too."

"We would be honored, your Highness," Grandmother said without hesitation. As we left, the young wife of Abd al-Aziz held up al-Jawhara, her curly-haired baby, to receive kisses from the departing guests.

"Well, my son, it seems we may have a decision to make."

"Oh?" Uncle Duhaim said before popping an olive into his mouth. "What decision?"

"The Amira Murjanah is interested in Nurah as a bride for her son Fawwaz, who fights at his uncle's side. She has asked us to supper tonight, but I suspect a proposal is coming."

"Isn't it possible she just wants to enjoy your company?"

Grandmother shook her head. "It was the way she spoke of Nurah's character. By my life, I believe she's assessing Nurah as a bride."

Nurah looked up in surprise.

Uncle Duhaim chewed another olive before speaking. "I dearly wish your cousin had returned from Bombay. Since he is delayed, my daughter, you are vulnerable to them. On the face of it, it would be a good proposal. But there are consequences of marrying into that family."

"What do you mean, Father?" Nurah asked. I think she was already fascinated with the idea of marrying Fawwaz.

"You'd be well cared for, certainly. Yet you wouldn't have the stability of a Qasimi husband. You might be divorced if you don't have sons, or if you displeased your husband. You'd live at the whim of your mother-in-law."

"How is this different from any marriage? Don't the same rules apply?"

"Well, yes, but they're not part of our family, our town. Your life would be so much easier with your cousin and his father's family. If you married this young man and moved to Riyadh and lived among strangers, how could we protect you?" Then he said, "Go tonight. I'll find out what I can about Fawwaz."

That evening, as we got ready to go, I watched Nurah apply kohl to her eyes with a small silver wand. Grandmother swept into the room and took her in her arms. "Don't worry, my darling. You do have a say in this. Remember, you are the equal of those women. Do not ever think otherwise. You are, after all, my granddaughter."

As we rode from home for the second time that day, I wondered what would happen to Mabrukah and me if Nurah married outside the family. Would we be sent away? Would we stay on with Uncle Duhaim?

The servants led us to a comfortable salon in the Amir's house, which was filled with women and girls, relatives of the royal visitor. Aside from us, the only local women in attendance were the wife of the Amir and the young local wife of Abd al-Aziz.

Massive tamarisk wooden doors opened at the opposite end of the room, and Princess Murjanah entered. We all stood to greet her. She sat next to Grandmother, and it seemed we were the honored guests. I began to think Grandmother had been right.

"May God give you long life," Grandmother began, "I trust you are enjoying your visit to al-Qasim."

"Yes, now I see why my brother loves this place so much. Your people are as gentle and as generous as your oasis gardens."

"We in turn are honored to be both your guests and your hosts," Grandmother said. "Your highness, I hope your family is well. With the sickness, we have all suffered so much this last year."

"I lost a daughter, about the age of your granddaughter here, God rest her soul. But He wanted to take her, as He took so many fine young ones. We trust they are in Paradise and someday we will join them. God willing it is over now, they all rest in peace," she said. Then she changed the subject, addressing me. "Salma, tell us the story of your journey, how you came to al-Qasim."

Grandmother smiled at me. She had warned me I might have to retell the tale. I sat up straight and took a deep breath. "Bismillah al-Rahman al-Rahim," I intoned, and the room fell silent. Then the strangest thing happened. For a few moments, I daydreamed I was out in the desert on a cliff, about to address a great crowd, thousands of people before me as far as I could see. They were waiting for me to speak. Then, in the next instant, I was back in the lamplit room, and the women were waiting. "It happened because of a poem."

As I told the story, Princess Murjanah couldn't contain herself and interrupted. "How did you manage to cross without a guide? How did you sneak through al-Jawf? How did you avoid robbers?" When I answered, she shook her head in disbelief, then waved her hand for me to continue.

After I finished the tale, we made polite conversation until we were called to a sumptuous dinner. Afterward, we returned to the salon for tea, but Grandmother and Princess Murjanah were missing. When they later rejoined us, something had shifted in the atmosphere. Princess Murjanah turned to me. "Your story brings me so many memories. No matter how grand my palace is, and how fine the comforts of the city are, I miss the open air, the smell of the wind after a rainstorm, clean and full of moisture. And there is, of course, nothing like fresh camel's milk when you are thirsty and exhausted from a day of riding. So many things. Each winter, we ride out to the desert and camp for a week, just so we can relive those days, to recapture that life, at least for a time."

"Funny how we only remember the good from our youth," Grandmother said.

We each reveled in our memories in silence. The happy days in my mother's tent washed over me, and my eyes teared up. I wiped them away, hoping no one noticed.

"Salma, I see you miss it, too," Murjanah said.

"Yes, may God give you long life."

Uncle Duhaim was waiting at the gate. Dusting off her cloak, Grandmother said, "It is as we thought."

She said nothing more until we were all seated in the women's majlis upstairs with the doors closed. "My dear granddaughter, Princess Murjanah is certain you would make an excellent bride for her son."

Uncle Duhaim put his arm around Nurah, and she burrowed her head in his shoulder.

Grandmother continued. "After dinner, Murjanah took me aside and told me her son had lost his bride, his first cousin, to the sickness. He's heartbroken, for they were in love and had been married only a few months. He asked his mother to find him a new bride, one who can read and write. He plans to live in the city one day and would like to be able to talk to his wife about the wider world."

"When she asked why you were still unmarried, I described your duties. She said you were a noble young lady, one she would be proud to have as a daughter-in-law. Then she said, 'Would you consider my son as a groom? I think they might be a good match.'"

"I said it would depend on you, Nurah, and of course you, Duhaim. She said Fawwaz is intelligent and considerate. He visits her often. This is a good sign, Nurah. You can learn a lot about a man from the way he treats his mother."

"My dear," Uncle Duhaim said, lifting her chin. "Perhaps I reacted too hastily before. Certainly there are good men among the al-Saud, and I'm told many of their wives stay with their own families. Of course, you might have to give up your children, especially your sons, when they get older, so they can go to school with the other princes. But you could still see them. I will only consent to this proposal if Fawwaz is suitable. If you want, we will insist you meet him first, and then we can decide. Furthermore, I will propose you be allowed to live here with us at first. Or if you prefer to wait for your cousin, just say so."

Tears filled Nurah's eyes. "I don't want to leave you all. I've never been so happy these last years, despite the war and the sickness. I could never go off with a stranger."

"Think about it tonight, give us your answer in the morning. If you say yes, we will make sure there are no surprises."

The next morning, zaghareed echoed through the house. It was Grandmother announcing Nurah's answer.

Princess Murjanah agreed to all the terms, and Nurah's bride price was very generous. Uncle Duhaim said it equaled the amount he would have to pay to buy his own house, one of the finest in town. Then, if she were later divorced, Nurah would receive an allowance that would support her well, even if she remarried.

Since Fawwaz would be off fighting with Amir Abd al-Aziz, it was agreed that at first Nurah would live at home. That meant, for the time being, Mabrukah and I would be able to stay on at Uncle Duhaim's. But for how long?

With potential terms agreed, the couple met. The marriage contract was drawn up and signed, and the wedding took place three days later. Yet even with her generous dowry, Uncle Duhaim and Princess Murjanah didn't spend much on the celebration, compared to what people pay for weddings today. Remember, Arabia was a poor country then. This was years before they discovered oil. Yet we celebrated that modest wedding with great joy. Having lost friends and loved ones in the epidemic, we were grateful for this occasion to celebrate life, and, in this case, what was to become a great marriage.

CHAPTER 31

THE WORD OF A KING

MOST PEOPLE don't know this, but Abd al-Aziz liked to spend time every afternoon with his female relations. It's true, for we saw it with our own eyes.

A week after the wedding, Murjanah invited Grandmother, Uncle Duhaim, Mabrukah, and me for a visit. When we arrived, Princess Murjanah turned to me. "Salma," she said. "My brother would like to hear about your journey. I'm afraid I couldn't resist telling him about you. Don't be nervous. Just answer his questions."

Though many amirs and shaikhs had visited our tents in the desert, we women had always stayed behind the tent dividers. This was different. I was to meet the Amir Abd al-Aziz, face to face, and I had to act perfectly, especially since he happened to be my cousin's new relation.

Sensing my unease, Murjanah put her arm around me. "Don't worry. He will direct the conversation."

Before I had a chance to grow any more nervous, the door to the salon opened, and Abd al-Aziz strode in. We stood at once. I was astonished at his great height. As Princess Murjanah presented us, we each said, "It is an honor, may God give you long life."

As he gazed down at me, his eyes filled with amusement and disbelief. "You are the Shamaaliyyah who rode across the Nafud on a hennaed white mare without a guide? And this is Mabrukah?"

"Yes, I take refuge in God." I bowed my head slightly.

"Well, I admit I am intrigued by what Murjanah told me about you two. She said you wouldn't mind telling me yourself. I hope that is true." I nodded.

He beckoned us all to sit back down. "Tell me something of your family."

I began to recite my lineage, stopping when he raised his fingers. "Ah yes," he said, "So you are Raghda's daughter, are you not?" I nodded. "Then you are a shaikhah of your own people."

"Yes, your highness, I suppose so," I answered, though for many months I had thought of myself as an outcast. I was amazed he knew my mother's name, but then she was so highly regarded. I'm sure I mentioned before that people used to call my Uncle Talal "Raghda's brother."

Heavy silence filled the room as he looked at me. I felt as if he would understand not only everything I said, but everything I left unspoken. Could he read my thoughts? They say he judged people in an instant. I looked down at my hands and waited for him to speak.

"You are a strong-willed woman. That is clear. But how can I be sure you really crossed the Nafud? After all, you are a storyteller, so you could have made it up!"

I liked the sound of his voice. Each sentence came out like a melody, and his hands swept through the air when he spoke. He reminded me of my Uncle Talal. I looked up at him and smiled, and my fear began to fade as I relaxed in the face of his charm.

"Perhaps there is a question you would like to ask to test me."

"Yes, good idea. You do not fear this?" I shook my head, smiling.

"Hah! You are brave! What is the most unusual thing about al-Jubbah, the village between al-Jawf and Hail, right in the middle of the Nafud?"

That was easy. "There are no flies there. Not a single one."

"Yes, that's correct!" he said, clapping his hands and smiling. Then he explained to the others: "It is so far out in the middle of the Nafud that even if flies travel with a caravan, they can't survive that long in the dryness of the desert. Strange, isn't it? So tell me, how did you manage to pass through al-Jawf and Hail without being discovered?"

He interrupted my answers with dramatic comments, "fantastic, unbelievable, by God," and my favorite, "by my beard."

Then he said, "Is it true, that two poems and an angry husband caused this great adventure?" At his insistence, I recited them both.

Before he spoke, Murjanah said, "You might have your doubts about her story. I know I did, but I confirmed it all through my own very reliable sources." She turned to me and winked. Then she went on, "Last year, her husband tried to take her back to the desert." She explained how Ahmad refused to divorce me, so I couldn't remarry.

"A hard-hearted man. And do you still fear him?" he asked.

"Yes, your highness, but this is a fear I must live with. Thank God I have had such a kind protector in Uncle Duhaim."

Abd al-Aziz was silent for a moment. "Salma, you are a brave young woman, though I wonder if you question your choice to run away." My head bowed, I nodded, tears filling my eyes. "Well," he continued, "this decision can't be undone, and now your husband has wronged you. It is indeed a difficult path you chose." He paused again, then said, "Perhaps I can help. I offer you my personal protection."

I never expected this. I looked up toward Grandmother, her eyebrows arched high in delighted surprise. It took me several moments to gather my wits.

"May God give you long life, thank you, and may God bless you for your kindness," I managed to murmur, before I turned to Princess Murjanah. "And may God bless you and grant you happiness and health." Kneeling before her, I kissed her right hand. It was improper for me to approach Abd al-Aziz like that, but I could express my gratitude to her. She gestured for me to sit down.

"What I ask in return," Abd al-Aziz said, "Is that you and Mabrukah stay with my nephew Fawwaz and his new family. Educate their children in the ways of the desert. Tell them the old stories and poems. Teach them the courage and morals of the tribes. I fear that, with time, we will forget the ways of our forefathers. The world outside is changing quickly. The electricity, telegrams, aeroplanes, automobiles—all these things will find their way into our land. The young generation will need strength to resist them, and to resist the Europeans who will bring them to us. I think we can make use of these new machines, but only if we are strong. The Ikhwan would have us keep all this change and all these foreigners out, while at the same time erasing our own history in the name of our faith. We must not do this. We must remember our old ways and our history, because along with our faith, those things will give us the strength we will need. So Salma, stay with them and keep this old world alive."

I nodded in agreement. "I will do it, Sir, God willing."

Then he leaned back and smiled at us all. "Yes, God willing. And may He make the newlyweds fruitful and happy."

"Yes indeed," Princess Murjanah and Grandmother said. "May God bless them with a fine family."

Then he turned to Grandmother and Uncle Duhaim. "You will be rewarded in heaven for taking in all these runaways. I wish all hearts were as open and genuine as yours. May God preserve you and your family."

"Thank you, your Highness," Grandmother said. "May God protect you and your family."

"May He give us all wisdom," he said. "Thank you for spending time with me. It is rare these days when I am able to rest in such a fine town among such fascinating persons. Now, if you'll excuse me, I believe it is nearly sunset."

As he rose, we stood with him and said, "In God's care, may God give you long life."

I knew his protection was important, but only with the passing of years and decades did its true meaning become clear. With that sentence, my life changed. No matter where I went in his realm, Abd al-Aziz, who later became the ruler of all Saudi Arabia, would personally protect me. No one, not even Ahmad, could harm us.

After the wedding, Fawwaz returned to military campaigns, and we helped Nurah furnish private rooms in her father's house. Fawwaz and his men visited every few months, and it wasn't long before the midwife confirmed Nurah was pregnant. Her first child was a healthy boy, named Sattam for his paternal grandfather. Nurah gave Fawwaz three more children – two more boys, and a girl named Asma, the mother of the young Amira Nurah you know today. These days, a woman is expected to have five or six children. But then, having four healthy babies was a singular blessing.

As each child arrived, the house grew noisier, and the pace of life quickened. The years flew by, and we married off all the Armenian girls but Makrouhi, who was still too young. Meanwhile, Princess Murjanah commissioned Mabrukah to weave a tent divider. That job took a full year, but it was well worth it, for after that, Mabrukah kept busy filling commissions for distinguished clients.

Nurah's brother Ghazi returned from Cairo after a five-year absence. He would laugh, saying that it had been so quiet at home when he was young that he could sit and read a book for hours, hearing only the cooing of doves. "Father," he would say, "I don't know how you can deal with all this commotion."

Ghazi announced that, seeing as he was nearly 30 and a successful merchant, it was time to marry. Grandmother and Nurah suggested several brides from the town's best families, but after considering them, he realized he'd been smitten by his second cousin Dalia, who he'd met in Medina on his way home. A proposal was set in motion, and, before we knew it, another wing of the house was filled with the furnishings of a young family. We were not surprised by his attraction to her, for she was a stunning beauty with wide-set dark eyes and milky skin.

As the al-Hamdan family grew, so did the realm of Abd al-Aziz. First, he and his men won the loyalty of tribes and towns to the east, all the way to the shores of the Gulf. In 1924 and 1925, the important Hijazi cities of Taif, Mecca, Medinah, and Jeddah all became part of his realm. The "taking" of Taif had been a disaster. The fanatic Ikhwan fighters had gotten out of control. They entered Taif ahead of Abd al-Aziz and killed hundreds of people before the town surrendered. Fawwaz told us the Ikhwan had become a big problem for the Amir, so we were all relieved to hear Abd al-Aziz entered Mecca in peace, on foot, dressed in the simple white cloth of a pilgrim. When news reached us that Medina and Jeddah had surrendered to him, I never imagined we would move there one day.

In the winter of 1926, it rained for two weeks straight, then the weather turned bitter cold. It even snowed, and the water in the courtyard pool froze. Grandmother began complaining that she couldn't get warm. She caught a severe cold, and a rattling started in her chest. We moved her to the women's salon and kept a fire going there all day. With our ministrations of broth and tea, she seemed to improve. Then she complained again of pains in her chest. She weakened, then started coughing up blood and said her time was coming. We never left her alone, not for a second. An Iraqi doctor, who was visiting relatives in Unaizah, examined her and said it was pneumonia. We did everything we could for her, but it was her time.

Uncle Duhaim kept a vigil on her last night. She stopped breathing an hour or so before dawn, a smile on her face. All night, she had been moving her lips in her sleep, as if she were talking to someone. May God rest her soul. It was she who gave me this golden cup. Each time I drink from it, I think of her and our stories.

Grandmother lived to be almost 80 years old. She was very ancient for those times, and she was the last living lady of her generation in town. After she passed away, the link to her generation and those old days began to fade.

Meanwhile, our world turned outward. When Fawwaz bought a home in Jeddah, Nurah agreed to move there. With Ghazi and Dalia firmly ensconced in the big house, Uncle Duhaim would not be left alone. Makrouhi was only 12, still too young to marry, and she preferred to remain near the other girls, so the newlyweds agreed to keep her. Dalia hadn't yet had children, and she adored the girl.

CHAPTER 32

HOUSE IN THE BALAD

Jeddah
Spring 1926

THE MORNING we left Unaizah, tears flooded the alleyway outside the courtyard, the same door through which the Armenian girls began their new lives years before. All of us– Nurah, Mabrukah, Dalia, all the Armenian girls, and Nurah's daughters– had slept in the women's salon the night before, talking long into the night, savoring our last hours together in the old house, promising to hold fast to our friendships.

As we rode toward the city's southwest gate to pick up the westward road to Medina, I tried to burn the sights and sounds of that dear place into my memory. None of us could know the way of life we were leaving behind would linger a while in the memory of a few old-timers and then fade away.

Moving such a long distance was not an easy thing, for there were very few automobiles in Arabia then, and no paved roads, so we rode camels and horses. Fawwaz hired men to transport all our possessions on camelback, even our beds and furniture.

All the women and girls except me rode camels, sitting inside litters draped with colorful tassels that swayed with each step of their mounts.

As for me, I rode out in the open on horseback, for Uncle Duhaim had returned al-Sahba to me as a parting gift. Though by then she was nine years older, the mare thrived on the road, and so did I. I felt free and triumphant on that journey, without the fear that cloaked us when we ran away from home. This trip was luxurious. Fawwaz's men set up our tents each evening, and one of them cooked for us, too. At night, I told the children about our Nafud crossing.

Once we left al-Qasim, our hearts were lifted by the excitement of seeing the holy cities of Mecca and Medina. All our lives, we had heard about these cities and the pilgrims they attracted from around the world. At Medina, we marveled at the five minarets towering over the mosque where the Prophet (peace be upon him) is buried. We couldn't help but stare in fascination at the costumes of the pilgrims from Africa, China, and Morocco.

After a few days' rest in Medina, we took the ancient pilgrimage road south toward Mecca, where we were guests of Princess Murjanah's family. There, we performed the minor pilgrimage and prayed at the Grand Mosque.

The ladies of the Hijaz seemed so different from those of al-Qasim! They wore delicate lightweight caftans of silk and cotton, and wrapped their hair in white cotton and linen. As you know, Mabrukah still prefers this style to modern-day dresses, since it's custom-made for our climate. And besides, it's elegant, don't you agree?

It was May of 1926 when we began our life in the city of Jeddah. We rode our mounts into the city through the Mecca Gate. Back then, that was the limit of the city. It seemed we had entered an oven. We navigated the maze of crowded city streets in the full heat and humidity of day, with the scent of cumin hanging in the air. At last we turned into a shady alley and arrived at our new home, high up on the hill.

The old house still stands behind Nassif House at the top of Gabel Street. It's easy to spot, a marvelous old mansion with white paint and green mashrabiyya shutters. Like in many houses in the balad, camels used to carry water five stories up its central staircase to a tank on the roof.

Though twice the size of Duhaim's, and with many bedrooms and salons, the house had no interior courtyard or garden. Thankfully, it had a rooftop terrace. Wooden carved wind tunnels caught the sea air from the roof and funneled it to the floors below. On the rooftop, a carved teak loggia lined the walls, and potted hibiscus and bougainvillea provided color and shade.

From the rooftop, we watched the turquoise sea shimmering beneath a sky milky white with haze. I was mesmerized, for until that day I had never seen the ocean. A wooden gate stood along one wall of the roof. Just like in Unaizah, it opened onto a walkway to neighboring homes.

Despite the mansion's grand size, Mabrukah and I felt closed in. After all, we still had the desert in our hearts, and we had just come from a town filled with gardens. Nurah announced to Fawwaz that the children needed goat's milk. If we raised our own, she reasoned, it would be more economical than relying on others.

Early each morning, Mabrukah and I dressed as Hijazi tribeswomen and took the goats out to find food and water. In this way, we explored the city. That, my dears, is how we have kept fit so many years. Those daily walks, up and down the hills.

You can still find the old house today. On its outside wall, you can even see the space where the sign once hung with Nurah's name on it. Yes, my dears, families then were proud to display the name of the woman of the house on each great home.

At that time, Jeddah had no paved roads, and we didn't get electricity until the 1930s. In summer, the heat and humidity were so intense we couldn't move. Fawwaz bought another house on the outskirts of Taif, and we moved there each summer. Once we got into the rhythm of this yearly trip to the mountains, we enjoyed the Hijazi life. Mabrukah set up her loom on the roof, and I told and retold the tales Grandmother taught me.

Nurah and her husband flourished as parents. Their boys attended the earliest schools, and their daughter Asma studied with private tutors. Fawwaz's businesses prospered. He assisted the Amir of Hijaz, Prince Faisal, in many of his projects, and became a regular visitor at Faisal's majlis. Nurah helped many poor families in the city. Each year, Princess Murjanah visited us for a month or two. Uncle Duhaim and Ghazi came many times. As the roads improved, the trip grew less arduous.

When Makrouhi married a few years later and moved from town with her groom, we lost track of the Armenian girls. You see, by then so many families had left Unaizah in search of new opportunities. Indeed, it seemed the whole city of Unaizah was disbanding. As you know, the Sulaiman family was put in charge of the kingdom's treasury. Other men from the town were tapped in the new Saudi state, for their industriousness and talent in commerce.

When the Americans discovered oil in 1938, many men from Unaizah moved to the Eastern Province to work in the oil fields, and they took their families with them. God only knows what became of our Armenian sisters, if any of them are even still alive. God bless them all, they were so brave.

As the years passed, and more of Fawwaz's northern relatives settled in Jeddah, the familiar accents of our youth began to echo in the house. Poets played the rababa and sang in the majlis. They danced the dahhah, and we sang the old wedding songs again. I was always introduced as a distant Shamaali cousin of Nurah's, and I entertained many visitors with stories. One night, Fawwaz invited us to the majlis so we could listen to a visiting poet recite the two poems about me. No one except Nurah's closest family knew my true identity, and my exile from my own people continued.

Jeddah welcomed us in its own way. Mabrukah and I found new friends in the city, and they became like a second family to us. Our life there has been richer than we could have imagined. Did you know, I even met the great Egyptian singer Um Kulthum when she came to Jeddah? Yes indeed. What an evening it was, being among the elite and artistic people of Jeddah, both men and women. It was like a dream.

In the 1950s, Fawwaz built the house in Ruwais. Nurah made sure that the grounds were shaded with many trees, and in time it blossomed into a lush reminder of our Unaizah days. It's the same house where we live now. Of course, they have updated it and added on. The family still keeps goats for their milk, so we can take them out in the morning on our walks. Then, it seemed, we blinked our eyes, and their children were marrying and having children of their own. By that time, I had become a busy storyteller, fulfilling my promise to King Abd al-Aziz by telling tales of the old days in the desert and the town.

Before we knew it, automobiles were speeding down the streets. By 1960, Fawwaz had two of them. That was the year Nurah died of cancer, God rest her soul. We never knew she was ill until there was nothing to do about it. We mourned her deeply, for, without her, we would never have survived even one day outside the desert.

Even though he was a white-haired gentleman, Fawwaz could have remarried a much younger woman, but he wouldn't have it. Luckily for us, his family never questioned our place and let us stay there. When Fawwaz passed away a few years later, his granddaughter, the young Nurah you've met, Fawzia, assured us we were welcome to live on as part of the family. She had always been close to her grandmother of the same name, and she grew up listening to our tales.

How quickly we have grown old, and yet I still feel like a young girl. And I still dream of al-Sahba, and our journey. Praise God for keeping us safe, I take refuge in Him, and may He have mercy on us all, and on the kind souls who helped us. He is the Victor, the Protector, who aids those in need. And unto Him we all return.

CHAPTER 33

GRANDMOTHER

Wadi al-Bu'ur
September 1980

WE SAT in silence, waiting for more. But there was no more. Salma had reached the end of her tale. The children slept, but the adults were wide awake. No one spoke, for we all knew the next words would seal the end of Salma's saga. We all preferred for it to echo on in our minds.

Without saying a word, Salim and the neighbors rose, nodded to Salma and Mabrukah, and stepped into the night. I remained by the fire, trying to hold onto her story. Salma and Mabrukah sat with me, and still no words were spoken, though I had so many questions.

Only when Mabrukah went off to bed, when Salma and I were finally alone, did I speak. "Did your family ever learn the truth?"

"Yes, God bless her, Nurah found my mother and we traveled to Amman to visit her. This was in the 1950s. At last I could tell her everything, and she wept when she learned that King Abd al-Aziz had protected me. Ahmad had indeed told everyone I had died running away, so this reunion brought my mother great joy. I reunited with my sister and met my many nieces and nephews. By that time, my father and Ahmad had passed away. Thankfully, their anger went with them."

"So that means you didn't die after all, to your people. They learned what really happened, after all those years."

"Indeed, that is so, you are right, my dear," Salma said. "How I miss them all." Then she began to cry. I went to her side and hugged her, trying to comfort the one who had given me so much comfort.

Another question jumped to my lips before I could stop it. "What happened to Abdallah?" Throughout Salma's story, I kept returning to this question. Would he find her again?

She sighed, then smiled. "You and your questions! I'm surprised no one else has had the courage to ask me. The answer is simple. I never saw him again. He truly vanished. And, since he had destroyed my young life with his indiscretions, I admit I had no desire to see him again. My anger toward him smoldered for years. Then, as the decades passed, my heart softened. We had both been so young, and we both made mistakes. How stupid I was to linger with him, to lead him on! I should have known better. Yet his words ruined my world, and forgiveness has not been easy."

She paused, and for once I had the sense to remain quiet, waiting for her to go on.

"Telling my own story has laid bare the truths of my life. There has been so much goodness. Despite my unwise decisions along the way, I was so lucky to find the good heart of Uncle Duhaim and his mother, not to speak of the great fortune of having the king's protection. Yet the bitter truth is that Abd al-Aziz gave me only one task, to help save our heritage. I have failed him in the end, for the stories are going to die with me."

"But I have it all on tape." My tape recorder had been running every night. I had gone through dozens of batteries, and Salim made several trips to town to buy blank cassettes for me.

"It's not enough to have them stored in a recording or even written on paper. You have to hear them told to you, so they become part of you. The last stage is that you tell them again, passing them on. It is not only the content of the stories, but the very act of telling and retelling them that is our heritage. Over the decades, I have told and retold them. But it seems now there is no one to carry this on. In the end, I have failed."

What could I say to her? She had shared every detail of her life with us, and it was her own story that mattered to me more than her folktales. She had given me this greatest gift, her own story.

For a second, I didn't know what to say. Then the words came. "I will never hear the voices of my grandmothers, but I have heard yours. I have never held their hands, but I can hold yours. And I can never know their stories, but now I know all of yours. So even though you don't have any grandchildren of your own, I would be honored if you would consider me your granddaughter, the granddaughter of your heart."

Salma smiled and held my hands tight in hers. "Which makes me the grandmother of your heart."

I kissed her hands in gratitude.

"How lucky I am that you found me that morning in Jeddah, and that you have these impulses to speak, and to ask. Never lose that, my dear. Praise God, to be so old and to find such a friend is a rare blessing."

I wiped my tears. "I wish I could live here with you both, for good."

"We wish you could stay, for you've brought us the hope of youth, but you must go on. Remember, even in our patched-together lives, with all our mistakes and regrets, God showed us our way. We found happiness and love, and friendships with the most unlikely people in the strangest places."

Salma's story had lit my days like a beacon, and, in its glow, I had let go of my troubles and worries. And it wasn't just me, for she carried us all away with her. We felt as though we were with Salma and Mabrukah at every stage of their journey.

I couldn't help thinking how lucky they were. What if Uncle Duhaim hadn't been such a good judge of character? What would have happened?

It was inevitable that I measured my own father against Uncle Duhaim. If I'd asked such a thing of him, would he have accepted me? Baba did have a loving heart, and watching him comfort Mama after Mecca proved it. But still, times were different, and running away for good would be far more complicated for me.

Compared with Salma and Mabrukah's daring and courage, and their unbelievable luck in finding those Ageylis who helped them make it safely to Unaizah, my problems seemed superficial in comparison. But then I remembered Ibtisam, and my heart opened up in sadness.

I often wondered what my family would say if they knew I was living a country girl's life. I was sure they would have been astonished to see me milking goats and gathering eggs early in the morning from the chickens we shared with Um Saleh. I learned to wash clothes the old-fashioned way, with a washboard, and to build a wood fire inside the hut, as well as out in the bath house where we did our washing.

My days were not filled solely with chores, as Salma and Mabrukah always gave me time to paint. I walked in the hills to sketch, but my favorite place to paint was on the roof, where I could catch the cool breezes and see everything just like a bird in flight. The roof became my private studio, open to the sky.

I made studies of the wildflowers and roses, landscapes of the farms, and watercolors of the sky at dawn and dusk. I sketched the women of the wadi working at their looms and made portraits of Um Saleh's children. I drew the rooms of the stone house, and Salim sitting outside his hut. After Mama sent Hamdi up to the wadi with art supplies, I began a large canvas in oils of Salma telling her story by firelight. Um Saleh and her children sat with Salim in the background, entranced.

I sketched scenes from Salma's own story, too, like the mare al-Sahba after she'd been hennaed, redrawing her until Salma and Mabrukah told me I'd gotten it just right. I made a study of the Armenian girls dancing around the fire on their last night on the road, trying to capture my own love for the dance in the canvas. Before long, paint decorated my dresses. Charcoal blackened my fingertips. Wood smoke and turpentine became my perfume.

"She's a storyteller. It's her art to make things up," Um Saleh said as I sketched her working in her garden one day. "I don't believe everything in her story. Really, how can we possibly know what's true and what isn't? Maybe it's all made up." Then she sighed and thought for a minute. "But you know, even if it isn't true, I want my children to believe it's possible those two girls were that brave."

Even though I'd extended my visit to last the summer, all too soon it was time for me to go home. Tarek arrived, seeming more relaxed than ever. He joked with the children next door and disappeared all day with Salim, doing who knows what. When he filled me in on news from home, I realized it would be hard to slip back into my old life as if nothing had changed.

On my last night, I sat alone on the roof and took up the burden of losing Ibtisam and Hisham once more. I would always hold tight to the sweet memories of my summer there, and of Salma, the grandmother of my broken heart.

Jeddah
1980

I don't believe in a land
Where thorns and cares
Are my share of its yield
While the harvest belongs to others.

- A Sailor's Memoirs by Muhammad al-Fayiz

CHAPTER 34

A Hallway Filled with Books

Jeddah
September 1980

JEDDAH SEEMED like a big anthill. Who were all these people and where were they going in such a rush? It was marvelous to stand in a hot shower and get really clean. As I dried off with a luxurious fluffy towel, my skin seemed rosier, my arms and legs more powerful. And I was happy the calm and strength I'd found in the wadi had stayed with me.

A few days later, the phone rang while we were having coffee after lunch. "It's for you, Fawzia," Tarek said, handing me the phone and grinning, he whispered, "She sounds so serious." I elbowed him in response as I took the receiver.

"Miss Fawzia? My name is Farhat, Farhat al-Batarji. Do you recall your family mentioning a young man named Marwan, who was with Ibtisam in the mosque? Well, he's my brother, and he asked me to find you. He needs to speak with you about her, in confidence. Please come to our house for tea. Don't worry, we are an honorable family, and I will be there, too."

Farhat lived in an old Mecca neighborhood of winding narrow streets. The directions were complicated, but Hamdi was sure he could find the house, having driven Ibtisam around Mecca for years. Even so, it tested every ounce of Hamdi's patience, and he had to ask the way three times. He found a parking spot in an alley. Wiping his brow with a handkerchief, he opened the car door for me and whispered, "O Lord." The house stood on a steep alley, and a handful of narrow marble steps led to a double door of intricate carved teak. Hamdi knocked, and a small door panel opened, just large enough for a person to step through. An Asian maid smiled and beckoned me inside.

"I won't be too long," I told Hamdi. "An hour and a half, maximum."

"Very well," he said, wiped his brow again, and walked back down the alleyway. He would wait in a nearby café.

Once inside, I took off my sandals and set them next to several pairs of small-sized men's and women's shoes. The maid led me along a hallway lined floor to ceiling with bookshelves and into a small salon furnished with low sofas of carved teak with inlay, cushioned in soothing moss green. The floor was covered with a thick Chinese carpet of sculpted flowers and birds. The house smelled of incense, an exotic mix of jasmine and patchouli.

Farhat and her brother Marwan entered the room. Their almond, upturned eyes and round faces bespoke their ancestors, Indonesian pilgrims who had settled in Mecca generations ago.

Once we were seated, Marwan smiled at me. "I can see you are Ibtisam's sister. You have the same nose and eyes."

"No, she was much more beautiful than me, and more courageous."

"How much time do you have?" he said.

"There's no place I need to be."

"Then I will tell you the important parts now. I hope we will continue to talk about her after today, that you will be our friend. Your sister made a great impression on me. She was a true Muslim, and I will never forget her or her courage."

"Our family had spent that night in prayer, just as yours had, and we were behind you when they shot your brother and took Ibtisam. I remember the rebel leading Ibtisam up the ramp toward the main courtyard. As they passed, she was scolding him, saying, "Shame on you for violating God's house!" Then, when it was our turn to climb out, a rebel grabbed me, just as I had pushed the last of my family through the window. My sister and parents screamed as the rebels took me away.

"Back in the courtyard, the rebels were trying to convince more worshippers to join them. Those of us who refused to join them numbered about a hundred. They held us in a group at gunpoint. I have never felt so alone, Fawzia, so afraid for my life. While we knew the government would overpower them, it was obvious the rebels feared nothing and would not hesitate to kill us if we got in their way.

"After the noonday prayer, the rebels shot at troops from the minarets. Then the rebel leader Juhaiman ordered the guards to blindfold us and bind our hands. They kept us in the courtyard until nightfall. Helicopters flew overhead. Men shouted, firing their weapons. Thus the rebels began their long and hopeless battle.

"The first night, they brought us to a carpeted room. It was not uncomfortable, save for the fact that we were tied up and blindfolded. The women hostages, along with the rebels' own small children, were nearby. We could hear them sobbing and praying.

"They removed our blindfolds to feed us some dates and give us water just before the evening prayer, but they kept us tied up. I'll never forget how it was to pray with my hands tied in front of me. Already the authorities had cut the power, so it was dark. I stayed awake all night, expecting it to end any minute. All night, men barked orders in their harsh desert accents, moving equipment and arms in preparation for the coming battle.

"Early the next morning, the sound of helicopters and explosions woke us. The government was attacking at last. I was sure we'd be freed any moment. But my hopes were dashed when they led us down two flights of stairs, the women behind us. They divided us, three to a room, in small offices along a single hallway, and removed our blindfolds. Dim light from the rebels' gas lanterns filtered through screens over the doors.

"We stayed down there for two more days, marked by moments of wrenching fear followed by hours of the worst kind of boredom. We heard bombs and machine gun fire, as well as occasional screaming, but we never knew who was winning. So many times, I was sure we'd be rescued, but government troops didn't come. Once in a while, young boys, the children of the rebels, walked down the hall and stood outside our room and stared at us, fear in their eyes. I wondered how much they understood about what was happening.

"Listening to the women down the hall was a welcome distraction. One of them challenged our captors over and over. In a calm voice, she admonished the rebel women. She said they didn't have to follow their men in sin, that God and the government would forgive them if they surrendered and freed the hostages. This, of course, was Ibtisam.

"A man interrupted her, shouting, 'Silence! Until you join us on the right path, you will remain silent. For "the sound of a woman's voice is shameful,"' he said, quoting from the old scholars. We heard the sound of a single slap, then silence.

"She kept quiet for a while, but then she began reciting from the Qur'an, loud enough for us all to hear. No one stopped her. Her memory was flawless, her enunciation impeccable. She recited from the Surah of the Cow, Verse 286.

> *On no soul doth God place a burden greater than it can bear.*
> *It gets every good that it earns, and it suffers every ill that it earns.*
>
> *Our Lord! Condemn us not if we forget or fall into error; our Lord!*
> *Lay not on us a burden like that which Thou didst lay on those before us.*
> *Our Lord! Lay not on us a burden greater than we have strength to bear.*
> *Blot out our sins, and grant us forgiveness. Have mercy on us.*
> *Thou art our Protector; Grant us victory over the unbelievers.*

"I answered her with a verse from the Surah of Imran.

> *O God! Lord of Power and Rule, Thou givest Power to whom Thou pleasest,*
> *and Thou strippest off power from those Thou pleasest.*
> *Thou enduest with honour whom Thou pleasest,*
> *and Thou bringest low whom Thou pleasest.*
> *In Thy hand is all good. Verily, over all things Thou hast power.*
>
> *Thou causest the Night to gain on the Day. And Thou causest the day*
> *to gain on the night.*
> *Thou bringest the living out of the dead, and Thou bringest the dead*
> *out of the living.*
> *And thou givest sustenance to whom Thou pleasest, without measure…*
>   (Surah 3, verses 26-7).

"Then she said, 'Thank you, my brother, may God reward you and keep you safe.'

"'And you, sister,' I answered. I wondered who she was, this spirit who kept us sane, who prayed with us.

"The next day, I believe it was the fifth day, the women rebels wailed, 'The Mahdi has died; he was martyred. God help us.'

"The rebels moved some of us deeper beneath the mosque, to the subterranean labyrinth of the cellar, and our guards disappeared. All the hostages gathered in the hallway and talked. There were 25 of us, all in our twenties and thirties. Six were women. An immediate bond formed among us. Strange, how I felt I knew the soul of each of my fellow captives in such a short time.

"That was when I first met Ibtisam. I had wondered who she was, this wise young woman who said everything I should have said, and recited what I should have recited. When I saw her face, the sun rose in my heart.

"'These people are out of their minds,' she said. 'With their mahdi dead, what are they going to do now?' Her defiance made her more becoming. I'm sorry, Fawzia. My words must be a shock to you. Please forgive me, but I know Ibtisam would want you to know how I felt. She was like a beacon of truth and uprightness that shone for all of us there.

"Someone started coughing and gagging at the end of the hall. It was tear gas. Reza, an Iranian student who had been in many riots in Tehran, called out, 'Cover your faces, quick, your eyes and mouth and nose! Try not to breathe once it comes.' We slipped back into our rooms. Since our hands were tied, all we could do was bury our faces in our sleeves and arms. Reza curled up and buried his face between his knees, and I did the same.

"'It's not too intense,' Reza said, sitting up after a few minutes. 'We're lucky, but we need to get fresh air if we can. Come on, let's look for some stairs.'

"We found a stairwell down the hall and called to the others to join us. We huddled in the stairwell, gulping the fresh air streaming down from a doorway somewhere above. I was sure the end of the siege was near. There were to be many moments like that, when we thought it was over. God tested all of us, in ways that we couldn't have imagined.

"A group of women rebels carrying rifles found us crouched in the stairwell. They had on full abayas and burqas, so we could see only their eyes.

"'You, all of you, come with us!" they shouted, pulling us down another hallway, clear of tear gas. It was pitch black, and I leaned against the wall. They lit a kerosene lamp, and one of them held it high. She turned to us. 'Come on, then,' she said. They were tough, those tribal women, used to dealing with men, not afraid of anything, including death. Yet they were women, and when I look back on everything I know, that was the moment when we should have tried to escape.

"They took us down sloping tunnel-like hallways into a large room. There were more hostages there, as well as rebel women and children we hadn't seen before. There were no carpets, no chairs at all, just bare linoleum. It was a kind of storehouse, stockpiled with bags of bread, crates of dates, crackers, and cookies. Between battles, the women filled jugs of water from the well of Zamzam.

"They moved the male hostages to a large adjoining room, leaving the door open, so some light filtered in. That night, our young bodyguards reappeared, one of them carrying a lamp. They crept into our room, shined the light into our faces, and counted us all.

"As days passed, we began to realize that the government's primary concern was regaining control of the mosque. We were secondary. What else could they do? They didn't know how many of us there were, or even if any of us were alive.

"Each day, the rebels moved us to new rooms, because the government was trying all means of forcing the rebels out of the lower levels. Once, we heard water rushing, as if a pipe had burst. The government had put firehoses into the hallways and tried to electrocute the rebels. They used tear gas again, and, we learned later, even poison gas. But our captors had learned the secrets of the hallways and passageways of the cellar. They kept pulling us with them, deeper and deeper under the Kaaba.

"In the final days, they kept us in two adjoining rooms. When the guards were away, we men and women mixed together. And the rebels' own children stayed with us.

"Deep in the catacombs underneath the mosque, held in darkness and filth, in a room full of strangers, Ibtisam and I became friends. We shared our hopes and dreams for our careers, our love of scholarship, and our thirst for knowledge and wisdom.

"Our friendship was clear to everyone, and I think it gave us all hope. Despite the fact that we ate only dates, drank only water, and slept on the hard floor, I felt as if I was in a sunny green garden full of birdsong. My heart glowed with happiness even as our days of captivity lengthened. We had been brought together in this terrible battle between good and evil, yet it seemed so natural and so right that we should be together. It was as if God had given us no options, and opened the path to our friendship.

"Ibtisam blossomed before my eyes. Even as the rebels forced us to smear black dirt on our faces so we could be disguised in the dark, she was still lovely. Her eyes sparkled, and her teeth shone bright. Our clothes got dirtier each day, but she remained beautiful. And nothing could dim the fire that burned in my heart."

"The crackle of gunfire woke us early on the last day. Rifle shots and shouting answered machine gun fire. One of the women rebels lit a candle. She looked around at us all and said, 'They are close. Inshallah we will find victory today.' Then she stood up and left the room, leaving us in darkness. The rebel children remained with us, it was the safest place for them.

We scrambled to our feet. I felt for the wall. 'Let's get out of here!' Reza shouted. 'This is it!' But the gunfire was too close. We all crouched down as far from the door as we could, using empty food boxes and foam mattresses for cover.

"Shots erupted down the hall, and someone shined a strong light in the hallway so we could see what was going on. One of the rebels, backing down the hall, walked past our doorway. 'Come on, cowards, show yourselves,' he muttered, then fired down the hall. The bullets whirred and ricocheted, then silence.

"'Now!' a soldier yelled. After a blast of machine gun fire, soldiers charged down the hall. I curled my body into a tight ball. Rebels shot back. A rebel stepped into our room. We could see only his feet as he took a shot down the hallway. Then he was picked off with machine gun fire, and he fell to the floor, facing us. A pool of blood widened around his torso where he'd been hit. Half noticing us, he said, 'O Mahdi, wait for me in Paradise.' Then his eyes became vacant. In the silences between rounds, shell casings clinked to the ground.

"The rebels shouted, 'The winds of Paradise are blowing!' as they ran down the hall all at once, charging straight at the soldiers and shooting their automatic weapons.

"One long burst of machine gun fire took the last of them down. Bullets ricocheted everywhere. It seemed to last forever. Then the guns fell silent.

"'That's it then,' a soldier called out. 'Leave the dead for now. There are more down here.'

"I yelled as loud as I could, 'We are hostages hiding in here! Help us!'

"'Stop, the soldier said. 'Did you hear a voice?'

"'Sir!' I called out, 'We are hostages, we're all tied up here. There are women and children. Please, help us!'

"The soldier called, 'All of you, come out slowly and raise your hands.'

"'All our hands are tied,' I answered. 'Some of us can't move.'

"'Ibtisam is hit!' one of the women cried. She had insisted on lying on top of two young girls, daughters of the rebels. The girls sat next to her, whimpering. Ibtisam was lying on her side. I rolled her onto her back and held her head in my lap. 'Hold on, my dearest, we're free, the doctors are coming!'

"'I can't,' she said, her eyes fluttering open. 'God is waiting for me. It is my time. I will wait for you in heaven. Fi amaan Allah.'

"'Stay with me. The doctors are coming!' I cried. I held her hand as she moaned with her eyes shut. Then she opened her eyes and smiled at me. The medics pulled her onto a stretcher and took her away. Soldiers prevented me from following. Somehow, I knew she had already gone where I couldn't follow.

"While a few male hostages had been hit with bullets, their injuries were minor. Ibtisam was the only hostage fatality in our group, though I have heard that many in other parts of the mosque were caught in the crossfire.

"As we emerged into the sunlight, it felt wonderful to drink in fresh air with each breath. Yet I knew Ibtisam was gone, that I would never see her again. I had found the most precious thing on earth, then lost it. We walked to freedom through the courtyard swarming with security forces and medical personnel. Yet a part of me yearned to be back down in the cellars with Ibtisam."

Marwan wiped his eyes and I started to cry, wailing for them both. "I'm so sorry for you. I'm so sorry. Ibtisam, why did you have to go! Ibtisam! God, why?" Farhat let me cry, but kept her arms on my shoulder as I rocked back and forth. Marwan sat with his head bowed, his right hand covering his eyes, catching his own tears.

After a while, Farhat coaxed me to drink some tea. "You know Ibtisam would want you to be strong."

"Do your parents know?" I asked.

"Yes," Marwan said. "They have been mourning with me, but, beyond these walls, no one knows of us. I try to distract myself with my studies, knowing Ibtisam would want this. I have one more year to go for my doctorate."

"Marwan wants to become a judge, someday, God willing," Farhat said.

A wave of sadness overwhelmed me, thinking of how perfect those two would have been for each other, and how Ibtisam's death was my fault.

Farhat comforted me, no doubt thinking I was mourning Ibtisam in innocence. And since he had told me everything, I decided to tell him and his kind sister the reason we were at the mosque that day.

Farhat kept an arm around me as I spoke, which comforted me as I confessed everything, looking down in shame. "It is my fault that we were at the mosque that night. I am to blame for my own sister's death."

Marwan spoke first. "God comfort you, my sister. You must remember that Ibtisam was so devout. She chose that auspicious night to visit the mosque. But she was not alone, it was not her original idea. Many students had planned to be there. I was among them. You cannot take the blame for that. Yes, you did disobey your parents' expectations for you, and you deceived them and lied to meet this young man. But it was Ibtisam who chose not to tell your parents. It was Ibtisam who chose to go to the mosque that night. And it was Ibtisam who chose to stand up to the rebels. Do not carry the guilt of her choices on your own shoulders."

"Ibtisam was so forgiving and brave," I said. "I didn't deserve her, not after what I'd done."

"Love is unpredictable, there is no telling what any of us will do when we find someone so special and true. You say you have broken things off with Hisham."

I nodded. "It is impossible for me to marry a Shia; my family would never approve. We should have never begun meeting in the first place."

"And you love each other?" Marwan asked.

"Yes, we did."

"Then this is a matter for your family, it's got nothing to do with what is acceptable in Islam, because you would not be the first Sunni to marry a Shia," Marwan said. "The fact that you met at school is not your fault, since your parents sent you to a co-ed university. What would they expect? That you'd not talk to any of the boys? You must have courage, for Ibtisam's sake." Farhat nodded in agreement, smiling.

As we drank our tea in silence, my strength returned. "There are no words to express my thanks for this, to know what happened."

CHAPTER 35

CAFÉ DE LA MER

Jeddah
October 1980

I FILLED my fall calendar and resumed teaching freshman English, still reeling from what I had learned about Ibtisam. If my family only knew that she had finally found love, I'm sure it would give them some comfort. But I kept her secret, as she had kept mine. It was the only thing we still shared.

One evening after dinner, I was correcting essays in the family room. Bashir opened the door of the men's salon. "Tarek, Hisham's here. We're ready to watch the movie."

Hisham. My head jerked up when I heard his name. Hisham. I hadn't heard it for so long. It was a fairly common name. You can find Hishams in every Arab country from Iraq to Morocco. But in Saudi Arabia, it wasn't nearly as popular. I liked the name; it spoke of urbanity and education, of sophistication. My curiosity overcame my shock. I walked to the kitchen to make a cup of tea and stood for a moment by the closed door to the men's salon, listening. They were watching the movie Raging Bull. They'd been viewing it night after night with their friends.

"Hisham, have another Pepsi?" Bashir offered.

"Sure, thanks." It was his voice, a thunderclap on a sunny day. What was my Hisham doing here, in my own house, with my own brothers?

I stood at the front gate and peered into the street. A dark red Impala just like Hisham's was parked under the streetlight, halfway down the block. I couldn't read the license plate number, so I couldn't be certain. Back inside, teacup in hand, I walked to the family room, pausing near the salon door to eavesdrop. I still couldn't believe it.

"Have you see the new model Range Rover?" It was him again. "What a car! I test drove one yesterday. I can see why you like it. It's high off the ground, you can see everything from the driver's seat, and it's comfortable. I think I'll buy one." It was true. Hisham had made friends with my own brothers.

I wanted to burst into the salon, but I couldn't—our relationship had to stay secret. Had he tried to contact me? How had they met in the first place? What were the odds?

The next day, I went to Salma's home and was thankful she and Mabrukah had returned to Jeddah. But they hadn't turned on the air-conditioning. "I prefer the fresh air, no matter how hot or humid it is," Salma said, fanning herself with the newspaper.

"Aha," Salma said, after I'd explained the situation. "This Hisham of yours. He's cleverer than I thought. I'm beginning to like him."

"What do you mean?"

"He has no doubt been trying to contact you," she said. Mabrukah nodded in agreement.

"But that makes no sense! My brothers will never introduce me to him, and what if they find out we were close at AUB and were seeing each other in Jeddah! Maybe he's just trying to find out if I'm engaged to someone else. I've heard of young men who are so mad when their girlfriends break off with them that they take revenge for their hurt pride by telling the girl's brother about their romance, so the girl ends up punished."

"Come now, do you really think he's that kind?"

"No, you're right." I trusted Hisham. Since I hadn't heard from him, I assumed he had decided to go his own way. But what if he was furious over our breakup and wanted to cause trouble? No, I had to trust my instinct.

"First, let me ask you," Salma said. "If you had your absolute first choice in life, Fawzia, would you marry him, or have you grown apart?"

"I'd love to be his wife. He makes me feel safe and comfortable, and he respects me. And besides, I think he would be an excellent father. But our families will never allow it. He's Shia after all. So what's the point? It can never happen, it's impossible."

"Forget what you think is possible and what isn't. If Hisham is like you describe him, sure as the sky he's trying to contact you, to tell you he's willing to try again. The question is, are you?"

After I nodded, she went on: "I think he's waiting for you to send him a signal, that you know he is there, that you want to see him again."

"What kind of signal?"

"Don't you have any ideas?" Salma said. "I'm amazed at you! Your generation is supposed to be full of all kinds of tricks, going here and there, doing this and that, to see your friends. You're creative, think of something! We're not going to tell you what to do!" The two of them laughed, making it seem like it was the most natural thing in the world, and that they would know what to do if they were in my place. I left with no solution.

At lunch, Tarek started talking about a project he had won with a new joint venture with the Triangle Corp, a company owned by Hisham's family. It was a construction job to build National Guard outposts along the Red Sea, north from Obhur all the way to al-Wajh. I pretended not to pay more attention than usual to business talk at lunch.

"Bravo. How close was the bidding?" Baba seemed delighted that Tarek had won the contract on his own, without involving him in the process.

"Really close. The winning bid's price difference was only 200,000 riyals. There was one really low bid, but it was thrown out as non-compliant. I heard they left off the transportation part of it."

"Who submitted that bid?" Umar asked.

"The Farhan Brothers. And it's a shame, since they had some influence with the National Guard. What a waste when they underbid like that."

"So you like working with Hisham?"

"Yes, we never step on each other's toes."

"May this continue during the job. Well, good luck, son. I'd like to meet Hisham. Bring him by my office sometime."

"I'm surprised you haven't met him," Bashir said, chewing a piece of bread as he spoke. "Lately he seems to be here every evening. This might as well be their second office. All they do is talk shop. They pour over drawings in the salon at night. Drives me crazy."

The phone rang, and Baba started talking to someone overseas. The rest of us moved to the sitting room, and I savored my coffee, thinking about my next move. Why was this so hard? Then it came to me.

I'd been daydreaming about Café de la Mer in Beirut. Hisham and I would watch the sunset from its lovely outdoor terrace, festooned with flowerpots and vines. Its décor of turquoise blue and orange echoed the colors of the sea and the evening sky. The owner's wife was a potter, and she made demitasse coffee cups with a brilliant glaze that swirled the two colors together on each cup and saucer in an earthy texture. I loved the pottery so much I had bought a set just before graduation. I'd forgotten about it until that moment.

Later that afternoon when the house grew quiet, I found the cups and saucers tucked in a shoebox, high up in the kitchen cupboard. Each cup and saucer was wrapped in pages of al-Hayat newspaper, dated the week of my graduation. I unwrapped and washed them all, then arranged them on a round tray from which we always served coffee to guests. I took the box and wrapping into my room and reread the newspaper pages, memories flooding back.

I had no way of knowing whether Hisham visited that evening, for Mama and I went to a fundraiser for the Faisaliyyah Charitable Society, a contest testing high school girls' knowledge of poetry. They knew their material through and through, reciting ancient love poems, religious odes, and modern free verse. All the while, I wanted to respond with a rhyme I had composed for my own particular, private occasion.

> I laid out the cups in hopes of an answer.
> He'll put his lips on them and drink.
> May those cups bring me to him,
> May they let me drink again from his lips,
> And taste the sweetness of his mustache,
> As dark and fragrant as Yemen's finest brew.

Hisham's car wasn't there when we got home, and they were watching Raging Bull again. This was the fifth night in a row. Hisham would only want to watch it once, perhaps twice at the most. But he wouldn't be back until they grew tired of the movie. I'd have to be patient.

Neither Tarek nor Bashir said anything about the cups. We had several sets of demitasse cups anyway, and they were changed once in a while for variety. Besides, the men would never question why such a trivial thing was altered. So they stayed there, day after day, being cleaned and rearranged for the next night. Halimah noticed them, though, and asked me if I knew anything about them. I explained that I'd brought them back from Beirut, that they brought back memories of old friends. Knowing that they had a special meaning, she began to serve me coffee in one of those cups each afternoon. Once she even winked at me when she handed me the cup. How much did she read into things?

A few nights later, I went shopping with Mama and Aunt Rosette. We were looking for outfits for my aunt to start off her trip to the Riviera. I always loved shopping with Aunt Rosette because she made every shopping trip into a party. First, we visited a French daywear shop that a Saudi woman ran from her home. It was a comfortable atmosphere where Rosette could try on dresses and debate the merits of each ensemble. Later, we went to some of the better shops downtown. We didn't set out for home until the market closed around 11 p.m. It was all I could do to keep from shouting when I saw the dark red Impala parked on the street outside the house. I was sure he would recognize the sign. This would be the test—would he signal me in return?

As I lay in bed that night, I imagined the impossible, being Hisham's wife. I prayed to God that the impossible be made possible.

The next day, Hisham was waiting for me outside school. Luckily, Mama needed the car that day, and I was going to take a cab home. He stood there like he used to, playing the grouchy brother. He turned as I approached him, and I followed him, my heart pounding. He opened the door to the car for me. The smell of the leather welcomed me as I sank into the luxurious upholstery. Just like old times.

The second he closed the car door and we were alone, he looked right and left to see if anyone was watching. Then he gazed at me with a huge smile and said, "Well, Fawzia, thank God! Do you know how long I've been working with Tarek and coming to your house? The entire summer. Why didn't you signal me sooner?"

"I've been up in Taif visiting Salma. I just came back last week, and heard Tarek utter your name when you were over watching Raging Bull. That was the first moment I knew you were around. Then it took me a couple of days to figure out how to signal you."

He laughed, pulling out of the parking lot and pressing down hard on the gas pedal to get away from the university crowds. "I can't tell you what was going through my mind when they served coffee in those cups, I wanted to scream your name. I tell you no coffee ever tasted so sweet. Bravo, brilliant signal! Can we go somewhere now? I want to hold you. It's been so long, you're driving me crazy."

"There is only one place we can go. You're going to meet my grandmothers." Always intrigued by adventure, he raised an eyebrow at me and nodded with a smile.

The Yemeni gardener at the gate was very discreet as he let us in the house. "I believe you'll find the ladies out back, Miss." I thought I saw the old man roll his eyes as he closed the door behind us.

A rush of cool air greeted us as we stepped inside. "Oh good, they gave in and put on the AC," I said. "Wait here a minute."

"Yes Ma'am," he said, grinning.

I found them behind the house, bent over a small rosebush with pruning shears. They hurried inside, wiping the dust from their caftans.

Hisham shook Salma's hand. "I'm honored to meet you, Madame." She sat between us. Mabrukah served us lemonade flavored with mint from Um Saleh's garden in the wadi.

"Well, young man," Salma began. "First, we know everything, and I mean everything. Second, your secrets are safe with us. Third, we want to help you both, but only if your intent is honorable—only if you want to marry Fawzia, and soon."

How could Salma put me on the spot like that? My face burned in embarrassment, and I wanted to cover my face with my headscarf.

Noticing my horror, Salma turned to me. "I'm sorry we are being direct, but we need to make sure, right now." She turned to Hisham. "From now on, no more funny business. We won't allow it, and neither will she. She deserves the best. So, young man, we want to know right now, what are your intentions?"

The hum of the air-conditioning filled the room. Hisham flipped up the edges of his ghutra and spread his legs far apart as he sat, pulling them in and pushing them back out a couple of times. He squirmed in his seat, and picked up his glass of lemonade. As he leaned his head back to drink, he looked at me from the side and winked at me. What was he doing? I started to fear he didn't really want to get married, that in a few moments we'd be throwing him out on his ear, and that my pillow would be soaked with tears yet again.

At last, Hisham stopped twitching and put down his glass. He winked at me again, then turned to the ladies and began to speak, while making a tent with his fingertips. "Madame Salma, Madame Mabrukah, thank you for the hospitality and for the opportunity to be frank. I assure you, marriage is my only goal, marriage to this wonderful friend of mine, Fawzia. We've known each other for four years. Since Ibtisam died, God rest her soul, we haven't seen each other at all. It was best to break things off, as it was becoming too dangerous for Fawzia. Though I agreed, I've mourned the loss of our friendship ever since."

"But then God seemed to want to help us," he continued. "I say this because by chance I met her brother Tarek last spring, and we got along. We were working on similar projects, as engineer and architect. We decided to bid on some work together. We just won a contract, and I have become good friends with Fawzia's brothers, and I even met her father." The smallest traces of a smile appeared on each lady's face.

"After Tarek and I first met," he continued, "I wondered whether I should stay away, out of respect for Fawzia's wishes to end our relationship. But it happened so fast that I found myself spending many evenings at Fawzia's home. I knew the door to the salon entered onto the kitchen hallway, so I assumed she had heard my voice but wasn't interested in rekindling our relationship. While losing hope, I continued doing business with her brother, as we really do work well together. I had almost given up on her when last week she sent me a sign. I now understand that she was gone all summer, visiting you. This made me very happy, and it has given me hope we might have a future together after all."

"Good," Salma said, but she wasn't going to let him slither away just yet. "Very good. But all this talk is just talk, empty words. Now's the time for action. What is your plan?" She folded her arms and gave him a fierce, smiling glare.

"Well, I," he cleared his throat. "Madame, we haven't had a chance to talk, Fawzia and I, about what to do next."

"Now, your family is Shia, is that right?"

"Yes, we are. And I know the possibility of me marrying into a good Hijazi Sunni family is slimmer than the crescent moon."

Salma shook her head. "As I have told Fawzia many times, let God decide what is possible. But if you don't try to resolve this, you have no chance at all. It seems you have bridged a lot of the impossible divide already. Fawzia's father and brothers have gotten to know you, and you are doing business together. Mashallah, what more encouragement do you need? It seems clear to me that a path is open, if you have the courage to take it."

The ladies excused themselves. "We'll be back in five minutes. Five minutes. We need to finish that rose bush." And with that, they went back to the garden, and the back door slammed shut. At last, we kissed.

CHAPTER 36

PROPOSALS

A FEW nights later, there was a knock on my bedroom door.

"Sweetheart, can your old Baba come in for a minute?"

He sat on my bed, his cologne filling the room with his signature scent. He had aged well, with curly sideburns edging his cheeks, his wavy hair cut short. The occasional white hair only added to his distinguished looks. He wore a puzzled, almost stunned expression.

"Your name came up tonight. I'm a little surprised by it all. You have heard Tarek talking about his colleague Hisham al-Saihati. Do you know him?"

"We were in school together at AUB. We were in a large group of friends."

Without revealing any suspicion at what I had just said, he continued. "Then, would you be surprised to hear that he and his father came to me tonight to propose your engagement to him?"

"Hisham? Really? Tonight? Here?" I had practiced saying these words for days and hoped my tone was convincingly surprised. Deceiving him made me feel guilty, but this charade was the only way.

"They left just now. Your mother doesn't even know yet. I wanted to talk to you first. What do you think?"

"Well, of course I'm surprised, though he's been on my mind since the moment I heard he and Tarek were working together. He's very nice. We always got along, too. I mean, in our group of friends, of course."

"And in many ways, his family is a lot like ours," Baba said, almost to himself. "They worked as traders in the Gulf, just as our family worked in the Hijaz. But their being Shia could be a big problem. I never expected one of them to come asking for my daughter."

"Yes, but why does it make a difference if Hisham is Shia? He is still a Muslim."

"But marrying him brings up so many issues, especially in how you'd raise your children, Shia or Sunni. He said he intends to stay here, that he'll buy a villa. Until then, he has a furnished apartment. He has offered a good bride price, half a million riyals. He seems to be a good man, and Tarek thinks highly of him. Yet… marrying a Shia. Fawzia, I want you to be sure."

"Didn't you raise us all to overlook things like this in our friends? We are all Muslims. To me, the most important issue is that we will live here and raise our children near you. So, to make sure we agree on these things up front, I would like to talk to him on the phone and to meet him. After we meet, I will give my answer." I hugged Baba, then said, "Do you think I could meet his mother, and his sisters too? I wonder how they feel about this gap between us?"

"Of course, darling!" He smiled and shook his head. "This is all happening in reverse of the normal routine. Usually, the women investigate the bride for the groom, then get the men involved."

"Baba, remember how your parents met? That was unusual, wasn't it?"

"But things were different in those days."

"Yet even then, it didn't go the normal way, did it?"

My grandfather had been a handsome young merchant down in the balad. Like his father and grandfather before him, he sold imported goods, including rare silks and hand-woven fabrics from Turkey. One day, a lady sent word asking him to bring dress fabrics to a well-to-do house on the hill. He and his shop assistant loaded a donkey with several bolts of popular silks and brought them to the customer's home. There, he met with a young lady and her mother, as was customary then, with their faces showing but hair covered.

At first, the bride-to-be expressed her opinions to her mother, who then relayed them to Grandfather. After a while, the mother grew exasperated. "Speak to him, daughter!" And so she did. She made him go back to his shop and bring three more loads of fabric bolts. The heat of the day kept rising, and he prayed they would make a decision soon, but they didn't. He did this three days in a row, until the young lady finally decided on a fabric she liked.

Which, he remembered, had been in the very first donkey-load he had brought to the house.

Grandfather was happy they had made a decision, and he assumed he would never see them again. Yet he remembered the young lady's smile, and how she laughed and made him go back and forth so many times.

Two months later, the girl's mother turned up in his shop. She was looking for fabric for a dress for herself. Her son was with her, but he left her at the shop for a few minutes. As Grandfather invited her inside, he said he hoped the marriage had concluded, and that the bride had liked the dress.

"Yes she liked the dress all right," the woman said, rolling her eyes. "But not the groom. It was a disaster, really. At the last minute, the young man announced he intended to bring her to a village in Najd. We hadn't agreed to that, so we cut it off."

Grandfather said he was very sorry. Then, in the next sentence, he asked if she was engaged to anyone else. The answer was no, and they were married faster than you could cut three yards of damask.

Baba, too, must have been thinking of the story. "I see what you are getting at. There is no typical engagement. Each one is, and has always been, unique. Just like every marriage, just like every couple in each generation. You, my dear, are a wise girl." He pulled me to him and hugged me. "But this will be a challenge for you. Are you sure this is what you want?" I breathed in his aftershave and felt the kindness in his strong arms.

"Yes, Baba, yes. But we need to be open with all the issues. I don't want surprises any more than you do." As I said this, I felt guilty at what I was still hiding from him.

"Good. Then, let me speak to Mama first. You may have to do more convincing in her case, let me warn you. You know she's always had her sights set on a groom from one of the Jeddah families."

"You say that, but none have come forth, have they? Let's face it. I really don't have any other prospects."

"Well, I'm sure if you made it known you were ready to marry, you'd have a lot of suitors, my dear. But the most important thing is your happiness. Twenty years from now, do you think you'll still be happy with him?"

"Yes, I think so." We hugged again.

"All right then, good night, my dear. I'll speak with Mama in the morning. She's asleep now, and I don't want to disturb her."

As I lay in bed looking at the ceiling, for the first time imagined that I might be Hisham's bride after all. Could it be this easy?

In the morning, Mama brought me a glass of fresh orange juice and sat with me in bed. She watched me drink, and when I finished she burst out: "Baba told me about Hisham's proposal."

I reacted with studied innocence, trying to keep guilt at my deception from giving me away. "I never thought that he would propose to me, Mama. He's a good boy, very kind and gentle. He's a lot like Baba, you know." How could she fault me for finding someone like her own husband, the father I loved so much?

"So have you thought it through? What do you think?" I could see she was trying to hold back her opinion of the proposal, which I appreciated.

"Mama, if he wasn't Shia, you wouldn't be concerned at all. Otherwise, he's a perfect match for me. He's educated, lives in the Hijaz, and wants to stay here. He has a successful business and is well-liked by Baba and my own brothers."

"But he's from the Eastern Province. Why not marry someone from a Jeddah family?"

"There's something about Hisham that's pure, that's clear, like a glass of cool water. It doesn't need any sugar, any color. When you talk to him, you are talking to his true self. That's a quality Ibtisam had too, don't you think?"

"Yes, dear." Mama's head was down, but I could see she was smiling. "Your mind is already made up, isn't it?"

"With time, I think I could learn to love him as a wife." I waited a few seconds. "But as I told Baba, I want to meet his mother and sisters, and to have a frank talk with him about what his plans are for us. Do you think I'm being wise? I don't want to hurt you, Mama."

She looked up, smiling at me, tears in her eyes. She reached for me, and we hugged. "My daughter, I wish for you only happiness. You are a modern girl, so sure of yourself. And I'm not surprised, for that's the way we brought you up." She hugged me again. "I wish I had been so strong at your age."

I leaned my cheek on her shoulder. "But you were, for your own times."

"Oh no, I wasn't. It was pure luck that I was matched with your father. It could have been a disaster. Well, maybe I should give some credit to your grandmother and the other ladies who thought we would make a good pair.

But I had known so few men that I had no way to judge. Even with my secondary degree, we were so sheltered, Rosette and me. But Baba was as kind and warm as he was handsome, and my young heart was taken with him in an instant. Fawzia, are you sure of this? I don't want my daughter to be in an empty marriage, especially one this risky."

"I think so. But I need to see him with his mother and sisters. Then I will say yes or no. They say you can tell a lot about a man from the way he treats his mother."

Tarek, Bashir, and Fahd burst through the door, each offering me a hug. "That sly fox!" Tarek said. "He knew you in college, right? Of course, why didn't I make the connection! I sure don't understand what he saw in you in Beirut, but you must have made an impression! This is so amazing, he never said a word to me about you."

Hisham's parents and sister flew to Jeddah the next weekend. By then, Hisham and I had spoken several times on the phone. He teased me like the old days, and I was always smiling. We would live in Jeddah, I'd get my PhD, and then I would continue working. Fortunately, he had a married brother whose wife had moved in with his parents. This took some pressure off Hisham to live with his parents. We would be among a growing number of young couples who were establishing separate households, away from the older generation. We were relieved that the family wasn't resisting our ideas. But all that was premature, as I still hadn't said yes.

We welcomed Hisham's mother and sister in the women's majlis with kisses on both cheeks. Up close, Hisham's mother seemed older than Mama, but that might have been due to her dark blue dress with a mandarin collar. She unwrapped her headscarf to reveal long black hair, streaked with white, wound in a chignon. His sister Reem jumped from the cocoon of her abaya like a delicate young butterfly and reached out to hug me. She had Hisham's chiseled nose and glowing dark eyes, framed by waist-long hair. She was more stylish than I'd expected, in a light purple Diane von Furstenberg wrap dress that complimented her golden complexion. She wore a classic gold chain with a diamond pendant and diamond ear studs to match. Hisham's mother wore understated but tasteful sapphire and diamond earrings.

We Bughaidan ladies had dressed with modesty, but we wanted to be festive and welcoming too. I wore a fitted pink silk blouse and had rolled the cuffs back as was the fashion, atop a long pleated ivory chiffon skirt. Mama loaned me her double rope of pearls and matching earrings. She followed my pearl-colored theme with an ivory gown in silk. On her index finger danced a large pearl and diamond ring that Baba had bought her in Switzerland. Aunt Rosette played her usual flamboyant role in a pink cocktail-length dress with short sleeves and matching pink diamond earrings.

I served the ladies the tea and sweets, a nod to a tradition, so the groom's mother and sisters could assess my abilities as a hostess. As I held the tray before each of them, my hands were shaking. I was afraid that something I'd say or do would give everything away. Or worse, that I'd trip and spill the tray. I was relieved to sit and talk once everything was served.

Pleasant conversation flowed between Mama and our guests. The adults seemed to be happy with small talk, but I was growing restless. We needed to get down to the reason for the visit, but I couldn't change the subject. One of the two mothers had to do it.

Um Hisham took the initiative. "We are happy to meet about this important matter. I understand that Fawzia wanted to meet us. Of course, if this were a typical arrangement, we would have already met. So, we are doing things out of the ordinary, aren't we?" We laughed.

"But then," she said, smiling at me, "No courtship and marriage is like any other. My husband and I met quite by accident. He came to our house seeking my brother, who was a scribe and a commercial mediator, helping people sort out their business differences. He was one of the first people in our village, Saihat, who could write. When Najib came to the door looking for my brother, no one was home except me. I didn't open the door, but I spoke to him, telling him to come back later. He liked the sound of my voice, and soon my mother called me into the salon one day to meet Um Najib. He had sent her over to see what I was like. We went from there!" From that moment on, I loved Hisham's mother for her directness and her kindness in telling us that story. I've always thought she was letting me know that she accepted the fact that I'd known Hisham in college.

They turned to me, expecting me to tell how we met. "We were in school together, as you know."

"Ah, Beirut. I miss it so much," Reem said, smiling, not knowing she had come to my rescue. "And now, with the war, we can't think of going back."

"One day, God willing, we'll return." Aunt Rosette sighed.

Um Hisham smiled at me. I felt she had, even then, accepted me into the family. "There was one more thing you wanted, my dear," she said. "I think it was to have a word with Hisham." Even though we'd all agreed to this, she still asked Mama: "Would you permit him to join us for a few moments?"

Hisham entered. "Son, come sit with us," his mother said. When she introduced Mama and Aunt Rosette, he smiled and nodded his head. "I'm honored to meet you both."

"Welcome," Mama and Aunt Rosette said in unison. Rosette winked as Hisham turned to me. Then Baba and Hisham's father joined us. His father looked just like Hisham, only more distinguished and somewhat frail. He was much older than Hisham's mother, I thought.

"It's good to see you," Hisham said.

I nodded. It was wonderful, in fact. I had only dreamed that we would one day be sitting in the same room as our parents, with me about to agree to an engagement.

The men stayed about half an hour. We talked about the old villa he was renovating and about his impressions of Jeddah. The adults agreed the Sunni-Shia question wasn't even an issue, given the compatibility of our families in so many respects. It was our happiness that mattered most. I'm sure no one was surprised when I said yes.

CHAPTER 37

UNRAVELED

HISHAM'S MOTHER, Mama, and Aunt Rosette dove into the wedding preparations. The invitations had to be reprinted twice, and we kept revising the guest list upward. The list was only constrained by the fact that the room for the ladies' party could hold no more than 350 guests. Flowers would be flown in from Italy. Madame Zeina Zahra traveled from Beirut to fit my wedding gown. She also designed dresses for Mama and Aunt Rosette, as well as for Hisham's mother and his sister. Aunt Rosette was one of Madame Zeina's best customers, so she fussed over us as though we were princesses.

Baba had rented a spacious new villa for a week at Obhur, so wedding guests from out of town could relax at the Red Sea before and after the celebrations. We would honeymoon in Istanbul.

One evening, Hisham called and asked if I could speak in private. Since we were engaged, private calls like this were acceptable, and I assumed we'd neglected to invite someone important. I carried the phone into my bedroom, pulling its long extension cord taut, and shut the door.

"Rashid's trying to blackmail me," he said. "He's going to tell Tarek everything about us, about our seeing each other last year. Everything. The bastard. He wants half a million riyals to keep quiet."

Rashid, our college friend, blackmailing us? "Are you sure he wasn't just joking?"

"Nobody jokes about this."

An icy wind began to blow inside me I imagined gossips whispering, "Oh you know they saw each other here in Jeddah. Yes, in restaurants and even in a private apartment. They're practically married already!" The implication would be that I was not a virgin. If our families found out, the engagement would be through, and I'd be an outcast.

I couldn't breathe, and a headache came on from the cold fear, spreading down my head to my fingertips and toes. I stared out my bedroom window as I listened, squinting into the glare.

"Fawzia? Are you there?"

I whispered, my hands shaking. "What did I ever do to him that he would turn on us like this?"

"He's jealous, no doubt."

"Jealous? Of what? He never ever made any advances toward me at school, or showed any interest in me. That makes no sense at all!"

"No, he's jealous of me and Tarek, of our business. You know he was also bidding on that contract we just won. Remember, one of the bids was thrown out because it was considered 'non-compliant'? Well, that was Rashid's company, it was very embarrassing. Rashid had tried to team up with your brother before, did you know that?"

"No, I didn't."

"A few months ago, he approached Tarek about forming a joint venture. By that time, Tarek and I were already working together. We even offered him a third of the company, but he wouldn't accept anything less than a 50% share. We didn't agree, of course. Then, when we won the bid and he was kicked out of the running, something must have snapped, and now he's threatening to tell Tarek that I only formed the company with him just so I could get close to you."

"How did it happen?"

"He called me at the office last night. First thing he said was, 'Congratulations on your pure and innocent bride.' He said those words on the phone. Then he said he was going to reveal everything to Tarek if I didn't pay him the money today."

"Allaaah. I can't believe this. How could he do that to us? I thought we were friends."

"So did I."

Another jolt of fear pulsated through my body, then everything collapsed and swirled around me. The next thing I knew, I was lying on the floor of my bedroom, and Mama was kneeling next to me, patting my hand.

I sat up, wondering how long I'd been lying there. Mama got me into bed and brought me a cup of tea.

"I'm just tired," I said. "I was talking to Hisham and stood up too fast, that's all."

She seemed to accept this, but made me promise to stay in bed. Hisham called back, but Mama wouldn't let him talk to me. Mama told him I'd fainted and that I was resting for the afternoon.

Once he learned the truth, Tarek would feel it was his right to punish me or to demand that Baba discipline me. Hisham was in danger too, for Tarek would feel he'd been betrayed personally by both of us.

What would Mama and Baba say if Tarek told them? They were modern, educated people, but how would they react? One thing was certain, if there were doubts about my purity, Hisham's family would have the right to call off the wedding. And the shame this would bring on my own family, once the gossips got hold of this, would be devastating. I knew my parents weren't the type to physically punish me. No, they were educated and would react with disbelief that their trusted and beloved daughter could have betrayed them, especially when they were open-minded enough to permit our marriage. After all they had been through with Ibtisam, I couldn't bear the idea of them being shamed by Hisham and me and our careless flaunting of social rules.

Hisham didn't call me back that night or the next morning. I phoned him, but there was no answer at his flat. I would have to wait to see if Rashid made good on his threat to talk to Tarek. Attempting to be brave, I went to class as usual. When I got home for lunch, Tarek was in the family room, arguing with Bashir about soccer teams. Nothing seemed out of the ordinary. I sat at the only empty chair at the dining table, to Tarek's right. The hairs on my arms bristled as I pulled out the chair. He didn't look up. He didn't say a word to me, nor look me in the eye. He knew.

We all moved to the salon for our afternoon coffee. Again, Tarek didn't speak to me and didn't once look at me, even though I glanced at him several times. When he went to his bedroom to take a short nap before returning to the office, I went to my room and prepared for the worst. I would have to face my fate. I expected Tarek to come after me any moment, so I propped my desk chair against my bedroom door under the door handle.

Nothing happened. As soon as I knew Tarek had gone back to his office, I told Mama I was going to Salma's. She was the only one I could talk to. Hamdi waited in the car while I rang the bell. Finally, the old gardener came to the door and told me Salma and Mabrukah were visiting friends. My head was about to burst. I told Hamdi to drive me to the balad, explaining I had to get Mama a present in the gold souq.

"But you'd be alone, walking in the market?"

"Don't worry, I'll take a cab right home. I have to surprise Mama, you see, so please don't tell her."

He dropped me in front of the Queen's building, on Abdul Aziz Street. I looked up at its curving modern façade of black glass, framed by white marble. Owned by the wife of the late King Faisal, Queen Effat fought religious conservatives to pioneer education for women, and all her life helped many needy families. Her name means "probity," and "good morals." How far I am from that, I thought.

I didn't know where I was going, but I needed to walk, to think. At least here I could disappear into the crowd. I drew in my abaya, reconfiguring my scarf so it covered my face with a single layer of fabric, so I could see yet would not be seen. I wandered into Gazzaz, where I was always dazzled by the quart-sized bottles of Chanel perfumes, the latest makeup from Yves St. Laurent and Guerlain. The young Lebanese and Syrian men behind the counter wore the top two buttons of their shirts unbuttoned, their sunglasses on top of their heads.

Since my face was veiled, they didn't speak to me. Otherwise, they were always very friendly and even flirtatious, if you were interested in that. In a daze, I watched Saudi and foreign ladies sampling and buying makeup and fragrances. I floated through the store like a ghost, observing, wishing I could be transported through a door in the back corner straight to Paris, London, or Beirut. I dreamed of sudden escape, of finding myself far from my troubles, standing in the cosmetics department of Harvey Nichols on London's Brompton Road, or drinking coffee at Café de la Mer.

I couldn't stay there forever, so I stepped back out to the shopping arcade, where the heat and humidity pressed in. The opulent fabric shops reminded me of how extravagant our wedding outfits were, of the happy activity that swirled at home as Mama and Aunt Rosette orchestrated more elaborate details of the wedding, unaware of the disaster that would halt it all in one moment. I kept walking, hoping my slow pace might calm the tempest that raged within.

Next, I turned down an old arched street – now just for foot-traffic — lined with gold shops. I hadn't been to the balad in so long, not since Ibtisam died. I stopped and stared at one shop after another, mesmerized by the glow of the gold in the display windows. Inside, the breeze from air conditioners made the delicate teardrop ornaments on earrings and necklaces dance. Veiled women with baby strollers filled the shops. They stretched their bare arms out as they tried on bangles and had earrings and gold chains weighed. The merchants worked their calculators as they bargained. Some merchants looked to be Javan, others Yemeni, and still others sported long beards, as if they were from conservative Najd families.

Watching the women go in and out the shops, I wondered if any of them had fallen in love. Were any of their hearts broken? I felt so alone, and wanted to connect to just one of them, as if it were possible to somehow scan their hearts and see if anyone else suffered as I did, and if they could help me.

"Cover your hair!" an old man's voice called out behind me. A scowling figure approached, carrying a long stick in his right hand as he admonished two ladies. They appeared to be Lebanese, judging by their knee-length dresses and lack of headscarves. He was a mutawa, a religious official whose job was making sure the shops closed for prayer. This was the first time I'd ever seen one admonish women about their clothes.

"You must be modest – go home and cover!" he shouted at them, as they stepped inside a gold store crowded with women. They slipped through the black wall of women wearing abayas and disappeared. The other women ignored him, dazzled by the glittering gold jewelry around them. The old man walked past me, still frowning. Since I was covered properly, I was invisible. After a few minutes, the two ladies reappeared from out of the crowded shop.

"It seems like they're everywhere now," one said in a singsong Lebanese accent. "Ever since Mecca. Cherie, before long even we will have to wear zee abaya."

"Don't worry, he went up the hill," I said in French. They nodded and hurried in the opposite direction.

I kept walking, comforted by the fact that no one knew who I was, or knew about the disaster that was about to ruin my life. I found myself standing in front of the Ba Humaid Gold Shop, its blue-and-red calligraphed sign faded with age. This was the shop where my grandmother, Baba's mother, bought her gold decades ago. I recognized the name from the old receipts she kept in her jewelry box. I had been wearing one of her bangles in honor of her memory and reached down to feel the simple designs along its surface. Its soft 21-karat gold was bent from the decades, but it fit my wrist.

An elderly merchant dozed behind the counter. His bald, skull-capped head was bent forward over his frail frame, his arms folded. He'd crossed one leg over the other to prop himself up against the wall. Beside him, a thick pair of glasses rested atop a folded newspaper on a stool. Unlike the shops in the busier part of the souq, his window and counter displays were only half full, as if he hadn't bought new stock in years.

"Excuse me, sir, good evening."

As if by reflex alone, the man stood up and pulled his glasses to his face. He didn't seem to resent being woken from his reverie.

"What can I do for you, my dear bride?" He blinked and rubbed his eyes. His glasses were thick from decades of staring at the tiny gold hallmarks etched in delicate baubles. He'd called me a bride. At first I didn't notice, since everyone at home was calling me that, too.

"I'd like to see your earrings, Sir. Those, in that case there." He nodded, slid the display case open, and took his time laying out five pairs of earrings on the glass. Evoking decades past, they were filigreed with a row of tiny, dangling seed pearls. "How long have you had this shop, Uncle, if you don't mind my asking?"

"Since I was a young man, but my father had it before me, and before him, his father. We have been here three generations."

"I wonder if you might have known my grandmother, Sir. She used to buy here. She passed away twenty years ago, God rest her soul. But maybe you knew her."

"There are so many customers: the princesses, the shaikhahs, the ladies of society. I can't remember them anymore, young lady. I'm sorry."

"Of course, Uncle, I understand. This bracelet came from your shop many years ago. It belonged to my grandmother." I took it off and handed it to him. He held it close to his eyes.

"Yes, yes, it is our work. I haven't seen one of these in years."

I turned to the earrings in the case and held up each pair to admire them one by one. "Are these Turkish?"

"Good guess, this is indeed the old Turkish style. The man who did this work learned his trade in Istanbul, but he was Saudi. No one else has this work now."

While I was still admiring it, I said, "But how did you know I am a bride, Uncle?

"Oh, I can always tell." He watched me put the earrings down and said nothing as I perused the bracelets and necklaces. I was swept up in the nostalgia of the old designs. "Excuse me for saying this," he said. "But something's wrong, isn't it? You are not a happy bride. There is a secret, a bad secret tormenting your heart. But it's not you who has been bad, for you are a good girl."

I looked down at the counter, feeling tears well up in my eyes. Two tears dripped onto the glass counter, and I wiped them with my abaya.

"No," he continued, gripping my arm, his voice rising in intensity. "It's someone else who is causing you trouble. Some devil, and you are afraid. Is this why you came here? Did you know who I am?"

"No, I...I didn't know where I was going, really. I just had to walk, and then there I was, outside your store. I thought maybe you knew my grandmother. But you don't."

"No, I don't remember her. But maybe she has brought you here. Listen to me. There isn't much time. My grandson will be back soon, and he doesn't approve of me talking about these things. This trouble, it is big. But you must face it, whatever it is. I sense you are a good girl, and you are surrounded by great love. You must trust that love. Everybody has troubles. But you are lucky because of this love." He patted my hand. "Dear bride, you must trust."

Before I could respond, a young man bustled into the store and went behind the counter. He was short like the old man, but wore a crisp new thobe and a headdress that towered on his head like the roof of a Japanese pagoda. He handed the old man a glass of tea and looked me over, smoothing his thobe, preparing to close the sale.

"Think about my price," the old man said, cutting him off. "And come back when you realize it's the best in the souq."

"Thank you, Uncle." I turned to leave.

"And greet your grandmother for me."

I stumbled out of the shop, stunned by the old man's words. Was he some kind of seer? They said there used to be people like that in the old days, like Salma's old Solubba woman. People used to tell fortunes using seashells, but now it was frowned upon. I kept threading my way up the hill, alley by alley, trying to calm my nerves. Dusk was approaching. Soon it would be time for the sunset prayer.

I walked through the Gabel Street underpass that was filled with shoppers hurrying to complete their purchases. Climbing the old stairs, I emerged from the crowds and reached my refuge, the old part of the city. Several muezzins began the call to prayer at once, their voices swirling from all directions. I stood in front of Bait Nassif, its massive structure glowing in the dusk. Small-time merchants selling cassettes and leather goods on the ground had covered their wares with sheets and left them unguarded while they went to pray. An old woman selling baby clothes on a blanket sat nearby. She lifted her veil to drink the tea she had poured from a thermos.

Usually, I would sit on the wall and think through my troubles. But I was too agitated, so I walked around the outside of Bait Nassif, hoping to find the home where Salma and Mabrukah had lived so long ago. It was there, just as Salma had described, its wooden mashrabiyya still painted bright green. Like many old buildings in the balad, its paint was peeling, and the stucco overlay on the walls needed repair.

I approached the door and, on an impulse, I knocked, suspecting there would be no one there. When no one answered, I caressed the wood. Had Salma's hands once run across it like this? I pushed the door open, amazed to find it unlocked. Then I pulled it shut again and walked around the building and looked up. There was no trace of the old walkways that once connected the rooftops.

Prayer time was almost over, and it was growing dark when I returned to the front of Bait Nassif and sat on the low wall near the towering neem tree. The merchants reopened their stores and switched on the lightbulbs outside their shops. Groups of women who had been resting on the wall during prayer time walked back toward the shops. Families paraded by, herding little girls in long crinoline dresses and patent leather shoes.

I sat there for hours, through the evening prayer call, my thoughts whirling in circles. My parents would be devastated if they found out how I'd deceived them. All their friends, all our relatives, had already received the wedding invitations. It was too late to undo the engagement without gossip and questions.

My tears dripped onto my lap under my veil, unseen. I prayed for a way out of the situation so my parents would not be hurt, particularly Mama. I found the prayer that Ibtisam had given me that last night we were together in Mecca, and I read it three times through.

By the time I finished, I was heaving quiet sobs, but no one noticed. I pleaded with Ibtisam for help, even though I knew it wasn't proper to ask for help from anyone but God. I called to my grandmothers, the old Princess Nurah, even Um Duhaim and Amina, the gentle wife of the Unaizah imam. As the hours passed, the maelstrom in my heart subsided and my tears stopped. I felt calm, though I knew the worst was still to come. But for the time being, I could think clearly. I lifted my head and looked around. It was the last hour of the market, and foot traffic had slowed.

The merchants began to close up for the night. The young men selling cassettes put them in boxes and carried them home on their heads. They would be back early the next morning, hoping to make enough to buy food or to pay their portion of the rent on a tiny apartment.

The old lady selling children's clothes had pulled the veil off her wrinkled face and was gazing at me. Having caught my eye, she came and sat beside me.

"Daughter, I've been watching you all night," she said. "You're in some kind of trouble aren't you. It's a pity, sometimes life is so difficult for us women. My dear, whatever it is that is bothering you, it will be all right. Don't be afraid. You must have courage and trust in God. Please, try to trust in Him."

Her words washed over me like warm light. "Thank you, Sister, thank you," I said. "God bless you." She offered me a cup of tea, and I accepted. It calmed me to sit with her, as we watched the city grow dark. Then she folded up her wares and bade me goodnight. After she left, I shut my eyes and sat still, as if I would hear the answer to my prayers in the air of the ancient city. But I found only the cold roaring of my fear.

"Fawzia, get up, come with me. We're going home. Now."

CHAPTER 38

ON THE ROOF

TAREK WAS standing in front of me. How had he found me?

"I know all about you and Hisham. It's over."

He expected me to follow him home with quiet obedience. But he was wrong, for defiance blossomed in me instead. Though my heart was pounding, I put my purse on my shoulder.

Tarek looked around. A litter of scrawny kittens meowed in the alley nearby. "This place is disgusting. It's so dirty. Let's get out of here."

He turned away, waiting for me to come along. Instead, I stood up and walked in the opposite direction, then broke into a run. I don't think he noticed I was gone until I'd disappeared around the corner of Bait Nassif.

The street was dimly lit, so no one saw me running, fully veiled, holding tight to my purse. It felt glorious to run, to fly from his trap. I had made my choice not to go with him, not to fall in line, at least not without putting up a fight. Those weeks in Taif had given me new physical strength. I could never have run like that before.

I reached the front of Salma's old house and opened the door enough to squeeze inside, then shut it behind me. A single lightbulb burned somewhere inside, illuminating rooms full of old furniture, relics from Jeddah's past. I crept up the stairs, hoping that Tarek hadn't seen me disappear into the building.

Crash! The front door flew open. I picked up my skirt and climbed as fast as I could to the next landing and listened.

He started searching the ground floor. "You can't get away," he said. "The family will find you. You know that. You've sinned, and you have to take your punishment. You've shamed our family name. Rashid told me everything. That you and Hisham were sneaking to his apartment, that he left you alone there for hours at a time. You've betrayed us, all of us."

I took off my shoes and began to climb again, grateful for the bare lightbulbs that lit the stairway. I tripped on a step, ripping my skirt. I fell to my knees, barely catching myself with hands now covered with dust and cobwebs. He started up the stairs.

I reached the third floor, feeling along the filthy walls with my bare hands. According to Salma, the house had five stories, so I kept climbing, waving my arms as I walked to keep the cobwebs from my hair and face. On the fourth floor, I hid inside an old wardrobe in a bedroom.

A door creaked. Tarek had made it to the fourth floor and was looking in the closets across the hall. He would find me if I stayed there, so I tiptoed toward the door. I had to sneak past him. As I crept down along the hallway, I stumbled on a piece of wood. "Fawzia?" Tarek said.

There was nowhere to go but up. I pushed the door open at the very top of the stairs and stepped onto the roof. Two old wooden wind tunnels still stood there, catching rooftop breezes and pulling them into the rooms below.

I backed away from the door, out to the edge of the roof and waited, trying to build my courage. I found an opening in the wall where coral bricks had fallen away. I crouched there, hoping this old house that once sheltered Salma would protect me, too, if only for a while.

I could see over the tops of buildings all the way to the sea, where several large container ships were moored offshore, their lights twinkling in the night. The markets had closed. The ancient mosque on Gabel Street was still lit up, its small minaret aglow with strings of white lights. All around me the ancient homes stood silent, glowing softly in the light from the newer parts of the city below. A crescent moon shone high above.

Was I about to have my love, my future, and maybe even my life torn away, like Salma? I remembered the sadness of Salma's eyes in the firelight, how she lost all hope of love in order to survive. Then there was Ibtisam, finding love only at the threshold of her death.

"It's over," Tarek said. He was standing nearby, watching me, his thobe covered with dust. One of his sleeves was ripped below the elbow.

"No, it's not over at all. It's just beginning."

He stepped toward me and tried to grab my arm.

I jumped back. "Don't touch me! You have no right!" I backed off, and he followed me. We circled the rooftop, facing each other. I was hoping to run past him to the door. First we would talk, then I would run. I was confident that even in my ripped dress and my abaya, I could still run faster than he could in his thobe.

"I certainly do have the right, especially now! You're not my sister anymore. No sister of mine is a cheap whore. Wait until Baba finds out!"

"But we're engaged, and we will be married soon."

"But that's the problem. Rashid says you committed sins with Hisham. That you're not a virgin anymore."

"That's not true! Do you believe everything you hear from him?"

"Well, how is this for truth? You and Hisham started seeing each other. You talked on the phone, went to restaurants, and you even went to Rashid's place and he left you alone in his flat. You've been alone with Hisham. You're not a virgin."

"No," I said. "Do you think I'm such an idiot as to not be a virgin? And do you think that Hisham would cross that line? Yes, I did meet with him, but I swear to you, by God, I am still a girl." He lunged at me, but I jumped out of his reach.

"How dare you mention God while you confess to these sins! For all I know, you've gone beyond even what he told me! Do you realize what you've done? You've shamed me, you've shamed all of us! How could you be so stupid?" He picked up an old piece of wood and swung it around, then threw it across the roof.

I backed away, waiting for a chance to run down the stairs. What could I answer to this? He was right. We had taken so many risks. We had been crazy, crazy in love.

"And how could I be so stupid!" he said, pacing back and forth in front of me, his fists clenched. I wanted to run, but I wanted to hear him, too. "Hisham proposes our joint venture, telling me he has so much respect for our family reputation. We even set up a company, and now I find out it was just so he could get close enough to propose to you! Dammit, do you have any idea how bad that makes me look? I get taken in by my sister the whore and her boyfriend. And I have to hear about it from Rashid?

"Rashid invites me to his house and sits me down at his bar, offers me a glass of scotch, shows me the alcohol he's got there, and even tells me about his parties. Then he tells me that you and Hisham spent several evenings alone in that very room. I tell him he's wrong, that you'd never do anything like that. Then he shows me a photograph of the two of you, taken in the same room. How could you be so careless with your reputation and our family name?"

My heart sank. The photograph. I'd forgotten about it. Rashid's manservant, the Filipino guy, took a Polaroid of us one night. I thought Hisham had taken it with him. That photograph was the evidence that made his blackmail threat real, and it could be my ruin. I gave up thoughts of running, sat down, and leaned against the wall. Tarek stood over me, waiting for me to speak.

"It's true, we were stupid, and I was stupid," I said, my fears rising with the thought of the photograph falling into Baba's hands. "It started out so innocently, but we kept on seeing each other. Ibtisam found out, and I promised to break up with him. She didn't tell Baba, and I ended it. I never expected to see him again. After Ibtisam died, I told Salma everything. That's why I went to Taif, to put it all behind me, to forget. I was shocked to learn that you were working with him. I had no idea. He hadn't been calling me. You have to believe me.

"I was so happy when Hisham proposed, and when it seemed at last we might be able to be together. Until then, it had seemed so utterly impossible for me to marry a Shia from the Eastern Province. But why would Rashid try to ruin everything? He was a good friend to both of us at school. And believe me, there was never anything between him and me. Maybe he's jealous of you and Hisham. Because he lost that big contract to you two."

"What's that got to do with it?" Tarek said, pacing again.

"Have you talked to Hisham about this?"

"No. It's between you and me."

"Well, no it isn't. He tried to blackmail Hisham first. He threatened to tell you everything unless Hisham paid him half a million. I'm sure you know that is the size of my dowry. Hisham denied his allegations, told him I was still a virgin, and refused to pay. So I see Rashid made good on his threat. You know what he said to Hisham? 'Enjoy your pure and innocent bride.' I've known for three days. I've been waiting for you to confront me ever since."

Tarek stood still, and the anger seemed to flow out of his shoulders into the air as he took this in. "He's trying to blackmail me too, Fawzia. He asked for the same amount and my 10% of Baba's company. He wants me to sign it over to him, and he wants me to get rid of Hisham and go into partnership with him! If I don't do all this by midnight, he's going to tell Baba what happened and show him the photograph. So I have two scores to settle, yours and his."

"There's something else. It's about Ibtisam." He slid down the wall and sat next to me. "She met someone in Mecca during the siege, another hostage, and they fell in love. Yes, Ibtisam fell in love, though she was so innocent, she probably didn't know it." I told him Marwan's story.

He covered his face with his hands. "Why didn't you tell me before?"

"You'd never understand. You might even have gone after Marwan."

Regaining his composure, he stood up and went to the opening in the wall. I followed him, and together we gazed down the hill to the sea. He rubbed his eyes with his thumb and finger.

"Please, for the sake of Ibtisam's memory, help us. Why would you deny Hisham and me our happiness? Rashid has tried to ruin the wedding, my reputation, and all our lives. Why give him what he wants? You know we love each other, and we will bring honor to the family as a married couple. Help us, please."

"What do you want me to do? Give in to his blackmail?"

"There is only one way out of this problem, and that is for me to face Mama and Baba. But I need you to trust that I'm telling the truth."

As I waited for him to speak, a warm breeze blew out of the wind tunnel from deep inside the house and caressed my face.

CHAPTER 39

THE TRUTH

"WHAT HAPPENED?" Mama gasped when we got home. "You're both covered with dust! And your dress, were you in an accident?"

Baba emerged from the men's salon, where he was entertaining friends.

"What's going on? You both look like you've been in a fight! Give me a minute, my guests are just leaving."

Mama followed me into the bathroom. "Was it a car accident? Was anyone killed?"

"No, nothing like that, but it's serious, and I need to tell you both something."

"It's about Hisham, isn't it? Oh no, the engagement," She grew silent and left the room, preparing herself for the worst.

I washed my face and hands, but left my ripped dress on. Pulling cobwebs from my hair, I prayed for strength. Then a fearlessness rose in me. Salma had not taken the chance to confess the truth and fight for herself, but now I had that same chance, and I decided to take it.

Mama, Baba, and Tarek sat on the sofa, and I paced in front of them, clasping my hands to keep them from shaking. "Baba," I began, "We're being blackmailed, and I'm afraid it's my fault."

I told them of our secret meetings, somehow bolstered, deep within, with courage from Salma's own story. I explained that we always wished we could marry, but assumed no one would approve of our marriage. Then I begged their forgiveness for flaunting their trust.

"How could you, my daughter, how could you?" Mama cried when I told them how I'd seen Hisham many times and had spent time alone with him at Rashid's apartment. I explained that Ibtisam found out and made me promise to break it off, and that we only took up again when Hisham started working with Tarek.

I cried as I finished. "More than any of my friends' parents, you were always the most trusting. And I took advantage of it, and now that trust is gone. I've ruined everything. I beg your forgiveness."

Baba glared at me with anger and sadness, and my heart broke. How deeply I had wounded them both. Then his face flushed. "What about blackmail?" he said, his teeth clenched with rage.

Tarek explained Rashid's threats and told them about the photograph.

Baba stood up and bellowed. "He wants half a million, 10% of my company, and Hisham's interest in your firm as well? The bastard. Who does he think he is?"

By then, I was drained of emotion. I was beyond crying. It was done. I had said it all, except the story of Ibtisam's love. That would remain a secret from them, at least for now. I kept my eyes lowered as Baba stood before me. I blushed under the power of his glare, losing hope that I'd ever be forgiven. What I had done was beyond anything they'd ever imagined.

Then Tarek stood between us. "I believe her. She is trying to move forward with Hisham, to be a good wife. Even though she was alone with him, I know him well enough to trust his self-control. You didn't ask for my view, but I want her to be happy. I've already lost one sister, and I don't want to lose another."

Tears of gratitude filled my eyes. No matter what happened, Tarek stood up for me, and he believed in me. The silence that followed felt like an eternity, although I'm sure it was really only a minute or two. I shut my eyes and prayed.

Mama stood up and whispered something to Baba, then squeezed his hand. I felt Baba's hand on my shoulder, and he took me in his arms.

"Although you sinned, in the end you're trying to follow your hearts into the honorable path of marriage. We love you and could never harm you. You are our only daughter now, and we want you to be happy."

Tears blinded my vision, and I began to cry. I couldn't speak as I buried my head in his shoulder. Mama's arms encircled me too. "Thank you, God, thank you Salma, thank you Ibtisam," I whispered.

CHAPTER 40

ZAGHAREED

Jeddah
January 1981

"HOLD ON tight now," Reem said, tucking my left arm in hers. Mama held my right hand. "I'll hold up the hem of your caftan, dear." They were leading me through Aunt Rosette's back garden. I couldn't see a thing, for they'd draped a silk shawl of muted gold over my head and face, a nod to an old tradition. I struggled to keep my balance as we walked along the marble pathway that still held the sun's warmth, then passed under an arched trellis of fragrant jasmine.

We walked toward muffled laughter and strains of Aboud Abd al-Al and his Golden Strings playing on a boom box. I inhaled the aroma of lamb shawarma cooking on a spit.

"Dear daughter," Mama said. "May you always walk in health and happiness."

"God bless you, Mama," I said, squeezing her hand. Someday, I would ask her to tell me the true details of how she met Baba. I was sure she too had a story, and once I was a married woman, she would share it.

"Wait a moment, bride," Aunt Rosette said, touching my shoulder.

"Bismillah," they intoned. Then my mother called out: "Blessings and peace upon you, O Beloved of God, Muhammad!" Joyous zaghareed spread from them in waves to voices all around me as they led me on.

"Step carefully, bride," Reem said. The soft wool of a thick oriental carpet caressed my feet. My friends' voices surrounded me as they clapped and shouted. "Welcome, bride!"

"Please sit, my dear, and may God protect you from all evil," Mama said.

They lowered me onto a pillow. The henna artist took my right hand and asked, "May I start now?" I nodded. I'd asked her to draw designs from weavings in the wadi. I watched her work from beneath the edge of the veil, listening to the guests enjoying themselves. Each delicate line of red-brown henna tickled and cooled my skin as the designs spread across my hands and feet.

When the henna artist had finished, Mama pulled the shawl away, and I began to cry. Until that moment, my henna night had seemed an impossible dream. Mama dried my eyes, since my hands were covered in moist henna paste. Aunt Rosette had decorated the patio with carpets and pillows. Small candle lanterns twinkled around the edges of the pool. Masses of red rose petals floated on its still surface. Strings of white lights hung between the walls and the cabana roof.

The sight of the ladies in costume bedazzled me. Aunt Rosette and Mama wore old-fashioned gowns of yellow and white and decked themselves in antique gold and pearls they'd found among my Grandmother's things. Badriyah and my friends from AUB dressed in caftans and costumes from their own grandmothers. My Najd friends sported long, gold-embroidered thobes made of black silks and chiffons. Reem and Um Hisham donned dresses from their village in purple and red. Salma and Mabrukah, sitting comfortably in armchairs, wore Banu Shamaal tribal dresses of dark indigo, accented with gleaming silver jewelry. Princess Nurah was resplendent in a turquoise gown her grandmother had worn on the night she met Fawwaz those many decades ago. Her matching turquoise necklace was a gift from him to her grandmother. Small crownlets of silver chains and delicate caps of gold and pearls decorated gleaming tresses. As for me, I wore the ivory brocade caftan that Mama's mother had donned on special occasions. It was elegant and simple, with matching pantaloons and a short vest.

With my sleeves and pantaloons rolled back, and my hair pinned up with jasmine blossoms, it was my turn to wait for the henna to dry while our guests danced and sang. Late in the evening after supper, Salma entranced us once more with tales from her youth. It was nearly dawn when the party ended.

I would leave home for my new life with mixed emotions. Even though we would live close by, I would miss my family. I would miss Tarek most of all, for he had supported me on that darkest night. On one of my last days at home, we walked at Obhur, along the same stretch of beach where Hisham and I had been together two years before.

"I'll admit you both owe me." He smiled. "Just pay me with romantic advice, when the time comes."

"Is there some news you want to tell me?"

"No, not yet. But you have given me courage that I can find happiness in this world."

"It's obvious you've never been short of courage," I replied, looping my arm through his as we walked in the reddening dusk.

There were tears from Mama and Baba when we left the house on my wedding night, for their days with an unmarried daughter at home were ending. But as Hamdi pulled the rented Bentley into the street, I forgot my wistfulness and was swept into the ancient marriage ritual. In my white wedding gown, with its billowing sheer veils and long train, I felt like a sailing ship gliding across a gentle sea. I wanted to enjoy it, not only for me, but for Ibtisam. I felt she was with me.

We arrived at the hotel around 10 p.m. and went to the room where the actual signing of the marriage contract took place. Some families did this weeks in advance, but given the distances between Hisham's family and ours, we did it the same day as the party. The imams from our mosque and the mosque of Hisham's parents witnessed. Each one said a prayer and read from the Qur'an. At our insistence, Marwan attended as well. At that point, Hisham and I were officially married, but we didn't kiss. That would come much later, when we were alone in the bridal suite.

Hisham smiled at me as we stood outside the tall double doors to the wedding hall. It was after midnight. The women guests had been waiting for hours, enjoying refreshments, conversation, music, and dancing. The men were being entertained elsewhere in the hotel, for, as always, the main event was the women's party.

We both said, "Bismillah al-Rahman al-Rahim." Then Hisham nodded, and the doors swung wide. A cloud of aloeswood incense mixed with expensive perfumes enveloped us, putting me into joyous delirium. This was our golden moment.

Drummers stood around us and began a slow pounding rhythm, as ancient as our bloodlines. Young cousins and nieces walked with us. They carried tall, lit candles and sang a song of blessing. Mama, Um Hisham, and Aunt Rosette followed behind.

As we made our slow procession through the crowd toward the stage, my wedding dress felt like a cloak of gratitude and happiness. Every few moments, joyful zaghareed punctuated the drumming. Our guests, wearing their finest gowns and jewelry, stood as we passed. With beaming smiles, they craned their necks to see us.

Marwan's sister Farhat sat with a group of Ibtisam's school friends. "God bless you both and grant you happiness," she called. My girlfriends from AUB whistled and cheered. Badriyyah smiled as I reached out to squeeze her hand. Um Saleh and her daughters were there too, and I caught a glimpse of them, wide-eyed at the boisterous crowd in their city finery.

Hisham's sister Reem waited for us on the stage, wearing a joyful smile. She'd told me she was thrilled that Hisham and I had met in school, though, like Hisham's parents, she didn't know the extent of our romance. Would we ever tell them?

Salma and Mabrukah sat in the front row, all smiles. Of everyone there, they could take the most credit for the miracle of this night. As we passed in front of them, I winked at them, and Hisham said, "God bless you both." Princess Nurah, sitting next to Salma, questioned her with her eyes. Salma just shrugged and smiled, rubbing her thumb across the mane of the carved horse head atop her cane.

Hisham and I took our seats on the stage and gazed out over the living bouquet of our family and friends. I thought of all the brides I'd come to know through Salma, of the heartache and tears, as well as the joy they'd found. Their courage had shown me the way. When I started to tear up, Reem raced to my side with a tissue. "Don't, bride, you'll smudge your makeup!"

Then the drummers, who were sitting behind us on the stage, began to play and sing lively wedding tunes, and the younger girls got up to dance. When Mama and Um Hisham approached the stage together to dance, the crowd went wild, for this was a sign to all that both families were delighted with the match. I whispered another prayer of thanks to God and said to Ibtisam, as if she was standing next to me, "Thank you dear sister, thank you." The zaghareed continued all night.

Toward dawn, Hisham and I went to the honeymoon suite and approached each other with a careful tenderness, fully aware of how lucky we were. Later, we slept, my head resting on his shoulder, my hand on his chest. Thanks to Salma and all the others, our happiness was not impossible after all.

Notably absent from the celebrations were Rashid and his family. The very night I confessed everything, Baba drove to Rashid's parents' home and confronted them with their son's attempted blackmail. He also divulged Rashid's social activities. Within a week, Rashid's father had banished him to a small town in Western Canada, where he was put in charge of a desolate, money-losing ranch. His Jeddah apartment was sold and emptied. I've always wondered how many bottles of Johnnie Walker they poured down the drain.

CHAPTER 41

THE GOLDEN CUP

DURING OUR first winter as husband and wife, cool weather teased us with the possibility of rain. High clouds veiled the city, turning the sea to silver and the sky to pearl. Some days, a fine dust filled the air, coating everything inside and out. Our 1950s vintage villa wasn't very airtight. The houseboy and I cleaned every surface again and again.

Salma had come down with the flu that winter, and remained weakened from it. The doctors suspected an infection of the heart, myocarditis. She was to rest until further notice, and there would be no more early morning walks. We weren't told her prognosis, so I called a Jordanian doctor, a friend from AUB. She said it could pass or it could lead to heart failure and other complications. There was no way of knowing.

It was disconcerting to see Salma so weak, lying in bed. To me, she was always an intrepid woman, charging through life's challenges. Yes, she had wrinkles, but until now she had always seemed ageless.

Salma's Jeddah bedroom echoed the wadi. The floor was covered with tribal rugs, and the bedspreads were of fine-quality hand-woven wool, with bright tribal designs. The walls were bare, except for one, where she'd hung one of my paintings, set in an expensive gilded frame. I'd sold it at a charity show, and I didn't know she owned it. It was a painting of the view from the terrace of their mountain home.

"Nurah got it for me," she said. "You captured the beauty of that place so well."

During my visits, Salma would always ask whether I still had the tapes of all the stories, and I assured her they were safe in my room at home.

One day, she squeezed my hand. "Don't let our stories die. Young people need to know that we, too, faced death and hardship, that we risked everything, even our lives, for love. We had to fight for our happiness, even though it might only bloom once or twice in a lifetime, like the wildflowers' brief dance in the desert. So gather the stories, the wildflowers, before they wilt and die. Promise me."

"Yes, of course." I didn't know what else to say. She and I both knew I was no storyteller. And she knew very well that it was impossible for one young woman to ensure that the wisdom of past generations was not lost.

"I'm sure you will find a way. When the time comes, you'll know what to do." She sighed and closed her eyes for a moment. "And yet, I sometimes think," she said, her eyes still closed. "Of what importance is one old woman's story? Who would care to follow the trace of my bare feet in the sand, or those of my mare who was the color of river stones?"

After a few moments silence, she opened her eyes and spoke with renewed strength. "Last night I dreamed I was with Mama and Baba again," Salma said. "Baba told me he knew I was innocent, and he cried. Uncle Duhaim, Nurah, and even Um Duhaim were there, too. We stood on a cliff overlooking a wide green wadi, only it wasn't our wadi. Um Duhaim said, 'You have done well, Salma. Do not worry, for the stories will live. But make sure Fawzia gets the other stories too. Their stories.' Then she waved her hand toward the sky. The white clouds above us were filled with the faces of thousands of women and girls. Their mouths were moving like they were speaking, but I couldn't hear what they were saying. I heard only the wind. It was a very strange dream."

Then, with deliberate effort, she reached into the pocket of her nightgown and pulled out her golden cup and pressed it into my hand. "This is yours now," she said. "You are the dearest thing in my life. Praise God we found each other, my dear friend, my granddaughter."

Mabrukah called me a few days later. "She slipped away last night. She's gone."

Together, we found the strength to carry out the rituals. We read from the Qur'an and prayed through the washing and the winding of her burial shroud. That evening, the imam said prayers for her at the mosque; both the men's and women's sections were filled. Then Nurah's husband and her sons took Salma to be buried.

Women, young and old, from many ethnicities and tribes, streamed to the villa to pay their respects. Her friends from all stations in life, from highest born to lowly servant, filled the salons in the big villa. It was only then I learned that many women used to come to her, just like I had, for advice on love and marriage. I wasn't the only one with a difficult love life after all.

We were honored when one of the most senior princesses in the city offered her personal condolences. Nurah introduced me as the one who recorded Salma's story and the stories she told.

The great lady held my hand and looked deep into my eyes, as if she was searching for something there. I asked her how she knew Salma. "She used to walk in our neighborhood, so sometimes, when I was out in my garden early in the morning, she would sit with me. We were great friends. She was a strong soul, and you are lucky to have known her."

As the last guests were leaving, Nurah asked me to stay behind. She handed me a thick envelope. "It's about Salma's property in Taif. She has left it to you, in her will. It is yours, the acreage and the house."

Jeddah
2019

Peace to past memories that loom
Like a covey of pigeons crossing the sky.

- A Sailor's Memoirs by Muhammad al-Fayiz

CHAPTER 42

THE THREAD

Jeddah
April 2019

WE'RE GOING nowhere, stuck in a traffic jam on a small one-way street, deep in the balad. The cars in front of us are stopped, their engines turned off. The morning sun beats down hard. Most of the antique coral-brick houses around us have been whitewashed and restored, their doors and lattice shutters replaced with new teak, glowing red. Little boys weave among the cars on foot, their arms full of schoolbooks on their way to Jeddah's oldest boy's school, just up the street. Once, Baba used to walk to school there, just like them.

I'm in a rush to get to the university. My students and I have been looking forward to this day for weeks, and I'd hate to be late. But I must rely on God's will and be patient. Everyone opens the windows of their cars to get some air while we wait. I do the same.

"Good morning, Ma'am." An old man sits nearby on a folding chair, in the shade of an ancient but well-maintained house. He's wearing an old-fashioned turban and a spotless white t-shirt. "I think you might be late today."

"Good morning, Shaikh," I respond, smiling. "Inshallah I'll not be late, but who knows, it is in God's hands."

"So true," he says. "Everything is in His hands, and we must be patient." I nod in agreement. He shades his eyes to look at something in the sky, up the hill over the center of the balad. I follow his eyes to a flock of pigeons circling high above. My memories beckon me, calling through the decades.

"Mama, are you awake? Traffic's moving," my daughter Nurah says, nudging me. The drivers behind us are honking. I turn the key and put the car in gear. At last we're moving. The thrill of driving never wanes, especially in that moment when the car starts to move forward, with me at the wheel. Aunt Rosette was right. I smiled, remembering the day when we got our driver's licenses. We stood outside the Traffic Department, hundreds of us, cheering and calling out zaghareed, waving our new permits in our hands.

"Sorry, I must have dozed off. I feel like I've had a very long, delightful nap. How long have we been sitting here?"

"Oh, just a few minutes."

"Good, then we're not too late."

There is not an empty seat in the classroom. I pause at the doorway, listening to the lively conversations of my forty-five students. A hush races through the room as I stride in. The video camera is set up, and its operator nods to me in readiness. I set my briefcase on the front table next to the podium, unwind my headscarf, and drape it over my chair. I smile at the girls, roll up my sleeves, and smooth my hair back into place. The students are quiet, waiting.

"Good morning. Choosing only five essays to be read today has been truly difficult, because you all did a wonderful job on this project. I am proud that our country is full of beautiful and courageous women like you, your mothers, your grandmothers, your sisters, and your aunts. The five who will read their essays are: Latifah, Madihah, Haifa, Khadijah N., and Maha. Latifah will start."

The girls whisper as they pat the shoulders of those who were selected. Latifah stands to her full towering height, gathers her papers, and walks to the podium while trying to smooth the wrinkles on her long skirt of dark green cotton. Conversations talk themselves out, and the room returns to silence.

Latifah places her essay on the podium with shaking hands. The sheets of paper are curled at the edges, as if they'd been read from a hundred times. She clears her throat, flips her long braids behind her back, and looks around the room. Then she takes a deep breath and tries to smile.

"Bismillah il-Rahman il-Rahim. My name is Latifah Faisal al-Uwais. My mother's name is Madihah al-Uwais. My grandmother's name is also Latifah; I was named for her. Our family comes from a small village near the northern town of al-Wajh, on the Red Sea coast. We moved to Jeddah in the 1970s when my father came here for work. Because we moved to the city, I was able to attend high school and join the University. I'm the first girl in my family to go to college. My major is economics and I hope to become a banker." Encouraging murmurs echo around the class.

"My sisters and I are the first girls in my family to learn to read. Though my mother can't read, she has many good qualities, among them: she is very funny and she always works hard. When we were growing up, we couldn't afford a maid or houseboy, so my sisters and I helped with the cooking and cleaning. Finally, three years ago, income from my brothers enabled her to hire a maid.

"My father is from the Bani Attiyeh tribe — they settled in the village after World War I. My mother's family lived in al-Wajh for many generations. How did they meet? One of my father's aunts met Mama at a wedding. She thought Mama was pretty, but was charmed by her joking personality. When she described Mama to my father, he wanted to talk to her, but you know in those days it was impossible. He only caught glimpses of her in the market, always with her family.

"He sent his mother and sisters to visit Mama. She suspected why they had come, so she was quiet and polite. They told my father she was a serious young woman, which intrigued him even more.

"'Which was it?' he said to his mother. 'Is she a serious woman or a prankster? I want a good woman for a wife, but she must know how to laugh.'

"So his mother went back to Mama's house one morning unannounced. Mama was doing the wash. When she greeted her guest, her arms were red and swollen from the hot water. In those days, they had to boil the clothes over a fire, you see. Then they would hang them out to dry.

"The old lady asked Mama what was wrong with her arms, not thinking that perhaps she would be doing wash. Mama responded, 'Oh, I was out washing down the donkeys with bleach to get them really cleaned up.' Of course she didn't have a donkey. No one had had them for decades. Even in al-Wajh, most families had cars by then. But being from the old generation who used to ride donkeys to get around the village, my grandmother believed her and didn't blink an eye. She decided Mama was hard working, but not very witty. She didn't tell my father that last bit of information, however, not wanting to pass up the possibility of having an industrious daughter-in-law. She only told him that she'd interrupted her in the middle of bleaching donkeys, so she must be hard-working. My father started laughing and didn't stop for a long time. He immediately sent out his sisters to find out more about this woman who bleaches donkeys. The more he heard, the more he liked.

"They were together for nearly 30 years. Then, five years ago, my father died in a car accident, may he rest in peace. My mother still runs the house, of course with help from my sisters and me. Over the years, she helped many women from al-Wajh who moved to Jeddah with their families, becoming kind of a guide to them.

"Since she never learned to read herself, she asks me to read to her from magazines and newspapers. And when I read from the Qur'an, she says it is the best thing I can give to her in all the world."

My students are paying more attention to her than they did to any discussion or lecture. No one is checking their mobiles for text messages, or typing on their laptops. Maha Umar is resting her chin on her hand, her eyes wide with interest. She will be next, for I can't wait any longer to hear this particular girl read her story. The students are clapping. I nod at Latifah, and she smiles with relief, then walks back to her seat. A nervous silence fills the room. Maha looks down at her paper and closes her eyes.

"Maha, please read your essay to us now."

She smiles at me and nods. She walks to the podium clutching her papers in one hand, carrying a paper bag in the other. As she tucks her shoulder-length hair behind her ears and looks at the class, I notice the bend in her small, hawk-like nose. "Bismillah al-Rahman al-Rahim," she says and then nods her head again and swallows. "My grandmother's story began in Turkey, in a small Armenian village. Her name was Makrouhi, and, when she was a little girl, she crossed the Nafud on foot with a band of Ageylis. I carry her name, I'm Maha Makrouhi Salma Sulaiman Umar." She reaches into her bag and pulls out a tattered doll dressed in faded indigo, setting it on the podium. "This was her doll." She pauses for a moment and swallows again.

The girls are drawn in at that moment, and no one breathes. She looks at me for permission to go on. "Please continue when you're ready," I say. "Relax, take your time."

"Thank you, Professor."

I hold a tissue in my hand, ready to stop the tears that will flow like a sudden rainstorm in the desert. As she continues, her voice grows louder and more confident. I close my eyes and smile, remembering.

Notes and Acknowledgements

This story is a work of fiction, the product of my imagination and my fascination with the people, culture, and history of Saudi Arabia. Since it is an imagined story about fictional characters, it does not represent Saudi society and culture. Wadi al-Bu'ur is an imaginary location, though there are many verdant valleys in the area. The character Salma is loosely inspired by the legend of Shoma, the niece of Huwaitat Chief Auda Abu Tayy.

My heartfelt thanks to the many people who have helped me complete the story's long journey toward publication. A thousand thanks to:

Editors Susan Leon and Marcia Lynx Qualey, for clear guidance and sound advice;

Early readers: Joyce Campbell, Art Clark, Liz Gordon, Jo Grossmann, Mary Gundy, Dorothy Hanson, Tricia Hanson, Marsha McDonald, Polly Robinson, and Cassandra Shore, for encouragement and feedback;

Kate Whouley, for reading the story, and for more than a decade of encouragement and insightful advice on writing and the publishing world;

Maha Akeel, as well as the members of the South Shore AAUW writers group (Beatrice Kelly, Susan Mahan, Patricia MacKay, and Gwen Sayian) for chapter feedback.

Cassandra Shore and the Jawaahir Dance Company of Minneapolis for staging two productions of my script "Shoma," a dance theater piece that rose from an early excerpt of the story. Seeing Salma come to life on stage was a dream;

Sarah Jones-Larson, for portraying Salma in "Shoma," and to Sarah and Hend Al-Mansour for character insight;

Kate Anderson and Susan Lind-Sananian of the Armenian National Museum in Watertown, Mass., for access to the collection;

Margo Nalbanian, for assistance with Armenian girls' names;

Dr. Saad Sowayan, for information on Unaizah folklore and storytelling;

Joy May Hilden, for expertise on Bedouin weaving;

My Saudi friends who shared their stories, culture and good humor;

And to Leif Hanson, for digital marketing.

Most of all, thanks to my husband Gary for his encouragement and boundless patience.

Historical Characters

This is a work of fiction, though it refers to and includes some historical figures. All the actions and speech of these characters in the novel come from the author's imagination.

Abadi al-Jawhar – (b. 1953) Renowned Saudi composer, singer, and oud player.

Abboud Abd al-Al – (1930-2009) Palestinian violinist, popular in the late 1970s.

Abd al-Aziz ibn Saud – (1876? - 1953) Founder of modern Saudi Arabia. Popularly known in the west as "Ibn Saud."

Abd al-Halim Hafez – (1929-1977) Egyptian singer and cinema star.

Abla and Antara – Legendary lovers of Arabic literature. Antarah Ibn Shaddad (525-608 CE) was a famous poet who fell in love with his cousin Abla, but could not marry her.

Al-Jawhara – Beloved wife of King Abd al-Aziz, d. 1919.

Al-Auruns –T.E. Lawrence, British officer who fought with and led the Arab Army in World War I (1888-1935), popularly known as "Lawrence of Arabia."

Hatim of Tayy – d. 578 Revered Arabian poet known, to this day, for his legendary hospitality.

Khalid bin Abd al-Aziz – (1913-1982) Ruler of Saudi Arabia from 1975 to 1982.

Nuri al-Sha`alan – (1847-1942) Leader of the Ruwala tribe and key figure in the Arab Revolt against the Ottoman Turks in World War I.

Queen Effat – (1916-2000) Effat al-Thunayan, wife of King Faisal, pioneer of women's education in Saudi Arabia.

Saladin – (d. 1193) Sultan of Egypt and Syria, founder of the Ayyubid Dynasty. He defeated most of the Crusaders' forces in the Levant.

Shaikh Falaby – (1885-1960) H. St. John Philby, British Arabist who converted to Islam and served as a personal advisor to King Abd al-Aziz.

Turki bin Abd al-Aziz – (1900-1919) First-born son of King Abd al-Aziz.

Um Kulthum – (1904-1975) Leading Egyptian vocalist who visited Jeddah at least twice.

Abridged Bibliography

In researching this story, I consulted the following English language works:

Almana, Mohammed, *Arabia Unified: A Portrait of Ibn Saud,* London: Hutchinson Benham, 1982.

Altorki, Soraya and Cole, Donald P. *Arabian Oasis City: The Transformation of `Unayzah.* Austin: University of Texas Press, 1989, 1994.

Altorki, Soraya. *Women in Saudi Arabia: Ideology and Behavior Among the Elite.* New York: Columbia University Press, 1988.

Dickson, H.R.P., *The Arab of the Desert: A Glimpse into Badawin Life in Kuwait and Sa`udi Arabia.* London: George Allen & Unwin Ltd., 1949.

Doumato, Eleanor Abdella. *Getting God's Ear – Women, Islam, and Healing in Saudi Arabia and the Gulf.* New York: Columbia University Press, 2000.

Doughty, Charles, *Travels in Arabia Deserta,* New York: Random House, 1937.

Helms, Christine Moss. *The Cohesion of Saudi Arabia.* London: Croom Helm Ltd., 1981.

Hilden, Joy Totah. *Bedouin Weaving of Saudi Arabia and its Neighbors.* London: Arabian Publishing Ltd., 2010.

Lacy, Robert. *The Kingdom.* New York: Harcourt Brace Jovanovich, 1981.

Lawrence, Thomas Edward. *Seven Pillars of Wisdom,* New York: Doubleday, Doran & Co., 1937.

Palgrave, William Gifford., *Narrative of a Year's Journey Through Central and Eastern Arabia.* London: MacMillan and Co., 1866.

Raswan, Carl R. *Black Tents of Arabia.* New York: Farrar, Straus & Giroux, 1935.

Reehani, Ameen, *Maker of Modern Arabia.* Boston: Houghton Mifflin Company, 1928.

Ross, Heather Colyer. *The Art of Arabian Costume: A Saudi Arabian Profile.* Fribourg: Arabesque Commercial SA, 1981.

Sowayan, Saad Abdallah. *Nabati Poetry: The Oral Poetry of Arabia.* Doha, 1985.

Trofimov, Yaroslov. *The Siege of Mecca: The 1979 Uprising at Islam's Holiest Shrine.* New York: Anchor Books, 2008.

Winder, R. Bayly. *Saudi Arabia in the Nineteenth Century.* New York: Octagon Books, 1980.

Made in the USA
Columbia, SC
09 April 2018